The
Other Side
of the
Coin

A NOVEL

By

Ci Ci Soleil

Copyright © 2026 Beach Reads Books
All rights reserved.
Published in the United States by Beach Reads Books
The Other Side of the Coin is a work of fiction. Any similarity to actual persons, living or dead, events or places, is purely coincidental.

ISBN: 979-8-9850660-7-4
Author: Ci Ci Soleil
Cover Art By: Danielle Hennis

Beach Reads Books
BeachReadsBooks.com

Books by Ci Ci Soleil:

VICTORY!

Finalist in the 2023 Next Generation Indie Book Awards

HOLY ORDERS

Finalist in the 2024 Next Generation Indie Book Awards

Facets of Love Series:

TAKEN BY THE WIND

THE OTHER SIDE OF THE COIN

Coming soon in the Facets of Love series:

ARC OF THE DREAM CATCHER

LOVE IN THE FISHBOWL

THE ART OF SUMMER

Connect with Ci Ci Soleil

www.CiCiSoleil.com

For Barbara Ann, so brave and so beautiful.
Everyone should get a second chance at life.

A Song for Jane
Music and Lyrics by Rory Watkins

I knew a woman once, wise beyond time
I asked if she'd explain to me the reason and the rhyme
"You are so sweet and innocent." And she said to me,
"What you don't know is that life and love hold no guarantees.
You must be careful how you love
For you give yourself like the sky gives its rain
Don't pour out your heart and soul
And get no love in exchange.
Yes, you must be careful what you do.
Learn to tell the truth from the lie.
For no amount of sacrifice and no matter how you try
You can't replace the rain once it's fallen from the sky.
It's time to learn the difference between the truth and the lie."

Well, I'm older now and a little wiser too,
Now I know better than to give my love to you.
The only guarantee we have is the one we give ourselves.
The only real freedom we know, we can't get from anyone else.
You know, I can still see your eyes and the way you looked at me
And I hear the echoes of those words come back, hauntingly, with
"You must be careful how you love,
For you give yourself like the sky gives its rain.
Don't pour out your heart and soul, until nothing does remain.

Yes, you must be careful what you choose.
Even the deepest well can run dry,
And no amount of sacrifice and no matter how you try,
You can't replace the rain once it's fallen from the sky,
No, you can't replace the rain once it's fallen from the sky.

Yes, I must be careful with this love,
For I love you like Earth is loved by rain.
But monsoons and floods
Washes it all away.
Next time I'll be careful what I do,
Learn to tell the truth from the lie,
Cause no matter how hard I loved and no matter how I tried
I couldn't find the truth buried in the lie.
Next time I'll be careful with my love.

Prologue

Jane chewed on a lone piece of ice from the margarita. She could both feel and hear it. It was one of those little things you never thought about, and then when you did you found that it was infinitely complex. The ice was cold and hard, and then soft as it melted and crushed. It was wet and smooth and sharp all at once. She could hear it, like a voice inside her head, a crunch and a dull squishing playing simultaneously off each other. And in less than a moment the whole slew of sensations passed into the nothingness of non-existence. It was just like everything else: so insignificant when you only glanced at it, yet so revealing when you paused to examine it. And all so very fleeting.

She touched the rim of the giant glass and then rolled the salt crystals between her fingers, feeling their sharp rough edges as she hummed the tune to a sad song she couldn't quite remember. The beach was hot and she was baking in the sun, the shade of the low-lying palapa not doing much to protect her from the blistering rays. Setting the minuscule salt cube down into a drop of sweat on her belly, she watched it dissolve. Everything seemed symbolic to her right now. She could look at sun, sand, sky, salt, or sweat and it all held messages and meanings. The white crystal dissolved in its pool of salty sweat and then moved as she breathed, sliding off her side, dropping to evaporate from some surface below her. Everything led to everything else. It was logical. That's what she needed: she needed to get back to logical. How did she end up here? Sitting here on this beach? Thinking about her life and what the hell she was supposed to do now? Well, if that was what she was going to figure out, maybe she needed to go back to the beginning…

Chapter 1

Paris. The Sorbonne. Dreams do come true. It was the first weeks of her semester abroad and life just couldn't get more exciting. Years of studying French had left Jane passable at the language, yet she was still an American in Paris, wide-eyed, running around in tennis shoes and taking selfies with every monument as if to prove that this was actually real. But at the moment, she was late for class and starving. The French were sticklers for funny things—how you ordered food, for one. How you appreciated the food you received. How you made every attempt to meet them at their culture, but then, of course, they would forgive you any fumble just because of your honest try. Her international marketing professor was not forgiving though. She hoped her attempt to grab something to eat as she ran to class would not be in vain or cost her points. She was top of her cohort and wanted to remain there.

The corner brasserie was as good a place as any to grab a sandwich. It offered a take-out window that the local student clientele loved, much to the dismay of the older and more traditional luncheon diners who had the luxury of leisure to enjoy their meal while they eagerly disparaged the younger generation their haste. She navigated the disapproving stares and dashed back to class. Rounding the corner, she got a brief glimpse of broad shoulders and then felt the crush of her body against someone very solid. The next thing she knew, she was staring up at the sky as knife-like spasms crossed her chest and she struggled to breathe. A man's face came into view, looking at her curiously. She felt dizzy and very confused, wondering why he was upside down. He helped her to sit up as she started to catch her breath again. She glanced around. Everything that had been in her arms or in her bookbag now lay scattered about on the sidewalk. As the man collected and stacked up the various items they had both been carrying, he mumbled something in French that she couldn't make out. The pains in her chest subsided, only to be replaced by a fluttering sensation as her heart beat wildly. She looked at this strange Frenchman and suddenly the earth moved. Her ears were still ringing, but now they were filled with some kind of celestial music.

She wanted to say, *Hello, I'm Jane. I'm the one you've been looking for all your life*, but she caught herself before the words could escape her lips. Never in her life would she have said anything like that.

I'm losing my mind. I must have brain damage.

She blinked and looked at him again. Instantly, her stomach filled with butterflies and she no longer cared about eating her lunch. She might never be hungry again. She shook her head gently and started to apologize profusely in French. "Pardonnez-moi, je suis desole! Es tu blesse?" She repeatedly inquired whether he was hurt.

The young man didn't even glance at her as he continued to gather their belongings, saying only "C'est bon, c'est bon," somewhat confusedly in answer to each question. He handed her the books, her bag, and her ruined lunch. She apologized once again, he nodded curtly at her, and they went their separate ways. Despite her impending tardiness, she watched him hustle off down the street until he disappeared around the corner.

"I love Paris." Her voice was breathy and caught her off guard. She looked around as if to check whether she had actually uttered those words and in that manner. Then she grimaced. "Ugh, I hope I didn't give him the concussion I think I just gave myself," she said as she put her hand to her forehead.

Pulling herself together, she took off at a clip to make it to class. Even more breathless, but this time from exertion, she plopped down next to Claudine, whipped out her book and the remains of her sandwich, and took a ravenous bite.

Claudine looked Jane up and down. As a Frenchwoman, she was totally put together—the only hairs out of place had been styled that way. Her heavy make-up was expertly applied. Everything about her signaled a confident, casual elegance that was no accident.

Jane, by comparison, was completely disheveled, with bits of her lunch partly smeared across her blouse. She ran her hand through her hair to push it back.

In heavily accented English, in which it seemed Claudine could pronounce no words that started with the letter h and all her th's came out like the letter z, she leaned over and hissed, "What happened to you? You are a sight, Jane!" Claudine picked a bit of lettuce out of Jane's hair, gave it a look of mild disgust, and flicked it onto the floor.

Through a mouth half full of food, Jane whispered back with great animation, "I think I just concussed a French movie star." Then she blinked a couple of times. "And I might have concussed myself in the process." She sighed. "It was amazing."

The professor started tapping his baton on the desk in an attempt to get the class to focus. Jane swallowed and leaned over to Claudine. "I mean, I literally ran into him. He was the most handsome man I have ever almost met." She took another huge bite of her sandwich. "I really hope I didn't give him brain damage."

"Oh, so you tackled the French movie star like you were an American football player? You did not stop to meet him?" Claudine asked as she reached over and smoothed Jane's still ruffled hair. "You should have gotten his number!"

Jane swallowed her current bite and took a big swig of her soda. "How in the world could I have done that?"

Claudine shrugged. "It would have been the French thing to do." She gave her friend a sly smile. "We don't give them a mortal wound by accident. Nor do we waste such an opportunity once it presents itself."

Jane just grimaced and shook her head, but she was wondering how the French girls could manage to snag a phone number when they were dealing with their heartbeat slamming, their breathing arrested, and that crazy celestial music ringing in their ears? "You French girls are super-human."

"Mon ami! You are such an American. I must turn you into a French-woman, and you must get me through this horrible marketing class this semester! Our professor, Monsieur Baton-Waver, is the worst teacher. I looked him up online. We are doomed, my friend."

"Oh, this class? Easy stuff. I can totally help you. I took a course on it last semester. I'm just taking this to practice my French."

"So, it is a deal? You will be my tutor?"

"Yeah. You teach me how to be French and actually get a guy's number and I'll make you a marketing genius. Guaranteed A in the class."

Jane reached for her marketing book as the professor called out, "Etudiants, classe, so tournez-vous vers le chapitre cinq," for them to open their books to chapter five. Jane pulled up her book and stared at it in confusion. She had never seen this book before.

"Mon Dieu! Mon ami, Jane! I think you might see your movie star again? This must be his book! Look, here is the name 'Nicholas'."

"Wow, Claudine, do you think this is his number?" Jane pointed to the digits scrawled beneath the name.

"Hard to say. If he is as good looking as you seem to think, it could be his boyfriend's number." She gave Jane a mischievous grin. "But fortunate for you he has some connection to the school! And very lucky for you, he likes the feel of actual paper! And it seems he likes to draw on his books." She gave the sketches an unsure look. "You know, Jane, most students get the digital books."

Jane ignored her comment. "He's a student here… I could call him…" Jane ran her finger over the name and number inscribed on the page. "We both love the feel of a real book. That's good, right?" Then she hesitated and looked over at Claudine. "He could have a boyfriend. That would be bad for me."

Claudine laughed out loud as their teacher continued to call for order. "You won't know until you call him. And see him again. Just to exchange books, no? And then you can find out much, oui?"

That night after classes were over, Claudine dropped by Jane's apartment with a question from the lessons that day. "And while we are here, let me ask if you have called your mysterious French movie star? I might like to get his autograph too."

"You're teasing me!" Jane said with a smile, but then it faded. "I haven't. I couldn't."

"Pourquoi?"

Jane looked anyplace but at Claudine. "I wouldn't know what to say."

"Oh, that is simple. You start with Allô."

"I mean I can't, I can't like, um… I can't talk to a guy. I don't talk to guys."

"What do you mean?"

"I just don't think I can. I get all tongue-tied and nervous. Zero confidence."

Claudine raised one eyebrow.

The words rushed out of Jane as she tried to both explain and defend herself. "You see, book-smart wallflowers like me are invisible to the handsome men on the street. Or who sit next to me in class. Or who I might try to get the attention of. I've just never known how to…" but Jane's voice trailed off as she realized she wasn't sure what the end of that particular sentence was.

Claudine nodded once and then picked up Jane's phone and dialed the number in the book, handing the phone to Jane when it started ringing. Jane shook her head vigorously as she backed up.

A deep voice on the other end of the phone said, "Oui?"

Claudine shook the phone in her hand, giving Jane a commanding look.

"Oui? Allô, oui?"

Nervously, reluctantly, Jane took her phone from Claudine. "Bonjour, je suis Jane Donahue. Je beleive nous aurions pu courir dans l'autre aujourd'hui. Je pense avoir votre livre et que vous pourriez avoir un des miens?" Jane's French was more than adequate for the occasion.

The voice on the other end of the line was slow and halting, "Oh, euh, pourriez-vous s'il vous plait, dire que sfai, euh… plus lentement?"

"Parlez-vous Anglias?" Jane asked.

"Oh God, yes! I do speak English," the frustrated voice said in a refined British accent. "English, please."

"Oh, sure then." Jane raised shocked eyebrows at Claudine.

Claudine mouthed back, "Il est pas Francais?" Jane shook her head. Claudine gave an annoyed humph and started writing on a piece of paper.

"Well, let's start again. Hi. My name is Jane Donahue and I think I might have run into you on the street today. At least I think I have your Green Architecture and Design book—and I'm very much hoping that you have my International Marketing textbook."

"Oh, you're that girl who could be a rugby player! Yes, I believe I'm still bruised from our encounter. And I do have this ridiculous marketing textbook that from the outside looks uncannily like my missing text."

"So, you are Nicholas?"

"Yes, yes, that's me. Nicholas Sutcliffe-Ashworth. You know, you sound like an American. I thought today that surely you were a French girl from your accent."

"Oh, well, um, thank you. I'm here on a semester abroad and hoping to improve my French."

"If mine were half as good as yours, I wouldn't have had to have come here at all," he said with a chuckle.

She immediately liked the sound of his laugh and those strange invisible butterflies started fluttering in her stomach again. Claudine was now holding up sheets of paper with large block printing saying:

Invite for coffee—return book—see him again! She kept scribbling out instructions and pushing them in front of Jane.

Jane took a deep breath and summoned her courage, glancing at Claudine's written notes. "Well then, Nicholas Sutcliffe-Ashworth, shall we meet up to swap our books back? I promise this time that I won't run you down. Actually, I'm not sure I could survive another encounter like that. Maybe I can buy you a cup of coffee by way of apology for the leaving you, uh, wounded?" Jane got her hopes up that he might just say yes. She thought she was handling this conversation quite well, marveling over how much easier it was without the guy standing in front of you and when your best friend was cueing you with lines like an expert wingman.

"What's your name again?"

"Uh," she said surprised at how quickly this sounded like a rejection, "Jane Donahue."

"And you're from America?"

"Yes, United States. North Carolina to be specific. Where are you from?"

At this he burst out laughing. "England. Are you surprised? No. Ha! Bath to be specific." He said Bath with an incredibly stretched out "ah" sound. And after a moment of silence he answered, "Well yes, Jane Donahue, I will accept your offer of coffee and if your apology is sufficient, I will ransom your bloody textbook back to you."

They agreed on a place to meet late the next afternoon when classes were over.

As she tapped the button to end the call, Jane melted to the floor with a big smile on her face. "Wow! I've never done that before. Thank you, Claudine. I'm so happy!"

Claudine pursed her lips. "You are not a French woman yet. You are very, very American." She picked up a strand of Jane's limp hair and shook her head at her friend's T-shirt and tennis shoes.

Jane looked at Claudine, a sudden expression of panic crossing her face. "I'm just a little Yankee goldfish in a sea of sexy French barracudas. I don't stand a chance here. Oooh nooo!" She put her head in her hands.

Claudine stood up tall and put her fists on her hips, looking quite fierce for such a small person. "Non! You, Jane Donahue, will impress this man or I am not Claudine Bellarose. I will turn you into a French woman. And you will help me get an A in international marketing!"

Chapter 2

"Oui, I will help you, but you must remember that love is not like in the movies, where you toss a coin in a fountain and make a silly wish. No, it is full of chance, like the toss of a coin. Sometimes you get lucky. Sometimes... eh." Claudine shrugged. "Not so lucky. Heads. Tails. Honestly, I think it is better to save your money and focus on your career. Keep the coin safely in your pocket!" She looked like Wonder Woman standing there with her hands on her hips.

"Oh Claudine... my career I'm not worried about. Top student always. Straight As. You could call me, well, yeah, driven. But I've never had a proper boyfriend. No one took me to prom."

"What is... prom?"

"Never mind."

"Have you ever... mmmmmm..." Claudine gave her a meaningful look.

"While I'm not precisely sure what you mean, I'm pretty sure I've never.... mmmmmm'd."

"Jane, tell me what you want. What do you really, in your heart, want?"

"I just want... I want the fountain and the wish! I want to toss that coin and have it come up heads. I don't want to be the book-smart librarian side character. I want someone to love me. To adore me. Like in the movies." She turned to look in the mirror. "My greatest fear is to be cast in the role of 'Jane the Spinster'."

"Spinster? What is this spinster? I do not know this word."

Jane turned to Claudine. "To face my life alone. No one to love me. No one to ever have loved me." She looked back in the mirror. "But how could they when I'm so aptly named Plain Jane." She sighed and fell into a nearby chair, melting into a little pool of despondency, and staring up at the ceiling.

Claudine leaned back, tapping her chin, and studied her friend. "Humph! That may be so, but you won't be 'Plain-Jane' by tomorrow afternoon." Claudine leaned down, putting her hands on the armrests on Jane's chair and made Jane look at her. "And Jane, just so you are aware, it is not plain or pretty that makes the difference—it is how you believe in yourself." She stood back up and started to pace. "I will let you in on the great secret of beautiful French women throughout history: it is all about confidence. Whatever it takes for you to feel confident."

Jane looked up at Claudine, a hangdog expression on her face. "One hundred percent confident with books. Zero percent confident with boys."

Claudine looked thoughtful. "Then you need a real dose of confidence à la française."

Claudine went to work immediately. First, she called her aunt who worked at a popular salon in the second arrondissement and by nine-thirty the next morning Jane had a new haircut and an enhanced four-color mix, making her hair look like it was ready to grace the cover of a magazine. Her formerly quite mousy brown was now a rich textured dark chocolate hue with subtle highlights and lowlights. Claudine then dragged her over to La Samaritaine, where her cousin worked at the make-up counter. Jane got a complete consultation and professional makeover, walking out a few hundred euros poorer. She missed all her morning classes.

Claudine waved off Jane's anxiety. "Oh, do not, what do you call it? Fray?"

"Fret. The word is fret. I do that a lot. I'm good at fretting."

"Do not fret. This is much more important than class. Besides, it is obvious to me that you could teach the classes, no? You are the brightest girl at school, I am sure. It is me we need to worry about! Men I have like flies, but I do not crave their adoration: what I want is a good career! Career is première. Personally, I would never accept a man who detracted from my success at work."

By two o'clock in the afternoon, Jane was wearing all new clothes, some of them Claudine's, and with her new look even her professors were doing double takes. As her last class let out, she met up with Claudine, who promised to accompany Jane and observe the rendezvous from a distance.

"Claudine, this is crazy! I think I've been asked out three times today. I haven't been asked out since I got to France. And of course, several years before then too."

"Mais oui. Yesterday they did not see you. Today, your natural beauty is shining. Natural beauty always needs a little helping hand. Boys are like that—they like 'natural' beauty. All Frenchwomen know this," she said, adding finger quotes around the last natural.

"Claudine, even one of my professors hit on me which, admittedly, was really creepy." Jane shuddered.

"Oui, they are like that, too. You must watch out."

"Really? That really did happen? I actually kinda thought that was my imagination. Wow, that would never happen in the States!" Jane felt amazed and simultaneously uncomfortable.

"No? Well, it is probably better that way. Here it happens all the time! I think I would like the United States."

"You'll have to come visit me and find out." Jane smiled at her friend. "Oh, there he is. Do I look okay?"

Claudine held Jane by her shoulders and looked into her eyes. "No. You do not look okay," she said with a haughty tone. "You look tres beau, Jane Donahue. You know this now. Act like it!"

Jane stood up taller and squared her shoulders, which was much easier to do with Claudine manipulating her like a marionette.

"Take the deep breath…" Claudine said, sounding like a sports coach. "And now your best smile… oui! That is very nice. Off you go! Bon chance! Be confident. Be your beautiful self. He cannot help but love you."

Jane felt a smile blossoming on her face that she couldn't have stopped if she'd tried. She had never felt this confident. Confidence and excitement were combining into a powerful cocktail; she felt wonderful and radiant. "Merci, mon ami!" She smiled at Claudine and then strode over to formally meet Mr. Nicholas Sutcliffe-Ashworth. She walked right up to him as he was scanning the crowd, his book bag slung over his shoulder. "Bonjour, Monsieur," she said, fully feeling Claudine's French restyling.

The man kept looking around and replied an offhanded, "Bonjour. Sorry. Looking for an American."

"Well, let's try this again. Hi Nicholas, I'm Jane." She gave a little wave. "I ran into you yesterday." She held out her hand and beamed at him. It felt as though she were radiating light, she felt so happy and confident. She could hear Claudine's voice in her head saying, *Oui, just like a French woman.* The tall man with dark eyes and light brown hair slowly turned to look at her.

At first it appeared as though he couldn't speak. He tried; it was just that nothing came out. Jane just smiled at him, holding her hand out to shake his. He looked down at her hand and slowly reached out his own in return. "Hullo," he stammered, looking back up to her face but taking her in as he did so. "So, you are… Jane? I'm… uh… I'm… sorry, I didn't recognize you."

"Well, I did hit you pretty hard yesterday."

"Must be the, uh, lack of lettuce in your hair."

She thought he had the most darling expression on his face when he was making a joke. She liked that he had a sense of humor. "Yeah, I decided to go sans vegetables today. Say, let me take you for that cup of coffee and see if I can wrangle my book back from you."

"Wrangle? What an American word. Oh yes, please! Now I'm most interested in being wrangled. Something tells me I'm going to like this."

She gave him a sweet smile and when he returned the look with a rather goofy grin of his own, she decided this wasn't as hard as she thought it would be.

"And call me Nick. Or Nicky. Nicholas is my grandfather."

"Nick then." She beamed at him. They headed over to a brasserie, sat down, and ordered. Three hours later saw them strolling through the Arènes de Lutéce. "These ancient ruins are one of the only Roman-era relics still to be seen in Paris." Jane described the scenery like a museum docent.

"As my grandparents would say, tickety-boo! You're just mad-smart, aren't you? I'm amazed at how much you know about the sites of Paris! It's like having my own personal tourist guide."

"I've dreamed of coming here all my life, so I suppose I am drinking it in. I've read about the city for years, and seen pictures and movies, but there's nothing like being here. It's as magical as I thought it would be." *Paris. Love. Magical. Nicholas… how all of those go together,* she thought.

"I'll have to start seeing the city through your eyes, then. It's more of a punishment for me."

"Oh, how can you say that? Nick, if this is your punishment, sign me up! What kind of crime can I commit so that I'm forced to study at the Sorbonne?"

"Well, my father imports wine and liquors to Great Britain and Canada. He loves wine and owns a part of a vineyard here in France. Has his own tiny little label, but it's his pride and joy. What he really wants is for me to follow in his footsteps."

"Oh, his pride and joy taking over his pride and joy then?"

"What? Who?" Nick asked, a bit confused. Then understanding her meaning he added, "Oh, right. I'm sorry to say I am not my father's pride and joy. Honestly, I think I'm a real disappointment to him."

"Oh, do you live in the shadow of your big brother or something?" She was curious and interested, glad that he was opening up. She'd been keeping the details of her life pretty superficial, afraid the mundane truth of her middle-class existence would be a turn-off to someone as fascinating and sophisticated as Nicholas Sutcliffe-Ashworth. She wanted him to think she was intriguing and mysterious and smart—and then was suddenly caught up in the thought that those qualities might not be the ones that attracted him. He seemed to appreciate an empathetic ear. Well, she could do that. Empathy was one of her strong suits. Years of practice as a wallflower had made her a very good listener.

"No, no, only child. But still, I'm afraid I'll never live up to my poor parents' high expectations." His dramatic sigh didn't quite fit with his rather lighthearted tone of voice.

Jane noticed the relative ease with which he made such a confession. Was it a joke? A self-deprecating type of British humor, perhaps? She decided to keep things light. Good wallflowers didn't ask overly-intrusive questions. "You're studying building and design? That's architecture, right?"

"Yes, building and design. I might go into architecture someday. Lots of maths there though. My parents might respect architecture, hmmm, perhaps, if they thought I would be another I.M. Pei that is."

"Wow. That's a high expectation! My parents just want me to come back alive. And without a ton of credit card debt," Jane added, thinking of her expenses of the morning.

He burst out laughing again. Jane thought that Nick was one of those rare kinds of people who just weren't brought down by life, they were simply happy—in Nick's case, even with those heavy thoughts about his parents. She felt an empathetic pang for him: how hard it must have been to live up to all that pressure. The only child with an upbringing that sounded so cold, so Roald-Dahl-kind-of-English, compared to what she had known. By contrast, her upbringing would seem a bit smothering, in that peculiar way that was characteristically southern.

"You know, you are beautiful and rather witty! Just charming. So, Jane Donahue, tell me all about your life in North Carolina, which I understand that despite the name, is actually in the South, and tell me what architects who specialize in green design do there!"

"Oh my, I'm sure I don't know anything about building and design. My dad's a dentist. I know kind of a lot about teeth. More than you'd want to know, believe me. And his only hope for anyone following in his footsteps would be my baby sister, Charlie."

"You have a sister... named Charlie? My goodness. Was she perhaps your brother at one point in time? I hear there's quite a lot of that going on. Really gets those American politicians' knickers in a twist—they seem to be so interested in what's happening in other people's underwear." He couldn't suppress the mischievous grin on his face and broke out in another laugh.

"Sorry to disappoint you, but there's nothing at all, um, 'knicker-twisting', about my family." Jane smiled at him and then wondered whether, strictly speaking, that was true. Her sister Summer wasn't exactly a conformist. In fact, she could be downright embarrassing when she chose to be. And she did own a superhero cape, not that Jane understood what that had to do with being an artist. Or, frankly, her actual bill-paying job as an underling in a microbiology lab. Jane decided to downplay the topic of her older sister. "Charlotta is my baby sister's given name, which she hates, so she insists on Charlie. She's the really brainy one in the family—wants to be a physician. A surgeon actually. And cut people up. My older sister, Summer, is a lab tech who really wants to be an artist. Me, I'm just the girl in the middle."

"Girl in the middle. What a wonderful place to be! In the middle. How I wish I had an older brother to be the complete oddball and take the heat! Or a younger one to be the eternal baby. But as an only, I have to be all things to my parents. They really should have had a swathe of children."

"Why didn't they?" Jane heard her voice ask the question before she realized how intrusive it was, but it was too late to draw it back.

Nicholas Sutcliffe-Ashworth seemed to be in a very relaxed and talkative mood as they walked through the beautiful streets of Paris. "Mum would have loved nothing but that, however I apparently tried to kill her when I was born. She was unable to have any children after me. I'm not so sure she's forgiven me quite yet, to tell you the truth."

Jane had heard the old adage about the British stiff upper lip and wondered if she might be seeing it in action. After all, the tone of his last statement sounded almost upbeat and she didn't know what to think, this decoupling of his affect from his words. "That's kinda heavy. A lot to be carrying on your shoulders."

"Yes, enlighten me a bit more. I've heard it a thousand times!"

Her heart skipped a compassionate beat as she concluded that he was putting on a brave face, but obviously, deep down, was suffering. She asked a bit tentatively, "But then why didn't they adopt? It kinda seems like the straightforward path if you'd like a bigger family."

"Mum wanted it. I remember raging rows when I was a lad. Mum wanted to adopt but my father wouldn't hear of having someone else's bastard in his house. Eventually it all died down, and by the time they realized that they were left with just disappointing little me—the boy who would never accomplish all their unfulfilled dreams—it was too late."

Jane didn't know what to say, so she just nodded.

Nicholas stopped walking and looked thoughtful. "You know, Jane Donahue, you are rather easy to talk to. I'm a bit surprised that I'm telling you all this." He looked somewhat abashed. "You can feel free to bill me for the psychotherapy, you're such a counsellor!" He gave her a little wink. "I'll have to watch out for you, you sly vixen, or you'll learn all my secrets."

She felt herself melt under that penetrating look he was giving her. "Your secrets are safe with me." She mimed zipping her lip and throwing away the key.

"Nice to know. I don't have that many people I can trust in my life." As the moment started to feel intense, he suddenly noticed a nearby hole-in-the-wall restaurant. "Might you be feeling a bit hungry? Would you like to step in here for dinner? This looks to be a somewhat decent place."

They were quickly seated at a small table in the corner of the Maison de l'Aubergine. It was clear the wait staff spoke only French, unusual for Paris in this day and age, even if it was simply to make a point. Jane found it delightful. In her short few weeks in the city, she found it disappointing when she tried to experience something French only to be enthusiastically greeted in English by the proprietor. Even most French menus came complete with English translations. The Maison de l'Aubergine was an authentic delight in every sense.

"It's quite rather, well, it's awfully purple in here, don't you think?" Nick asked.

Indeed, the interior of the tiny eatery felt drenched in purple. "Well, given the name, I half expected the entire menu to be eggplant dishes." She gave him a smile and looked at the menu. "And it looks like a fair number of the items do indeed feature that vegetable."

"Eggplant?"

"Yes. Aubergine. Eggplant." She saw the look of consternation on his face.

"Oh, right! Jolly good." He gave her a smile. "Eggplant's all right."

"I'm sure it's great. Just check out who's here—strictly locals. This is the real deal. Not a tourist trap. I mean look—not a single meal comes with fries!"

"Fries?"

"Yeah, Pomme frites. They're on the menu of every cheap eatery in the city. We call them French fries."

"We call them chips."

"That's so cute. Our chips are the very thin, potato, uh wafer-like things. They're, well, crispy." She was surprised at how hard it was to describe a food once you took away the name for it.

"We call those crisps."

"Oh, yeah, right. For obvious reasons."

She smiled and hoped she wasn't sounding as stupid as she felt. She looked again at the menu and had to catch her breath. It was classic old-world French, looked fabulous, and was completely beyond her student budget. The expenditures of her early morning had totaled over five hundred dollars. She expected a harsh text from her father before noon the next day, shortly after he got the call from the credit card company about the "unusual activity" on the account. She wasn't sure if Nick might be expecting this dinner to be a continuing part of her apology, which would make it the nicest apology she had ever made, judging from the debt she would incur. She hadn't been planning on more than the coffee, but she didn't know how to bring it up without completely embarrassing herself in the process. For the first time in her life she was experiencing magic—like she was starring in her very own movie with Nicholas Sutcliffe-Ashworth as her leading man. She wasn't willing to risk anything that would break this spell.

"Let's get the bay scallops on cailloux for starters, shall we? By the way, my lovely French tourist guide, what does cailloux mean anyway?"

She looked down at the menu. "I think that means pebbles or some type of small rock? I can't think what they mean by that though. Is that supposed to be a euphemism for on a bed of small gnocchi, for example? I'm trying to think of what food is small and round like that. Peas? Beans?"

"Oh! Let's be adventurous and find out!" Nick gave her his dashing white smile and she melted, nodding her assent. She would just have to apologize to her father later, probably have to work it off in the dental office filing tedious paperwork in the summer. For an entire summer. Maybe for all the summers for as long as she lived.

The waiter came over and Nick ordered a bottle of wine. Jane swallowed hard. He ordered the intriguing scallops, and then turned to her for her choice for dinner. Since the waiter was ignoring her, she said to Nick, "I'll have the smoked duck breast."

"Smoked duck breast?" He studied the menu as if to verify the selection actually existed.

"Yes, it's listed as being prepared with huckleberry preserves atop the duck confit and accompanied by duck with goat cheese wrapped in pastry. It sounds absolutely divine." She pointed it out on his menu.

"Oh! Is that what that is? Well, that does sound marvelous." He pointed to her selection on the menu, not daring to pronounce it, and then to his choice. The waiter smiled generously at them, nodding his head and glided off to put their order in with the kitchen. Nick turned to her, "I got the pentard." He smiled and added, "Love it, just love it."

"You know, I've never tried pheasant."

"Then I'll make a deal with you, I'll give you a bite of the pentard if you will give up a bite or two of your duck-two-ways."

She nodded at him thinking he was far too handsome to be British. And his teeth were far too perfect. She gave herself a strict reminder to stop thinking like a dentist's daughter.

"So, Jane, tell me all about your life in that mythical place of the South that is North Carolina and all about this quaint family you come from with two other sisters, you girl in the middle you!"

Jane regaled him with stories of growing up in the New American South, watching his face grow ever more puzzled. "So, something obviously isn't making sense to you?"

"No, your stories are delightful. I suppose I thought it would be more like Gone with the Wind or Diary of a Vampire or something. You know, trees dripping with Spanish Moss and Southern gentility and all that."

Jane thought about the good old boys who drove around in their jacked-up trucks with offensive stickers on them. "Um, it's not quite like that."

"And I'm confused about who all these people are? You told me you're the girl-in-the-middle, but it sounds like you have a mess of brothers."

"Oh yeah, them. You know, I sort of do have brothers. My mom's best friend is Mimi. She and her husband, George…"

"Good old English name, George!"

"Yes, I suppose. Well, Mimi and George divorced when their three kids were young. George moved overseas, and Mimi had to raise Caroline, Rory and Chase."

Nick nodded his head sadly. "There must be some terrible karma between 'George's' and Americans. It never seems to work out, does it? George-the-third became rather a stalker of America after their little rebellion caused their great divorce. I hope this modern-day namesake behaved a bit better?"

Jane laughed. "Oh, Nick, you're so funny. So very funny. Anyway, after Mimi became a single mom, her family kind of blended in with ours. It was always my two moms, my dad, and what felt like my five siblings. Every Christmas. Every Easter. Every Fourth of July. Any Hallmark holiday you can name. Lord, you should have seen us at Halloween! We were quite the crew. There was so much chaos that the parents called these get-togethers 'WMD events', because it was like weapons of mass destruction had been detonated by the time the evening came to an end."

"I can imagine with six children! How wonderful! It sounds like an absolute circus. It must have been delightful! You always had playmates growing up, didn't you? And you always have companions now."

Jane smiled as warm memories flooded her. "I'm not sure I have a childhood memory that doesn't have Caroline, Rory, and Chase in it, in addition to Summer and Charlie. Oh sure, I'm exaggerating, but yeah, we were together a lot. Caroline is one of my best friends now. Just like a sister to me. Like my oldest sister."

"Well, you show off, you, just be ready to be jealous! I—" he paused for dramatic effect, "…had lots of empty rooms to play in, and when my father wasn't home," here he dropped his voice to an excited whisper, "his prized car collection was always great fun for an imaginative and lonely little boy. But that was only if I wouldn't be caught. They weren't supposed to be touched, those cars. But in them, me and my imaginary friends went everyplace a little boy could dream of. I can tell you since you are the keeper of my secrets!" He mimed zipping his lip and throwing away the key.

"And are you still an imaginative and lonely little boy?"

He gave her his best roguish grin and she felt her heart quiver. "Imaginative always! Never lonely, if I can help it! Tell me, does your father collect cars as well?"

Jane gave an involuntary chuckle. Her father, John, had often remarked on the motley crew of cars that they did seem to collect. As each daughter came of age, she needed "an old beater" to drive, and all too often those cars seemed to come back home to roost after their owners moved on to school and didn't need a car there or abandoned them as they got jobs and cars of their own. Audree, her mother, would bemoan the line-up of junk cars, all next to John's old beat-up green and white relic of a truck. "Uh, yeah, but not quite like what I think you're talking about. I don't think my mom, in particular, would call them 'beloved' automobiles. Not quite that. And it was okay if we drove them. It was okay if we drove them into the ground actually."

"Well, lucky you, once again! My dad has six cars from the nineteen-thirties and nineteen-forties. Real collector's items, in stellar condition, every one. The only time their motors ever run is when they're rented out for movies and period pieces on the BBC. Gods, they make him scads of money at the prices he charges."

The scallops came as their first course, and they were indeed served on a bed of actual pebbles which were quite hot. "I don't recommend eating those, by the way," Nick said to Jane with a wink.

"No risk there." Jane pointed to herself. "Daughter of a dentist!"

They proceeded to finish the bottle of wine, dinner, and dessert. When the waiter brought the check, which Jane was afraid to see, Nick smiled at her and said, "I hope you don't mind if this evening is on me, in payment for the private guided tour of Paris. All the psychotherapy earlier. And… and… oh, I can't think of another reason but do let me pick up the tab."

"Thank you. I do feel, though, that I owe you at least another tour. This was such a lovely dinner and there's so much of Paris that I haven't shown you." She felt that queer sensation of radiating light again, she was so happy. She felt confident, both in her ability to make smart conversation and now to also look good while she did so. He smiled at her and seemed at a loss for words. They left the restaurant close to nine o'clock. It took an hour to walk back to her apartment, as they talked the entire time. At her door he gently lifted her hand and kissed it.

"May I see you again? Perhaps next weekend? You know, there are some awfully touristy things I've never done in Paris. Perhaps we could be tourists together? Maybe there is something for me to appreciate about my internment here, after all?"

* * *

In class the next morning, Jane could hardly pay attention. As the professor called out, "D'accord, la classe est teriminé," Claudine gently shook her friend. "If this is how you pay attention, then I will be sorry I made our deal!" Claudine sighed with mock disgust. "How will you help me become a marketing wizard, so I can head my own firm someday, if you are all dreamy and don't pay attention."

"What? Huh? Oh, nothing to worry about. Like I told you, this is all intro stuff. Took a whole class on it last semester." Jane waved off her friend's worry. Then she proceeded to tell Claudine all she could of her rendezvous of the previous evening as they walked to their next class together.

"Oui. From what I saw, he was quite taken by surprise—and that is a good thing. You are a good student of La Femme Francais, Jane. A good student."

Jane stopped and thought for a moment. "It's amazing what a little bit of confidence can do for you. I never had the confidence before."

"Oui! That is the heart of je ne sais quoi."

Chapter 3

"Earth to Jane? Allô? Are you there?" Claudine asked, irritation evident in her voice.

"Huh? What? Oh yeah, sure, I'm here! I'm here! What do you need?" Jane snapped to attention, having been called out once again on her daydreaming.

"I thought we were supposed to be on a team creating a marketing plan for this… eh… not a real one… what did you call it?"

"Fictitious. It's a fictitious company."

"Oui! Fic-ti-tious," Claudine sounded it out. "That is a good English word. I will have to remember that one. Fic-ti-tious. Our fictitious company. And its fictitious product that we are supposed to say will bring you a real relationship." Claudine rolled her eyes. "All this obsession with relationships! Jane, our assignment is not fictitious. It is due next week and I am reading, reading, reading and you are someplace off in the clouds! We need to figure out how we are going to market this fictitious product that no one in their right minds could believe is required for their happiness."

"Sorry. I'm focused now. I'm on it." Jane turned her attention back to her textbook and their scattered papers sketching out their plans. She had to admit, she loved how Claudine translated ideas into English. So often they came out hilariously twisted and yet also dead-on target, full of insightful wisdom.

Claudine looked carefully at her friend and at last let out an exasperated sigh. "It is no good. You will not be able to focus until you have got it out. I know you, Jane—you must talk about what is bothering you. You cannot keep it in until you explode like the firework."

Jane looked up at Claudine, putting a hand to her chest in defense. "I don't explode. I have never in my life exploded."

Claudine shrugged. "Eh! So maybe that is me who is the firework. But you know what I mean. You are sad and you cannot focus. If you cannot focus, we will never develop a brilliant but devious campaign to convince people that they must have something that does not exist and, more importantly, I will not get an A in this class. So, this is about that Nicky-boy, is it not? I can tell by the look on your face. We will take a break from being marketing wizards. Go ahead. What is happening now?"

Jane blew her bangs out of her eyes. It would be good to talk about it. And who better than Claudine? She was the savviest person at relationships that Jane had ever met, even if a bit cynical. "I went to the art gallery opening last night. That new artist. Very avant garde, not that I cared about her work, but I knew Nick would be there."

"Oooh! She is supposed to be very good. A bit disturbing, but if you are not prone to nightmares, I have heard her work is worth seeing!"

Jane shook her head. "If you aren't prone to nightmares already then you will be after seeing her show." She shuddered. "But Nick was there. Thought it was amazing stuff... and apparently, I was hardly worth the conversation."

"He didn't talk to you? Did he ignore you?"

"Well, yeah. Pretty much. There had to be four women who were just hanging all over him. He certainly didn't notice me. I could have been art on the wall." Then she added, "Bad art that no one was noticing." She looked up as she thought. "Let me rephrase that. Everyone was clamoring over, well, whatever that scary crap was that was splashed up all over the place. Ugh!" she shuddered. "So, I felt more like ignored, boring-yet-normally-adjusted, wallflower art."

"Oui, people seem to like art that makes them feel destabilized and uncomfortable. I think it gives them something to talk about. So that they can feel smart and special because they can talk about it."

"Let's just say it wasn't a winning night for normal."

Claudine shrugged it off. "You are already smart. You do not need avant garde to make up for the fictitious things you think you lack." She looked at Jane judiciously. "But he ignored you. Hmmm. Is there any chance you were you wearing your horrible American clothes? The ones that look like bags?"

"They don't look like..." Jane started but Claudine cut her off.

"So that is a yes." Claudine sighed. "And you are jaloux?" Then she added in English, "Jealous is, I believe, the translation?"

Jane looked down at her textbook while a tear slid down her face. "Oui," she answered dejectedly. "We've gone out four times in the past six weeks. And we've had a wonderful evening every time. He talks so much about his life. I mean, he really opens up. But when I saw him surrounded by those girls…"

Claudine looked at her curiously. "Just what were those girls doing?"

"Well, for one, they were fawning all over him."

Claudine shook her head. "Faux-ning? Is this like 'fic-ti-tious?' I do not know this word."

"Faw-ning. It's like, like how a dog is excited to see you."

Claudine looked blank. "A dog wants food. A scratch on the head. Then it goes about its business. It's a dog."

Jane couldn't help but chuckle. She thought that it should have been obvious that Claudine wasn't a dog person. "Like a cat," she said, and then mimicked licking her hand like a paw.

"Oooh! I know just what you mean. I had a cat like that. Loved me very much. Was insecure. Sticky."

"Clingy."

"Oui, 'cling-gee'. Used to bring me dead things and beg me to love on it. It was very annoying."

"Right, like no self-respect. They were clinging to him and honestly, for a moment I wondered if they were hookers, given what they were wearing. Or maybe I should say weren't wearing." Jane shook her head in disapproval and shuddered slightly. "I just couldn't do that."

"And… was Nick happy? Did he look like he was enjoying himself with all the…" Claudine mimicked licking her hand like a paw, "fauxning?" The distaste in Claudine's voice surpassed mild.

"Oui." The word came out weighted down and heavy. "He was like a fish on the hook. And if I'm being really honest, which I always am with you, those women were so sexy and so pretty and… and I was so intimidated." She sighed heavily. "I lost all my confidence and I couldn't even speak to him or approach him. It was like seeing how they had raw power over men. And he… he left with them. I don't even know if he knew I was there."

"All of them?"

"All of them. Laughing and giggling. And wiggling. Them, I mean. Not him." She sniffled. "I don't have that kind of power. I'm just a wallflower. Guys have to like me for me, but I don't have bait on my hook like that! You know, Claudine, I think Americans are the ones who are crazy for Europeans, but I'm pretty sure it doesn't work the other way around. Nobody loves Americans."

"Hmmm. I don't think they were 'Little Sisters of Hearts', as the working girls are sometimes called. I think they were just girls hungry for the attention of someone like Monsieur Sutcliffe-Ashworth. Jane, because Nicholas is a very handsome man, he is likely to have the attention of women. And he is riches, so they will lay themselves down at his feet. They will ask to be walked on. They will enjoy being walked on by him."

"Handsome, yes. Too handsome. But wait, what did you say? Rich? Uh, I don't know about that."

"Jane, you are naïve. He is British and here at school in France and he does not care much about his grades. He is twenty-three. He should be done with his school by now. If he needed schooling to find his place in the world, he would care more about it. His parents must be sending him here to either let him grow up someplace not a risk to their reputation or they want him to have some type of pedigree, also for their reputation." She shrugged like it was obvious. "Therefore, he is riches."

"He's wealthy?"

"Oui. Or he is stupid to still be in school at his age, and Jane Donahue would never fall in love with someone stupid."

There was no arguing with Claudine.

"Love? I'm in love with him?" Jane stared at Claudine and then with dawning recognition became wide-eyed. That little girl crush she developed at first sight was growing into something much more consuming. "Oh my God, I'm in love with him. Help me, Claudine!"

"Jane, you are a fool to think that other women will not, what is the saying? 'Throw themselves' at him? They will. They will be doing the faux-ning. A man who has both good looks and a good bank account is beyond reproach for some women. He will always have candy at his feet. He can have anything he wants. All that attention will teach him that he can play by his own rules, make up his own rules, treat women as he wishes—and they will thank him for it." Claudine looked hard at Jane, and then she sighed and her expression softened. "But, if he is to love you, he must feel that he needs to 'step up his game a notch', as the British say. He must want the thing he cannot seem to have. And that special thing is you, Jane."

"Oh, he could have me in a heartbeat if he wanted. That's the problem." Jane shut her textbook and slumped back in her chair.

"Oh, so you have become like those girls? Throwing yourself at him? Becoming his doormat? His little cat?" Claudine looked at Jane, eyebrows raised and teasing her with little tsk, tsk sounds. "Jane, I am not sure this Nicholas is worth the wanting. Oh arrêt! Stop! No more crying. I will help you. I just hope you don't hold it against me someday. Jane, you need to be more Français! You are too Américain. You need that je ne sais quoi. Be not so direct. You always look at him right in the eye. You always look everyone right in the eye."

"Yes, of course I do. It's honest. It's forthright. It's trustworthy. It's me."

"Ah Jane! You do not understand: this is not a business deal. This is amour. There is nothing honest about amour."

Jane looked at Claudine, total incomprehension in her eyes. "He was initially wowed by your quickly applied veneer of glamour and class, but the real American book-smart girl beneath the classy French shine…"

Claudine waved her off, a bit impatient. "Okay. Let me put it another way. It is fictitious." Claudine gave a sigh. "This is marketing."

Slowly Jane sat up. "Huh? I mean, I get marketing."

"Apparently not when you are the product. Now you watch how I am with you now, you see how I talk to you now? I want you to pay attention. This is important," Claudine said, but as she spoke to Jane, she looked away, and then looked sideways at Jane out of the corner of her eye, a sly smile on her face. She slowly tucked her short bob behind one ear and looked away again as she spoke. Her long fingers and painted nails almost stroked her own face as she drew them away. At "important" she looked Jane directly in the eye, held her gaze for a moment and then looked away, turning her shoulder slightly as if to shut Jane out.

"Oh my God!" Jane leaned back in her chair.

"So, you feel it? You feel it?" Claudine asked, once again herself, leaning forward towards Jane, the excitement resonant in her voice.

"I felt as if you were flirting with me. Oh my gosh, that was so… awkward."

"But you felt it. Jane, je ne sais quoi is not something you do. It is something that you feel. Like confidence. And because you feel it you do that something undefinable that captures his attention, no?"

"Whoa, it was like you were flirting with me. Another woman."

"Ah, Jane," Claudine sighed loudly with a look heavenward, "you have so little idea of how the world works. Of course, I was flirting with you. Interested… and maybe not. Dangled in front of you and then drifting out of reach. Elusive. That was the point. But can you do it with him? That is the question." Claudine sighed, somewhat exasperated. "Let's talk parfum."

"What?"

"You need a parfum."

"Oh my God, do I smell?" Jane asked, raising her arm to sniff, trying to be subtle but making sure she didn't have body odor. Given how the French were not nearly as appreciative of the advantages of deodorant products as the typical American, she thought the accusation about her "scent" was rather a low blow. All she could smell was her Power Fresh Secret, which she had brought with her from the U.S.

"Jane! What are you doing?" Claudine said, horrified as she looked around the library. "Get your nose out of your armpit! Don't ever let anyone see you do that!" She shook her finger at her friend. "Ach, Mon Dieu! No, you need a parfum. You need a special scent that is you."

"What is that? A scent that is me?"

"Oui, we will go to La Samaratine. Or maybe Printemps. Or maybe we will have to resort to Le Bon Marché. Bring your credit card!"

Jane swallowed hard.

"We will try many scents. Nous allons en trouver un qui est vous."

"Find one that is me?" Jane asked, mystified.

"Oui. Napoléon loved Josephine. She wore the scent of violets. It drove him crazy because he could sometimes smell it and the next moment not. And then it would be back. She was smart to do this. A woman should drive a man crazy. It is je ne sais quoi. A woman should look at a man as if to steal a glimpse. It is je ne sais quoi. A woman should care but not too much. She should be confident in herself. It is je ne sais quoi. Jane, you will have je ne sais quoi and I will have a top grade in international marketing!" Claudine said triumphantly. "And after school, I think I will come and find a job in your Charlotte." She gave Jane a wink. "You will help me."

Jane diligently sought out "the scent of Jane". After patiently trying about a dozen different parfums she found it. In a very un-French-like move she finally tried a signature fragrance from an American designer and suddenly she understood what Claudine was talking about. Sometimes she could smell it and sometimes not, but it was all the more delicious on her for that elusive quality. Even Claudine noticed it.

Jane took on "marketing Jane" like a project, tackling it with the same intensity she devoted to all her schoolwork. She wrote up plans, made drawings, put swatches together, planned outfits, practiced in the mirror. She practiced on the guys in her class and suddenly became quite popular, with invitations for coffee or museum excursions abounding, which she went on as a form of research so that she could experiment and learn what worked and what didn't. She was amazed at how men noticed her even without her dressing as a "Little Sister of Hearts"—she could do je ne sais quoi without mimicking a prostitute. Or a doormat. Men noticed her everywhere she went. Much better than that, so did Nicholas Sutcliffe-Ashworth. And he certainly noticed the competition.

Most importantly to Claudine, they both got top marks in International Marketing.

Chapter 4

"Earth to Jane, Earth to Jane…" His deep rich voice called her to the present. "Are you almost ready? Darling…?"

She loved how he said *darling*. With his accent it came out as daahling. It was like when he said shed-jewel. That one actually took her a couple of times before she understood he was saying "schedule". Early on in their relationship she could easily miss what he said, either because she was lost in his accent or sometimes because his words and phrases just didn't translate to American English. He always laughed at her and said she had a French je ne sais quoi and a real American witchcraft about her that he found absolutely enchanting.

"I'm under your spell, as apparently are all of your male classmates! And even, I might say, some of the teachers", he'd remarked quite a few times. That sense that Jane was a woman in high demand, someone special who garnered attention far and wide, had served to accelerate his interest. Jane had learned that you could have anything you wanted, provided you wanted it badly enough. Marketing made all the difference.

"My little daydreamer—we're joining my parents for the theater in less than fifteen minutes and you're not ready. Your zip isn't quite up. Did you know?"

Jane smiled at the memories and brought herself to the present. "My what? My zip?" She craned her neck to see her backside in the mirror.

"Here, silly. Let me help you." He came up behind her and zipped her dress up the rest of the way, kissing her on the neck as he did so. "You speak four languages and yet you can't get yourself properly dressed! My silly girl!" he said, as he kissed her on the forehead.

"Oh! You mean the zipper!" Jane smiled at him.

"Yes, your zip-*per*, you call it. Well, if we look the dashing pair, then we should be ready to endure the evening with Cressida and Colin. At least we'll have the theater to, what is it you Americans say, eat up the time?" Nick smiled. Giving her a wink he added, "Enjoying limited time with my parents is always a good plan. With Cressida on the scene, you never know when everything will go all pear-shaped."

"Nicky, you're too hard on your mother."

"Oh, just you wait until she finds out we upgraded our room. I expect a real wobbly with that one."

Jane glanced over at the bed. "You know, I have to say, I just didn't think hotels still offered rooms with twin beds. That was so weird to walk in and be greeted by a nineteen-fifties sitcom set. Of course, we had to upgrade to something normal. That was… that was a kiddie room."

"She's a woman who absolutely must always be in control. Well, time to go, my love." He tapped on his watch.

"Let me put on my lipstick and I'll be ready." As she bent over to the mirror in their hotel room, she puckered and highlighted her lips with a pretty poppy color, catching the glint from the sparkling jewel on her hand. It was like nothing she'd ever seen before. Nick said it was a very special ring, and she agreed with him. A large diamond, pink in color and oval in shape, was tucked in a filigreed platinum nest studded with tiny diamonds, which themselves gave off bluish hues. It looked so old world and so very British. She couldn't imagine where he'd found it and made a mental note to ask him at some point. She took a moment to gaze lovingly at its artistry. She was going to marry Nicholas Sutcliffe-Ashworth. He had asked her just last night, on Christmas night, and she had accepted his proposal. She was on cloud nine: the happy ending she had doggedly pursued and poured herself into despite the hardships and challenges along the way. Indeed, there had been dark days when she thought her heart's desire would elude her.

Nick's entire experience with women was simply total capitulation to his whims and desires. *He will always have candy at his feet—*Claudine had certainly read that situation correctly. Nick had been stunned when Jane accepted a full ride scholarship to NYU for an MBA, instead of her finding "Some convenient position, anything close by. It's just a job, after all" near him. In truth, Jane had surprised herself with her independent decision, but Claudine had threatened her with an American-style intervention if she passed up such an opportunity.

With a tsk, tsk, tsk, sound, Claudine had said, "I am sure he is most astonished that anyone would choose something—like their education—over him, but never let a man deter you from your career. I know you love him, but you must love yourself first and most! Jane, do not be candy at his feet. If you are to be candy, be the fancy box on the high shelf that he has to work to reach. Make him 'step it up a notch'. Or several."

Jane had taken the scholarship and the relationship risks that came with it. Time and distance had been daunting, with bumps and break-ups that shook her to her core, but she had prevailed and seen her way through. One more semester and her degree would be complete—and she already had a post-graduation job offer from her internship last summer. A position with a bit more security and a much bigger paycheck than Nick's, actually. With approval, Claudine had assured her that she was far beyond being any type of candy for anyone. The candy was going to be at her own feet.

But her heart had made its choice. And apparently, so had his, despite the odds and the three thousand, four hundred and fifty-nine miles between them. "We are two halves of one whole. No matter what happens, we will always find our way back to one another." That was the promise he had made her. And now she was living her own personal fairy-tale ending: wearing his ring, putting on lipstick in a room at the Intercontinental Hotel in London—a room with a king-sized bed in it—about to spend the evening at the theater with her fiancé and her future in-laws.

He brought her coat and held it up for her. "It's beastly cold out there. It would seem that global warming is on holiday as well. Let's hope my parents are warm tonight." He grimaced. "And don't forget the gloves that Mum gave you for Christmas! Wouldn't do to leave them behind."

"I've got them right here," she said unenthusiastically as she pulled a pair of white gloves out of her coat pocket and held them up. They looked like they would have been the height of fashion in the nineteen-fifties, right in keeping with those twin beds. "Do people still wear white gloves?" She shoved them back in her pocket. "I mean, like does the Queen even do that?"

Nick sighed. "I'm sure she's making a statement."

"Yeah, maybe one about the mid twentieth century." And then muttered, "like those twin beds". Changing the subject, she asked, "Your parents love the theater, don't they? And visiting London? It's such a nice Christmas present to bring us here and do the whole theater tour together this week as a family. I feel like they're really finally accepting me. We'll see, what? Six shows in the next few days?"

"Yes, and by design have hardly any time for only the two of us. Honestly, I think that is part of their plan. And I must confess, I did make one little change to the schedule without consulting you." She loved it when he said shed-jewel. "I exchanged some boring drama here in town to go out to Stratford-Upon-Avon for Shakespeare—a Much Ado About Nothing matinee to be precise. I hope you don't mind. I wanted to give us a little respite and have some time on our own."

"Oh Nicky, that's terrific! Wow, seeing Stratford-Upon Avon!" He opened the door for her and escorted her down the hall to the elevator. "I can't wait to see Wicked tonight. I've wanted to see it for years."

"Yes, that's a good choice, for us anyway. I'm sure Mum's going to be on edge since it's 'modern theater' and such popular musicals aren't considered 'proper' theatre at all. My mother can really throw a wobbler if provoked, so we want to avoid that on all counts! God forbid any children are there tonight." The elevator door opened with a cheery *bing!* and they entered. Nick pushed the lobby button. "And please don't tell her about the new room. They can just find it out when the bill comes due."

"Oh, Nicky, she's just old-world conservative. She probably knew we'd change the room, but now it's not 'on her' that we're sleeping in the same bed. Maybe it's a generational thing. My parents can struggle with that stuff too." Jane waved off his concern. "I'm sure she meant well."

"Nice of you to defend her so, but you sound like you've forgotten the very first words my mother said upon meeting you."

Jane shifted uncomfortably on her feet as the elevator descended. She did remember. Cressida had not said Hello or Nice to meet you. She had walked up to Jane and, putting her two hands on Jane's cheeks, she studied her face and said, "Colin, she is pretty, she is pretty," her voice filled with a great deal of relief. Later she had declared her son's girlfriend to be 'very French', but given the way it was uttered, Jane wasn't sure whether that new assessment negated her previous praise.

"Yes, I remember." Jane forced herself to shake off the memory. You marry the man, you marry his family. She had to make this work. "People are who they are, and we have to accept them that way. She's not going to change. I'm sure if I just understood her perspective, her point of view, it would all make sense, the things she says. Or does."

"I think you could forgive any insult could you only understand the poor perpetrator against your person. You are undoubtedly the most compassionate woman I've ever met. So empathetic: the most generous explanation to the core. I've never been able to share with anyone the way I can with you. I just hope you don't bestow that kindness on an unworthy recipient. Jane, really, you are an angel incarnate. You have more patience with my mother than do I." He picked up her hand and kissed it. "My angel."

Jane chortled. "Not quite an angel. There are some lines that can't be crossed. But you know, people value different things. I'm sure that… that… well, if you pit higher education against attractiveness, I would guess that beauty just looms larger for her, with her upbringing and her social set, and it wins every time." She felt around in her pocket. "As do, uh, gloves."

"Her upbringing. Wouldn't that be interesting to talk about? She's quite the pedigree person now, but yes, looks have been more important to her than she might like to admit. I don't think you'll be able to pry open that oyster though, all your most wily interrogation skills notwithstanding."

"I think a lot of women equate their worth with their looks. And while that's not my family, people are different. My parents aren't perfect. They value being smart. Surely you must have felt how they tested you when you came to visit that first Easter? I was mortified."

"Well, perhaps," he said. "But I'm always dashing, I'm always smart!" He pretended to straighten his tie.

Nick's reference went over Jane's head. "I was amazed they weren't pulling out an IQ test and making you take it."

"Oh! You don't mean smart. That would be my mother. You mean intelligent! Well, disappointment for them, they're going to get a swotting son-in-law, rather than some type of natural genius-in-the-making like their daughters are turning out to be. Sorry, darling, if they were checking me out, I missed it. Tell me, did I pass the test?"

Jane put on her best Southern drawl and said, "Honey, you pass my test, and that is all that matters." She pulled the new and unfashionable theater gloves out of her pocket.

"Well, that's all I need to know then, is it not? And here we are, apres vous, mon Cheri," he said with almost no French accent at all. With a smile and a small bow, he held open the elevator door for her. "Steel yourself."

"Oh, honey, what could possibly go wrong?"

He made a non-committal grunt. "Now pop those gloves on your hands and look posh, even if in a toffee-nosed kind of way, and everything will be top notch. At least for Mum."

Not sure what he meant and slightly worried about her nose, she reluctantly pulled the stiff white gloves over her fingers.

Chapter 5

Jane and Nick walked into the lobby of the Intercontinental Hotel, joining Cressida and Colin Sutcliffe-Ashworth, the elder.

"Ah, brilliant! Right on time. Aren't you smart-looking tonight, Jane!"

"Why thank you, Colin," Jane gave Nick's father a warm smile.

"You look so French, my dear," Cressida said, giving Jane a near-kiss on the cheek. Jane kissed back, taking care to make sure her lips didn't touch Mrs. Sutcliffe-Ashworth or leave any lipstick marks on her coat.

"I must say, you two certainly look the dashing couple." Nick's voice was pleasant and upbeat, betraying none of the hesitation he'd expressed on the lift.

"What a splendid evening," Colin said with a little clap of his hands. "We should have a car waiting. We have a reservation at 190 Queen's Gate over in Kensington. It's a bit early to eat, but we'll have plenty of time to make the show tonight."

"Sounds lovely. What drew you to this particular restaurant?" Jane asked. "What are they known for?"

"Haven't the slightest idea. It was just on The List!" Colin said, still jovial and excited.

Jane hoped the unknown restaurant didn't surprise them by being a gastropub or a burger joint, given how they were all dressed for the evening. "I'm sure the list was full of enticing possibilities. The theater we're headed to is down by Victoria Station, isn't it?"

"Oh, I'm sure I don't know," Colin chuffed. "Never bothered to learn London. The driver will take us where we need to be. After the show we'll come back here and have drinks in the bar."

"Yes, Father, that sounds just fine." As Nick helped his mother with her coat, Jane noticed that she pulled on a lovely pair of navy gloves that looked to be a soft lambskin and which perfectly matched her coat. Nick then offered his arm to his mother and escorted her out and into the waiting car.

Colin followed suit, offering his arm to Jane, remarking, "Your gloves are so quaint, my dear. Rather reminds me of my own mother. Is that the latest American fashion? They say it all comes back around again, don't they?"

When they walked into the restaurant, Jane noticed that the only people wearing white gloves were certain members of the serving staff. She slid hers off and shoved them back in her pockets.

190 Queen's Gate was a quaint, nostalgic place that felt exactly like the kind of English restaurant Cressida and Colin's social set would enjoy. Dinner started off reasonably well. Jane had the roast parsnip velouté while Nick and his parents all ordered pan-fried foie gras with macerated cherries. It was during these first courses that Cressida nearly choked as she sipped her wine. A waiter ran over to assist; the restaurant stilling as patrons were riveted by the drama. As Cressida at last caught her breath she spluttered out, "Oh, I can't breathe! Do you see that!" Then she pointed to Jane, her finger flailing wildly. "She is wearing a... a... a ring. Tell me, is that my family heirloom on your finger? Why does she have my ring on her finger?" For some reason, Cressida seemed to direct her question to the waiter, rather than to anyone at the table.

Jane felt a sense of shock jolt through her body. She slowly looked around the restaurant, realizing that everyone was now looking at her, including the waiter. She was not used to being the center of such public curiosity, and the tables were indeed close enough together that neighboring parties didn't need to strain to eavesdrop. Slowly, it dawned on her that Nick might not have informed his parents about his intended proposal. Here she'd been waiting for the happy moment when they gaily announced their news, with his parents smiling and making some joke like "about time!" and "welcome to the family" while they ordered champagne. Nick had also encouraged her to wear those ugly gloves, which Cressida never noticed, even though the gift tag had identified them as a present from her. Jane felt very awkward to be the one breaking the news to them—not to mention to the room full of complete strangers now staring at her. The waiter's initial look of surprise had morphed into one of accusation: he was standing behind Cressida and looking daggers at Jane, as if she'd stolen the ring.

Cressida thinks this ring is hers and a family heirloom? Jane's head was spinning. She could hear her voice, timid as a mouse. "It's lovely, isn't it? It was actually a, well, sort of a Christmas present." She looked over at Nick, feeling the need for rescue. He should be the one to give full voice to their plans.

"A Christmas present? Really?" Now Cressida stared daggers at Nick. So did the waiter.

Nick took a deep breath. "Yes, Mother." He tried to hold his voice steady. "I proposed yesterday, on Christmas day, and Jane has accepted me."

"With my grandmother's ring? And without consulting me?"

Colin looked puzzled. "But the two of you broke up last summer—what about Ashlyn?"

"Who's Ashlyn?" Jane asked, looking from Nick to Colin to Cressida.

"You're completely rushing into things! You've hardly resumed your relationship. Why, just last summer you were apart and seeing other people. After all, Jane ran off on you to earn that New York MBT thing." Cressida was nearly squawking, seemingly having started her wobbler already.

"MBA," Jane said. "New York University." Jane looked around the table and said, more defensive-sounding than she intended, "I only have one semester left."

"That's a quick turn-around. You were seeing Ashlyn," Colin said to his son, far more interested in the other woman angle than anything that had to do with higher education. "Now she's a looker, that one."

"Who's Ashlyn?" Jane asked, now looking directly at Nick.

"And the two of you so young? Why Jane isn't even out of school yet!" Cressida shifted tactics from not knowing what degree Jane was earning to now being worried that she wasn't yet finished. The waiter crossed his arms, letting out an audible "humph!" as he tossed his floppy hair and gave Jane a look.

Jane felt so many shockwaves that she hardly knew how to process them all. The jolt of finding out that the ring might not have been Nick's to offer was only the start of it. Who was Ashlyn? By comparison it seemed mundane that Cressida worry about Jane completing her MBA, when she hadn't seemed supportive of it in the first place. And what the heck did that waiter have to do with anything?

"I'm twenty-five years old, Mother. I think I know what I'm doing." Nick huffed. "And Jane is twenty-three. We're not children." He took Jane's hand.

"I'm going to finish school, Cressida. No worries about that. That's a priority. It's only another few months after all. And I have a great job offer already."

"How could you do something so drastic without consulting me?" Cressida said to Nick, ignoring Jane. "And with my ring?"

Jane glanced around. It seemed that no one in the restaurant would need to go to the theater—they were getting dinner and a show right at 190 Queen's Gate.

"I didn't consult you because: a, this is my life, Mother. And b, because it's always been a given that my wife would wear that ring, continuing the family tradition. And c, because I didn't want to create a scene." Nick answered her levelly through gritted teeth as he glanced surreptitiously about the restaurant. Then he met the stares of the other guests, causing them to look away guiltily and resume their own meals. He took a rather large sip of his wine.

Cressida immediately reached for her glass and took a few deep sips herself. She looked up at their waiter and gave him an almost imperceptible nod. He returned the gesture, gave another harsh look at Jane, and then strutted off.

Jane had to hand it to Nick, now that the ball was rolling, he seemed to have nerves of steel. She couldn't imagine surprising her parents with something like this. Then, with a sinking realization it dawned on her that her parents would be surprised to get her call with the news of their engagement, particularly given the on-and-off relationship between Jane and Nick over the past two years. And they would probably share similar concerns, although mostly about where the young couple would eventually live. She knew her parents would be ecstatic about solid jobs for either of them.

Colin gave an inappropriate chuckle. "Well, in my day we were never hasty about marriage. We waited until we were… um, how old were we when we got married, my dear?"

"You were in your thirties. I was twenty-six," she answered. "And in hindsight that was too young," she said quickly as if realizing her argument stood on a weak foundation.

Suddenly they were interrupted. "Oh, Cressida, *dahling*! There you are. You weren't on the transport over to the restaurant earlier. My dear, the whole point of group excursion is to be with the group. We worried you were going to miss the whole of the evening!" A very tall woman swept up to the table. "It's not good to worry us, after, well, you know." Cressida, Colin, and this new stranger exchanged meaningful looks. Suddenly, in a much lighter tone she said, "Now, I know you're upset that it's modern theater, but I'm sure it will be all right." She placed a few comforting taps on Cressida's shoulder. The woman turned to Nick's father. "Hello, Colin, dear." Colin and Nick both immediately stood up. Jane noticed how frozen Cressida looked.

"Julia! Aren't you looking just smashing tonight. Where's Simon?" Colin said, looking around.

Very formally, Nick said, "Good evening, Mrs. Stuart."

"Well, hullo! Of course, Simon is off drinking single malts with the boys in the bar. I'm surprised you haven't joined him. Oh, Chip! Your mother had said you would be tagging along this year. We are so looking forward to having you join us. You know, when it's only all the old folks it's not nearly as much fun, but I'm sure you'll be the life of the party!" The woman named Julia laughed loudly. "And who is this charming young lady?" she said as she turned her larger-than-life personality onto Jane, who felt as though she had just been thrust under a microscope.

"Mrs. Stuart," said Nick, "allow me to present Ms. Jane Donahue."

Jane stood up to greet Mrs. Stuart. "Very nice to meet you."

"Oh, my goodness, you're an American! I had pegged you as French!" She went on to remark on Jane's hair, her dress, her boots, all very kindly but still it somehow made Jane feel like a horse up for auction and being appraised. There wasn't much opportunity to get a word into the conversation while Julia was holding court and Jane noticed that Cressida didn't even try. And then Mrs. Stuart spotted the ring. She picked up Jane's hand and held it firmly. "Oh my, darling, just look at that! My dear, what a lovely ring!" She shot a glance at Cressida who looked ready to eat bullets. "Is it possible that the two of you are engaged?"

Jane nodded meekly, completely overwhelmed by this woman.

Nick jumped in to save her. "Yes, Mrs. Stuart. Jane and I became engaged just yesterday. We met as students at the Sorbonne. Jane is now a student in New York, getting an advanced degree. We are, um, celebrating… with my parents."

"Oh! Chip! Chip, you're engaged? I never thought to see that happen. And to a highly educated, ah, American. I particularly never thought to see that happen!" She winked at Jane, who didn't feel this at all lessened the impact of her words. "Cressida, you must be beside yourself… beside yourself with joy!" Now Julia turned her attention to Nick's mother. "And planning a wedding! How splendid. I'll tell the others, shall I? Waiter!" She snapped her fingers loudly several times. "Please bring a bottle of Moët here to this table and put it on my bill. Lovely, lovely. Well, I should be getting back. They'll wonder what in the world has happened to me. No good in making any of them worry. See you at the theater! Wicked! How perfect! How perfectly suiting. Ta, ta!"

And the whirlwind that was Julia was gone. Somewhat awkwardly, Jane, Nick, and Colin resumed their seats, just as their dinners were brought to the table. A bottle of Moët & Chandon quickly followed, the ice bucket being carried by the snooty waiter. No one spoke as the sommelier opened the bottle with a cheery *pop!* that was completely discordant with the moment. He poured glasses for each of them.

Nick broke the silence first, raising his flute. "To my lovely bride-to-be," he murmured a bit awkwardly. He nodded to Jane and sipped. Jane gave him the strongest smile she felt she could muster at that moment, although the feeling of an unwelcome tremor in her lips was distressing. She really didn't notice whether his parents joined in the toast or not.

"Well, that cat's out of the bag, whatever your plans to the contrary," Colin said to his wife as he threw back a good amount of his glass of champagne.

"I take it she's a family friend?" Jane asked.

"She's my best friend," Cressida answered as she, too, threw back her glass of champagne.

"Nick, why did she call you Chip?" Jane asked her fiancé.

He shrugged at her. "Oh, that. Ages old. I was called 'Chip' growing up. You know, 'Chip off the old block', that sort of thing. It helped keep all the men in the family straight."

Jane was confused. "Why would you need to be kept straight? I'm sorry, I don't think I understand the confusion?"

"Because my father and I have the same name."

Jane felt thick-headed and stupid. "But he's Colin and you're Nicholas."

Nick's father jumped into the discussion to clarify. "Like my father, I am Nicholas David Colin Sutcliffe-Ashworth, only I am the third. We didn't want to go by 'two, three, and four', so my father was always known as Nicholas, I was always known as Colin. And Chip here was always called Chip. It wasn't until he came back from school the first time that he insisted on changing his name to Nick, but we ended up calling him Nicky."

"So, you're the fourth?"

"Yes, a wonderful English tradition, isn't it?" The sarcasm was dripping off the younger Nick's voice. "I am Nicholas David Colin Sutcliffe-Ashworth the fourth. Otherwise known as Nick."

"My dear," Cressida managed to purr. "I must say I'm rather shocked that you would be marrying my son and still not even know his name!"

"I didn't know the English still did that. I mean, follow names for generations. I haven't even heard of the royal family following that track…" Jane's voice trailed off.

"My father-in-law insisted," Cressida managed to say, but then added, "and it's tradition."

"Oh, it's a silly tradition, a silly old British tradition, but we followed it nonetheless. We're all about British tradition. And now that you're wearing that ring, you'll have the fifth!" Colin said, holding up and waving his refilled champagne glass at her, causing a little bit to spill out over the top. He didn't seem to notice it splash on the table.

Jane gave him an enigmatic smile, not quite knowing what to say or what to think. She took a small sip of her champagne, hoping that "tradition" didn't interpret that she'd just agreed to Colin's statement. She glanced at Nick, who looked as though he was losing his nerve.

"Mother, why is Mrs. Stuart here? And what did she mean about 'tell the others'?"

"Oh that, it's nothing," Cressida said evasively and waved him off.

"Mother?" Nick asked again, "Why would your best friend be here at the same restaurant and going to see Wicked tonight, on the same night that we are? I find that to be quite a coincidence. She lives in Bath after all. It's not exactly around the corner, is it? Who else is here? Who is she telling in the group dining room?"

"Well, Nick, your mother and I didn't think you'd want to sit with the old hen party, not on the first night anyway, so we reserved a table. The rest of the gang are in the party room dining together," Colin said. "But we got a car. They all rode the tour package group transport."

"Do you mean to tell me that you have booked us onto this theater tour with all your friends? This isn't a family excursion at all. You're actually out with your friends and having us tag along? I've got that right, haven't I? It's a group tour package?"

Cressida looked uncomfortable for only a moment. "Chip, dear," she said placatingly, "after Nelson Wycliffe had his stroke, he and Lydia couldn't use their tickets, so I thought it would be nice if you two joined us. We got them at a wonderful discount."

"Mother, are you telling me that you bought discounted tickets off of an invalid, taking advantage of the misfortune of your friends, and gave it to us as a bloody holiday present?"

Colin had the decency to look abashed. Cressida did not.

"I thought you'd enjoy it." Cressida looked directly at Jane, putting her in the position of either defending her soon-to-be mother-in-law or joining with her future husband in condemning her.

"I'm sure it will be a lovely week, and that your friends would have wanted their tickets to be used, and not go to waste." Jane stammered out the words. She didn't know how they made it through dinner. Nicky seemed to sulk, and Jane didn't know whether it was because her attempt at peace-making had left him undefended or because his mother's friends were slated to be their dinner and theater companions for each of the next seven days. She wouldn't have a moment alone with Nicky to find out until they returned to their hotel room, hours from now.

At the theater, Cressida's friends hovered around her, pulling Jane into their midst. Jane thought she counted eight other couples, who were so alike she had a hard time telling them apart or remembering their names. They all examined her ring and pronounced it gorgeous, even as one of them made a side comment that "didn't little Chip change horses quickly?" Another murmured back, "Advanced degrees? That seems a bit excessive, doesn't it?"

Julia looked at the ring for a particularly long time and then kissed Jane on the cheek, using the opportunity to whisper in her ear, "If you ever divorce him, she'll want that back. It's a family heirloom on her mother's side you know. She'll want to keep that in her family line."

Jane returned her sweetest smile and replied, "I think I am her family line now, Julia."

"Oh, well, yes, of course," Julia replied with a thin-lipped smile.

* * *

Hours later, back in their hotel room, lying on their upgraded king-sized bed, both of them stared at the ceiling. Nick hadn't touched her, not even tried to kiss her goodnight. She wasn't sure how much she wanted to kiss him either. The bed was so big, it was almost like they were in the separate twin beds originally planned for them.

"Who is Ashlyn?" Her voice came out in a whisper.

"Well, bugger me!" Nick's tone was scathing.

"Is that a request?" Jane's voice was flat. She felt drained of emotion.

Nick sighed, "Some girl I dated after we broke up. Quite obviously impressed my father with her breast implants. Not much else to tell about her though. Not too much in the upper stories."

"Oh." Jane didn't think she could manage to say anything else. She hadn't dated anyone when they broke up. She had been too consumed with being miserable.

"We were apart at the time, as you might remember. And I did show up on your doorstep again, begging you to take me back. After all, I needed someone to be on my side."

She reached for his hand. "I'm always on your side. And yes, that was very dramatic. And sweet. Three A.M. Your text. Well, all eight of them, if I remember, waking me up. You asking me to open the door. I really didn't expect to see you there, suitcase in hand. And I don't know where you found those flowers in the middle of the night."

"You can find anything in the city that never sleeps. Just ask a cabbie. They're all tickety-boo to be your personal shopper."

She sighed heavily.

"You made the right decision, you know. Saying yes. Even if my parents are a part of the picture."

"If only I'd known what you were begging me to come back to."

"Yes, it seems I begged you to come back to save me from the wonders of my dysfunctional family. And all their even more dysfunctional friends. Oh, save me, Jane." They started laughing and he put his arms around her. "Only you could make me laugh after a night like this! That was bloody awful. If I'd had any idea, I would've flatly refused the week with them."

"I do think they meant well. I mean with the theater tour. As for dinner comments, I'm still on the fence about those. But I get it, they were in shock. We didn't really prepare them." *And that shouldn't be a surprise,* Jane thought. She had this idea that most women knew when the proposal was coming, that there were signals or hints, but opening that gaily wrapped present and seeing the ring had caught Jane by surprise. She was delighted, cloud nine to be sure, but surprised, nonetheless. Trust Nicky to decide on impulse that Christmas night was the right time.

"Just proves you're an angel incarnate that you can be so forgiving. And that ring is for me to give to my wife. I've been told for forever that it would be worn by the mother of Cressida's grandchildren. Me being an only child and that being the future you, it seems appropriate that you're wearing it now."

Jane looked at the beautiful ring once again. "Cressida actually seemed to enjoy all the attention at the theater, even if she hated the show." Jane was quite sure that she herself had not enjoyed that particular scene, although she found Wicked to be nothing less than brilliant.

"Yes, her friends started planning our wedding. She certainly loved being the center of that hen party. Wouldn't surprise me in the slightest if by the end of the week they have the date set and the guest list drawn up."

"Oh my, we haven't even started to think about how we want to get married. I'd like some time for the engagement to soak in before we start planning things. And we have to see where we're going to live and decide about jobs. Oh, it's too much to think about. Let's just enjoy this for a while. I can't plan anything until I finish up school."

"I'm afraid that ship has sailed. The hens are off to the races! And I suppose you didn't catch the fact that my father just named our first born."

"First born son. Luckily, we have daughters in my family." Jane smiled at him.

"But since your girls go by boy names, I'm not sure it will matter much to them whether it's got all X's or a Y for chromosomes, as long as it's the fifth in the line."

"I'm getting the feeling this is going to be a longer week than we'd imagined." Jane sighed and closed her eyes.

"I can imagine this becoming a very long week indeed."

Chapter 6

"Jane! Jane, honey, what time are you leaving for the airport?" Audree called up the stairs. "What time does Nicholas' flight get in?" The anxiety in her voice was insufficiently masked by her southern drawl.

"Not until four-forty-five, Mom," Jane called back down. "Plenty of time!"

Audree walked around the house again, making sure that everything was ready for company. John joined her as she was inspecting the living room.

"Triple checking?" John said, teasing her. "Everything looks particularly nice. The place couldn't be more festive for Christmas." His soft Tennessee accent lilted his words and betrayed no tension whatsoever.

"I've just run out of things to do. And it makes me a bit nervous not having something to occupy my mind, particularly when we are about to be descended upon by guests."

"What guests? Everyone is family. Jane is home for Christmas and with her being engaged to Nick for the past year, that makes him family, too, even if he's so very far away. Hector is married to Summer, which makes him family. I've forgotten if there ever was a time when Mimi's brood wasn't a part of our own. Nothing to stress about, my dear."

"You're right. When you're right, you're right." Audree gave a sigh and shook her head. "I meant to say thank you for closing the office for the afternoon. I feel so much better when you're here. I know you hate it when you have to do that."

"The office staff were thrilled at having an extra afternoon off so close to the holiday. I suppose everyone can use more time. I just rolled it into their bonus. We got all the patients taken care of, so no worries there. It'll be good to have Nicholas here for a long visit. I think I need to know my future son-in-law much better than I do now."

"Yes, I feel the same way. Although I'm not quite as sure I'd like to get to know his parents much better than I do now." Under her breath she added, "Bless their hearts."

"Amen to that. Sometimes it's hard to imagine that boy turned out as well as he did." Concern tinged John's expression for a moment. "And yet I find myself called back to thoughts of apples and trees."

Audree bit her lip. "Well, if our happy couple chooses to live here, at least his apple won't be anywhere near that proverbial tree." A look of distress crossed her face. "John, I do feel, well, awkward, putting Jane and Nicholas in the same room. I know they're engaged. I know they've… they've… I'm sure…"

"Spent a little bit of time together?" he offered, sparing her the necessity of finishing her sentence, "during all those intercontinental trips?"

"Yes, that's one way to put it. But I feel so awkward putting them in the same room under our roof when they're not yet married." She brushed her hair behind her ear. "What my mother would have said." She shook her head again. "Am I so out of step with the times?"

John put his arm around his wife. "I remember when we were engaged, visiting your family, and being in separate bedrooms." He leaned over and whispered in her ear. "And I'm sure you remember how we used to sneak out at night to be alone in the backyard gazebo."

Audree squirmed away as he pinched her bottom, saying, "You were such a bad influence on me, you bad boy!" But she leaned into him and kissed him. "At least with them being in the same room, we don't have to worry about any climbing down vined terraces from the second story!"

John laughed. "We're fortunate neither one of us ended up with anything broken! Neither our bones nor heads nor hearts. But young love seldom sees straight and clear nor does it heed danger. Don't worry, Audree—your mother is not here to scold you. You don't have to listen to that voice in your head. Our children aren't children anymore." He kissed her on the forehead and whispered in her ear, "It'll be all right my dear. After Summer getting married almost two months pregnant, I'm not sure I have an apple cart left to upset! Maybe you and I; maybe we need to come into the twenty-first century."

"And then losing the baby at five months. That was dreadful. Thank goodness for Hector. He pulled them both through that."

"That Amish upbringing of his shows through." John nodded. "A true man of faith, that boy. Amazing he was shunned."

"Now shush, John! We don't talk of that."

John nodded. "Hector is a good man. He gives our Summer strength still."

"Yes. And it could happen again. Life holds no guarantees, a situation I find woefully inadequate, were I of a mind to complain to a higher power. Nothing is guaranteed us but this minute that we're in."

John smiled warmly at his wife. "And that alone is an understandable source of anxiety! I think one guarantee is that Hector will be by Summer's side come what may. She's a fortunate woman."

Audree's brow creased and she frowned slightly as she looked at the top of the stairs. "And do you think Jane will be similarly fortunate? Nick seems... well, all that British refinement is certainly impressive, but has she found herself another Hector?"

"Hector was a diamond in the rough while Nicholas certainly has plenty of polish and sparkle."

"But is he a true diamond?"

Before John could answer, a resounding "Bang! Bang! Bang!" shattered the relative quiet. Four-year-old Ty came peeling around the corner of the living room, on a tear through the front hall and into the dining room, passing Audree and John.

Close on his heels came Charlie, long blonde hair flying behind her, slipping and sliding as she tried in vain to gain some purchase on the wooden floors in her stocking feet. "You missed me. I'm gonna get you, you stagecoach robber! You're going to jail!" She turned the corner too quickly in her socks and fell over. Ty screamed with laughter and tore through the house ahead of her, continuing to shout "Bang! Bang! Bang!" wildly shooting his imaginary finger gun behind him as he made his escape on an invisible horse.

"Is that my son making all that noise?" Caroline asked as she came down the stairs.

"No, that's my sister doing most of the yelling," Jane said as she trotted down the steps behind Caroline.

"Ty, don't you break anything at Miss Audree and Dr. John's house! You be careful now!"

"Bang! Bang! Bang! I got you!" echoed from someplace close to the kitchen, followed by a loud crash. "That was my fault," came Charlie's voice. "Nothing broke! Not really."

Caroline stared upwards for a moment and then called out loudly, "So help me, if you break anything, Ty, I'm not taking you to see Santa tomorrow. I'm serious."

Charlie appeared around the corner. "You guys are going to see Santa?"

"Uh, we're supposed to. Why? What did he break?" Caroline asked, an undertone of dread in her voice.

"Nothing. Nothing broke. Dented maybe, but not broken. It's just that I've read about Carolina Place's display. Are you going to that mall? Can I come along? I really want to see it."

Jane joined in, "I saw that on the news. I'd like to go too. Sounds crazy over-the-top."

"Looks like a whole party, then." Caroline chuckled. "I'll text Summer to see if she might wanna come too. Audree? John? You game for joining the happy hoards lining up to see old Kris Kringle tomorrow afternoon?"

"Hmm, no, but thanks. I'll be making Christmas cookies. And please take Summer. I don't want her popping by and helping me out. She thinks it's funny to decorate the gingerbread men as scary Christmas clowns!" Audree walked over to Jane. "My, my, my, Janie! Just look at your hair. That's a right beautiful job with the color. Caroline, you have a special talent. I think there must be three shades of brown in here?"

"Four actually!" Jane said with a big smile on her face. "I think Caroline is missing her calling!" She swished her multi-hued chocolate-colored hair from side to side. "You could be a professional."

"Well, I must've done it ten times for friends over in Japan. It's very popular over there. I'm glad the color looks so good on Jane! It's such a rich, dark brown. Lots of highlights and lowlights."

"It reminds me of France!" Jane beamed. "And it looks like it did when I first met Nick."

"At least this was not as expensive, I assume, as the new look you got in Paris?" John asked.

Audree rolled her eyes and said good-naturedly, "That was a necessity, John." Turning back to her daughter, she said, "We are looking forward to having Nick arrive tonight." She smiled. "And seeing you all again in a couple of days, Caroline. Your mother and the boys will be joining us, won't they?"

"Absolutely, we'll be here. Rory and Chase both got home from college last week. I'm not sure how Mom's managing it with her baby boy finally gone off to school," Caroline said. "I kinda worry about her."

A soft and slightly sad smile grew on Audree's face as she looked at Charlie. "Yes, now that Charlie is off at college, I find empty nesting to be the hardest thing I've ever done. Mimi and I are coping together."

"It seems to take a lot of meeting up for glasses of wine," John said, giving Ty's mother a wink.

"Lucky for you, Caroline, you have many, many happy years before crossing that bridge yourself." Audree took John's hand. "C'mon, honey, let's go make sure the decorations look all right outside and haven't fallen over, en masse. After all, Ty and Charlie were playing out there just a little while ago. Who knows what disaster ensued."

"Once a weapon of mass destruction, always one. Some children never grow up." John laughed as they disappeared through the front door.

Caroline turned to Jane. "I won't let Ty run around screaming like that when Nick is here, I promise. I'm sure he'll appreciate some peace and quiet upon arrival. I bet he'll be soooooo jet lagged." Caroline grimaced. "It's always a killer for me to make the trip from Japan. Ty, too. Oh God, it's torture."

Jane put a hand on Caroline's shoulder. "Getting to Europe is only half the time of the trip to Japan. Trans-Atlantic is nothing compared to Trans-Pacific."

"Your new job sends you over a lot, doesn't it?"

"Oh yeah. Working for Airbus has me trotting off 'across the pond' pretty regularly, which is great. I'm at the bottom of the ladder but I volunteer for every assignment. It's funny, cause they think I'm a workaholic, but really it's about racking up frequent flier miles and sneaking off on weekends to see Nicky. And still, it's not often enough. Seeing him, I mean. Seeing his parents, errrrugh?" She shrugged and Caroline laughed. "The flight's exhausting though. God, I'm glad he's making the trip this time. I expect he'll be a wet noodle by the time he arrives. He can't sleep on planes at all."

"Airbus. What an awesome job." Caroline sighed heavily. "If I'm being honest with you, I'm so jealous."

"Huh? Jealous? I didn't know you were that into the airline industry? I thought you were kind of a nervous flyer?"

"Very funny!" Caroline chuffed and started to reinspect her job on Jane's hair now that they were in a room with more natural light. "No, I just wish I'd had a work life, you know. Like any kind of a work life."

"But Ty..."

"Being a mom is great. Don't get me wrong. Wouldn't change that for anything. But somehow, I wish, I wish there was more. Motherhood is wonderful, unless you actually want to use any higher order cognitive functions... or interact with any adults at all.... or have friends."

"He's getting older. You can get a job, even something part-time, once he goes to school."

Caroline shook her head. "My dear, have you met Sasutki? Mr. Don't-Embarrass-Me."

Jane's eyebrows furrowed. "I don't get it? Wouldn't that make it easier, I mean the whole two income family thing?"

"Now you sound like an American. But where we live, the wife needing to work means the husband loses face, which is pretty dire to my dear spouse." Caroline shook her head again. "Not happening." She shrugged. "I probably couldn't get a work visa anyway."

"What about Chicago, the promotion? Is that gonna happen?"

"Yeah, he got the offer, but he's really dragging his feet. We'll have to go before Ty starts first grade. He goes to a Japanese school now and even with four-year-old's it's intense! It's not what I want for my son. It's too much pressure to put on a baby. I can't wait to get to Chicago."

At that moment Ty and Charlie made yet another round of the house, riding imaginary horses and pretending to compete in the equestrian Olympics, complete with mock British accents.

"Charlie, do not have him jumping over the furniture. Mom will ground you!" Jane watched them disappear around the corner again. "That baby sister of mine. She's as bad as your baby—but he's not really a baby. He's a little boy, rapidly on his way to being a big one."

"Yeah, you're right. I'd better get him back to Mom's before he breaks something here and I have to make good on my empty threat about not seeing Santa. No way we could miss seeing The Big Guy. You and Charlie joining us tomorrow then?"

"Yeah, sure. Charlie will be into it. Maybe Nick will come along as well. He'll get a taste of some true American culture."

Caroline snickered. "I think I might enjoy seeing all that proper British upbringing at an American shopping mall at Christmas time. Not quite Dickens, is it?"

Jane opened her mouth to respond, then realized she couldn't really think of anything to say. Nick was likely to have a lot of opinions about the ostentatious and gaudy treatment that Americans gave such a classic holiday. Not quite Dickens, indeed.

Chapter 7

As predicted, Nick arrived utterly exhausted. Jane was shocked at how thin he looked as he dragged himself through the arrivals gate. He smelled vaguely of cigarette smoke.

"Your luggage should be coming out soon. Oh my God, love, let's get you home and get you a shower. Did you have to hang out with smokers during your New York layover?"

"Oh, those would be my parents. Mr. and Mrs. Chimney Stacks. What I want is a bed. I had several scotches on the plane, and they failed to knock me out. I still couldn't sleep." He groaned. "I had a couple more on my connecting flight. I'm totally knackered. I'm a cream-crackered mess."

"So, you're under-slept and hungover? Lovely. What a way to start the holidays."

"Oh, please, please, I've just come from bastille de la Cressida é Colin. Please let me have two weeks without any criticisms." He had a beaten-down look that tugged on Jane's heart.

"Of course, honey, I'm sorry. I didn't mean to give you a hard time. I was just teasing. We'll get you home and you can take a nap. No plans for tonight, just rest. Tomorrow, I thought we could join Caroline taking her son to see Santa. The decorations are supposed to be spectacular." She noticed he didn't look even remotely interested. "And Rory and Chase are home for the holidays, I know you'll like to see them. They're coming over the day after that."

"Oh yeah, I do like them. Fun chaps."

"So, your mum and dad have been… difficult?"

"Oh, you don't know the bloody half of it." He sighed heavily. "They are quite outraged at the wedding plans. My mum has a list nearly four-hundred people long, who 'must come'. Most of them I'm sure I don't know. Actually, I'm not sure that she knows some of them! I'm buggered if I know what to do with her. It's like she thinks it's her wedding and not ours."

Jane's heart sank. "Cressida has shot down nearly our whole arsenal of wedding plans."

"Yes, she's thrown a classic wobbler at each and every proposal that we've come up with. I'm so tired of hearing how our wedding is going to kill my father. Just planning it is going to kill me. And four hundred hugs and handshakes! Bloody hell!"

Jane swallowed hard. "Four hundred?" she said in a squeaky voice. While her family was reasonably well off, they couldn't afford to throw a society wedding in England hosting four hundred strangers.

Nick took her hand and kissed it. "We have pledged to stand united against the hostile takeover of our wedding and stand united we shall! Death threats notwithstanding."

Jane nodded as she looked into his eyes. "How?" She felt hopeful.

"Oh, bugger me. I don't know."

She could see just what a toll the whole situation was taking on Nicky, all the constant badgering about the wedding plans, and probably, she assumed, about his intended bride as well. Being based in the U.S. gave her a thick layer of protection that she appreciated. She looked down at the engagement ring on her finger. Generations of his maternal ancestors had worn that ring.

He was slowly pulling his two bags off the carousel in baggage claim. "Here we are. Oh, please take me home!"

"Of course. And when we get there, I'll make you a nice cup of tea and you can lie down and I'll rub your shoulders and your neck." She took one of his bags.

"Oh, you are my angel incarnate. That sounds like heaven. And then sleeping. I feel like I could sleep for an entire day!"

* * *

Jane walked through the mall feeling a bit sad that Nick was too exhausted to join them. However, there was no point in staying at home and watching him sleep off his hangover, his jet lag, or his parent-induced exhaustion; so she decided to join the excursion without him. If and when he woke up, her mother would be more than happy to dote on him, offering him Christmas cookies that didn't remotely resemble scary clowns. She looked over at Caroline. "You seem more wide-eyed than Ty."

Caroline blinked a couple of times, staring about her. "You know, living in Japan, you just forget how things are back at home. This is… I don't even have a clue how I would describe this to people back in Tokyo." Turning to her son, she said, "Hey, Ty, are you happy to see Santa today?"

Ty squirmed in his excitement, proving to be a challenge for Charlie to hold onto. "Santa. Want to see him. Tell him… want for Christmas!" Then he spoke in rapid-fire Japanese, making his mother laugh.

"What did he say?" Charlie asked.

"More of the same. And Ty, don't pull Miss Charlie's arm off. Honey, we'll get there. Be patient." Caroline sighed. "Uh, good luck, Charlie." She turned to Jane. "So, what's the status with the nuptials? You guys have been planning for what, eight months now? You've made a lot of reconnaissance trips to check out venues. Figure anything out yet?"

Summer and Charlie both turned to look at Jane, who began to feel nervous being the center of attention. "Um, apparently that's the million-dollar question. I'm tempted to say 'don't ask' but as you'll all be my bridesmaids, you have every reason to want to know. Nick arrived here absolutely demoralized. Turns out Cressida is adamant that the wedding happens in England and that it's some type of high society affair. She vehemently rejected every venue we've looked at. She gave him a guest list nearly four hundred people long."

The other women gasped. "Million-dollar question is right!" Summer shook her head. "That's a million-dollar wedding. Mom and Dad love you, Jane, but not that much. You know, hate to break it to you." She gave Jane a playful punch in the arm.

"Summer, maybe it wasn't fair of you to set the bar for your wedding at fifty bucks?" Charlie said as Ty tugged on her arm. "It kinda disadvantages the rest of us."

Jane laughed at both the tease and the truth in Summer's statement, as well as the insight of Charlie's. "Let's be realistic: this is Nicky talking. He's exaggerating, but if he's exaggerating by half, that's more than twice the size we ever imagined. We don't want a huge affair."

"What're you gonna do?" Charlie asked.

"Just plan what you want." Summer waved off any concern. "Absolutely no need to follow anyone's path in life but your own." Petite and pixie-like, she could have passed for one of Santa's elves, except for her striking red hair and noticeably pregnant belly.

"News flash: turns out when you actually have a plan, there's actual costs. And it's not like we haven't tried. We've planned this out four times. Each time it turns into a huge fight between him and his parents."

"Not her wedding." Summer absentmindedly rubbed her abdomen.

"Easy for you to say, Miss Independent, getting married on a twenty-four-hour notice, and, oh-by-the-way, two months pregnant." Instantly, Jane was sorry she'd said anything at all. They just never talked about the baby that Summer had lost but, to her relief, Summer just laughed.

"Miss Independent. I like that." Summer nodded to her younger sister and ran her hand through her hair with the result that it was spiky

62

and nearly standing up on top—a look that reinforced the whole pregnant Santa's elf vibe. "So, what's preventing you from being independent of the groom-to-be's parents?"

Jane blew out her breath, puffing up her cheeks. "There are some complicating factors that I haven't shared with you all yet. You know how last spring Nick was working for that green design-and-build firm in London?"

Charlie, Summer, and Caroline nodded.

"Well, last summer it went bankrupt. A huge mess apparently. Nick calls the guy who ran it 'a real tosspot'. But it left him without work. After a couple of months with no other prospects, he finally agreed to help his father with the wine import business. He didn't want to do it, but his father had that cardiac arrhythmia and what could he do? Of course he had to say yes. He's been running the whole enterprise, supervising the staff, traveling back and forth to France, seeing customers, and it's been beating him to a pulp. He's not really a businessman and he's not really a wine guy. That's why he begged to stay home and just sleep today. Poor Nicky's absolutely wiped. On top of all that he has to be around his parents nearly all the time."

"Whoa. That gives them a lot of pull. They employ him. They're his parents. And daddy's ill." Caroline nodded sagely. "Nick's between a rock and a hard place."

"Cressida is really tough to manage. As the only kid he's not like us. I have all my sisters here." Jane reached out and took Caroline's hand, including her in the family group. "I have you all to help me muddle through everything. But he has no one."

"I don't know how you do it, managing over such a long distance," Charlie said. "I think it's great that you guys are so tight! You don't have to worry about Nick at all. I mean, he's just devoted to you." She gave a heavy sigh. "I wish someone would be devoted to me like that."

"Can't imagine who…" Summer said with a smirk on her face.

Jane felt a wave of discomfort. Sure, Nick could be doting, but other women seemed to materialize out of thin air, quickly becoming outrageous flirts with him, not seeming to mind or even notice that he was standing next to Jane. And the man did seem to enjoy the attention far more than Jane thought was appropriate. She considered telling the girls about her last trip to Bath and one of the characteristically weird contemporary art openings that always seemed to draw Nick in. He was suddenly surrounded by three lovely young sirens. Gently and with subtle grace the girls surrounded Nick and quietly shouldered Jane out. Nick was barely holding her hand through a wall of strongly-scented, clingingly-dressed, heavily-lacquered belles who were flocking around him. He seemed to be enrapt in the conversation, laughing with the trio of adoring vixens without noticing when Jane went back to the refreshment table to get another glass of wine. That moment was pivotal: it was the instant she decided that she loathed contemporary art.

Devoted should feel different, but she didn't bring it up. The wedding planning was torturous enough, and besides, this was Christmas. Nick was here in the US, safely away from any moths to his flame. She was going to focus on the positive and be happy.

Chapter 8

Ty kept pulling Caroline and Charlie's hands as they walked through the Carolina Place mall. "Where is he? Where is he?" he asked over and over again, alternating between English and Japanese.

"Ty, honey, we'll find him. Believe me, it won't be hard." Caroline laughed as he dragged the women along in his excitement. She said something back to him in Japanese. He stopped pulling quite so hard on Charlie.

"These decorations are… over the top," Summer said, nodding. "I'm impressed. And I mean 'wow!' This is me saying it and I'm an artist."

"Yeah, I read about this online," Charlie said, "but seeing it in person is just a whole 'nother thing. Know what I mean?"

"You don't say." Jane was starting to feel glad that Nick hadn't joined them after all. He wasn't big into holidays anyway and this ostentatious display would certainly fail to bring out the best in him, snarky as his humor could be. "I have to admit though, from a marketing standpoint, they're fabulous. Just look—even the marble floors are so polished that they reflect that artificial greenery on the curved stairwells. It's like there's twice as many of those giant red and gold bows on the escalators, just because of the shine. How do they keep it so clean?"

"It's the elves," Summer replied with a grin.

Charlie pointed up. "I like the lights. And the clouds." Huge gatherings of tiny white lights hung from the ceiling looking for all the world like stars twinkling three stories above them—some were even embedded amidst suspended angel-hair clouds.

Their little group passed a stage where children as young as Ty were playing almost-recognizable Christmas carols on tiny violins before an enrapt audience of parents and grandparents. The performance was joined by passersby who listened with delight until, one by one, they hit the number of off-key-induced winces that reminded them of their shopping. Another display had three-foot tall nutcrackers dressed in red or green, and set up on a giant tic tac toe board. Children were moving the lightweight pieces, ostensibly playing the game, although it quickly devolved into toy soldier battles, drawing several intervening elves. Ty was entranced by everything.

"Wow, talk about seeing the magic through a kid's eyes!" Charlie laughed as she once again caught Ty when he escaped from his mother. She clipped a lead to a beltloop on his pants.

"Charlie, please tell me you did not just put a dog leash on a child." Jane was horrified.

"Future surgeon. Always prepared." Charlie nodded with satisfaction.

"Brilliant Charlie. Absolutely brilliant!" Summer nodded with approval.

Caroline mouthed an "It's okay," to Jane, and then added, "No place in the world does Christmas quite like the U.S."

Ty started to drag Charlie a few meters in front of them. Jane pointed to the two of them, looking at Caroline, who just shrugged. "You wouldn't see it in Tokyo, sure, right, but Ty's energetic little self needs a measure of corralling. He's just not like the other kids over there. He overwhelms them." She looked thoughtful. "He overwhelms me!"

Summer's oversized smile lit up her face as she turned her head to take in the decorations. "Speaking of overwhelmed, I don't think

Hector should ever see this. I think this might be consumerism beyond what his little post-Amish heart could take." She threw back her head and laughed out loud.

Surprisingly, the line for Santa was not the lengthy nightmare they had been expecting, perhaps because the lure of the diverse attractions had children spread out through the mall. Ty talked on and on, partly in Japanese and partly in English, about what he wanted to tell Santa.

Charlie slipped off the dog leash when she got a dirty look from one of the older, supervisory elves. "I guess we're pretty safe from him running off here," she said under her breath.

When his turn finally arrived, an unexpectedly speechless Ty dutifully had his picture taken with Old Saint Nick.

"That's weird," Caroline whispered to Jane. "He's not talking. He never stops talking." She called out to her son, "Honey, smile for your picture with Santa! Smile! Smile?"

"Why does he look like a deer in headlights?" Charlie asked. "I mean, this is what he wanted, wasn't it?" She felt in her pocket. "You don't think it was the... the dog leash?"

"I don't know what's up with him. Not the leash, Charlie, don't worry." Caroline's voice was a quiet murmur and she looked concerned.

"Hey, Ty, do you want us to get in a picture with Santa too?" Charlie called out.

A grumpy old woman dressed as a Santa's chief elf said, "Santa is just for little children. You grown-ups don't need a picture."

"I'm sorry?" Jane said, incredulous at this lack of holiday spirit and exceedingly poor marketing. "I think we do."

In the end, in addition to the solo picture with the shell-shocked looking Ty, they paid again and the four of them had their picture taken with Santa.

"Oh my gosh! This is the greatest keepsake ever! Look at us!" Jane laughed. "We should do this every year!"

Summer snorted. "We look like Santa and his backup singers."

"Hmm. This picture of Ty." Caroline looked at her five-by-seven print out. "Santa hypnotizes little boy."

Summer peered around to see. "Oh yeah, that's a classic. We've got a ton with Jane looking just like that from when we were kids."

Caroline looked at Summer. "I'm sure you were always smiling brilliantly."

Summer pointed to her mouth. "Oversized mouth. Big smile. I might look like a mutant, but it really works for Santa shots, even when you're a kid."

"Was I always smiling in those pictures?" asked Charlie.

"Oh, Charlie, you were always smiling at Chase." Caroline winked and Charlie blushed furiously in return.

"Honey, what did you tell Santa you wanted for Christmas?" Summer leaned down and whispered to Ty.

Ty was quiet, and then his lower lip started to pout, and then it started to tremble. Suddenly, he burst into huge sobs. Caroline swept him up into her arms, comforting him. She finally managed to understand that he couldn't speak to Santa—he'd been too afraid.

Loudly, Ty wailed out something in Japanese.

"What did he say?" Jane asked her sisters, who all shrugged in response. Everyone turned to Caroline.

"Oh, honey, Santa knows you hate red bean cakes. He won't bring you those just because you didn't talk to him." She turned to the trio of women. "His equivalent of coal in the stocking is getting red bean cakes. I'll never forget that one," she said with her eyebrows raised and she blew out a breath. Ty continued to bawl and bury his face into his mother's shoulder.

"Hey, Ty." Charlie got around behind Caroline, attempting to catch his eye. "I have really good news for you: Santa can't find red bean cakes in the U.S. Nope—they don't make them. Never, ever does he bring those to kids here. And since you'll be here for Christmas, you'll get only American candies in your stocking. Those don't have any vitamins, minerals, fiber, or any redeeming features at all. They're just sugar!"

Summer rolled her eyes. "Honestly, Charlie, do you really think that's helping?"

But Ty was sniffling now and looking at Charlie over his mother's shoulder. "Just Sugar? Mommy, can we go there?"

Caroline turned around to face Charlie. "He's seen the store called Just Sugar. Apparently you've got his riveted attention."

Jane spoke up in Charlie's defense. "Hey, as an expert, I have to say: I know marketing genius when I see it," Jane said with a smile. "Just sugar. What it lacks in being good for you, it makes up for in sheer brilliance."

"And by way of apology," Charlie said with a grimace, "you know there's more than one way to let Santa know what you want for Christmas."

Ty blinked and looked at her, but he was paying attention.

"You can write him a letter. And I read online that the other end of the mall has a letter writing station, staffed by more elves." Then she added quickly, "But nice ones! Happy elves this time. No stern, grumpy elves, no sir!" She mimicked the dour face of the judgy-elf with the poor upselling skills. "We just have to look for the big gingerbread house."

Ty instantly started squirming in his mother's arms until Caroline had to put him down. He started to take off, but Charlie caught him. "Whoa there, tiger. Let's get you hooked up." She re-attached the dog leash to his belt loop. Ty was off, leading them all like an excited reindeer, determined to write a letter to Santa. They found the giant gingerbread house, staffed with elves who were marginally more well-adjusted than those attending to Santa himself. There were kiddie-sized tables with paper and crayons scattered across them. An over-sized red and green mailbox stood next to the gingerbread house—the mailbox was even taller than Ty himself. An opaque plastic tube ran out of the back of the mailbox, all the way to the upper story of the mall, ending in one of the largest of the angel hair clouds as it floated in the imaginary starry sky above them.

"Well, hey there, partner!" A pretty, blonde elf came over. "If you want to write a letter to Santa, you just put it on one of these pieces of paper here." She showed him over to a table. "You can use whatever crayons you like—Santa loves all the colors! Tell him what you want, or draw pictures of your wish list, and when you're ready we'll put it in an envelope and you can mail it in our Santa's Super Special Delivery Mailbox!"

Summer leaned over and said quietly to Caroline, "Wow, that elf has had a lot of caffeine today." Charlie overheard and burst out with a loud laugh. "Come to think of it, Charlie's had a lot of caffeine today, too."

Jane shook her head. "It's the sugar. All those complicated coffee drinks are made with a ton of sugar."

Caroline nodded. "Sugar and caffeine turn Ty into a little hyper monster."

Charlie crossed her arms. "I'm just in training. Future doctor. Future surgeon. I figure highly caffeinated specialty drinks will be an important tool of the trade."

A sudden *whoooooop!* caught their attention and all five of them turned their heads towards the mailbox, where a little girl had just deposited her letter into Santa's Super Special Delivery Mailbox. Tiny white lights began to glow on the tube behind the contraption, lighting in succession all the way from the mailbox to the "sky" and ending in a large, angel-hair cloud. They all looked up, watching the lights as the little girl started to shout, "My letter to Santa made it! He got my letter! I texted my letter to him!"

Summer leaned into Jane and whispered. "Anything about that strike you as morbid? Like Santa's at the Pearly Gates? The Big Guy's dead and now he's an angel in the clouds or something? And you can text him letters?"

"Shut up, scary-Christmas-clown-cookie-lady. You're ruining the magic," Jane whispered back.

Ty gasped. Then he rushed over to a chair and started to work furiously on a letter of his own.

Jane took a good look at the design and layout of the decorations. "Quite the contrary: these people are beyond marketing geniuses. They're marketing wizards. Wow." Her voice held true admiration. "I'm getting so many ideas... I should carry a little notebook with me so I don't forget any of these absolute fireworks going off in my head." Jane sat down at a kiddie chair and started to capture her thoughts in crayon.

In a few minutes Ty brought two pieces of paper to his mother.

"Mama, I want to send these."

"Two letters, Ty?" Caroline smiled at him.

"One is for you." He smiled shyly at her, not a sign of a tear now.

Caroline took the two letters, first reading the one in pictures with rudimentary Japanese lettering. "Okay, I think Santa will understand these pictures. Sure, this is good. I'm so proud of you, Ty!" She flipped to the next piece of paper then she froze as she stared at it. On it was a picture, a stick figure with bobbed brown hair and the Japanese symbol for "mama":

マヾ

In the picture the Mama looked very sad, standing in a pool of tears. Then there were arrows to another picture of the stick figure woman with a big smile on her face. Ty hugged her and said, "Mama ga shiawase ni narimasu".

Jane was shocked to see a tear slide down Caroline's cheek.

"I am happy, Ty. I am happy." He buried his face into her chest and she kissed his hair as she hugged him, a few tears escaping and running down her cheeks.

Jane, Summer and Charlie all shot looks of confusion and concern to one another. Caroline looked up at them.

"His wish for me is to be happy. I am happy." But as she said it, her lip trembled. She looked like she was struggling to keep it together. "I'm just a bit homesick living in Japan. I miss my family. That's all." She kissed him again, hiding her face in his hair as she took a couple of deep breaths. "Relationships are complicated, Ty."

"Tell me about it," echoed Summer, Jane, and Charlie.

Summer and Jane turned questioning looks at Charlie. "And your complicated relationship?" Summer asked. "Something we should know about?"

Charlie shrugged nonchalantly. "Merely observation."

"Yeah, right," Jane said, but she was too distracted by Caroline to wonder what was up with very-single-Charlie, who only had eyes for Chase. She and Caroline got one another in so many ways, both living trans-global lives with different cultures and travel and juggling too many balls in the air. They were in touch with one another all the time, but the depth of emotion Ty had just wrenched from his mother was uncharacteristic. *People can hide a lot in a marriage.* Jane bit her lip at the thought.

Another elf, a college boy suffering through a necessary holiday job and obviously wishing he were somewhere, probably anywhere else, helped Ty "mail" his two letters. He flipped the sparkly "Special Delivery" switch after Ty dropped his first card into the slot. Suddenly, tiny white lights began to glow on the tube, lighting in succession from the mailbox to the "sky". A whooooop! accompanied the lights as they shot skyward.

"There you go, little guy. Now you've seen your letter get to Santa." Despite the elf's deadpan voice, Ty was entranced by the spectacle, but to be fair, so were the adults.

"You guys need kids," chided another close-by mother who was there with her three small children.

"Awww, c'mon! Don't you think that's endearing?" Jane defended this marketing marvel to the stranger, her eyes still on the heaven-directed tube.

"Yup," the other mother replied. "The first ten times we came down here and mailed letters to Santa it was endearing. The second ten times it was cute. Now it's sorta lost its edge. Can't imagine why."

"Just be glad you aren't an elf," mumbled the college boy with the artificial pointy ears before he turned to help another child, his stiff elf smile re-plastered to his face.

Chapter 9

The day after Christmas, Rory walked into the kitchen as Chase was helping himself to coffee. "Jane asked if we wanted to do something for New Year's Eve with her crew."

"And just how would that be different from any other year?"

"Well, we've been invited instead of packed up and hauled off somewhere by mom," Rory answered as he pulled down a cup for himself.

"Sure, and Nick's fun, so I'm cool with that. But I want to go out this year. I'm finally twenty-one and I can actually go out for a New Year's. I don't want to stay at home and play board games and watch the ball drop on TV while our overly-restrictive parents serve us Shirley Temples."

Rory laughed. "You know, most places you'll go, like a bar, which I'm sure you're thinking of, watch the ball drop on the big TV screens. It's not that different. It's just louder and the bathrooms are dirtier."

"Whoa, you just sounded so much like Caroline, it was scary. So, it will be you, me, Nick, Jane, Summer, Hector…"

"No way Summer or Hector will come, given that everyone's on pins and needles about the pregnancy and all."

"Oh yeah. Well, maybe she can hang with Audree and John and Hector can come with us?"

"I'll ask, I'm just not sure that a New Year's Eve at a bar is exactly Hector's scene." Rory looked at his brother. "Amish?"

Chase sipped his coffee and looked at his older brother over the rim of his cup, all innocence. "Not anymore."

Rory sighed and shook his head. "Moving on. I do notice that plan leaves Charlie out of it, since she's only nineteen."

Chase shrugged, unperturbed by Rory's concern.

"I don't think she'll take it too well to be left at home and she's not really a child anymore either." Rory looked impatiently at his brother. "We can't leave her out."

"Does she have to come? Do we have to bend all our plans around her? She's so, she's so… clingy. She's like an annoying little sister I can't shake. Geez, if I didn't know better, I would think she actually followed me to UNC. I bump into her all the time, Rory, I mean all the time. I know Chapel Hill is a small town, but it's kinda creepy how often we see each other. She's like my stalker. I always wonder if she's going to tell her mom where she's seen me and what I'm doing… and Audree will tell Mom and then I'll get a call…"

"Why?" Rory asked, "What are you doing?"

"Nothing," Chase shot back but looked defensive.

Rory gave him a look and raised one eyebrow.

"I mean really, nothing. I'm just out with the guys, or on a date, or at a party. It's not like she sees me in class, I mean I'm an accounting major and… and…" Chase looked pensive, "and I don't actually know what she's studying."

"Pre-med," Rory answered. "She's studying pre-med."

"Oh, well that would explain why I never see her in class. I only bump into her when I'm having fun… and that's not quite the whole picture of my college experience. And not the snapshot that I would want sent back to Mom."

"So, back to the New Year's plans. I don't think we can run off with Jane and leave her sister behind. I think we need to find something that includes everyone who wants to come."

"How about First Night Charlotte?" Caroline said as she came into the kitchen. "Sasutki will be here tomorrow, and he might enjoy it. Ty's napping, thank God. The time change is still plowing that little guy under. And me too. Thanks," she said to Chase as he handed her a mug. "Somehow that trip to Disney with Grandpa George only hyped the little guy up. And now we're paying the price."

"First Night. I like that idea. Could be cold, but still fun to run around and see the events and attractions," Chase said. "I've always wanted to do that. Why haven't we ever done that?"

Rory thought for a moment. "You know, I could call Tony and see what he's planning to do at his place."

"Oh, I like Tony! He's that guy with the pizzeria slash bar, slash empanada place? The one that has the open mic nights?" Caroline asked as she sipped from her mug.

"Yeah. He appreciates when someone, anyone, can sing. They seem to get a lot of American Idol rejects. It's sort of open mic meets unintentional stand-up comedy. It's both hilarious and simultaneously pathetically sad."

"Hey, you could be more generous to your own sister about her debut there!" Caroline said; they all laughed.

"That could work. I know Tony's got teenagers and he likes to keep a more family atmosphere, so let me give him a ring and see what he's doing with the place for New Year's. We could do First Night and then head to his place later on, before midnight." Rory left the room.

Chase turned to Caroline. "Did you know Rory was so particular about clean bathrooms?"

Caroline looked at her youngest brother, opened her mouth a couple of times, but no words came out. Thinking a moment, she gazed curiously at Chase as he loomed over her, his six-foot-three frame causally leaning against the counter. "That's a good thing, Chase. A good thing. A part of adulting. Someday, I predict that you will meet this thing called adulting, and it will completely transform you." She nodded at him a couple of times and gave him a teasing smile. "I look forward to that day, baby brother. Yes, indeed! That'll be a day to remember. Might even make the news."

He grinned back at her. "International headlines, to be sure."

Chapter 10

Jane's phone buzzed and when she saw who it was, she excitedly excused herself from the group, grabbed a coat and went for a walk. She was eager to talk and process some of her thoughts with Claudine—after all, she'd been with Jane since the start of this relationship. After catching up on Claudine's holiday, Jane plunged in. "Well, he slept for most of his first twenty-four hours on American soil. I had to reassure my parents he didn't have dengue fever or anything. You know, I was a little concerned when he arrived—he looked a bit like he'd been a political prisoner."

"That lovely woman will be your belle-mère, your mother-in-law. I imagine that will be a delight. Like living your own fairy tale."

"Don't remind me, only that's evil stepmothers, not belle-mères."

"What is that lovely American expression full of violence? 'Horseshoes and hand grenades'."

Jane sighed. "Right. Only so much of poor Nick's condition could be blamed on the multiple scotches he had on the flight."

"So how did he do with the big family holiday?"

"All in all, I would say he navigated pretty well. I mean, he's in a house full of relative strangers who all treated him as well, as a relative. Everyone hugged him like they'd known him since childhood. Kissed him on the cheek like germs don't exist and lipstick marks don't matter. They threw their arms over his shoulder while they walked from room to room, corralling him into conversations he only partly grasped. Oh my God, you should have heard Chase talking to Nick about accounting. And my dad, he is so excited about dental implant technology! Honestly, I don't think anyone noticed Nick's frozen expression or how I was wincing in sympathy for my poor, out-of-place beau."

"Oui! As an only child I am sure he was used to quiet holidays where he was the sole focus of attention. I imagine it was quite *accablant*. Jane, what is that en Anglaise?"

"Um, overwhelming? Yeah, you'd say overwhelming. And I think you're right. He rose to the occasion for the twenty-fifth, but something's bothering him now. I'm so glad I have you to talk with about it. I can't really talk to my family."

"Why? What is wrong?"

"Well, I don't know what's wrong, but he's been distracted again, and if I'm being honest with you, I'd describe him as a bit short tempered."

"I think that boy was born distracted. Focusing is not his strength." Claudine's voice didn't hold judgment. She just said it like it was fact, as though she was describing the weather.

"What I'm really worried about is, well, maybe he doesn't like my family. He's jumpy as a cat, Claudine. I know my family is overly expressive. Terribly nosy. And they don't feel like they're connecting with you unless they're touching you. But they all mean well! They're very loving and loyal and steadfast."

"It sounds like how the American family should be; like a family without their own television show sharing with the world how *dysfonctionnel* they are. Do you understand my word?"

"Perfectly. Something's bothering him. I've tried to venture into that conversation once or twice, but no luck. He wouldn't go there."

"Well, let him be. When he is ready, he will confess."

"Confess? What do you think he has to confess about?"

"I only mean he will open up to you. Don't you become *dysfonctionnel!*" Claudine laughed into the phone. "Do not make a mouse-hill into a mountain. And remember, my Anglaise, she is imperfect."

* * *

For three days, Nick was edgy and off. For three days Jane mulled over every possible meaning of the word confess, but she kept herself under her usual tight leash and betrayed no outward sign of her anxiety. She was sitting in the sunroom, a book in her hands which she was pretending to read when Nick peeked in around the door, looking a bit abashed.

"Jane." Nick spoke quietly. "I need to talk to you about something."

Jane put down her book. "Yes, Nicky?" She commanded herself to be as neutral as possible. *No mouse-hills becoming mountains,* she told herself sternly. She took a couple of deep calming breaths. He could be a bit tricky to handle when something was bothering him.

"I have to tell you something. I'm sorry I didn't tell you before. But this is important. Don't be mad at me that I didn't tell you before."

Jane felt her stomach do a little dance, like it suddenly realized that out of thin air a tightrope had materialized and was swaying beneath her. She swallowed. Unbidden, her mind brought back the image of the three hardly-dressed-harpies from the art show who had so expertly shouldered her out, encircling her man, excluding her even though the ostentatious, old Victorian ring on her fourth finger screamed out that he had made his choice. Women were drawn to Nick like moths to a flame, just as Claudine had predicted. Of course, some of those women weren't moths, but rather peacock butterflies: beautiful to behold. Intimidating to stand next to; impossible to compete with. Looking at his face, at how he held his shoulders, Jane decided she couldn't speak, shouldn't speak. Her voice would betray her fears and to hear the tremble, the dread, the disappointment in its timbre would make it real, as if to open that door would call the impossible into being. No, it was better to keep that unspoken possibility at bay. It wasn't reality. It was just the suspicious nightmare that haunted her sleep and kept her on her toes around the man she loved more than life itself. Her first love. Her only love. There would never be another Nick. The other side of her coin. She took a deep breath to steady herself and composed her face to calm… and waited.

"It's about…" He looked around the room uncomfortably. He walked back over to the door and closed it quietly after he looked up and down the hall, as if to ensure that no one was near. He took several steps towards her and then froze. "I… I need to confess something."

Jane could feel an acid taste in her mouth. She breathed deeply, thinking of how she would do absolutely anything for this man, her man, and breathed again. She nodded slowly.

"It's something you should know." He sat down in a chair opposite her and looked out the glass walls of the sunroom.

She noticed he didn't make eye contact. She could feel her heartbeat in her ears now, and it made his words hard to hear. She had to concentrate, which was a challenge because a huge part of her didn't want to hear anything he had to say. A part of her wanted to run from the room, her hands over her ears, not listening; or, alternatively, to tackle him, seducing him on the spot to distract him away from the thought of anyone else. To prove to him that she was the more loveable, the sexier, the right choice. She was the one he'd been looking for all his life.

"It's about…" He sighed in exasperation. And then he blurted all in a rush, "It's about my family."

Jane could feel that false composure on her face melt into a look of complete bafflement. "Your… family?" She searched for what new revelation this unexpected turn could be leading to. "Like your name being 'Chip'? Or 'Fourth'? Or the expectation to produce… the 'Fifth' at some point in time?" She hoped her voice sounded light-hearted. Certainly, none of the rest of her felt that way.

Nick looked relieved. "You are the most perceptive woman I have ever known, Jane. You're remarkable. Really, you are. It's just uncanny!

We are two halves of a whole, you and I. Two sides of the same coin. And yes, actually, it's a bit like that. Something I don't like to talk about. I don't really want people to know. But now that it looks like we finally will be getting married..." Jane noticed he stumbled the tiniest bit on the word married. "...we have this, this thing you should know. I'm, well, I'm... I don't know quite how to say this. And I'm really not supposed to talk about it either. Mum and Dad really don't want you to know."

Jane's fears of moths and peacock butterflies instantly dissolved and were quickly replaced by new fears for his health. "Nick, are you all right? What's wrong? Are you ill?" She got up and moved over to sit beside him, placing her hand on his knee. Jane suddenly envisioned Nick with a horrible genetic condition that she couldn't imagine, something that would alter his life, or possibly their lives together. Perhaps he couldn't have children, and that was behind all that stressful talk of the "Fifth" which was incumbent upon him to somehow magically produce from the universe so that his parents could feel secure in their posterity.

"Ill? Ill? No, I mean yes! Sometimes it drives me round the bend. Yes, I suppose sometimes it makes me sick." He turned to look at her again, "You know, you're right. I can't believe how insightful you are, Jane. You're simply amazing. That must be why I love you so much. You are such an angel incarnate. Yes, of course, it makes me ill."

Jane was totally mystified by this line of thinking. "Nick, just tell me what's going on."

"Jane, my darling: steel yourself for this. I didn't tell you before because, well, I couldn't. It's a matter of some delicacy. I really don't want people to know. It could change so much. For you, I mean. I'm not sure how you'll take this."

"What could change so much?" She found she was breathless. Her heart was pounding. Her ears felt like they were stuffed with cotton. She teetered on the edge of panic, suddenly now waiting for him to deliver a blow that was made for reality TV. Claudine's voice rang in her head: *Dysfonctionnel.* Scenarios of stories she'd seen crossed her mind, like the fiancé admitting he was secretly gay and his girlfriend had merely been a desperate, but cruel, ruse to divert his parents. That thought felt like a knife sliding between her ribs. Or there was the ever more common story where the groom-to-be decided he really was a woman living in a man's body and he'd made the decision to transition. What would she do then? That sharp sensation in her ribs made her catch her breath. There were so many vicissitudes of life for which she was wholly unprepared.

Jane, get a hold of yourself! she told herself sharply. *Sure, those things happen, but they happen to famous people… and people who become famous because of them.* She shuddered. *Crazy shit doesn't happen to boring wallflowers. Crazy shit doesn't happen to me.* She couldn't imagine, wanted to stop imagining, in fact, what was about to come out of his mouth.

"Jane. I'm a bit of a… of a… well, a fraud. There. I've said it. It's out. And now you know."

A fraud. A confession. A fraud. *Dysfonctionnel.* She teetered again, waiting for the proverbial other shoe to drop. She decided to just ask questions and use all her power to stop short of slipping into accusation. He got up and started pacing around the room in an agitated fashion. She couldn't tell whether Nick seemed at all relieved to have made his confession. "You're a what? A fraud? You mean you're not really…" *straight?* she almost said but caught herself. "An architect?" Sure, that seemed like safe ground, if ridiculous. It was all she could think of at the moment.

"No, what? No, I'm doing that. At least I was before the shop folded." And then he added, "Tosspot!" under his breath. "And I will again. Oh yes, I'm that! It's just that… my family… well, we are…" He took a deep breath, as if to steel himself. "We are not… British." He looked at once ashamed, yet also curious how she might take such devastating news.

Jane felt her brain freeze. She stared at him, her thinking sluggish as it slowly dawned on her that her worst fears weren't going to be realized in this moment. "Not British?" She couldn't make sense of the words coming out of her mouth, but she was more distracted by her heart rate, which felt like it was at least considering recovery from its perilous high. "How can you be not British. Just listen to you. Of course, you're British." She was bewildered. "You live in Great Britain. You're British."

He fell to one knee at her feet and picked up her hand. "Oh, Jane, it's a huge family secret. We are actually…. not British. We are… Canadian." He whispered the last word.

"Canadian?" She looked down at his hand holding hers and then back into his eyes again. "But you grew up in Bath? Didn't you tell me about going to your prep school there? Then your parents sent you away to some boarding school when you were like eight—and then they only saw you on holidays after that. You were effectively raised by strangers. English strangers. Your parents have a home in Bath. I don't know that you've ever been to Canada? Have you ever been to Canada?"

"Well, I have. To see my grandfather and extended relatives. But not since I was about ten. You can't tell anyone about that, that we're really…" He looked around the room as if there were someone there to hear them, "…Canadian." He said it like there was something wrong with it.

"Where were you born?" Jane asked him directly. "I mean really."

Nick let out a big sigh, slumped his shoulders, and admitted the fact like it was a huge confession. "Toronto. We moved to England when I was five—for my father's business. He broke away from his father's business and set up his own line of work. Had to move to another country to really get away."

"What? And they give you all this shit about not following in the family tradition? You don't actually have a family tradition!" Jane was stunned. "I can't believe your dad is making you work for him!"

"Well, I'm working for him now because of his heart condition. You know, Jane, tradition is a funny thing to the British…"

"But you're not British…"

"Fair. And, we Canadians in the family have something that binds us much more than tradition."

"Hockey?" She was completely confused by this conversation.

"What? No! My great-grandfather's legacy. His fortune. It binds us all."

"Your what?" Jane asked blankly.

"I'm an heir, Jane. To a fortune. To my great-grandfather's Canadian fortune. Thirty million dollars—um, that is Canadian ones, to be specific. So not quite as impressive in U.S. currency. And, uh, quite small once it gets, uh, translated into pounds sterling." He actually sounded apologetic.

"What? Not only are you Canadian, but you're a… a… what did you call it?"

"An heir," he said calmly and with an aura of great pride, as if he had actually done something to earn the title.

"You're an heir?" Jane put her face in her hands and let out a huge sigh of relief. "Oh my God, Nicky, I thought you had some horrible diagnosis!" *Or worse,* she thought to herself. "I think I need a moment to wrap my head around this. You mean to tell me that you're faking being British? And… and… and just why is that?"

"Oh my gosh… what a good thing to ask. I don't think I ever questioned why. I was just always raised that way. We were always trying to prove how British we were and not wanting anyone to find out the truth."

"And you're feeling sick about being Canadian? I don't really get that. It's cool to be Canadian. They're the polite ones. They're nice. Where does the fortune come into all of this?" She was struggling to make sense of it. She thought his family was comfortably off, despite being what her own mother would have called cheapskates. "I thought your father was, well, successful. You know, with the whole wine and liquor importing… thing. You know, with a little wine label of his own in France?"

"Well, he's marginally successful. Just successful enough, perhaps. And, oh, the label, well, it's just a small thing. Actually, kind of amusing you know," he said with a chuckle. "Quite enterprising, the French. You can devise your own label and there are wineries which will put it on as many bottles of their table wine as you'd like."

Jane burst out with a laugh. "A vanity wine press? Your father has a vanity wine label? How many bottles does he have made?"

"Oh, I don't know. Maybe a hundred. Maybe less." Nick stretched the collar of his shirt a bit and swallowed. "Whatever he can afford. You know, mostly they've been flush because of Granddad and the stipend he gives them all. Helps everyone buy a house. He's the one with all the cash, but he's in an awful row with his own brother, my great uncle. They're ninety years old and at each other's throats over the fortune. But it should come down to me… eventually. There's not really anyone else left at the end of the line but me… and a second cousin over on the Canadian side."

"So, you're feeling sick about being Canadian? Or about this being a secret? Or the family winery that is actually a total sham or over the fact that you might stand to inherit some family money?"

Now he was all animated. "The pressure is immense, Jane! Thirty million is not chump change. Even after you translate it to pounds sterling."

"Thirty million?" She could feel her lips forming the words but wasn't sure that anything was actually coming out of her mouth. Thirty million in any currency at all was hard to wrap one's mind around. A cascade of thoughts avalanched through her brain and it was as though she could see missing pieces of some crazy puzzle all falling into place. The image was so clear she could almost hear the snapping sound as each piece clicked. Her interactions with his parents suddenly seemed to make perfect sense. With her new-found clarity she understood much more about their relationship with their son. The underlying currency of their bond was their expectation that Nicky prove to them that he was worth the inheritance. They loved him as the heir to the family fortune and as the fourth namesake of the line, but not so much as the actual person he was. She had seen that they used money as marionette strings on him, which he resented and rebelled against, but she saw that it also bound him quite effectively. "Thirty million… strings?" she said, that image of puppets still in her mind, but she said that last word very quietly.

"Yes, it's awful, isn't it? And it's tea. Bloody Canadian tea!"

"Canada produces tea? You can grow tea leaves in Canada?"

"What? Grow tea? Well, I'm sure I don't know. I've never been interested in *that* side of things."

"But your family owns a Canadian tea company?"

"No, no, my great-grandfather sold that in the late nineties. We haven't run that trolly in decades."

"Tea…?" Jane said, still lost in the avalanche of her thoughts, including now some about climate and growing conditions.

"Yes, Fouchada Tea to be specific."

"Fouchada Tea?" Jane asked.

"Yes, Fouchada, surely you've heard of it. Huge company."

"Never heard of it," she said while she wondered just how much tea one could grow in Canada.

"How can you not know Fouchada tea? It's simply huge. That's why we're so bloody rich!" He looked exasperated.

"Look, Nicky, I'm an American. I know Lipton tea and anything Starbucks carries." Jane sat back in her chair. "Nick…" She turned to look at him.

He sat down on the ottoman next to her chair, took her hand in his and said, "Yes, darling?"

"I don't think I can marry you."

Nick stared at her, speechless. Several moments passed without a word. Jane could feel her heart racing, her pulse in her temples was pounding. The pieces were falling into place about his family. They were so damn dysfunctional and, given her rather normal and unremarkable upbringing, she had no compass to navigate the dynamics of his kin. But at least she finally understood why. She pulled her hand out of his.

"Because I'm... Canadian?" He looked terribly hurt.

"No, I think it's wonderful that you're actually Canadian. I don't care where you're from. I'm an American. How could I care where you're from? And Canadians... compared to Americans, well, they're the good guys."

"Because you... you hate tea or something, is it?" he asked, confused. "You would break up with me over tea. My love, you don't have to actually drink it."

"No, no, it's not that. Tea is fine. Canadian tea is fine. It's the money, Nick. Money like that... that's crazy money. Thirty million? That's not healthy. Money like that corrupts people. It drains away your reason for living. It leaves you with nothing left to accomplish. People who have that kind of money... they feel the rules don't apply to them. It's... it's toxic." She felt the words pouring out of her in a rush.

"It hasn't ruined me."

"It's ruined your parents. Just look at the way they live. Nick, they have a fake wine label and pretend to be British, living on a stipend from your grandfather in a fancy house that he bought them... I mean at their age! Do you see the way they make you prove yourself to them over and over again, and yet you'll never be good enough in their eyes. They're the most screwed up people I know. Everything about them is for show. Nothing is authentic. Nothing. And apparently even you live this bizarre double life, of being a secretly rich Canadian masquerading as a... as a... a British, oh my God, I'm not even sure what to call you."

"We don't have to live in England. It's cold and rainy there. We'll live here, in Charlotte. The land of eternal sun and infernal heat. We'll live far away from them. Or maybe Colorado. I've been reading about green design in a place called Boulder."

While she was glad to hear it, she wondered what brought on this sudden burst of flexibility about where they would eventually make their lives together. He'd been adamant that they live in Great Britain since the start. It was always Jane who would eventually need to make the big move. "But can you live far away from the money? Nick, can you live without that money? They control you like you're a puppet on their strings. You'll never be happy until you stand on your own two feet—completely and totally independent of them. Financially independent of them."

Nick laughed and then realized that she wasn't laughing with him. He looked at her for a long time. "I'm sorry I lied to you about it. I should have told you earlier. I should have told you at the start. But I couldn't. I had to know that you loved me for me, and not for… well, my assets. And you make such a good living now, that it didn't feel like such a risk to tell you—I mean, you have assets of your own!"

"If you had told me, I would never have become involved with you." Jane thought back to how Claudine had pegged him early on as being "riches". And the problems that flowed along with that. Well-off was one thing. "Riches" was another.

"This is so ironic." He gave a sarcastic chuckle. "My mother always lectured me to never tell anyone about the fortune because I would be besieged by girls from poor families with good names in need of refurbishing their family security. She assured me they wouldn't love me, just the money. Or actresses. My mother was always terribly afraid of me becoming involved with an actress. Equates them with prostitutes, I believe. And here I'm being rejected by the girl I love because of the money." Then he looked down and muttered "Well, it should make the pre-nup she's demanding ever so much easier."

Jane jolted at hearing the word "pre-nup". Never in her life had she anticipated hearing those two syllables in a sentence directed towards her.

Nick turned back to Jane. "You do beat them all, Miss Jane Donahue." Nick got down on his knees again, so that he and Jane were eye to eye as she was sitting. "Dahling, you are absolutely perfect for me. Just what I need. You keep me so grounded. You keep me honest. Do tell me that you won't leave me over something stupid like money? I know you, you wouldn't leave me if I were poor. How can you leave me now that you find out that I'm not poor? It would be just too prejudiced of you! Besides, I need you to save me from the taint of all that wealth in my life. To keep me authentic. I promise it won't corrupt me! Say your heart will find its way back to me and that we're still getting married." He looked at her deeply, and picked up her hand and kissed it. "Say you're still the other side of my coin. Two halves of one whole."

Jane felt herself melting under his gaze. "This…money…" she could barely spit out the word, "is with your grandfather. And you have a second cousin on your great uncle's side…"

"Yes, so the money might never come to me after all. We might be free of it. I might actually be poor!" He said it like it was a badge of honor. "Except, once we get married, Grandad will give us a living stipend as well! He's a big fan of marriage. So, nothing's really changed, since you don't care about me being… Canadian." He kissed her hand again, kissed up her arm and then swooped her into a passionate embrace for a long minute. Jane felt herself melting into his arms as her fears of tabloid headlines faded into a dim memory and relinquished their hold on her.

Suddenly startled by a noise, Jane and Nick broke their kiss and turned their heads, their lips still touching. There stood Ty, staring at them curiously.

"Are you practicing for New Year's Eve?"

Chapter 11

New Year's Eve dawned a cold day. Jane was excited for activity and getting out of the house. While the days were relaxing, there really wasn't a lot to do. She was used to the intensity and excitement of a fast-paced job, and all this quiet was a bit unnerving. The holiday was a lot of down-time that just felt like an empty space of waiting for the next thing... or anything, to happen. Sure, she and Nick had seen a few movies. They had gone indoor rock wall climbing at a new rec center. And they'd been through what felt like a million-and-one family events. But the time hung heavy. She snuck away on a few occasions to check email, but her workmates were on holiday too. She finally had to admit to herself that without her work, she was bored.

Happily, tonight was going to be yet another Watkins-Donahue cross-family affair. The whole crew was meeting to go out for dinner at seven. Nothing fancy, just local Italian. Then Summer and Hector would head home to watch a movie and make an early night of it. Summer was just past the point of her last tragedy. While her anxiety was more well-controlled than her parents', she was still taking a laid-back, low-risk approach to life. The rest of the crew, including Sasutki, who had arrived on the twenty-seventh, and Ty, would do First Night Charlotte, enjoying a few ice sculptures as they melted away, the street musicians and magicians, and any other surprises the festival had to offer. Ty and his Nana would head home before ten o'clock, and Jane was pretty sure her parents would disappear then too if Mimi was calling it a night. Any remaining party members would go to Tony's Pizza & Empanadas. Rory's friend had agreed to include them in his private event for the evening. Best of all, Charlie could join because the group wouldn't end up bar hopping. Jane heard from Caroline how that decision sent Chase sulking for a bit.

"Welcome! Welcome my friend!" Tony said to Rory as their party arrived shortly after ten o'clock. "You got here in good time! Welcome, come on in everybody! Any friend of Rory's is a friend of mine! Get warm! Coat hooks are over there if you want them." He pointed to the far wall. "Everybody gets wristbands at that table over there, where my wife, Frannie, is. The kids are going to open the side room as a dance floor at some point tonight. Those kids!" Tony laughed heartily and was so engaging that everyone laughed along with him.

Tony's Pizza & Empanadas was a cozy place with a lot of warm, exposed wood and music memorabilia decorating the walls. Clearly, it was the couple's friends who made up the party-goers, with a variety of folks aged from just one decade to about seven. Rory introduced his group to Tony; they hung up their coats and made their way over to check in with Frannie and get their wristbands.

"Indebted to you, sir." Nick nodded as he was introduced to Tony. "It's brass monkeys outside! So nice to be in your lovely establishment." Nick blew on his hands to warm them up.

"Brass monkeys?" Tony said as he went to the door and looked outside, presumably for monkeys.

"Oh, you've got to be kidding me!" Charlie stomped back from Frannie's check-in table. "I'm the only one with this construction-cone-color monstrosity on my wrist!" Charlie showed them her neon orange wristband, designating her as a no-alcohol guest.

At that moment a child ran past them, proudly brandishing a replica orange wrist band, shouting to his mother, "Mommy! Mommy! Look at my glowy wristband! Cool!"

Chase turned to Charlie. "That's because you're the only one under twenty-one. You're lucky to be out at all tonight." He admired his neon green band that allowed him to order whatever he wanted. He went up to the bar, followed by Charlie and Jane.

"Happy new year! What can I get for y'all?" the bartender asked with a smile.

Jane surveyed the drink menu. "I'd like a cosmopolitan please, Dirty Pelican Cosmo if you can." Turning to her sister and Chase she added, "I'm going to see what Nick wants, I'll be back in a mo." She walked over to a table where Nick was standing and talking to Sasutki.

"Coming right up! And for you my dear? Diet Coke or Regular?" the bartender asked Charlie.

"Diet," she sighed. "With a lime, if you can."

"No problem. Soda is free tonight. All designated drivers drink free." The bartender turned to Chase. "Have you decided yet? What can I get for you?"

"Uh… um… I'll have a… a…" Chase was stuck, frozen by too many choices in front of him. For the first time he could order anything he wanted, but he had no idea what he liked. "A Bud. Uh, yeah, a Bud."

"On tap or in a bottle?"

"Uh…"

"He'll have it on tap. And make it a Bass Ale," Charlie said, scanning the tap heads.

"Yeah, what she said." Chase nodded as he pointed to Charlie with his thumb. Turning to her, he asked, "And just how do you know about Bass Ale, Miss Under-Age?"

She shrugged. "It's Rory's favorite. It has to be good. Everything Rory likes is a class act."

"Make it two Bass Ales. I'll get one for Rory too," Chase called out to the bartender.

The Diet Coke with a lime wedge and two beers showed up and Chase paid the bill, stuffing a few bucks in the tip jar to boot. He carried the drinks over to the table Tony had reserved for them and presented Rory with his beer.

"Wow, Chase—this is unusual. Thanks. Wait a minute, did you make Charlie pay for it?" Rory held up the glass. "What is it?" He tasted it. "Wow, Bass. I like Bass. Good choice."

Charlie punched Chase in the arm while she gave him a look.

Nick came over to the table with a Guinness Stout and Jane had her special Cosmo. Soon Caroline and Sasutki joined them, Caroline with a sidecar and Sasutki with a double shot of honey whiskey.

"You know, this is the life. No homework. No semester starting up in a few weeks. Making a decent salary. I love being out of school!" Jane said with a smile. "I love being a part of the working world."

Rory laughed "Are you rubbing it in that you so wisely chose a two-year MBA while I chose to go back for a doctorate? If I'm out by the time I'm twenty-eight, I'll be lucky."

"And just what do you read there? In Princeton, is it?" Nick asked.

They all looked at one another and then at him. "Sorry, Nick, I'm not sure what you just asked me," Rory answered. "What do I read?"

"Yes, what kind of doctor are you studying to become? What do you read?"

"I bet he means, what are you majoring in?" Chase said.

"Oh, that would be data analytics. It's like how your phone knows what ads to show you based on the websites you've visited and what apps you use. That kind of thing," Rory answered, and Nick nodded.

"But I think you're wrong, Rory." Chase teased his brother. "Obviously Jane's freedom comment was directed at me! I have a whole 'nother year after this… and I haven't told Dad yet, but I think I'm going to need to go for a fifth year." He winced as he said it.

"Oh, you're kidding?" Caroline asked, "Why, Chase?"

"When I changed into accounting I was behind, so it's gonna take more time to catch up. But I can pick up a minor along the way, so it'll be worth it. And I really like Carolina. The B-school's great."

"Actually, I think Jane is teasing me!" Charlie jumped into the conversation. "I think she's rubbing it in that I'm a just a sophomore and with medical school I have at least six years of education still on the horizon!" Charlie groaned dramatically. "I will be so old by the time I get out. Oh my God, I'll be old like… well, like you, Rory!" Everyone laughed.

"Thanks a lot!" He raised his beer in mock toast, but he was smiling. Nothing ever ruffled Rory. "I like Princeton, I like what I'm studying. In the last year I've made some new friends—mostly data analytic types like me, so, that is to say, real geeks. I found some guys who like to fool around with music, cool guys. One dude is Indian and sometimes brings a sitar. One is Scottish. He can really hold a tune and he's ace of bass, but I have no idea what he's saying."

"Snap! I have that problem with Scotsmen too!" Nick nodded knowingly. "It's like they're speaking in tongues. Well mates, I'm going to spend a penny. See a man about a dog. Be back directly."

As Nick left the table and walked over to the restroom door, Chase turned to Jane, and in his best fake British accent said, "Blimey, Jane! How you understand what-it-is he means? And he complains about the Scots!"

"So," Sasutki asked, "you all play music?"

Rory smiled, pushed his shaggy blonde hair out of his eyes, and continued, "I've always enjoyed tinkering with the guitar, so we mess around together on Tuesdays and Fridays. It's a good excuse to drink beer and hang out. We're thinking of playing a couple of gigs at local bars."

"At Carolina, I just drink the beer and leave the guitars out of it!" Chase said with a laugh.

Sasutki laughed too and looked at Charlie. "Beer or beer and guitars?" he asked jovially.

Charlie held up her obnoxious construction-zone-orange wrist band. "Neither. I only get Diet Coke."

Conversation turned to the Watkins' family Christmas trip with their father, George. Typically, he took them skiing or to some warm and sunny beach for four days, either just before or just after the holiday. Since Ty was four this year, he had taken them to Orlando.

Even Chase had enjoyed doing kiddie things with his nephew at Magic Kingdom and Rory and Chase got some time to enjoy older kid attractions together too, while George, Caroline, and Ty played at Seuss Landing at Universal Studios.

"Something's really different with Dad," Chase said. "No girlfriend with us this year."

"Yeah, it was just us and him, that was really nice." Caroline smiled. "Ty had a wonderful time. He kept asking where Nana was and why she didn't come. That was just a tad awkward." Turning to Sasutki, Caroline put a hand on his arm, "And I think you would have loved it, honey. I know you said you weren't interested, but it wasn't all Magic Kingdom. We went to Epcot and Universal Studios. We'll have to go there sometime when we come back to the states."

Sasutki nodded non-committedly and sipped his whiskey. "We can go to Tokyo Disney if you want."

Nick returned to the table and pointed to the dart board on the far wall. "Would anyone care for a spot of darts?" Chase agreed and the two men went to play, followed by Charlie. Rory and Caroline talked about the trip and the time with their father. It wasn't long before Nick returned, having been soundly defeated by Charlie at darts. She was now taking on Chase.

"I didn't think I was quite so knackered as to be beat by a little girl," he said in a mutter. Then he called out to Chase, "She's a shark! Watch out for her!" Turning to the rest of the table he added, "Frankly, I'm chuffed she didn't beat the pants off me! Embarrassing, that, as a Brit. I think I need another Guinness!" He held up his nearly empty glass to a passing waitress who nodded at him and headed off to get another round.

"I want to see your brother get beat by a little girl," Sasutki giggled to Caroline and Rory, and left to join the darts game.

"That bloke doesn't stand a blooming chance against her! She's got mad skills," Nick said draining the last of the beer in his glass. The waitress showed up with his replacement and set it down. "Cheers then," Nick nodded to her.

"You know, on our trip, Dad talked about the weirdest stuff," Rory said. "Going to Nepal. Mountain hiking. Going with a friend. I mean a guy friend, so a real friend rather than a girlfriend."

"Your dad is going to climb Mount Everest? That's the dog's bollocks!"

"The dog's what? Never mind. No, he promised us he isn't having that kind of mid-life crisis. He's just going hiking and adventuring with a friend, sometime this summer, but it's not like him. He's all Vegas and younger women." Rory was definitely not smiling.

Caroline added, "Or Miami sun… and younger women." She was also not smiling.

"Yeah, he's definitely not the hiking-mountains-in-developing-countries-type-of-dude. I don't know what's up with him." Rory stared at his beer, a serious look on his face.

"Oh well, it would still sound brilliant even if he just saw Everest! I say, let's get some nosh, shall we?" Looking at the menu, Nick pointed out a couple of options to Jane. The waitress came back over and they ordered late night snacks. Chase let out a cry of defeat from the dart board, and Sasutki stepped up to take his place.

Nick glanced over at them. "That little girl is something else," he said and took a swig of his beer.

"In what way?" Rory asked, looking a bit uncomfortable and staring at the liquid in his own glass.

"Well, don't let my mother see her for one!" Nick exclaimed. "She would love her to bits!"

"Why's that?" Jane asked in surprise.

"Well," Nick laughed, "I'm quite certain she would steal her from you all, lock her in a closet until she lost a stone or so, and then turn her loose on the runway."

"What?" rang out in chorus from Caroline, Jane, and Rory.

Rory looked confused. "How would that be 'loving her to bits'?"

"What's a stone?" Caroline asked.

"She would turn your baby sister into a model," Nick said to Jane as if it was the most obvious thing in the world. "Of course, she's far too fat right now, but I bet my mother would be just drooling over her."

"Why would Cressida think Charlie could model?" Jane asked doubtfully, looking back over at Charlie full of skepticism. She certainly didn't see that in her sister, nor did she see that Charlie was any amount overweight.

"Well, because she was one. Yes, I don't think even you know about it, Jane, but my mother was a model in her day. That's how she and my father met. She was really quite dishy. The woman has smoked like a bloody chimney for decades to stay thin. I'm afraid that hasn't done her any favors, but she was quite the looker at one time."

"Cressida a model?" Jane said, the shock apparent in her voice. "Like in magazines?"

"Oh yes. Clothes, cosmetics, perfumes, a few magazine covers."

"Wow, not that she isn't still attractive, but I just wouldn't have guessed about… the… yeah, modeling thing." Jane smiled and was trying not to laugh.

"Oh, I've heard boatloads about bone structure and big eyes and straight noses the whole time I was growing up. She's got an eye for picking a winner, I'd give her that. But she's a stickler for girls being awfully thin. Completely not into that whole body positivity thing." Nick sipped his beer and watched the darts match from across the room.

"Completely not into positivity could fit as an apt general description," Jane said lightly, trying to look her most innocent as she caught Caroline's eye.

Caroline tried to not laugh. "Wow, a real model. That's interesting! Why'd did she give it up? Did she ever make the jump to acting?"

"No, never acted." Nick shook his head. "In fact, she lost a lot of jobs once actresses started getting the magazine covers and the cosmetics sponsorships. Seems the marketers decided that people wanted a face they knew and liked rather than one they just liked and wished they knew. Jane, as a marketing expert, would know all about that!" Nick said and Jane nodded. "Mum hates actresses, says they ruined her career, but I have also heard her say that getting married was a career-killer as well."

"Yeah, I could see that," Caroline agreed, nodding her head. "And not just for models. Me too."

"She had to give it up once she got serious with Dad. And of course, having me really ended any hope of ever getting back into it. Says she was washed up before she was thirty. Honestly, I don't think she's gotten over it quite yet."

"And she would say little Charlie has potential?" Caroline asked.

"Like I said, get the baby fat off her, give her a decent haircut, or maybe any haircut at all, and make up, and my mother would turn her into a professional. That bone structure. That smile. She's like a flower about to bloom. Of course, she's late in the game, what is she? Seventeen?"

"Nineteen." Rory was the first to speak.

"Well, a bit too old! But my mum would have a hay day with her!"

"I think Charlie is into school. She wants to be a physician. I don't think anything would pull her away from that. Certainly not something like being a... a model." Jane shook her head and was almost laughing, dismissing the idea.

"I suppose she'll see her at your wedding?" Rory asked, looking over at the darts game as if deciding whether he wanted to play.

"Perhaps. Let's not talk wedding plans." Nick sighed heavily. "My parents are throwing wobblers over the whole idea."

They were saved by the waitress bringing over three large platters of "nosh" as Nick called it. Charlie, Sasutki, and Chase returned to the table and started to dive into the food.

After a while the music began blaring from the next room as Tony's kids started the dancing portion of the party. After a couple of songs and finishing his second Guinness, a slow song started to play, and Nick turned to Jane. "Would you care to dance, my love?"

"Oh, that's so romantic!" Charlie said, her voice gushing.

Chase looked askance at Charlie. "What? He only asked her to dance."

"No, not the dancing. Okay, well, yeah, the dancing, sure, but he called her my love. That's romantic." Charlie sighed, looking back at Chase. He shrugged and turned back to the plates of nachos and wings.

"Charlie, my love, would you care to dance?" Rory asked her, rolling his eyes at his brother.

"Yes, I would adore that." Charlie turned her nose up at Chase and took Rory's hand.

"As long as you don't mind dancing with an old man like me."

The two couples went over to the dance floor, quickly followed by Caroline dragging a reluctant Sasutki. Chase was left at the table by himself with the now quite cold nosh.

There were about a half dozen couples on the floor, including a pair of ten-year-olds who were moving about like stiff toy soldiers.

"Jane," Nick whispered in her ear, "while we're alone out here, I would like to talk to you."

"Nick, we're hardly alone. There's a dozen other people on the dance floor."

"True, but it's not like we're sitting around with your family. I want to talk about the wedding plans."

Jane felt her heart sink. "Okay." She was going to be firmly in control this time and not let her imagination run away with her. No being dysfunctional allowed.

"I wonder if you... well... given how difficult it has been to come up with a reasonable plan, well, what I'm trying to say is...." Nick sighed.

"What do you need to tell me, Nick?"

He looked her right in the eye. "How about if we abandon the whole big wedding thing and just go to the Pyrenees and elope in some small town? Would your parents murder you? Mine will surely murder me, but I can't stand their interference. I'm tired of their meddling. How about we just run off?" He smiled at her.

"Oh, Nicky!" She breathed, happy to feel such a sense of relief. "I need to let that sink in. Maybe? Let me think about it."

"We'd have to give up having our families there, but I suppose that's what eloping is all about, isn't it? The Pyrenees are beautiful. We could do it in April?"

"Wow. Mountains. April. That sounds pretty wonderful. Okay, let's look into it."

"And we could stay in a mountain cabin for our honeymoon and hike a bit in the hills? With your excellent French I'm sure we'd get along smashingly well."

"Oh, Nicky! It sounds romantic. It sounds perfect!" She smiled and then kissed him.

"Hey, you're supposed to hold off on that until midnight!" Rory laughed as he and Charlie fox-trotted past them.

"Where in the world did they learn to dance like that?" Jane laughed at them and kissed Nicky again.

Chapter 12

The first couple months of the new year flew by. There was so much to plan, and so much to get ready for. Unfortunately, most of it fell on Jane's shoulders. She wished she could spend some real time with Claudine. Now there was a woman who always saw straight through the hype and was never bothered by emotions. She didn't have a great sense of romance, true, but Claudine was ever the voice of reason. Objective. Logical. Happy to be outraged on your behalf when you were being a passive doormat. Jane checked the time and decided that it wasn't too late to ring her friend in Paris and gave her a call.

"Oui? Allô? Jane, mon ami, how are you?"

"Hey, Claudine! I hope I didn't get you up."

"I am not yet in bed, so all is good." They caught up a bit on general news and Jane filled her in on the elopement plans. "But why is Nicholas not helping you?"

Jane sighed heavily. "He's swamped in his attempts to run his father's business while Colin's doctors are still trying to solve his atrial flutter. From what Nick described to me, I'm not sure whether the heart condition, or the fear of it, is going to do poor Colin in first. But he's effectively abandoned Nick at the import business. Since it's not anything Nick went to school for or knows how to do, he's drowning with the learning curve. And it's completely undermining Nick's attempts to get his own career going again. So, he's been just useless when it comes to planning the elopement he so desperately wanted at New Year's."

"Can you not talk to him about this? It will be a real problem if he is still trapped at the business when you are married. That will put chains on you as well."

That prediction sounded all too on-the-money to Jane. "He's been so hard to reach. I leave him messages all the time."

"And he calls you back?"

Jane made a non-committal sound. "I think he needs a new phone. I've gotten a lot of 'sorry, low battery' responses, several 'poor cell signals' and those automatic 'I can't talk now' messages. And then later on he'll send, 'too tired' with an apology that comes in after midnight, his time."

"Oh really? And he is nose to the millstone, like his workaholic fiancée?"

"Nose to the grindstone," Jane corrected without even thinking.

"Grindstone, oui."

"Not always," Jane admitted, a bit uncomfortably. "There were a few times, okay, maybe more than a few times, when he answered and the background noise was deafening. He was with those friends I told you about, Greigh, Sean, Emily, Astrid, Trevor, and a few others."

"He is running with a fast crowd. A trust-fund baby crowd."

"Yeah, they aren't really my type. But if they're around, they always pile on the phone to ask how things are on the other side of the pond. And that Astrid, in particular, is always putting her face too close to the camera and screaming things like 'All right, Janie? We're having a piss up! What are you doing?'"

"I imagine you are not having 'a piss up'," Claudine said.

"No. definitely not. I'm usually at work and not having a 'piss up' at a bar. I'm not even doing that after work." Jane had met this particular crowd from Bath quite a few times on her visits to Nick. They were a rowdy group full of self-described artists embracing "alternative lifestyles." To Jane, they mostly sounded like spoiled rich kids who could afford to be edgy and "alternative" because they didn't have to worry about paying their bills. She was sure that none of them were a good influence on her fiancé. "Nick told me the strangest thing: this girl, Ashlyn, the one he dated briefly when we broke up, was offered a job by Nick's father. Old Colin had become sweet on her for two very obvious reasons and was impressed with her assets, if not her talent, if you know what I mean."

"I understand you clearly. While I never would bother to have them, I have always been amazed at how breast implants more than pay for themselves in unexpected ways."

"Yeah, right," Jane answered uncomfortably. "And now Nick, rather awkwardly, has to work alongside the impressively-breasted Ashlyn. He assures me that it's not a big deal since she's dating 'we're-having-a-piss-up' Astrid. They're really quite serious. He said they make a good couple."

"Hmm. Janie, I do not know whether to say 'marry him quickly' so that you can drive those other women away from him or to say that…"

"Don't say it. I love him. I trust him. He's just overworked and busy. And life is weird, I mean you just can't make this stuff up. But if you could help me with making the right plans for the honeymoon, all these troubles will be just little bumps in the road that will go away soon."

"All right. I will do everything I can to help you. But mostly I want to help you open your eyes."

* * *

Despite her frustration, Jane plowed on without any credible help from Nick. With crucial help from Claudine, she researched all she needed to know about marrying in France. In a way, Jane felt like she should be marrying Claudine, since that's who she made all the plans with. Claudine even found a romantic cabin in the French Pyrenees just a couple of miles outside the mountain town of Prades. The hiking would be wonderful in the beautiful hills and the town was a short half-hour walk away. It was perfect for a honeymooning couple who wanted a remote location but with fine dining just down in the valley.

Jane booked her flight for the twenty-fourth of March to meet Nicky in Paris for two days. Then they would take the TGV high speed train to the mountains and finally pick up a car for the last leg of their journey. It was the faultless two-week elopement and honeymoon which would allow them to reconnect and truly leave the world behind. Between her hectic job and spending all her free time planning their trip, Jane was really looking forward to some rest and relaxation. She was in sore need of some good old-fashioned fun. She tried to ignore the feeling that planning the trip without Nicky was more depressing than it was exciting, and she resolutely blocked out thinking about the second half of Claudine's unfinished sentence.

One Sunday, as Jane was pouring over online ratings and comments about restaurants, shops, and hikes, putting the finishing touches on the plans for each day of their trip, the phone rang. She looked at her caller I.D. "Hey, Summer! What's up? How are you feeling?"

"Oh, I scared you. Sorry. I can't even call Mom these days, it sends her into a panic. I have to text her first and tell her I'm going to call and that there's no emergency. But no worries—I'm good. Yeah, really good. I feel great. I was just wondering if you wanted to go to a movie? I've stayed in for so much of this pregnancy and I kinda have cabin fever. Hector's on a job, building some lucky family new kitchen cabinets on an impossible deadline. It's all late evenings for him, but the surcharge for overtime will be great for us. Will you see a movie with me?"

"Oh yeah, Mom and Dad are in D.C. with Charlie." Jane looked at the clock on the wall, seeing it creeping up to noon. She knew Summer would want to see an early matinee, which would mean leaving soon. Summer was always so spontaneous, while Jane was the completely plan-ahead-and-check-the-boxes type, but she really needed a break from all her researching. "Yeah, sure. Want me to pick you up?"

"No, I'll drive. I'm feeling the need to get out. Feeling restless. Maybe that means the baby will come soon."

"Or maybe it means you've been kind of cooped up during the icy weather we've had for the last two weeks!" Jane laughed. "It's March fifteenth and that baby isn't due for another month!"

"You know it's not true what they say about pregnancy. It's not nine months. It's more like ten. It's a really long, long, long time." Summer sighed. "I'll pick you up in about a half hour—sound good?"

"Sure, see you then. We'll get some cure for that cabin fever." Jane smiled as she hung up the phone and went back to her travel guide. Summer was never on time. Jane figured she had about an hour before her sister would actually arrive.

Much to her surprise, in twenty minutes Summer phoned from out in front of Jane's place. The unseasonable cold was hanging on, so Jane grabbed her coat and bag, and met Summer in the parking lot.

After the movie and hitting Cup-A-Joe's for Summer's favorite decaffeinated-skinny-no-artificial sweeteners-caramel latte, she dropped Jane back by her apartment at four o'clock. They were still laughing about the movie and their coffee conversation. Jane felt more relaxed than she had in the last several weeks.

"Thanks so much for coming, Janie!" Summer said as Jane got out of the car. "It was so good to get out! Just what I needed."

"Absolutely! Let me know if you want to go out to dinner on Wednesday. God knows, with Nick in another country I have no life at all. All I do is work and wait for him. Maybe I can get in touch with him now—it's not quite ten for him. I'm sure he'll still be up."

"I'll let you know about Wednesday. You stay warm! Bye!"

Jane shut the passenger door and as Summer zoomed away, she turned to walk up the sidewalk to her unit. She chuckled to herself, happily distracted and lost in her thoughts about the movie. Then all of a sudden, she felt it: a swoop. The earth moved underneath her and the world slowed down. She had that odd sensation of both being in every second as it ticked by and also observing it objectively. It was as though time was suspended. In striking detail, she saw the bare tree branches above her: naked, inky fingers reaching across an ice blue Carolina sky, like they were grasping for her—but to rescue or threaten her, she couldn't tell. The contrast of the puffy white clouds looked strangely eerie and suddenly she felt a wave of abject fear. Then she was on her back. More knowing than thought, more like a whisper directly into her mind than any kind of logical reasoning, came the quiet words *it will never work*. It loomed in her mind, large like the sky above her and etched in darkness, a reflection of those skeletal branches. Everything hung for a moment, suspended like time was. Then she felt it. It rushed up her leg from her ankle, racing past her hip, and then registering in her brain with the screaming realization that she had slipped on black ice and had possibly broken a bone. Or maybe more than one. Pain. She screamed out, "Ouch! Ahhhh! Shiiiiit!"

She wasn't sure whether her scream was from the pain in her body or from the dead fear of the thought that had just exploded across her awareness.

It will never work.

What will never work?

I think you know.

She chose the pain in her body, resolutely turning a deaf ear to that voice in her head. She reached for her right ankle and cried out again—her left shoulder was immobile. She lay on the sidewalk like a turtle on its back, breathless for a few moments, trying to regain any semblance of self-control. "Okay, Jane, all you did was fall," she said aloud through her panting breaths and gritted teeth. "Oh, shit, you might have a broken ankle, just breathe, just breathe." She panted a few times. "And a busted shoulder. Just breathe, just breathe."

She wished somebody would come out of their door or drive up. "Stupid, quiet, secluded condo complex." The exact opposite of New York City's hustle and bustle: that's why she had chosen to live here after her MBA—to get away from people. "Seemed like a good idea at the time," she grumbled, her eyes watering with the agony. She remembered how one afternoon she'd pulled a chair out here and read for more than two hours without ever seeing anyone out and about. That day she'd counted herself lucky to live here.

"You're on your own, Jane. Figure this out." She took another slow, deep breath and gently rolled over onto her right side; there was no way she could put any pressure on her left shoulder. "Assets. Think assets. One good arm. Two good knees. One good foot. So, not totally fucked, just about fifty-percent. You can do this." Gasping in pain, she managed to get up on her knees and, keeping her right ankle off the ground and her left arm curled against her body, she managed to crawl very slowly over to her door. It was exhausting. By the time she got there she had accidentally bumped her ankle once or twice, allowing herself to curse like a sailor. Her knees were now scuffed and bleeding in a couple of places. Pulling herself up by the door handle, she clung to the knob as she gently moved her right ankle. She panted with the pain, but she could it move slightly. "Okay, so maybe not broken?" She looked down. "Oh shit, look at that swelling." Even though it had only been minutes since her fall, the size of her ankle was already impressive.

She tried to move her shoulder and swore once again, but at least it was responsive, not the frozen immobility so common with breaks. She fumbled for her keys, opened her front door, and hobbled inside until she could ease herself down into a chair. She pulled out her cell phone and looked at the numbers programmed into it. Her parents were still on their trip visiting Washington, D.C., for some cultural event on Charlie's spring break. They would be gone all week. Summer, who she had just left. *Last resort. Don't want to put her into early labor or anything,* Jane thought with a guilty pang. Hector—on a job, but that was the same as calling Summer. Then there was Charlie—*nope, right, she's with Mom and Dad.* Chase. *Who knows where he is? Probably at some sunny beach surrounded by admiring, bikini-clad strangers since it's spring break for UNC.* She wondered, would she have called Chase if he were here in Charlotte? *Yes, of course. Chase or Rory. Absolutely. They're like brothers to me.* But Rory was in New Jersey, also at school. Cross him off the list. The boys weren't technically family but certainly, she could call on them for anything. Then she touched the icon for Mimi, the obvious answer now that she saw it. Mimi was her "other mother" in every way.

"Hi Mimi? It's Jane. Oh, yeah, of course you know that. My picture came up on your phone."

"Jane? Honey, you sound awful. You're crying! What's wrong?"

"Well, I had an accident. Not a car accident, but I just fell on some, well, I guess it was black ice. I don't think I broke my ankle, but I can't walk."

"Your ankle?"

"And I've hurt my shoulder. I'm so sorry to impose on you, but Mimi, is there any way you can, well, I guess I'm really asking if you can drop everything you're doing and come over here and mother me. I don't know if I need to go to the ER and get an x-ray or if I just have a really bad sprain. I have no idea what's up with my shoulder." Jane could hear the whimper in her voice and knew that Mimi heard it too.

"We'll be right over. Chase is home for spring break this week. Until we get there, can you put ice on it? If it hurts too much to move, then you just sit tight until we arrive. We are starting the car now and we'll be there soon."

Jane looked across her living room to the kitchen. She wondered if she could crawl that far on one hand and two bloody knees or if it would be better to hop over on one leg—and what would happen if she fell? She wanted to avoid getting blood ground into the carpet. In the end she made it to the kitchen and then to her freezer by a combination of methods. By the time Mimi and Chase arrived she was sitting on the floor in the kitchen with little freezer blocks stacked around her ankle, one pinned between her shoulder and the wall behind her, a beer in her hands, and tears on her cheeks.

"Thank you for coming." Jane sniffed as she used the back of her hand to wipe away some of the wetness from her face. She was so embarrassed to be crying in front of them.

"Oh, my darling! Just look at you!" Mimi rushed over to her. "You must be in such pain!" Mimi glanced down at the red streaks on the carpet.

Jane wasn't about to admit that the tears weren't because of the pain in her body. Pain was pain, but it was nothing compared to that thought, that awareness, that whisper she had heard as she fell. That scared her. Eerie fingers reaching out to steal away all her happiness. It was something she wasn't ready to talk about, something she wasn't ready to even think about. It was easier to let Mimi and Chase assume she was crying from the pain of her physical injuries rather than some unexplainable psychic one.

"Chase, put that bag down and then you come over here and carry her. Move her to the couch. Watch out for her shoulder; which one is hurt, Jane?"

"Left." Jane said, gesturing with the beer bottle in her right hand.

Chase gently picked up the freezer blocks and maneuvered around to Jane's right side. "Wow, Janie, you're kind of a mess. Hold on to my neck." He took the beer bottle out of her hand. "Good choice, but I brought you something better." He gave her a wink and a comforting smile.

She did as he said and he very gently picked her up, carrying her as his mother instructed. He was careful when he set her down to make sure her left shoulder didn't brush against the back of the couch. He took a couple of cushions and rested her ankle on them, elevating her leg to help with the swelling. Mimi came over and started to inspect and wipe off the blood. "Oh my. Well, with two boys of my own... I've seen a lot of these. And these. And those."

"Just us?" Chase called out from across the room where he was sifting through the satchel he had brought with him. "Not Caroline?"

"Ha!" Mimi laughed. "Caroline was the ideal child. Never put a toe out of line, that one. I mostly worried about her because she seemed to have no mischievous streak at all. Honestly, I wondered how she could be my child!" Mimi clucked as she examined Jane's ankle, moving it ever so slightly. "But she's George's girl, through and through. Very careful, very detailed, very meticulous." She smiled at Jane. "So much like you, Janie. It never surprised me that you two became such good friends, even though you had a bit of an age difference between you."

"Yes, Caroline and I always got along well. She's like a sister to me." Jane gasped in pain with Mimi's touch.

"And as you get older age differences just don't matter. Good news, Jane! I don't think your ankle's broken. I think you do have a whopper of a sprain. I'm going to put a very loose ACE bandage on it, just for some support. I want you to ice it in cycles. Let it rest. Rest. Ice. Compression. Elevation. You'll need crutches."

"Ha!" Chase said as he came back to Jane's side. "You'll need this." He handed her a little shot glass of whiskey.

"Where...?" Jane asked, looking with confusion at the glass.

"Oh this? I brought this from home. It's honeyed whiskey. Believe me, you'll need this. Beer is way too wimpy for that ankle."

Mimi looked at him sternly. "Actually, I was going to say six-hundred milligrams of ibuprofen every six hours." Then she looked back at Jane. "But the whiskey won't hurt, and it probably will help you before I check out that shoulder. Honestly, Chase, you do beat all."

"Mother, I am twenty-one now and I do know where you keep the whiskey." He turned to Jane. "I'm kinda surprised there's any left after Sasutki visiting for Christmas."

"Chase!"

"You know it's true." Chase turned again to Jane. "Ages ago, when Dad crashed his bike and hurt his arm, Mom gave him a lot more whiskey than that! Probably because Dad was a way worse patient than you are, Janie!"

Jane laughed at the two of them and Chase went to get a warm, wet washcloth.

"Now, that's a good sign! I like to see a smile on that face." Mimi gave Jane a reassuring pat on her good shoulder. Chase returned and pulled up a chair to sit next to Jane. He started to gently dab at her face, wiping up her tears and smudged make-up. Then he cleaned up her bloody knees. Then he went and cleaned up the carpet.

In the end, Mimi's declaration that nothing was broken turned out to be right. Chase went out and got Jane crutches while Mimi continued to help Jane get cleaned up. The next day, Chase took Jane to her doctor's office, where they gave her an air cast for her ankle, put her shoulder and arm in a sling, and gave her something quite a bit stronger for the pain.

As Chase drove her back home, Jane sighed and said, "Chase you are just the sweetest. How come I never knew you were this sweet before?"

"You're welcome! And I've always been sweet. I just get overshadowed by Rory. He's got this insane ability to mount that white horse in about two seconds. By the time I realize anything's happening, he's already ridden in to save the day. And I just look like Mr. Clueless on the sidelines."

"Well, you look like a very handsome Mr. Clueless." She laughed. "And right now, you are my Prince Charming. Thanks so much. Hey, it's spring break. How come you aren't at the beach?"

"Sensitive topic," Chase said in a mutter.

"Oh, I'm sorry, Chase. I didn't mean to offend you."

Chase shook his head. "Nah, nah, it's all right. It's just I have to do a fifth year and Dad's pissed. So, I'm grounded from anything like spring break. He seems to think I'm not working hard enough. If I were, I'd be more like my older brother."

"Geez, Chase, I'm sorry. That must be heavy. I never had that with Summer. She was always so wild and unpredictable. Honestly, I think I was a breath of fresh air to my parents. You know, I'm not the

Donahue sister who could have grown up to speak to school groups as the superhero Bacteria Babe." They both laughed. "I mean, I appreciate that she teaches kids the importance of washing their grimy little hands and not picking their noses and all, but the whole costume-and-cape thing? Yeah, my parents breathed a sigh of relief when unexciting little me came along."

Chase glanced at her as he drove. "You know, it's nice being somebody's Prince Charming, and not just the pageboy in the shadows."

Jane was about to make a remark that he was quite obviously Charlie's idea of the knight on the white horse, but he caught her off guard when he said:

"And by the way, don't let Nick know you said that. I think he's counting on being your shining white knight."

"I hope so," Jane said, distracted, once again feeling haunted by that voice in her head and it's ominous message.

After they arrived back at her place, Chase helped her inside and got her settled. "Before I go, I'll get you a cold soda." He was back in a moment. "Jane, you have like three oranges in your fridge. Girl, you have no food. You're even out of milk."

"Oh yeah, I was going to go to the store yesterday afternoon, then Summer wanted to see that movie. And then I fell. I used the last of the milk at breakfast…" Her voice trailed off.

"You sit tight. I'm gonna run to the grocery store and get you set up. I'll pick up some dinner while I'm out. What are you in the mood for? Mexican? Chinese? There's this great place I love called Village Pizza—best calzones in the world."

"Wow, I haven't had a calzone in ages. That would be great. Is this what it's like having a brother? Chase, you're amazing. My sisters are always so involved in their own lives. I mean they're sweet, but I can't imagine them even thinking of checking the fridge."

"Jane, from what I've seen growing up, you're always the caretaker of everyone. You were the quiet voice of reason in the background countering every wild idea Summer offered. Good thing I paid attention, huh? You sit. I'll go and try to avoid buying exclusively college-boy food. No ramen, I promise. Just healthy, easy meals for you to microwave and stuff for the next few days until you're more mobile."

"Let me give you some money."

"Hell no, I'm charging this to Dad!"

Chapter 13

Jane woke up when she heard the front door open. Chase came in with several bags of groceries, set them down and then went back to the car to get more. She yawned. "I can't believe I fell asleep. How long were you gone?" She looked at her wrist, forgetting that she had left her watch on its charger—even her watch bothered her left side.

"A little under two hours. Sorry it took so long."

"No worries. Apparently, I sacked out while reading my book. Wow, Chase, when you spend your daddy's money, you really spend it!" Jane said, amazed as Chase started showing her what he'd purchased. He was a guy with a big wingspan and could wrap his arms around a lot of grocery bags.

"You know, I actually had a really good time. I remembered that you're a fresh fruit fanatic, so I got you lots. And easy dinners for you to make. And your favorite beer." He presented her with a six pack of a locally brewed red ale. "Goat cheese, dried cranberries—crap for salads, French bread, you know, 'girl food'… and this!" With a flourish he pulled out a bottle of Black Label Tennessee Honey Whiskey. "I can buy this now!" he said excitedly, relishing in the power of being twenty-one.

"Ooohhh, I thought that was great!" Jane smiled and got up, using her crutch to hobble over to the kitchen as he unpacked his finds.

"Yeah, Dad will be pissed at that, but he'll turn into a marshmallow when I tell him it was for you. He loves you," Chase said over his shoulder with just the tiniest hint of a sneer in his voice. "Speaking of people who love you, what did Nick say about his betrothed getting mega-lamed?"

"Who knows? He's in Spain," Jane winced. She still hadn't quite gotten the hang of the single crutch and she felt like an over-sized Tiny Tim. "On a trip for his dad. I left him a message. Just like always. But I didn't tell him what's going on. I didn't want him to get that in a voice mail or a text. You know, it's really going to play havoc with our plans. That's just not text-message fodder. We have a phone date set up for tomorrow. This cross-planet love affair is a pain! I am really looking forward to living in the same country."

"Which is where?"

"Eh? We've both been trying to find jobs, me a transfer to there and him getting anything here, but nothing's clicked yet. I can't imagine how he's going to get his dad to take back the reins, though." Jane shook her head.

"Well, you'll cross that bridge when you do. I'd better pull the calzones from the oven; I put them in to keep them warm first thing when I got here. Where will I find a hot mitt?"

Jane pointed to a drawer.

"Oh, yeah, and I got you a white—you like pinot grigio, right? I have no idea how to judge this stuff, so I got one with a monkey on the bottle."

"Yeah, how can a wine not be truly great if it has a monkey on the label? It's a sure sign!" Jane smiled at him, but she found herself wondering what was on Nick's father's private vanity label. Certainly not a monkey. Monkeys weren't British. Well, maybe they had been Colonial British? Then she thought Colin might be just the type of man to have a monkey on his fake private label.

"And it was twice what Mom would usually spend on a bottle of wine, so I figured if the monkey wasn't the tipoff then the price sure was. But I also bought you this one." He pulled out another bottle of wine, also with a monkey on the label. "This one was one-third the price of the other. I thought we could do a taste off." He laughed, making Jane laugh too.

Jane started to direct Chase where to put the groceries away. Then he pulled up the barstools to the kitchen island and pulled out four wine glasses, setting them up in a tasting flight. After he opened up the pair of monkey-emblazoned bottles, he brought out plates and silverware and served up their calzones, not letting her lift a finger to help. Since she had the use of just one arm, he even cut her calzone into convenient bite-sized pieces for her. As they ate, they talked about their childhoods and shared memories. Jane was amazed at how you could hang out with someone for years in a group and never really know them. Or maybe it was that "knowing them" took on a totally different meaning as you both grew up? Maybe as a person grew up, the child you knew was only tangentially relevant to the adult they became.

"Hey, Chase, let me ask you something." Her second glass of wine was making her feel braver than usual. "Have you ever had a perception that defied logic?"

He looked at her, eyebrow raised.

"Okay, I mean, have you ever known something to be true, had all the facts in front of you, but then for some reason felt it should be different? You know," she searched for the word, "intuition?"

"Oh, you mean what does your gut say? Yeah, I know exactly what you mean. I always go with my gut."

"Always?"

"Yeah, sure. I mean, why wouldn't you?"

"Well, what if you had a crazy intuition? A crazy gut feeling?"

"Crazy? Yeah, you go with your gut."

He said it so confidently.

"Really? What if your gut told you something that completely made no logical sense? Something you just couldn't explain to other people? They would think you were crazy or that you believed in, I don't know, magic or the supernatural or something weird like that?"

"I'm not following you. Like what?" he said, his voice rather flat.

"Well, say like your gut told you to...um...," she searched for something that would be really out there for Chase, "to quit school and head out to New York or California and become a... a model." Jane saw the scowl on his face. "Or an actor?" she added quickly, and then saw from his face that that option wasn't any better. "What if your gut told you to do that? What would you do?"

"My gut would never tell me to do something like that." He took a sip of his wine. "Never."

"Uh, Chase?" She was surprised at the vehemence in his voice.

"I would never, ever do something like that. Jane, let me ask you: would it surprise you to learn that I'm at the top of my classes? I am going to pass that CPA exam, all four parts, on the first go."

Jane was caught off guard by the intensity in his voice and wasn't sure what to say, not helped by her two glasses of wine on top of her painkillers. "Chase, I know you're more than just a pretty face."

"Yeah! Thank you! It's weird to talk about it, but Jane, girls are just freaks. I'll be at a bar, maybe out to eat and if I haven't turned Air Drop off on my phone, you wouldn't believe the pics that pop up. Of them. Or, more technically speaking, of parts of them. Like they think that crap would be enticing?" He shook his head, clear disgust on his face. "No self-respect at all. Shit, makes me feel like I'm part of the wrong generation, like some Southern gentleman from a past century. I rarely meet anyone I could, how should I say, bring home to my mother? I mean, what if they accidentally Air-Dropped some of their hot shots to her? I'm pretty sure Mom doesn't know how to turn those options on or off. That's too techie for her."

Jane looked at him with wide eyes. "You're kidding." In truth, she didn't understand just what these young women were dropping to him that showed up on his phone, but she was too embarrassed to ask.

"C'mon. You're a pretty girl. Surely you had guys who were only interested in you for your looks?"

Jane nodded, mostly because she felt she should, but she wasn't sure she'd ever had any guys interested in her just for her looks. She might be okay looking, maybe pretty on a good day, or with Claudine's magical assistance, but she could admit that on her own she was far from beautiful.

He didn't seem to notice her consternation, and continued, "It's just so fake. I understand how women get annoyed at men hitting on them. I get it because there's more to me than just my face."

Jane smiled and thought, *And your body. And your smile. There's the hair. Yeah, and the deep voice doesn't hurt.* But she said, "Yeah, I know what you mean."

He looked at her intently. "I knew you would understand. It's the drool that's really the turn off, isn't it?"

"Yeah." She laughed. "The drool, so gross." She agreed even though she wasn't exactly sure what he meant, never having seen "the drool" herself. While she'd had her short fling with attention from the opposite sex during her self-marketing experiment, Nick had really fallen for her over time. It was their conversation and ability to deeply connect, how she intensely listened to him, how he could tell her anything. He trusted her and she never judged or berated him. He called her his "angel incarnate". He said he needed her. She made him a better person. So often ignored or shipped off as a child, Nick felt seen and heard by Jane, safe to be who he was. He didn't have anything to prove with her. It was a novel sensation to him. But it was novel for Jane, too. Quite the wallflower all her life, over-shadowed by her two more extroverted and energetic sisters, she had never known anyone who felt that need to be seen quite so acutely. But she saw him. She heard him. She felt him. She loved him. They were two sides to the same coin.

And now here was Chase, someone else who wanted to be seen, not for the obvious, but for the hidden. His obvious obscured his rather interesting depth and kindness. Chase's experience was foreign to her. She'd never had a man follow her like a puppy dog. Apparently, Chase was swarmed by puppies. She reflected that while most women—and probably a majority of plain-looking men—would give a lot to be so sought after, for Chase, at least, it seemed to have some serious drawbacks.

"So why the question?"

"What question?"

"The intuition question."

"Oh, nothing. Just something in that book I was reading." Jane thought fast for an excuse, now that she'd lost her courage to delve into the topic. "Something about a character… yeah, in a book. It was nothing. Fictitious. And a little bit dysfunctional." She thought of Claudine.

Chase stayed late and before leaving got everything "sorted out", as Nick would have put it, had he been there for Jane rather than four thousand miles away. Chase examined all the food he'd purchased and anything that took two hands to prepare—washing and cutting the lettuce, opening the package of goat cheese, preparing a huge salad—he took care of. He made sure everything was set up so that Jane could do what was needed with her one good arm. She felt so cared for. She felt so loved. And yet somehow, it made her feel sad and lonely. She hobbled off to bed like Tiny Tim on her singular crutch.

Chapter 14

At ten o'clock in the morning, Jane logged in to meet Nick virtually. She had moved most of her meetings to the virtual world since going into the office was still too painful and she didn't feel confident about driving yet with her right ankle still so swollen. Taking Tylenol with codeine for the pain also prohibited her from getting behind a wheel.

She made sure she looked extra nice this morning. She wanted to wear a clingy, sleek shirt, something a bit sexy for Nick, but the arm sling ruined the whole effect. The cold snap was still exerting a tight hold on Charlotte, so Jane ended up pulling a cardigan-type sweater over her shoulders anyway, conjuring a look that was far from sexy. She thought "crippled granny" was a more apt fit.

Her computer beeped and there he was. It was late afternoon for him, but he looked tired. Even through the internet and with all those Astrid-set up filters to make him look "peng", which he explained meant "dishy", he still looked tired. He sounded tired. He talked about work in great depth and didn't seem to notice her sweater or what it was hiding.

"The trip to Spain was smashing. We can make a blend there and import it at a good value. Old Colin is just so damn blinkered, he can't see it. It's French or nothing for him, but the business has got to expand. He's left it stagnant for so long. Thank God I have the chance to save it all. He's hired this, well, um, a manager, who's a wizard, just totally brill. Anyway, that's how I know about the Spanish deal. It's bloody good value but he can't see it. And I think we should offer personal wine labels for our best customers. We can play off their vanity and do it at a huge mark-up, at virtually no cost to us! I mean, why not be inspired by how my own father's been played all these years? He's certainly spent a fortune on his personal label."

Jane couldn't help but be distracted by his comments about vanity. In February, he had started to get Botox injections to prevent aging—again, a thing popular with his social crowd and some of his coworkers were joining in, like it was the equivalent of meeting for cocktails or watching a football game together at a bar. *If they are so concerned about aging, maybe they should all quit smoking?* she thought, but held back that opinion after he mildly suggested she should check it out as well. Why anyone in their twenties would need to be concerned about anything other than adequate use of sunscreen, Jane couldn't imagine. And as for video filters, the only one she really knew how to use was for video-chats with Caroline and Ty when they would all become cats during those precious minutes when Ty would join the call. Apparently, turning into a cat was a great motivator for the little guy to engage in a conversation with otherwise boring adults.

Nick went on with details about the sixty-hour work weeks, the endless travel and meetings for ten more minutes while Jane listened patiently, if somewhat uninterestedly, to his frustrations about the wine importing business. He didn't seem to remember that he was searching for a job in the US or that he even had a passion for green building and design.

"But at least we're off on our trip soon. Gods, but I could bite your arm off for a vacation! And, my dove, we'll be heading off to the French countryside in just a few days now! I can't wait to see you!"

"I miss you too. Like crazy." She paused. "I have some bad news." She reached for her crutch and pulled it into view of the camera eye. "I have this brand-new wardrobe accessory."

"Blimey, Jane! Why are you holding… is that a crutch?" Nick asked in slow amazement.

"It's not just that. I also have this." And she slid the sweater off her shoulder to reveal her sling.

"What is that?" Apparently, it was difficult to tell through her no-filter-enhanced video connection.

"My shoulder is in a sling. I fell on the ice on Sunday. I blew out my ankle and shoulder, but the good news is that at least nothing is broken."

"Broken?"

"Honey, there is no way I can hike. I can't manage a suitcase. I can't sit for that long on a plane. It's some type of a blood clot risk. Oh, Nick!" She burst into tears. "I can't make the trip! I can't come and meet you in France. I can hardly get from room to room in my own home!"

Nick just stared at the screen, blinking a couple of times. "Jane! Well, bugger me!" And then he slumped back in his chair and just stared, opening and closing his mouth a few times, unable to speak.

"Oh, honey, I'm so sorry. I'm just devastated. I can't believe it." She was wiping tears from her cheeks.

"It's dreadful. Ice in North Carolina? Who would've thought? Hard lines, that's for certain," Nick said. "The honeymoon… is in a bloody shambles. Oh, Janie, don't cry, my dove. Well, we'll cancel and when you're better we'll go again."

"We can't cancel. It's non-refundable. It's use it or lose it."

Again, Nick just stared, once more opening and closing his mouth a few times, unable to form coherent thoughts. Finally, he said, almost in a whisper, "Bollocks. It's like someone doesn't want us to get married."

"While that would be your parents, I'm quite confident that they had nothing to do with that particular patch of ice." They both laughed at the absurdity of the thought. Then Jane got a sudden inspiration. "Nick, you should go."

"What?"

"Yes, you should go to the cabin and enjoy it. Rest up. You've been working so hard. You need a break. Go and get a break from work. Enjoy it. Otherwise, it'll just go to waste."

"Go? On our honeymoon? Alone? Without you? And, what did you say? Enjoy it? You are barmy! Did you hit your head too, perchance?"

"Yes. I mean, no. I didn't hit my head, at least I don't think so, but you should go. Send me pictures! Enjoy it for the both of us. I would say take your mum and dad for a vacation, but I think you really need a break from them. I've got it all planned out. You should make use of it. Let me know how it is. We'll go someplace else for our honeymoon. Someplace we can both experience together. Once I'm healed."

"Oh, Jane! Without you?" But his voice sounded uncertain. "You've undoubtedly got the gen on what to do, where to go, what to eat. Oh Jane, what will I do there without you? I'll be so lonely."

"Hopefully rest. I hate to say this—and in my condition this is a bit of the pot calling the kettle black, but Nicky, you really look awful—I mean in a way that Botox just can't address. You look tired. You sound tired. I think you should go and just recover. Take a bunch of books with you. Relax. You've already got coverage at work, so you should go, at least for a week. Sleep. Rest. Miss me."

"Jane, I'm gobsmacked. You are an angel incarnate that no living man deserves!"

"Well, it's either you go and enjoy it or we waste all our money. I'll heal up here. You rest up there. And we'll start over with another plan. It's not like we aren't experts at starting over by now." She couldn't help laughing through the tears on her cheeks.

"We will always find our way back to one another. No matter what ice or oceans try to keep us apart. We are, the two of us, absolutely perfect together."

"Two halves of the same whole."

He sat up and looked more resolute. "When do you think you'll be better? By June? Want to get married in June? My angel, I'll come to you this time. We'll run away and get married in America. Yes! I'll come to you. No risking you on long flights."

"Oh, will you, Nicky? Really? Oh, that would be terrific!" Jane felt an immense sense of relief. Planning something at home didn't sound nearly as daunting as starting over in another country. The more she thought about it, planning something here at home sounded just right.

In the end, Nick took a ten-day vacation in their cabin in the French Pyrenees. He sent her pictures of him everywhere—hiking in the mountains, dining at quaint little restaurants, even a couple in cute little shops. At first these were obviously selfies with his long arm holding his phone, but eventually it looked like he was able to get some locals to snap some shots of him as well. He told her about a few presents he shipped to her and he texted her quite frequently, particularly at first. The only problem was that the cabin had no wi-fi and they found the reported cellular service was, in reality, non-existent. He had to hike into town to send her messages and pictures, which he did eagerly in the first four days but then those trailed off to a tiny stream.

"At least he's really resting. If he can't contact me he can't be working either," she reassured herself. She kept busy by re-planning their wedding, this time right at home in Charlotte.

Chapter 15

Jane taped up the pictures of Nick on their honeymoon—by himself—all around her desk at home. At first, she thought it was hilarious and she liked seeing the pictures of him. But with the passing of each day that she didn't hear from Nick, the images became a downer. By the end of the month, when he was long back at and consumed by work, all the pictures were tucked safely in a box of old photos up on a shelf in the closet.

With her dual injuries, she found that she needed to work from home for weeks and surprisingly discovered that she got twice as much done without all the distractions of the office, so she kept telecommuting. She pitched a new marketing concept—a plan her boss thought quite ingenious. Her inspiration came from hobbling around on her Aircast and crutch, playing on the idea of inferior flight craft crippling an entire airline.

> She texted Claudine:
> In the end, I was awarded a promotion for the success of the campaign I designed while under the influence of Tylenol with codeine! I mean, go figure. Who would've thought?

Claudine texted her back:

> And to think, we spent all that time choosing to study instead of relying on drug-induced hallucinations! 😊 😊 While I am glad for your promotion (*toutes nos félicitations*), please do not become addicted to the medicines... 😁 😁 just to your success, mon ami! ♡ ♡ ♡

Jane found it funny that Claudine loved emoji's, since at first glance she really didn't seem like the type. Then she thought, *but we are millennial women, and we practically invented emojis. Of course she does.*

There was the wedding to plan—and this time Claudine could provide no helpful insider knowledge or advice whatsoever. Unfortunately, Jane's mother wasn't as much help as Jane would have liked, as Audree was completely distracted by the impending birth of, and then the taking care of, her granddaughter. Weddings were nice, but clearly the grand prize was the grandchild. Summer and Hector's daughter came along in mid-April, right on schedule. Much to everyone's relief, the delivery was uneventful and the only real drama in the offing was Summer's decision to name her daughter Echo. And Grace, as a middle name in homage to Hector's mother, who would never see this little girl, but where "Echo" came from, Jane could not imagine. She hoped the little girl was born supremely talented since, as Echo Grace, she already had the name of a movie star or perhaps a famous gospel singer.

Mimi happily stepped into the mothering gap vacated by Audree and lent her artistic talents to Jane's wedding plans. She made everything easy for Jane, always presenting her with multiple choices, all of them perfection in themselves. Jane found it surprisingly challenging to choose between the two or three compelling options Mimi lay before her. Cake—Jane opted for a beautiful basket weave topped with giant rolled chocolate pieces in dark, rose, and white chocolate. Flowers—Mimi showed her the most gorgeous arrangements of hydrangeas which Jane fell in love with. The frail flowers wouldn't last for days like roses, but they would hold up beautifully for the ceremony and reception. Nick agreed with everything. In fact, he was so agreeable as to seem barely interested.

"Whatever you want, darling. It's your wedding, your special day!" he would say.

Jane just kept assuring Mimi, "Oh yes, Nick loves all the plans!" as she shushed those inner voices that were whispering annoying sentiments like *your strength seems to be in overlooking problems.*

April and May flew by, leading to that oft-rescheduled wedding day, which loomed on the calendar on the third of June. Scheduling on short notice at a traditional kind of venue simply wasn't going to work for anyplace that was deemed suitable. The guest list was small, family and very close friends only. After exploring many futile options, Jane accepted Mimi's offer to have her wedding on the grounds at the Watkins' place. While her own parent's house couldn't accommodate that kind of event, the Watkins huge old house and surrounding yards and gardens could easily manage a group of up to even moderate size. And Mimi seemed so eager to host.

"Venue secured!" Jane puffed out a breath. "Now we just need an officiant." She was surprised that ministers, a justice of the peace, and judges seemed to be in even shorter supply than venues on short notice.

"How about Pastor Jefferies? You could always ask him to officiate?" her mother suggested as Jane recounted the details of her search.

Jane shuddered. "You mean that fire-and-brimstone dude who livened up Hector and Summer's impromptu ceremony? Uh, no thanks. This is not a one-day notice needing any breathing officiant with a pulse and a shotgun. I want something normal."

Audree gave Jane one of those mothering looks. "He did not have a shotgun! Well, not one he took out of his truck anyway. He's a nice man and he'd be willing to do it. I'm not sure where you're going to find a traveling Justice of the Peace. They don't exactly show up at your door like those folks who always want to come and clean your gutters."

Jane might be stumped, but she was not yet desperate enough to reach out to Pastor Jefferies, shotgun or no. The shortage of qualified officiants was merely a temporary setback. She texted Summer, who, while quick to respond, was less helpful than Jane had hoped.

> I thought Pastor Jefferies was entertaining! And better yet, Hector thought the whole thing felt just like home ☺

"Yeah, Summer, I bet you found the whole thing downright hilarious," Jane said aloud as she read her sister's text. She thumbed in:

> I know this is going to sound strange, but most brides, this one included, aren't looking for any kind of drama. 😬 😬 I just want a nice, calm, 'no shouting' kind of ceremony. Memorable... but not family-legend memorable, if you know what I mean.

It didn't take long for her phone to give a cheery ping!

> Most brides take their weddings entirely too seriously. It's about the guy, the life together—and that doesn't require an aisle, dress, flowers or ceremony. You have all you need because you both show up for each other, every day. ♡ ♡

Jane had to chew on that one for a while. Before she could compose an answer, her phone pinged again.

> You could always pop down to city hall the day before and do the deed. Just hire an actor as your minister for the big show. That way, you'll get what you want. Mom'll be happy. And your pictures will be perfect. 👍

Jane put down her phone. "Performance wedding" wasn't the feel she was going for. And the whole idea of some America's Got Talent wanna-be conducting her wedding made her shudder. It felt so impersonal.

* * *

In mid-May, as the days were counting down, Jane's cell phone rang, and much to her surprise it was Hector's face that showed up on the screen of her iPhone.

"Hey, Heck, everything all right? How's little Echo?" Jane was still trying to get used to the name. "How's Summer?"

"Everything is blessed! The baby's nursing great. Summer's enjoying being absolutely waited upon by her mother and she's healing very well. No one's sleeping but no one cares—we all just want to look at Echo Grace. She's an absolute miracle." Hector gushed on about his daughter for several more minutes. The way she breathed so peacefully. How she slept so deeply. How she nursed so hungrily, and then how her eyes would roll back and she would simply pass out, sated and happy, drunk on mother's milk. Jane had seen the baby a couple of times, but her shoulder was still quite weak and despite her dedication to physical therapy and yoga, might need surgery given that she'd torn a rotator cuff. She wasn't in a position to be of much help to the new parents. Besides, her own cup of joy was running over. Running over and spilling on the floor with a mess she didn't quite know how to clean up, if she were being honest.

"Yeah, thanks for the last pictures you sent. She's a darling little peanut. I love how she has Summer's bright red hair! So, uh, what's up? Is there anything I can do for you?"

"Actually, I'm calling to offer to do something for you."

"Really? Well, thanks. I'm moving around pretty well now..."

"Oh, not that. I have news! I have recently, as of this afternoon, become a Reverend in the Church of the Moon."

Jane stared at the wall. She had no idea how to respond to this piece of information. Years ago, Hector had left his restrictive Amish community, but to Jane he seemed to be fitting in with regular America. He seemed to be pretty normal in fact. Not like he was missing his old home, or anything. Still a man of faith, sure. Jane wondered how her sister was doing with a new baby and a husband suddenly joining a new and different kind of cult. "Oh. Wow. Gee, Heck, um, that's... that's... gee, honestly, I'm just not sure what to say."

Hector burst out laughing. "I did it for you, Jane!"

Again, she found herself at a loss for words.

"It was all Summer's idea!" he said excitedly.

At least that made sense in the way that nothing Summer did ever made sense.

"I got a mail order instatement into the church. It's in California, of course, but as a reverend in the church I can perform marriage ceremonies in California."

"Are you moving to California?"

"For you, Jane."

"We're getting married at Mimi's. Like you guys did. In Carolina. Not in California."

"Yes, but luckily North Carolina has reciprocity with the other states. Because I'm recognized, as of this afternoon, as a minister in Southern California, I'm also a minister right here in Charlotte! I can officiate at your wedding."

"You can?"

"Now, Summer told me that you probably had your heart set on Pastor Jefferies, but in a pinch, in case you can't find anyone else, or maybe don't actually want a shotgun brought to your wedding or have hell mentioned frequently, or perhaps even not at all as you say your vows, well then, I would be more than happy to do the ceremony for you and Nick. And if I'm not what you want, no problem. It only cost fifty dollars and now I'm going to do the baptism for my own daughter, so we're good all 'round!"

He certainly sounded happy in an over-the-moon kind of a way. Jane wondered if that was how the church got its name, and she started getting ideas for the next Airbus advertising angle to their major buyers that she would pitch to her boss. She reached for her pen and notepad. She could feel a huge smile break across her face. "Wow, Hector, I think that would be awesome! Let me check in with Nick about it, but it sounds like a great idea! I can't believe you're so busy with a new baby and you and Summer would even have the energy to think of us. Thank you!"

"Well, there is the happy convergence of many wonderful events. It's a great spring. Just let me know what you and Nick feel comfortable with. No pressure, really. If you want me, I'll get ready."

Predictably, Nick agreed with the plan, almost too willingly. She asked him, "So what did your parents say when you told them we were definitely getting married in Charlotte? They've never come to the U.S. It's a gorgeous time of year here. I'm sure they'll love it and maybe they can see some of the country while they're stateside."

"Oh Cressida? She hung up on me."

"She what?"

"Hung up on me. Says they won't come. Says Dad's too ill to travel. Actually, he seems fine, but he's timid as a hare, afraid to try anything or exert himself in any way. His cardiac procedure was a success and his doctors keep telling him to get back to a normal life. At least he's working half days, well, some days that is. He turfs most of the business decisions to me, still. It's like he's lost interest in it. I tell him about the new product lines and the partnerships I've developed, and he says, 'Oh, that's fabulous', but it's like he's not even listening. I told him about one total disaster of a plan, and he gave the same answer. Any time he gets a sniffle or feels a moment of dizziness he's back in the A&E department in a flash."

"The emergency room? Oh, poor Colin! He's just scared to death."

"Yes, I tell you it's a bit like I've become the parent with him. Mum's not handling it well at all. She says there's no way they're leaving the country, even though the doctors have all blessed the idea. They say it would actually be good for him! But they won't come. So, it's you and me."

"Oh Nick. I'm so sorry. How are you with this? I mean really?" Jane was afraid he would say they had to cancel everything and move the plans back to England. She didn't know if she could face it again. The invitations were long since sent and the RSVPs were all in.

"I say what she told me the whole time I was growing up: rubbish and codswallop! If they don't want to come, they don't have to. We're marching forward, come hell or high water, so I'm just 'aces', to quote a phrase," he said stubbornly. "And I find I am rather wanting to get out of England at the moment."

"Well, it's going to be a small affair, family and close friends only. You'll know nearly everyone there, but I'm so sorry your folks won't be with us to celebrate. Have you asked Greigh or Trevor to stand up with you? Who will be your best man, now that we're having a real ceremony and not the equivalent of a Justice of the Peace in France?"

"Actually, since we're having a U.S. Southern home style-wedding, I thought I'd ask Rory. Would you mind terribly? I know he's like a brother to you. I'm not sure about dragging my British contingent across the pond. Do you think he would say yes?"

Jane sat in stunned silence. Rory as best man? She might have chosen him were she the groom, but it seemed an odd choice for Nick. They were almost the same age, she reasoned. They'd talked easily the few times they'd been together. And Nick was right, Rory was like a brother to her. She did find it more than curious that none of his friends would be coming to the ceremony. But then again, Claudine was struggling to make it as well. She had started her marketing career in fashion, which paid quite poorly at the entry level. It was just thousands to make the trip and the average young person fresh out of school didn't have that kind of disposable income.

"So, you don't like the idea of Rory?" Nick asked in response to her silence.

"No... no, it's fine. It's great. Um, let me text you his number and his email. You'll need to speak with him yourself, of course. Summer can't be my Matron of Honor since the baby will be less than two months old. She's got too much going on as it is. I guess I'll ask Charlie. Caroline is trying hard to get plane tickets back for her and Ty. Turns out it's somewhat complicated, but she's doing everything she can to be here. Not sure about Sasutki yet. So, Rory and Charlie will stand up with us. Okay." While Jane felt sad that it wouldn't be Summer, Caroline, and Charlie all serving as her bridesmaids, she had the wry thought that Charlie would be bummed to be standing up with Rory rather than Chase. Jane and Rory were close in age, but she felt a new closeness with Chase and was a bit sorry that it wasn't Chase who would be their best man. *Chase really does exist under Rory's shadow. Well, for everyone except Charlie,* she mused.

"Sounds wonderful," Nick said agreeably. "Just totally brill. And what are you thinking about for the honeymoon?"

"I've found a great resort in Cabo San Lucas, at the tip of the Baja peninsula of Mexico. It's not that long of a flight, at least not compared to your trip here, and just one change of planes. I have tickets on hold for us, which I have to buy by ten o'clock tonight in order to get at an unbelievable price. And then, I'm getting us in first class by upgrading with my ten zillion frequent flier miles."

"Sounds totally brill. What's Cabo-San-what-did-you-call-it? You know that neither of us speaks Spanish, right?"

"It'll be fine. One of my four languages is English, which is pretty universal. Cabo's a resort town. It's small. The hotel looks beautiful. It's on the cliffs overlooking the Pacific Ocean. Beautiful sandy beach down below. Tons of sun. You can sit under private palapas where they serve you fun drinks with little paper umbrellas in them. Perfect honeymoon spot. Looks like it's not at all crowded."

"Sounds wonderful. Sounds perfect. You're an angel incarnate."

"Yes, and just the opposite of that cold, lonely cabin in France. I was trying to find something very, very different! Sun, rum, ocean. I'm so looking forward to getting away, although I probably won't be up for much hiking yet."

"And no more ice!"

"Not unless it's in a margarita glass."

"No more accidents!"

"I promise. I'm being ultra-careful. But you'll probably have to carry my bags, with my shoulder still not back to one hundred percent."

"Oh yes! For sure! I'll do all the heavy lifting. Nothing but good from here on out, I promise! I'll be yours to command."

"Nothing but smooth sailing from here on out," Jane said agreeably. "And you don't have to worry about anything. In fact, the plans for the ceremony are all coming together. Mimi's been amazing; really shouldered the lion's share of it all. This will be so easy for us compared to the other half dozen attempts we've made at getting married." Jane tried to laugh, to be light and bright in the moment, to be easy be with, but she felt a sense of heaviness. Must be the pain in my shoulder, she thought as she rubbed it absentmindedly. After all, there isn't much left that can go wrong.

Chapter 16

Four days before the wedding Nick arrived in Charlotte. He was loaded down with masses of luggage. Wedding clothes. Honeymoon clothes. Gifts for everyone. British tea and teapots for Audree, Mimi, and Summer. A pretty pendant of ruby-like stones set in gold filigree that was a replica of some ancient crown jewels for his new mother-in-law—a present particularly to Audree's liking. A pearl and gold necklace for Charlie. Cufflinks for John, Hector, Chase, and Rory, all from the same collection. Bottles of his new liquor with his own vanity label.

"Everyone loves the gifts you brought."

"Well, my dove, I have something extra special for you." He handed Jane a plain, brown paper-wrapped rectangular box.

"Extra special? I like the sound of that!" Jane giggled as she unwrapped her gift but quickly found herself speechless. She stared at a blue sapphire and diamond necklace and earrings. "Oh, Nick, they're beautiful!"

"Now these are the real thing." He whispered in her ear as he attached the necklace around her neck, "but please just let the others enjoy thinking their stones are genuine."

"So gorgeous!" Jane stared at her reflection in the mirror, her finger running along her collarbone where the jewelry sat. "Genuine stones? Oh my, thank you. Not a, well, a family heirloom, is it?"

He smiled. "It our family heirloom. Yours and mine alone."

She smiled and made a mental note to have the set appraised so she could have it insured. He must have spent a fortune on it. She had never owned anything like this.

"Well, your present simply cannot be outdone—you're giving me the wedding and the honeymoon! It will be a wonderful trip."

Jane was so pleased she didn't bother to ask why all his clothes smelled of cigarette smoke. She just unpacked everything and washed it all again. Two days before the wedding, John, Rory, and Chase took Nick to get their tuxedos. It was a particularly long visit for Nick since he hadn't been pre-measured, and the tailoring had to be done while they waited.

"Well, fellas, much as I would like to stay with you, I've got patients in the office." John looked at his watch for the fourth time.

Rory nodded. "Sure, Dr. D. We've got everything covered here. We'll get Nick back to the house when we're done."

"Thanks boys!" Turning to Nick he said, "See you at dinner!"

Nick gave his soon-to-be father-in-law a casual wave and watched him drive away. As soon as John was out of sight, Nick turned to Rory and Chase. "Mind if I nip out for a smoke?"

"What? You smoke?" Chase asked, surprised.

"Don't tell Jane. Just a tad. I was with Mum and Dad so much I picked it up."

"Wait, your dad has a heart condition and he smokes?" Rory was clearly trying to control the expression on his face, having failed to control the judgment ringing in his voice.

"It's not a blockage, so it probably wouldn't matter." Nick shrugged. "But no, he mostly gave it up this winter. Mum'll never be able to break with it though. Now that I'm running the business, I understand why they smoke—gods, it's a stress reliever. Really helps you think. Amazing after sex. And it's the way you get business done in France, Spain, and Italy. All deals are brokered over fags." Nick winked and then ducked out the door to have a "fag" on the sidewalk.

Chase looked at Rory, shock and confusion evident on his face.

"Cigarettes, I believe he means," Rory said in an aside, not commenting on the other statements but looking distinctly uncomfortable.

"Well, that's better, I guess." Chase said without conviction and stared at Nick outside. "But Jane won't be happy."

"It's not like he can really hide it from her. I don't know what he's thinking." Rory studied Nick through the window.

"His new job must be something else. Look at him pacing out there. Who's he talking to on the phone?" Chase looked at Rory.

Rory shrugged. "Beats me. I think I liked him better when he was an architect."

"Yeah, it's quite the transition from environmental-maniac to sidewalk-smoker. Hey, he's lighting up another one."

"Yeah. From the butt of his first."

"Uh, excuse me," A petit Asian gentleman interrupted them.

"Yes, Mr. Lee." Rory stood up.

"Did Dr. Donahue return to office?"

"Yes, sir."

"Your father, good dentist. I've seen him since I came to America. Nice to have you in my shop. I need foreign man for next step in fitting. No smoking in store." Mr. Lee wagged his finger at the boys as though they had been on the sidewalk puffing away with Nick.

Chase started to explain that Dr. Donahue wasn't their father and that none of them smoked, but Rory shook his head indicating it wasn't worth it. They'd already had their challenges with understanding one another. "No need to make things more complicated." He turned to Mr. Lee. "I'll get him." He went to the door, opened it, and signaled to Nick that he was needed. Nick nodded, ended his call abruptly, threw his cigarette down and crushed it out with the toe of his shoe. As he came inside, Rory watched him as he walked past, and then went outside, picked up the two crushed butts off the sidewalk and threw them in the cigarette disposal tube, standing right next to the trash can, only fifteen feet away. "Europeans," he muttered and went back into the shop, heading for the bathroom to wash his hands.

After the fitting was finally complete, the three boys decided to grab lunch at a hole-in-the wall carry-in place called The Loop. After placing their orders, they went to find a table until their buzzer came alive with its blinking and buzzing dance, indicating that their meals were ready for pick up. As they walked by tables filled with young women, a lull in conversation quieted the dining area, blanketing the room with an unexpected silence. Older diners looked around, confused by the sudden lack of noise. Then the background buzz started up again, as conversation resumed.

One young attractive blonde who had tried to chat them up in line walked by with her tray and stopped at their table. Even the aroma of the food failed to compete with her perfume. "Y'all can come and join us if you like." Her southern lilt made the words melt off her tongue like sweat on a hot day. She inclined her head towards a table of three other women, all equally coiffed and adorned with heavy makeup. They giggled and smiled at the three men.

"Thanks, nice offer, but we're working on some wedding plans here, so we really need to… to… ah… focus," Chase said.

"All right. If y'all change your minds, we'll be right over here." She smiled coyly. She said the word "here" like it had two syllables.

"Missed opportunity," Nick said with a wry smile. "I'm a nearly married man." He looked wistfully at the table of women who were looking right back at him. "Not quite though. But you mates have no excuse at all."

"I live here, Nick. I've fallen for that trap before. There's a lot of drool you have to clean up after hanging out with those types." Chase answered in a tight voice, not looking at the women.

"Drool?" Rory asked.

"Yes, I know," Nick said with a sigh. "I rather like the drool." He fumbled with the settings on his phone. "Always wickedly fun when they air drop you pictures, isn't it?" He still had that wistful tone in his voice. "Oh well. While we're out, I have a favor to ask: I need to go by a jewelers."

"You didn't bring enough bling with you from England?" Rory laughed.

"Oh, I brought it for everyone but me. I forgot my bloody wedding ring! I can't very well marry your sister, well, she's not your sister, but you know what I mean, without the ring. And I don't want her to know that I forgot it. So, I have to find something as similar as I can and hope she won't notice."

Rory and Chase exchanged a quick glance. "Sure," Chase said. "We can help you with that, uh, problem."

"Nick," Rory said, "not that this will matter to you, but our father will be at the wedding."

"I've never met your father. That will be lovely." Nick smiled. Then his smile faded. "Oh, do I stand corrected, that won't be lovely?"

"It'll be all right," Chase said flatly.

"Dad and Mom divorced when we were kids. Things are pretty calm between them now. He was great friends with Jane's parents," Rory said.

"Still is," Chase added. "And he adores Jane like his own daughter."

Rory nodded. "Yeah, okay. He just doesn't come around much for family events. Rarely at the house. You'll meet him at the wedding. I know he wouldn't want to miss Janie's wedding. He's flying in today."

"Staying at the house?" Nick asked, taking a bite of his sandwich.

"Oh no!" Chase answered emphatically. "Hotel. Never the house."

"You'll just meet him at the wedding. Probably never see him again after that," Rory said.

They ate lunch as the talk turned to bike racing and music, but Nick was greatly distracted by the table of giggling girls who continued to steal glances at them, wink, and wave. Rory was somewhat distracted but being in a band made him a little more used to people giving him attention based on their own agendas. Chase resolutely ignored them.

"Those birds not dishy enough for you, Chase?" Nick teased as they finished lunch and piled the trash on their trays. "You must have exceedingly high standards, mate!"

"Plenty dishy. But dime a dozen. And if you talk to them, they won't have anything to say. They'll just make noise and it will be about nothing. Or all about them."

"There's options beyond talking, mate!" Nick winked.

"Uh, we need to get going," Rory answered, his voice quite flat.

It turned out that Nick had neglected to bring a very special band, created to reflect the design of his great-grandmother's ring, now Jane's engagement ring. As the wedding was happening in two days, he had to purchase a ring that got, hopefully, close enough to that design and in addition fit him. They found their best match at the third store they went into. Nick thought it was hilarious, just "the dog's bollocks" that the clerk at the second jewelry store thought Nick and Chase were the couple and buying rings for their ceremony.

When the clerk stepped away, Nick turned to Chase. "Well, Chase, I have to say that you seem most out of sorts! I have loads of friends with alternative lifestyles and lovers and each of them are great fun, head-to-toe. You don't need to be biased, mate! It's all right. Doesn't diminish your masculinity one bit." Nick put his arm around Chase's shoulder.

Chase stiffened and blinked as Nick's breath hit him in the face. "Not that, Nick. Not that. Sorry, man, but I would never marry a smoker. Not sure that Jane will, either."

Nick withdrew his arm and looked concerned. "Oh, that could be a problem."

They swung back by Mr. Lee's store to pick up their now-finished tuxedos.

"Final check. Make sure all perfect. Please try on." Mr. Lee nodded and smiled at them. As the three men passed his inspection, he asked them to stand against a green photo screen and he snapped several pictures with a special camera—individual shots, shots together, even close ups. "You, very handsome men," he said in his heavily accented English as he scanned through the shots. "You make good picture. May I use?"

"Use for what?" Rory asked.

"Show my customers! How good they look in suit tailored by me." He pointed to himself and nodded enthusiastically. "Help my business grow."

The three men looked at each other. "Yeah, sure." Rory nodded.

"I'm game!" Nick said cheerfully.

Chase shrugged. "Whatever."

When they finally left the enthusiastic Mr. Lee, they took Nick back over to Jane's condo. "I'll pick you up at ten A.M. tomorrow," Rory told him. "You're spending the night before the wedding at our house. We'll do the rehearsal early tomorrow afternoon. I think Jane will be at her parent's place tomorrow night, but in case the girls need someplace to go, they don't want any guys over at bridal central. Besides, Mom will have tons for us to do to get the house and the grounds ready, I'm sure."

"Yeah, she's nearly killing me with work already," Chase said in a low mutter.

"I think she's making up for the missed opportunity of not having Caroline's wedding at home, and having Summer's be such a surprise that she couldn't plan. She sees this as her last chance to have a wedding there and man is she going all out."

Chase got a worried look on his face. "Or she's rehearsing for our weddings. Oh, I don't even want to contemplate that."

"Huh. You don't say. That's a good thought, Chase. You're probably right. This is all dress rehearsal for Mom."

"Well, cheerio, you pending grooms. Getting a little crystal ball into your own happy futures, are you? Maybe one of those 'dishy dames' from lunch? Did I sound like an American there? Dames?"

"Maybe an American gangster," Chase replied.

Nick laughed heartily. "Like the moonshiner that I am! Much gratitude for all the help today, gents!" He started to walk towards the house.

"Uh, Nick?" Rory called out the window. "Did you want to take your ring? Or did you want us to take it to the house with the tux?"

"Oh! The ring! Right. Bollocks!" Nick looked thoughtful. "Just pop it in the pocket of the tux. That way I won't lose it or forget it again. Cheers!"

As Rory drove back to their mother's house, Chase shook his head. "Whoa, that dude seems... I don't know. How would you describe that? What was all that?"

"Wedding jitters... I guess."

"Yeah, I guess." After a long silence, he said, "Do we tell Jane?"

Rory's lips tightened. "I don't know, man. I don't know. She's known him for years, she must know that he's, he's..."

"A bit of an asshole?"

Rory shrugged. "They say that love is blind. I tell you, when I get married, I'm going to be all in. Eyes wide open and all in. No secrets. No weirdness."

Chapter 17

The third of June arrived sunny and warm. The wedding was planned for three in the afternoon, with a catered dinner and dancing afterward under the big tent by the flower garden. Mimi, with the eventual support of Audree, had outdone herself. It was as if the two best friends had the chance to plan their dream wedding, albeit quickly. The affair, initially intended for twelve people, somehow mushroomed to fifty-five. Somewhere along the line, she wasn't quite sure just where, Jane had relinquished control to her mother and Mimi. The pace had been so fast that planning was a whirlwind, the choices were overwhelming, and there was always the echo of that disturbing voice in the back of her head. But it was a voice she would be proving wrong today.

By noon, Jane only needed her dress to be ready to go. Her hair, nails and make-up were done. The gown was hanging upstairs in the guest bedroom. The only dampener to her day was that Claudine could not make the ceremony. After scraping together the money for the ticket, she was down with the flu, stuck in Paris, and had to miss the whole event. Jane felt like something was missing. Claudine had been there from the start. Summer would fill in for Claudine's reading, but no one could fill in for Claudine's presence. It couldn't be helped though. Things happened. For now, she had to focus on her big day.

Jane and Caroline strolled through the grounds. Ty ran around counting the torches, pretending to fly like an airplane through the grass between them. He was already at the far side of the yard, gliding along the perimeter where Caroline and Jane couldn't hear him anymore, but he would circle back and give them the final count when he was done. "Don't touch them!" Caroline yelled out to her son. She said more quietly to Jane, "Oh my God, I feel like a terrible mother that I'm not holding his hand and keeping him away from all those cylinders of flammable liquid."

Jane watched Ty run. "Well, they aren't lit yet. And honestly," Jane said studying Ty, "I think he's moving too fast to get burned, even if later on tonight he lets his fingers pass through the flames."

"Not helping, Jane, not helping!"

"I'm kidding! They won't be lit until sundown! And all the activity will keep him close."

"I can't help but worry about moths to a flame…" Caroline gave a heavy sigh and looked around at all the wedding paraphernalia. "My God, Jane, you've been the victim of my mother! I'm so sorry and I'm so happy for you," Caroline chuckled. "You know, I'm sure she wanted to do this for me. My tiny East-meets-West affair must have been such a disappointment. Kind of like how my in-laws felt about Sasutki marrying out." Caroline sighed deeply and then looked around at the grounds again. "This, however, could be in a magazine."

Jane decided to avoid talking about disappointed in-laws. "Yeah, I'm glad Dad is at least pretending to be okay with it. I sort of broke Summer's budget here."

"Her budget of, what? Sixty dollars? Her big plan of, 'Hey, Mom, never mind that tomorrow is Christmas Day but we've decided to get married. Can we use your living room?' Yeah, I bet you did break that budget. I mean, the only flowers we could even get for Summer came from the grocery store."

"Mimi's been amazing! I know she ran options by me, but all this is like experiencing it for the first time. I mean, after the accident, I spent the first two weeks high on codeine and not exactly decisive. And then I was so behind at work—and I'm absolutely eating up my vacation time between my weddings that weren't."

"That wasn't"

"What?"

"Wedding that wasn't. Singular. Not weddings that weren't. Those 'others' that got shot down were ideas only—no contracts signed, no guests invited, credit cards charged, or cake cut. Not the real thing. Don't jinx this one! Besides, I don't think anything could stop your wedding from happening today. Come hell or high water, girl, you're getting hitched!"

"Yeah, nothing can stop it now." With a shiver, Jane heard the echo of that voice in her head from when she fell just a few months ago.

"And it's going to be beautiful."

With a deep breath, Jane surveyed the grounds. "It's almost like I'm a guest at my own wedding." Sure, she had said yes to the tent. She knew there would be a tent. She did not know there would be a veritable fairy castle set up in the yard, sparkling with crystal chandeliers and tiny white lights everywhere. Two of the sides were up and open to the yard, the two that were down had arched windows, which enhanced that fairy-tale effect as they looked out over the rose garden and the patio with the fire pit. She'd known there would be some torches set up around the perimeter. She didn't understand that the entire grounds would be staked out in torches to mark the boundary of the celebration, making her small affair look more like a giant festival. She knew that hydrangeas were the selected flowers. She didn't know there were that many hydrangeas in bloom in all of Charlotte.

"That would be my mother." Caroline pointed to some new plantings. "I think Mimi used this as an excuse to put into play a lot of plans she'd had in mind for the garden too. Let's walk over to the sculpture piece. I bet she got Dad to pay for that. One of her friends made it."

"Uncle George paid for that? How'd she get him to do that?"

"Dad is still very involved in everything. Even things at the house. Hell, he still owns the house. Mom could never afford this place on her own. Mom could probably make it as an artist, but not here, not like this," Caroline said matter-of-factly. "He gave Mom everything she asked for: gardeners, plantings, sculpture, new paint, some new curtains. You name it, all in the run up to the wedding. He loves you like his own daughter."

"He and Mimi? Partners in the house? I never knew. Rory and Chase...." And then she wasn't sure how to finish the sentence.

"Oh, the boys complain about Dad a bit overmuch. They were too young to understand. I mean, it was rough on me too, but at fifteen, I could see that there was nothing left between Mom and him; she'd had it with his equating fatherhood with being a good provider and smiling in family pictures. She needed more and wanted more for us. But good ole' George is a product of his own upbringing. To him, that's what a man did: provide. He was role modeling for his children, and I hate to say it, in the best way he knew how. I mean, that's all he ever saw. All he ever knew."

Jane mused on the adage that a woman often marries a man very much like her own father. Given what Caroline was talking about now, she had indeed wed a partner who shared key traits with her dad. Working hard and providing for his family was an immutable part of Sasutki. Smiling in family pictures, not so much. But in a lot of ways, George and Sasutki sounded cut from familiar cloth. "I guess Rory would've been about, what? Ten?"

"Yeah, and little Chase about five years old. So young to miss the father figure he wanted and unable to understand Dad's view that creating security was expressing a whole lotta love. But both boys wanted a dad who was there for them in different ways. John really stepped in. Your dad was great. Never missed one of the boys' ballgames or bike races. But it's an exaggeration to say that Dad wasn't still our dad. It was all those overseas assignments—and since he and Mom were divorcing, of course we didn't move with him, which was good, because we never would have seen him. They just spent too much time apart with his job. They were both incredibly lonely in their marriage."

"I have to say, that gives me the shivers. It's been a struggle for me and Nick too. I think it's been easier on me. I mean, I have you all around and, to be honest, it's really easy to just lose myself in my work."

"Some people are born workaholics, Jane." Caroline gave her a wink. "I know and love them, even so!"

Jane laughed. "I am a workaholic. Oh my God, it's true! But Nick's world isn't like that. I think he's been much lonelier, suffered a lot more than I have. I'll be so glad to be living in the same place at last!"

"And that's the U.S.? Right?"

"Yes, by the end of July he will have handed the company back over to his father. He finally committed to leaving England. They're interviewing now for someone to take on most of his responsibilities. I think it's going to be that Ashlyn girl." Jane shuddered, but Caroline didn't notice. "He'll come here and we'll live at my condo until we decide where we want to go. I think he wants to move to Boulder. There's a strong green design movement there and he wants to get back into his chosen profession."

"And if you go to Boulder, you'll apply for a transfer? Or get a new job?"

"Working on it."

Caroline looked toward the house. "Hey, I hear commotion. I bet the cake arrived. Have you seen it?"

"Are you kidding? Of course not. All of this is new to me. I know I said yes, but really, I'm in the dark. Mom even picked out my dress and Mimi my shoes. When I went to try on the selections they had on hold for me, I still needed the cane because of my ankle. I fell in love with the dress the moment I saw it. Mimi got me the most beautiful little ballet slipper-type shoes. Those women are simply unbelievable."

"No heels for you."

"Uh huh. Bad sprain. It's still not terribly stable. I'll have a brace on it for the ceremony. I have one now." Jane pulled her pantleg up to show Caroline the flexible brace peeking between her very loosely laced tennis shoe and her pant cuff. "And I had the weirdest experience when it happened…" Jane hadn't told anybody, although the memory of it had dogged the back of her mind constantly. She thought she could confide in Caroline now. Given how the day was flying by it felt like a last chance, but then she was distracted by Nick coming out of the house with Rory and Chase at his side. They were heading off to the patio and fire pit area with what looked like small, fat sticks in their hands.

"There's Nick and his bodyguards," Caroline said. "They took him out last night," and then added quickly, "not too late, don't worry. What in the world are they doing? Oh my God, they're smoking cigars. And there's bodyguard number three," she said as Sasutki came out of the house carrying a cigar and a bottle of some type of liquor.

"Oh, he's definitely a bad influence on them." Jane sighed.

"Nick or Sasutki?" Caroline asked and they both laughed.

Jane paused a moment. "You know, Nick confessed that he started smoking. Promised me he'll quit. He said it's rare, just the stress of his father's business. I can't wait to get him out of England. It's been a toxic year for him. I'm looking forward to getting my old Nicky back!"

"I hear more big trucks. I bet the caterers are here. And I'm dying to see that cake," Caroline said and then called out to Ty to join them. "You leave Daddy and the boys alone right now. Grandpa George is going to be here any minute."

"Grandpa George! Grandpa George!" Ty shouted excitedly as he ran off to the house in search of his grandfather.

Jane and Caroline turned away from the rose garden and walked towards the house. "Grandpa George visits us in Japan at least twice each year. That man is always on the move. Work sends him everyplace. It's been wonderful to see him. Now that he's retiring, I don't know that we'll see him that much. I can't imagine why he retired so early, the boredom of it will drive him round the bend. My dad taking time for reflection and relaxation? Exotic trips to Nepal? That is so not him."

"Maybe he's having a late man-o-pause?"

"I wish. I worry more that he knows something we don't, and it's made him get much more serious about life and not just serious about work. But no dark talk today. Let's go see that cake!"

Jane and Caroline went toward the house, where Jane assured Mimi for the twentieth time that everything was beyond perfect, looking like it was straight out of a magazine or a dream. The caterers were bustling about and all the final details were being attended to. Outside, waiters were putting tablecloths on the tables, both the ones under the big tent and those set up in the yard, all under Mimi's expert direction.

"Oh, my word," Caroline said, as she grabbed Ty and held him back from the cake as it was being set up. It was four tiers tall, palest blue and done in the basket weave Jane had selected. On the top, the caterers were carefully placing giant shards of white, rose, and dark chocolate, rolled and curled, some as big as Ty's forearm. They delicately arranged fresh flowers to look like they were spilling out from the top of each layer, completing the effect of the basket weave. It was classic and yet contemporary at the same time.

"Wow!" Jane said, her face lighting up. "That's amazing. That's got to be, what? Ten pounds of chocolate on top of that cake? Twenty? How will we eat all that?"

"I hope your guests are hungry. Really hungry. Who all's coming?" Caroline asked.

"No idea," Jane whispered, staring at the cake and shaking her head. "You pegged it. It's my wedding, but it's not really my wedding."

Caroline gave her a sideways glance. "You okay with that?"

"Oh yeah, under the circumstances, it's a huge gift. I love it. I'm grateful to be getting married at all. It's just… weird, that's all. It feels weird. Like I won it in some kind of nuptial lottery."

"You could use a cup of something hot and strong," Caroline said, putting her arm around Jane and steering her towards the kitchen in the house, her other hand still on Ty, who was trying to squirm away to get to the cake and any rolls of chocolate that were not yet out of reach. "Tell you what, Ty—if you can not touch the cake, not at all until it's served, then, and only then will I let you have one of those giant pieces of chocolate on the top. Any piece you want."

"Any piece?" Ty's eyes were round as saucers and he started murmuring softly in Japanese. Then he said, "I like chocolate way better than red bean cake."

Caroline turned to Jane. "I just struck a deal with the devil. Kitchen. Coffee. C'mon."

Jane nodded. "He's gonna be really hyper on that much sugar."

It was one-thirty in the afternoon. Guests were expected at two for cocktails, the time at which Jane and the girls would retire to Caroline's old room to put on their dresses and add their final touches to hair and make-up. The moment was almost upon them.

"Gotta love the calm before the storm."

Chapter 18

At two-thirty Nick was standing by the unlit bonfire with his bodyguards, Chase and Rory. He wore the vague look of a deer in headlights. Rory had removed the bottle of scotch Sasutki brought out earlier in the day, thinking that two drinks was plenty for any groom-to-be. If that couldn't steady the man's nerves, then nothing could do the trick.

"I could use another hit of that scotch," Nick said with a sigh.

"Bottle's empty. You'll have to wait." Rory's voice was calm and smooth despite his lie. "Audree and John are having a full bar, but it won't be set up until after the ceremony."

"Yeah," Chase said with a frown, "when they said cocktails at two they should have said girly drinks beforehand. Did everything have the flavor of spring flowers? Rose, violet, hibiscus, lavender. Uck. I'm going in to check on things. Find out when Mom wants me to seat the guests."

As Chase walked away, Rory took a long look at Nick, who appeared a little green around the gills. "You okay, man?"

"Me? Sure!" Then Nick paused and looked around him uncomfortably. "John had the talk with me a little while ago."

"Yeah? I saw you two walking around the grounds."

"Told me all about how wonderful his marriage is with Audree. How much they love each other. How they're best of friends, to boot.

How much he loves his little girl. How a marriage is based on respect and trust and honesty and all that."

"Okay. That must have been… interesting," Rory said. "I mean, it sounds like good advice and all, but, uh, yeah, wow."

"Yeah, 'wow' is one way of putting it. It was a bit like being put under some type of microscope or… or being dissected like a frog."

"Did he ask you any questions?"

"No. And yet somehow it was an interrogation just the same." Nick breathed heavily. "Do you have any cigarettes?"

"Nope. Jane said no more smoking after the cigars this morning or she would refuse when Hector says, 'You may kiss the bride'. And that would make a scene."

Nick laughed. "Oh, I suppose she's right. She's always right, you know. Always an angel incarnate. Always my better half." His voice drifted off as he said, "She's my angel, she is… I'm sure I don't deserve her."

Chase came back out to join them. "It's time. Sasutki and I will start seating the guests. Rory, you and Nick need to get the minister and head to the flowered canopy. Glad we got such good weather today!"

Chase left them and Rory gently took Nick by the arm, rousing him from deep thoughts, and started steering him over to the concentric circles of draped chairs decorated with generous bows. A pale blue runner created an aisle between the chairs, a straight line cutting through the circles.

"Ye gods, that looks like a bullseye." Nick looked pale.

At the start of the runner, a graceful arch was completely covered in flowers. The runner led to the flowered canopy, a small pergola at the center of the circles, under which Jane and Nick would exchange their vows. Mimi had the white wooden structure built just for the occasion, and it, too, was draped in flowers and growing vines which sprouted upwards from large white ceramic glazed pots standing sentinel at the four corners of the pergola. At the end of each curved row of chairs, a wrought iron shepherd's hook stood in the ground and held a basket of potted flowers. Nick and Rory both stopped and stared for a moment.

"Gods," Nick stammered out, looking like he was trying to find his breath. He ran his finger around his collar, trying to loosen it. He swallowed hard. A string quartet played over to one side, making background music punctuated by birdsong from the forest.

"My mother is not to be outdone by anyone. Not even by Martha Stewart." Rory shook his head. "If this is her warm-up act, makes me scared for what she'll do when either Chase or I get married. You all right, man?"

"I'm brilliant," Nick said, but he didn't sound it. The two men walked over to the tent where Hector was waiting, obviously rehearsing his lines.

"Hello, Reverend," Rory said respectfully, but with a wry smile.

"Ha, ha," Hector said. "My debut as a minister and this is the setting! It's a little intimidating for a first timer like me. I thought there would be twelve people. Simple little backyard wedding." He ran his finger around his collar to loosen it slightly and cleared his throat, mimicking the move that Nick had made only moments before joining him. "Now I'm wondering when the paparazzi are going to show up?"

"Tell me about it." Nick mirrored Hector's gesture.

The guests, led by Chase, Sasutki, and John, started pouring in, materializing from different parts of the house and grounds, and were being seated. Waiters whisked away trays filled with the remnants of the flower-themed cocktails, getting the pre-party cleaned up in preparation for the wedding ceremony itself. In the distance by the sunroom, Rory, Hector and Nick could see the bridal party come out of the house and get ready to make their grand entrance.

"Take a deep breath, boys. It's almost time to go," Rory said encouragingly.

"I hope I remember my lines!" Hector said, his voice trembling.

"If you can't remember your lines, then there's no hope for me!" Nick said in a panic. "I'm counting on you, Hector!"

Hector blinked a few times and started breathing deeply. After the guests were seated, the quartet struck up Pachelbel's Canon in D Major, which signaled Rory to spur Hector and Nick to move to the end of the runner. Sasutki and Chase, both in tuxedos, stood there, waiting for them.

"Sasutki, you didn't come to the fitting with us." Nick looked him up and down, eyeing his tux. "Where'd you get a tux so fast?"

"Who me?" Sasutki smiled. "I own this." He nodded knowingly.

Mimi and George were the last guests to be seated, right in the front row, escorted by Sasutki, who seated them next to Caroline and an already squirming Ty. Sasutki walked around the outside of the circle and re-joined Hector, who was trying to not look nervous. John and Audree started their approach across the yard towards the entryway arch, where the groom stood by Rory and Chase. Chase nodded, the tallest and most athletic looking, with his dark hair cut short on the sides with a bit of curl on the top, his gray eyes nicely balanced by his high cheekbones and cut jawline. Rory, shorter than his brother and stockier, his blue eyes shining, his normally shaggy blonde hair now slicked back—looked more like James Dean than he did his usual self. Nick, almost as tall as Chase, brown wavy hair and brown eyes, angular face, broad shoulders, completed the trio of poster-perfect men. Rory and Chase broke out in big smiles as John and Audree approached. Nick was trying to smile despite his nerves.

"My goodness boys, y'all look like an advertisement for tuxedos!" Audree smiled warmly back at them and winked. "Very handsome, very handsome, all of you."

Chase held out his arms to them and escorted the parents of the bride down the aisle and they took their places in the front row. Chase looked around for Sasutki. Seeing him back by the entranceway arch, standing with Hector and Rory, Chase also walked around the circle of chairs and joined them.

Hector took a deep breath and glanced at the sky for a moment. Then with a calming exhale, he nodded at the three other men and he walked slowly up the aisle. Nick followed Hector, then came Rory. Quite unexpectedly, Chase, who had never paid much attention to all the instructions and not quite remembering what he was supposed to do, followed Rory. Sasutki simply followed Chase. Although it was supposed to be just Nick and Rory standing up front with the minister, Nick now had three groomsmen all in a line, rather than his expected one. But he didn't seem to notice as his eyes were fixated on the approaching bridal party.

Jane crossed the yard with Charlie and Summer, with baby in arms, alongside her. "Jane, you look unbelievably gorgeous. Like you're in a fairy tale!" Charlie said, and Jane beamed back at her sister.

"Absolutely! Here, let me fix this." Summer reached up with one hand to adjust one little blossom in Jane's hair. "Perfect."

As they approached the flower-and-vine-covered arch marking the entranceway to the ceremony, the women paused to wait for the music that was their cue to start their slow bridal march down the blue runner. Charlie arranged the train on Jane's dress as Summer, holding Echo, whispered pointers.

Jane felt beautiful. The beaded dress with the train must have weighed twenty-five pounds, but the sweetheart neckline showed off her figure well and showcased the stunning necklace Nick had given her. Her ankle was tightly wrapped in athletic tape, and so far, holding up just fine.

"Wait a minute…" she whispered to her sisters. "Why are there four of them lined up like that? That's not what we practiced."

Summer and Charlie looked over. The three girls whispered together and nodded.

Sitting with the guests in the front row, holding Ty's hand, Caroline looked over, curious at the activity. She, too, had wondered why the boys weren't following what they practiced at the rehearsal. In fact, nearly everyone was looking over at the bride, who was conferring with her bridesmaid.

Charlie beckoned to Caroline. Then she beckoned again more emphatically.

Caroline pointed to herself and couldn't fail to notice that most of the guests had turned to look at her, following the pantomimed conversation. Seeing Charlie's emphasized nod, she slid Ty's hand into Grandpa George's and got up. She walked back up the aisle with as much dignity and grace as she could muster, feeling that every eye was on her.

The four women whispered again, quickly conferring and nodding, while all of the guests looked on curiously. The Canon ended and the bridal march began to play. At the front of the line, Charlie handed her bouquet to Caroline and then quickly stepped up to the flower-covered arch, studying it. With an audible grunt, she forcibly yanked two large bouquets of flowers out of the decorations, teetering the arch mightily. The whole audience gasped a collective "Oooohhh!" as Caroline dove to steady the structure.

Charlie heaved the flowers off their mooring, leaving two large blank spots in the floral decorations. She handed one each to Summer and Caroline. Summer held the baby in one arm and took her flowers in the other. Then Caroline lined up in front, with Summer behind her, followed by Charlie and then, at the last, Jane. One by one they did the slow walk up the aisle and lined up. Summer handed Echo to her mother as she passed her in the front row before taking her place.

Nick took in an audible breath when he saw his bride walk up to him. Rory and Chase also gasped as the bridesmaids and bride approached, while Sasutki just had a faraway, rather dazed look. Jane felt absolutely happy. The day was perfect. Her dress was gorgeous. The necklace Nick gave her sat at her collarbone, nicely echoing the bouquet of hydrangeas she was holding. She walked up and took Nick's hand. She handed her bouquet to Charlie, just as they had practiced the previous afternoon in the rehearsal and looked at the lineup of her unexpected bridesmaids. She smiled at how perfect it turned out to be. Without planning, just spontaneously, it became perfect. All her sisters, there in line, standing up with her. It was all going to work out in the end. Everything was going to be okay. So much for scary visions. So much for frightening voices in her head. The day was warm and beautiful with no black ice in sight. She dismissed all her concerns, feeling deeply happy and relaxed. She turned back to her groom. He stood next to Rory and Chase, the closest thing she would ever have to brothers, and Sasutki. She could feel the tremble in Nick's hand. Hector waited until the music ended, then he began to speak.

He gave a short homily on marriage and the most important friendship of one's lifetime, a relationship built on trust and mutual respect as well as love. He talked about God's grace and the sanctity of the union. It was beautiful and meaningful without a hint of the fire and brimstone Jane had wanted to avoid with Pastor Jefferies. When it came time for the exchange of vows, Jane's voice rang clear. Nick's was much quieter, he was almost breathless, and he continued to tremble through the entire service.

Like all ceremonies, it flew by, and all too quickly Hector was announcing the first kiss of Nicholas David Colin Sutcliffe-Ashworth and Jane Audree Donahue as husband and wife. Then he presented Mr. and Mrs. Sutcliffe-Ashworth to the applauding guests.

When it came time for the first dance and the band started to play, Nick still had that shell-shocked look about him. "Well, Mr. Sutcliffe-Ashworth, you old married man, are you having a lovely time at your wedding?" Jane's voice was teasing as he took her in his arms and they started to sway to the music.

"What? Oh, that, yes. I'm ace. Just tickety-boo, as they say."

"Do people really say that?"

"Oh, I don't know. But it does sound so quintessentially British, doesn't it? And how are you holding up, Ms. Jane Donahue?"

"Mrs. Sutcliffe-Ashworth, you mean?" Jane laughed. "Hasn't this afternoon been magical? The dinner was wonderful. At least, I think it was. Maybe it just looked wonderful. You know, I can hardly remember eating."

"Right. I had a hard time eating too. Who can eat at a time like this?"

"Of course, who can eat? There are so many people to talk to, to thank for coming, so many relatives and old family friends I haven't seen in years. You must have met dozens of them. I don't know how you'll keep them all straight."

"Not possible," Nick said, glancing at the gathered crowd watching them dance. The emcee called for the best man and maid of honor to join the floor, then the rest of the bridal party. Rory led Charlie out and they resumed their foxtrot from New Year's Eve. Chase came out with Summer and Sasutki with Caroline. Ty came out leading his nana and grandpa, and John led Audree out to the floor and danced. Jane was sure it was the most spectacular evening that she had ever experienced.

An hour later, as she was happily chatting with old relatives, Chase came and asked her for a dance.

"And how does it feel to be a married woman?"

"Delightful. I hope you find the woman of your dreams someday, Chase. I hope you're even happier than I am."

"That's a generous wish. I think the woman of my dreams is probably out of my reach. And you look like you're on cloud nine."

"I am. Thank you. Are you having a good time?"

He paused.

Before he answered, she asked, "You're not?"

"Oh no! I am. I am." He spun her quickly so that she would be facing the photographer who was trying to get a shot of them on the dance floor. "It's just that between that photographer, who should be dogging your heels but weirdly seems to be following me around, and that line of single women—who I'm sure I'm related to one way or another—but who all want to dance way too close to me, I'm just a little bit out over the end of my skis, as it were."

Ty walked past them with an arm-sized curl of dark chocolate, much of it smeared over his face and suit. Caroline was in quick pursuit and rounded him up, disappearing into the house. Chase and Jane laughed.

"I see the torches are being lit. That means the bonfire will be lit soon. I'm not sure how a bonfire and a wedding dress fit together."

"Just roll with it. I bet this party will go on long past when it was planned to end. My mother will be thrilled." Chase did a quick spin again so that Jane was facing the photographer. "Does he actually know that I'm not the groom? I shouldn't be in these pictures—Nick should be. Hey, where is Nick?"

They looked around. "Oh, I see him," Jane said. "He's at the bar. Again."

Chase looked into her eyes. "How about I go and bring you your groom? I think it's time for that photographer to get more pictures of the two of you on the dance floor."

Chase dutifully retrieved the groom and delivered him to Jane's arms.

"You seem more relaxed now, honey."

"What? Oh, top notch! Yes indeed. While I'd murder for a cigarette about now, I haven't had one. I've been a good boy."

"I appreciate that." She laughed at him. "I can't imagine how you've coped."

"Oh, that was an easy solution! I implemented a liquid strategy. At the bar."

At the end of the very late evening a limo took Nick and Jane to their hotel for the night. They were leaving for Cabo the next day. Nick helped Jane out of her dress, although he fumbled quite a bit with the long line of tiny fabric-covered buttons down the back. As it turned out, he'd done quite a bit of coping at the bar, which was not helping his fine motor skills at the moment. Jane hoped her parents hadn't noticed how drunk he was. She was sure Chase and Rory had. One or the other of them seemed to be at Nick's shoulder much of the night, trying to steer him to where he needed to be and away from temptation.

After finally getting out of her dress they both flopped over onto the king-sized bed. Jane was wearing the sweet nothing undergarments, garters and all, that she had suffered through all day. She curled up against Nick. "Wow. Married at last. That was an amazing evening, honey. Honey?"

Nick answered her with a soft snore. He was fast asleep.

"And thus starts our passionate marriage. Oh well, see you in the morning." She kissed him on the cheek and went off to take a hot bath, hoping he would wake up in a bit.

Chapter 19

The next morning, John Donahue picked the newlyweds up from the hotel at eleven A.M. to deliver them to the airport for their flight. He would take Jane's wedding dress and fancy necklace and earring set back to Audree, who would see that the dress was appropriately cleaned and stored and the valuables taken to be appraised. He took Nick's tux and added it to the collection of everyone else's, which he would return on his way back.

After wishing the new couple bon voyage at the airport, John drove to the shopping center where Lee's Suits, Tailoring, and Tuxedos was located. Opening the trunk, he pulled out the four tuxedos and, humming the country tune that had just been on the radio, he walked up to the store. A soft clinking sound caught his attention. He looked at the pavement around him to see what he'd dropped. Sunlight glinted off the metal of a rolling object. John stepped quickly and caught it under his shoe before it disappeared down a drainage grate. Examining the object he said, "What do you know. It's a ring. Looks like a man's wedding band." He looked around, but he was the only person in the parking lot. He looked at the suits. "Huh. I wonder…" his voice trailed off as he once again started towards the store. Then he stopped in his tracks and stared at the windows.

Three large posters hung behind the glass, advertising the tuxedos available inside. Without thinking about it, John slid the ring into his pocket as he slowly walked over and stared first at one poster then another. He didn't know quite what to make of it, so he took out his phone and took some pictures.

Forty minutes later when John walked into the house, Audree met him with a smile. "Did they get off to the airport all right, dear?"

"Oh yes," he answered. "But I had the most interesting stop at Mr. Lee's. When I took all our tuxedos back, well, their new advertising caught me by surprise. It was… hmmm, I would call it different than anything I've ever seen. A real attention getter. For me anyway."

"Oh my, what weird thing is Mr. Lee doing now?" Audree asked. "Those comics he ran in his windows were just…" she paused, searching for the right words, "not funny for an election season. What tone-deaf step has he made now?"

"I think in this case a picture is worth a thousand words." He pulled up the image on his phone and handed it to her.

Audree looked at the phone, started to say something and found that nothing was coming out of her mouth. At last she said, "But that's…"

"Precisely. There are three huge, and I mean huge posters of those boys filling the windows of Lee's."

"But when…? How…"

"I asked him. Says he took them at the fitting. Said the boys were okay with him using the shots to show customers how good they would look in his suits." John nodded his head. "Said the boys gave him permission."

Audree looked at the pictures again, scrolling through them. "My, my, that man is talented at more than tailoring. You know, this is terrible to say, but I don't think I ever realized those boys look that good. Yes, indeed. Rory with his blonde hair slicked back like that. Nick with that brown wavy hair, and then little Chase. My goodness, little Chase has really grown up, hasn't he? If accounting doesn't work out for Mimi's little boy, he could model tuxedos full time. Are his eyes really that gray?"

"I was wondering if we should point this out to Mimi?" John asked.

"For some reason, I think Mr. Lee believes the boys are mine, but Mimi would want to know about this."

"Perhaps you're right. I wonder how she'll feel about it? For my part, I'm just relieved Mr. Lee doesn't have any cartoon bubbles filled with statements lost in translation. That's a fine art, I tell you! You know, if it's just Mr. Lee's store, it's a local little thing and will blow over. I'm sure this won't be anything to fret about. This won't go anyplace."

Charlie came down the stairs. "Hey, Mom! Dad!" she called out as she rounded the corner. "I got the weirdest message. Look what my friend Kitty sent to me." She handed her phone over to her parents. "She just posted this on her socials. Like all of them. Don't those guys look so exactly like Chase and Rory? And the guy in the back, the one you can see in profile, he looks kinda like Nick. Kitty saw this in a digital ad and grabbed an image. I mean, isn't that a crazy coincidence?" She showed them a casual, outdoor shot of the three men all dressed for the wedding; a large white event tent was just discernable in the background at the edge. The rest of the surroundings indicated a lovely, park-like ground.

"Just where is your friend Kitty right now?" Audree asked. "What store is this for?"

"Says it's at a place called Lee's Bridal and Tuxedo of Raleigh. That's where she lives now."

John looked at the phone and then back at Charlie. "You mean to say she saw these advertising a store three hours away from us? And she posted these photos?"

"Yeah. And she Insta'd it. Said she was making a TikTok, too! She remembers the boys from high school. She always had a major crush on Chase. Said she just knew he'd become a model someday." Charlie shrugged and looked back at the phone.

"I don't think this is gonna blow over, my dear," John said, turning to his wife.

Audree nodded. "Maybe we should call Mimi right now."

Chapter 20

The first-class flight to Texas was a treat for Jane. The flight attendant brought her a Bloody Mary, which added to the vacation feeling of the trip. Still green from his hangover, Nick just waved off the offer of a cocktail, with his gesture catching Jane's eye.

"Nick! Your wedding band? Where is it?"

"Well, bloody hell! It's not on my finger. When was I wearing it last?"

"Uh, that would be last night."

"It must be in my luggage, darling. Where else could it be?" He stroked her cheek. "Nothing to worry about. I'll pop it on when we get to the hotel. Until then, I'm going to have a quick kip." He closed his eyes, put his seat back, and quickly fell asleep. Jane stared out the window for the duration of the flight, her Bloody Mary practically untouched when it came time for the attendants to prepare the cabin for landing.

Their connection turned out to be a tiny prop plane for the rest of the journey into Mexico. Jane was surprised that aircraft with propellers were still in service in this day and age. It was a bumpy flight, the choppy air creating a lot of turbulence. The plane jostled and shook, an experience of torture for Nick, given his hangover. Sleepless and miserable, he mostly laid back in his seat by the window and groaned.

With her new spouse basically incoherent, Jane engaged in conversation with the older gentleman sitting in the seat across the aisle from her. Gregg Talbot was an American married to a local from the tiny town of Todos Santos.

"Your coconut plantation sounds like something I've only ever dreamed about!" Jane found Gregg to be gregarious, friendly, and fascinating. She kept thinking how much her parents would enjoy meeting him. He was like a mythical uncle who lived an impossibly idyllic life.

"My wife would love you. We never could have kids. For me, well that was sad, but she's Mexican—for her that was like a curse." He paused for a moment. "You know, you and your husband should come by our farm." He leaned around her and looked at the incoherent Nick. "I mean, if he ever recovers," he said, giving Jane a wry look. "You're staying in Cabo?"

"Yeah, a hotel called Rui Sol del Dolphin."

"That's a nice place. A couple of miles outside of town, proper. Very isolated. Nice and quiet. If you want to see authentic Mexico, you should visit us. It's so easy. About an hour away. Here, let me show you." He picked up the small square napkin on his tray table and took out a pen and started to draw. "See you just go north here, on Mexico Carretera Federal 19 the whole way." He drew some more squiggles. "And once you get into Todos Santos…" he explained some turns but didn't write down any street names. The drawing might have made sense to Gregg but with no directional signals, no road names, and no scale, it was just a bunch of intersecting lines with an "X marks the spot" for his farm. Jane thanked him graciously, amazed at the warmth and generosity and wondering if everyone they met in Mexico would be so welcoming and friendly. She slipped the map into her pocket, thinking nothing of it and with no plans to follow up. She was on her honeymoon, after all.

After they landed, Gregg reiterated his offer while they waited for their luggage in a shed-like structure that passed for a baggage claim. Nick, still not recovered from the bumpy flight, stood there deaf and numb to the world around him, mumbling something about "Hoping

I don't chunder, oh gods!" Jane didn't even want to know what he meant.

She ignored Nick and thanked Gregg warmly. "I've got the map!" she said brightly as she tapped her jacket pocket.

After what seemed an age, given that their plane was so small, their luggage finally arrived. Nick picked up his bag and stood, looking around, quite fascinated at how little there was to see.

"Nick, honey, that's my bag. Uh, Nick?" Jane sighed as Nick made no movement. She went to retrieve her own luggage, happy she'd packed lightly for honeymoon-attempt-deux. "So much for yours-to-command," she said under her breath.

While she was concerned about Nick's degree of distraction, her unease evaporated when they got to the hotel. As advertised, it was right on the cliffs with a spectacular view of the ocean. The rooms were traditional, adorned with rustic tile everyplace, and huge by any standard. Their furnished balcony, also impressive in size, overlooked the Pacific. It was paradise.

From the hotel, a steep wooden stairway led down to the beach, a blazing white stretch of pristine sand adorned with a dozen palapas dotting the landscape. Waiters popped by the low shelters to take orders and she soon discovered they would bring any number of icy drinks with umbrellas or "scrummy" appetizers in pressed eco-paper take-out containers. As they lay on lounge chairs under their favorite palapa, Jane remarked, "You know, you can get absolutely anything on a quesadilla. This place could not be more perfect. Don't you think, Nick?"

"Hmmm…" he said, but he wasn't really answering her. He was on his third cigarette since they'd arrived at the beach. Once again, he was staring at the ocean in between texting people back at the office.

Jane reached for his left hand and stroked his finger. "You know, with my beautiful wedding rings and your bare finger, it's almost like I ran off with someone instead of my real groom! I wonder what the people in the hotel are thinking." She tried to make light of the situation but in truth, the fact that his wedding band had never materialized bothered her.

"Are you going to go off on that again?"

Who is this stranger? Where is the man I know and love? She reasoned with herself that he was struggling with guilt: his parents unable to come to the wedding, his imminent abandonment of his father's firm. No wonder he was moody and distracted. At least he seemed eager enough to make it up to her at night. She reminded herself that these were big changes for him and that people from supremely dysfunctional families needed time to process and a bit more support and TLC. She could do that. She could support him. She could love him through this. On the third day his disposition seemed to be much brightened, and he surprised her.

"Let's rent a Jeep and drive around today."

"Are you bored in paradise already?" Jane laughed, happy to see a hint of the old Nicky making a reappearance. "The beach too perfect? The rum too wonderful? The sun too hot? Your new bride too sexy?" she said, thinking of the previous night's lovemaking.

"Right, I am rather bored." He stared at the ocean and failed to notice the hurt look crossing her face. "Let's go find a private beach or something. I'm sure if we can get away from all the people there are bound to be amazing finds in little coves along the coast."

Jane looked at the nearly empty beach. "What people?" There might be four other couples under the dozen palm tree umbrellas. This was no Miami beach crammed with tourists. She hated the thought of leaving their palapa, not to mention the palapa bar. With the wave of a hand, margaritas and food would soon appear. It was a heaven of a beach. She looked back over at Nick. He looked restless.

"Okay. We can rent a Jeep and drive around. Tomorrow will be another perfect day on the beach. And the next day another. We can go adventuring if you want."

They were surprised to find a Dollar Rent-a-Car in town. The fire-engine-red convertible Jeep Grand Cherokee looked new and shiny, a vast difference to the old relics anyplace outside the four or five exclusive resorts that dotted this end of the peninsula.

"Can you believe the brilliant deal we got? No banger this!" Nick said as he pulled out of town, driving a bit over the speed limit posted on the signs. "That was brilliant. I feel a bit as if we're pinching it."

"Apparently, going adventuring isn't very popular here." Jane sighed as she watched the small town whizz by.

"I can't imagine why!"

"Probably because the hotel and beach are too perfect for anyone to want to leave," she shouted, but it didn't seem like he could hear her over the wind rushing past them as they raced down Carretera Federal 19.

While the Jeep was clean and seemed almost unused, the roads, however, fit neither of those categories. They bumped their way north with a full tank of gas, but no particular destination in mind. Just a "truly secluded beach" was Nick's oft-repeated goal. Jane couldn't imagine what he wanted to do there.

Almost an hour into the drive, and a quick stop at a tiny bodega, Nick said, "Let's try this road." They'd been searching for the road which "they absolutely couldn't miss" that led to the ocean. A woman at the store had told them about it, speaking mostly in Spanish, and had drawn Nick a map on a little sticky note.

"What is it with Mexicans and their sticky-note-maps?" Nick asked Jane as he passed the scrap of paper to her. "You're our navigator."

"I don't know, Nicky. This looks more like modern art, or, uh, like a child's scrawl than a map." She mused that it looked a lot like the map that Gregg from the plane had drawn for her. No north indicator. No names of roads. Not even "top" or "bottom". She turned the square piece of paper over and over in her hands and tried to answer Nick's questions about the directions. Suddenly it slipped from her fingers in the wind of the open car and was gone.

Nick rolled his eyes. "Can't you pull up a map on your phone?"

"I told you, no cell signal." In frustration, she shoved her phone into the glove box. "Are you sure that's a road?"

"It looks like a road," he said, but then when Jane looked at him dubiously, he added, "Well, it'll do for one anyway. Besides, it's just a rent-a-Jeep."

"I don't know if that's reason enough to destroy it."

"Such a party pooper. C'mon." He put the Jeep into gear and drove down the dirt lane.

While the sandy peninsula known as Baja was famous for sun baked dunes and fields, arroyos abounded, as it was also a land carved by monsoon rains and the occasional hurricane. The flat expanse of smoothed stones the car was now travelling down created a pathway to the ocean, but it was a pathway intended for gushing water, not for cars. The bumpy, rocky access eventually diverted onto something that seemed more like a real dirt road. Nick drove for several minutes parallel to an ocean he and Jane could only at times glimpse, never finding anything even remotely like the *pequeño camino de la playa*, which they took to mean "an unmistakable little beach road" that the friendly native had recommended. The view of that inaccessible ocean was maddening for Nick, who felt like he was being taunted by the deep blue water that he couldn't reach. There had been so much out of reach for Nick in the past couple of years—his career, his out-of-country fiancée, his dignity what with having to put up with his parents' demands and machinations. Jane thought that the universe taunting him must feel like another straw added to his load, and at some point, he too, would suffer the fate of the camel.

"Tell me again what that woman said?"

"Honey, my Spanish comes from three weeks of listening to my local library's Let's Speak Spanish! I only know how to plead for my life and ask where the bathroom is! I don't know what she said."

"You understood pequeño!"

"So yeah, I guess I could plead for my small life or need to take a quick pee. My Spanish is just not helpful here."

"But you speak so many languages! You're fluent in French. You've got quite a bit of German down. Even that Chinese language you speak. Why couldn't you translate what she said back there?" The frustration in his voice was palpable.

"Um, probably because she didn't give us instructions in Mandarin. Can't imagine why, here in Mexico, that they'd expect us to speak Spanish." She rolled her eyes, feeling that thick shag carpeting of her empathy starting to wear thin.

"Yes! Why do they speak so much Spanish here? It's a tourist area. You'd think everyone spoke English, just like on the continent!"

While Jane was tempted to explain that he was well on his way to being an ugly American, she did have to admit that she was also just a bit surprised at how little English was spoken. For most of her travels, it was hard to use the language you were trying to learn. As soon as people figured out you were an American, which they quickly surmised just looking at the way you dressed, they jumped in to practice their English. But not here. Once you got outside of Cabo San Lucas proper, it really was like being someplace back in time in a foreign country.

They passed several farms. At least that is what they must have been, but the tobacco and chicken farms that were outside of Charlotte were nowhere to be seen here. She wasn't sure she could recognize the crops in the fields they passed, but she was a city girl after all. Coconut groves were easy. Coffee plantations were harder, and some of the crops were just plain unfamiliar to her. One thing she did notice, however, was that the field workers were nearly all women. Bright scarves tied around their heads framed their rich skin beautifully. They wore colorful long wraps as skirts. Those few in jeans wore bright blouses. She thought Mimi would love to paint them: they looked like flowers dotting the fields here and there as they worked under the afternoon sun, picking beans and peppers, or whatever one harvested from those bushy trees. By comparison, Jane felt small and plain. She was dressed in all tans and olives: colors of earth and sand. Her skin was pale, as if she was meant to fade into the background rather than decorate it.

Right now, being with Nicky made her want to fade into the background.

Nick turned down another dusty lane and the Jeep bumped and rolled for several minutes before he stopped on a wide, dry mud flat sprawling beneath a large dune. It was a wall of golden sand separating them from the perfect blue ocean under a clear blue sky on the other side. Here and there were stray tracks of wide tires crisscrossing the dunes, looking like scars interrupting the wind-swept smoothness of the sandy surface.

"Blimey! Look at that! People have been driving here already. This is it! The dunes must be worth giving a go! Brilliant!" Real enthusiasm rang in Nick's voice. Jane had almost forgotten what that sounded like. Then he added, "I hope no one's here now," suddenly sounding much more like the man who had shown up with her on this trip. He put the car into first gear.

Certainly, they'll be no one here. There's no one anyplace. There's not a road in sight, much less a house, Jane thought, but she didn't say anything. There was something odd about Nick's wanting to be away from people, from everyone. Maybe even her. She didn't want to fight. She was sick and tired of the senseless bickering that had characterized the last three days. It was easier to give him what he wanted than it was to argue. Jane fleetingly wondered what kind of mother she would be, the mother of Nicholas David Colin Sutcliffe-Ashworth the fifth, if all she could do was fold. But then the tracks caught her attention, and she studied them for a bit. For some reason they looked familiar, but the answer was on the edge of her memory, like an itch in her brain. They didn't look quite right but she couldn't say why, distracted as she was by Nick's moodiness. Nick moved the car forward. Halfway up the dune the car started to slide backward, losing traction.

"Bloody hell," Nick said as he put the car in reverse and backed down the dune. He backed up further and got a stronger start. This time they got about two-thirds up the hill before being forced to retreat. Jane suddenly remembered Summer working with Rory and

Chase on an old Volkswagen bug they wanted to turn into a dune buggy. Summer had found the plans on the internet and had talked the boys into trying it. It was such a typically "Summer thing to do". Jane looked again at the tracks crisscrossing the sandy mountain before them and she felt her heart sink.

"Are you sure this is a good idea?" She asked the question tentatively, not wanting to set Nick off. Nick had been so touchy. She didn't want to tell him what to do. She didn't want to fight about it.

Nick put the Jeep into four-wheel drive. "Hold on, darling. We'll make it this time!" he shouted excitedly, getting a good start and charging up the hill.

"I really think those look more like dune buggy tracks than Jeep tracks!" Jane shouted back, each hand clutching the interior around her. Perhaps her voice was drowned out in the roar of the engine or perhaps he just ignored her. Either way, the Jeep charged up the hill.

At exactly the half-way point, the car sunk straight down into the sand like the earth was trying to swallow it.

Nick screamed in frustration. "Bloody hell! Bollocks! What a cock up!"

Jane bristled at the hostility in his voice and realized she was clutching the interior around her so hard she might damage the surface with her nails. Nick put the car in reverse. She instinctively turned around to look behind them as Nick put his foot on the gas pedal. Sand met her face with thousands of stinging little beads. The tiny pellets rained on her head, pelting her hair. It went down the collar of her shirt. It went up the legs of her shorts.

"Stop!" she screamed, spitting the sand out of her mouth.

The roar ceased and car stopped rocking. Nick looked at his wife. "Uh. Sorry." He didn't sound at all sorry. He looked at her with an angry expression, as if this were her fault.

Jane stared at this stranger sitting next to her, then slowly, carefully, she stepped out to brush off the sand and shake it out of her clothes. Before she took two steps away from the vehicle she stopped, frozen in mid-motion. "Oh, uh, Nick. You'd better look at this." The concerns she'd had for the driver were now vastly outmatched by those she held for their car.

Nick climbed out of the Jeep and stared wordlessly at the helpless vehicle. His mouth hung open.

Jane shook her head and ran her fingers through her hair furiously to get the sand out. The shower of sand released from this movement sounded like distant rain as it fell on the passenger seat and the door of the Jeep. She stepped further back and shook again. No sense in putting more sand in the car. She looked again at the Jeep.

Their once shiny new Jeep was now buried up to the axles. Each of the tires was bent outwards in a different and unnatural direction. It looked like the desert version of Chitty Chitty Bang Bang floating across the sand, except that this was not funny or cute. This was not child's play. They were in a strange country, in the middle of no place, not a house in sight, maybe fifty miles from their hotel, and they didn't speak the language. There was no cell signal. Their car was half buried in a sand dune and it wasn't going to magically start flying anytime soon.

"Oh fuck!" Nick stalked around the car, staring in amazement and kicking one of the unnaturally angled tires with a vengeance. "Oh, bugger, we're fucked! Bloody hell! Fuck off, you goddam bitch of a rubbish heap! Fuckety-fuck this!" he said over and over with such hostility that Jane cringed and stepped back.

She stared at him and felt helpless. If he were a cat, every hair would be standing on end, tail bristled, and she would be fearing some type of rabid attack. She'd never seen him like this before—never seen this side of him, and it scared her. Truth be told, she had never seen anyone act like this before. She'd trusted that Nick knew what he was doing on their "adventuring"—and he'd let her down. Colossally so. She trusted that he was being sensible at the very least. But he hadn't been. Had she overestimated him that much? What had happened to him?

"Oh my God, this is going to cost a fortune." She ran her hands through her hair again.

Nick continued to spit out his curses as he stalked around the half-buried Jeep, encircling it as if he was in some kind of hostile trance.

Jane took another step back as she struggled with her own emotions. She was scared of the situation, didn't know what to do, but she was angry too. Angry at Nick. Angry that he would have gotten them into this mess in the first place. Angry that he was now breaking down, seemingly only able to scream obscenities at the useless vehicle as he paced around it. On top of that, she was scared of him. It was a morass of emotions that she didn't know how to deal with. She would've liked to scream back at him, telling him how stupid it was that he buried the Jeep, but it wouldn't make a difference to those dazed, unseeing eyes. Screaming at him would do no good. He was like a person controlled by strange forces, unable to shake it off, unable to function.

"Bloody hell! Bloody hell! Bloody hell!" he shouted. "Damn fucking shit!" echoed through the air, over and over again as he savagely kicked the car. "Bugger! Bugger! Bugger!"

"Oh my God, we're going to die out here."

Chapter 21

"Yeah, we're gonna die out here," Jane said again, baffled by what she could possibly do. Clearly, Nick was not going to get them out of this mess. She gritted her teeth, spat out some more of the sand and shut the lid on her fear so suddenly she thought for a moment the *bang!* must have been audible. There was no rational adult around right now but her. She would have to take care of this. She didn't know how, but she didn't have the option of being afraid—either of Nick's condition or of the situation. With a deep breath and a silent-but-heartfelt prayer, she stepped back into rationality and set her feet firmly on the ground. "You're on your own, Jane. Figure this out."

She walked over to the Jeep, pulled out her butt-pack, put some snack bars and the water bottles in it, and strapped it around her waist. Without a word she took off alone down the dirt path to what she hoped was a real road. She was glad she had firmly taped up her ankle this morning. Who knew how long her walk was going to turn out to be?

About a half a mile or so later Nick caught up with her. "And just where are you headed off to?" At least he was a little more focused now. She noticed the words, "bugger me", "bloody hell," "shit," "damn" and that new classic, "fuckety-fuck," weren't part of his question. Certainly, their situation was anything but "tickety-boo."

"I'm going to get help." She didn't look at him. If she were being honest with herself, she was afraid what she would see if she did. Afraid she still wouldn't recognize the man walking next to her. The man who just days ago had said "forever" with her. She was afraid that maybe this wasn't the man she wanted to be married to.

"Where?"

"I dunno. But at least it has a better shot of producing results than chanting 'bloody hell' and 'oh fuck me' over the car." She bit off the words, far less steady than she had hoped she would sound. A second deep breath and a little prayer steadied her nerves before she continued. "There were some farms back up the road. Maybe someone can help us." Jane instinctively felt this was the right thing to do. Farmers were good people. They lived close to the land. They cared for living things and right now she was a living thing that needed to be cared for. They would help stranded strangers. Someone would help them. "I know Baja is a small area, but there's got to be a tow truck someplace."

Nick didn't say anything. He just walked beside her in silence. After a full five minutes broken only by the dull shish and thud of their shoes on the dirt road, Jane pulled out a snack bar from her pack. She tore the bar in half and handed one portion of it to her husband, partly as a peace offering, but partly against her own will too. Really, she wanted to punish him for ruining their honeymoon. Without a word, he accepted it and ate. She pulled out a water bottle, took a swallow, and then offered it to Nick. Maybe it was the food or maybe it was the movement forward, but something seemed to have a positive effect on the man. He grew more focused and regained some semblance of normal; more the person she had always known him to be anyway. Jane took a deep breath and decided to venture speaking.

"Did you notice that I didn't say anything about burying the Jeep?"

"Right. That's because you're an angel incarnate. You never make a step out of turn. Always my better half." Did he sound sheepish? His speech was somewhat halting. "I do appreciate that. I know I, what do you call it? Freaked out back there..." His words drifted off as he looked around at the scrub grass, the sky—anyplace but at Jane. "It was a barmy thing to do. I'm sorry, darling, I'm really sorry. I just really freaked out. It was really… stupid."

"Yeah, I thought you probably knew that already. At least I was sure that you didn't need me to explain that fact to you." She found a half-smile crept across her face and in return he ventured a half-smile back. She breathed a deep sigh of relief, seeing some part of the Nick she knew and loved. *Maybe things are going to be okay after all? Maybe this is just one of the challenges newly married couples face?*

She couldn't figure out what was up with Nick, what would cause him to react like that. He treated the car mishap like his whole world was crashing down around him. Sure, the situation sucked, and admittedly he'd made a series of rash, immature, and stupid mistakes. And potentially dangerous, given their situation now, but it wasn't like anything life-altering had actually happened to them. No one was bleeding. Nothing was broken. Like many hardships, someday, this would all make a great story. Someday they would laugh about it.

"I think those might have been dune buggy tracks on the sand."

"Dune buggy tracks? Why would you think that?"

"Summer and the guys worked on one way back when, in one of the Watkins' barns. I mean, it's not like the thing ever ran or anything, but those tire tracks on the dune looked vaguely familiar. I think that might be the kind of tracks a dune buggy makes."

"If you thought that, why didn't you tell me?"

"Oh, I shouted it out. Believe me. Top of my lungs." She turned to look at him as she trod on. "I thought you knew what you were doing. I was trusting you."

He was quiet for a few moments and muttered something under his breath about that being totally daft. She didn't take the bait. She could hear his heavy feet against the dusty earth. "I'm sorry, darling, I'm really sorry. Really sorry... so sorry..." His voice took on the quality it had had when he was circling the stranded vehicle, almost on autopilot of repeated phrases.

"Okay, okay, just don't start that chanting stuff and freak out on me again. That's much worse than being stuck here in God's no-place. And, uh—one more thing..."

"What?"

"Next time I do something stupid, I mean really, really fucking stupid, you don't get to say a thing. I get the equivalent of burying a Jeep... for free."

Nick smiled at her. "No worries. Right. Stiff upper lip and all. After all, how bad can this be?"

"Well, let's think about that." She tried to avoid sounding too antagonistic. "You saw those tires. They look a bit like a T-Rex used the jeep as a chew toy. And we may have damaged the axle to boot. In fact, we may be buying that lovely Jeep as our souvenir from our honeymoon." She smiled at him in mock sweetness. "I thought I would turn it into a planter."

Although she had sneakily checked the box for the full insurance package with the rental after he insisted they didn't need it, she didn't bring that up now. She decided to let him stew in the implications of his actions.

Nick looked at his wife, gave half a laugh that died out quickly as the realization hit him, and then just turned his gaze ahead. He didn't say another word.

After a couple of miles, they came to the driveway of a farm. Now Jane's ankle was starting to have some serious discomfort. As they walked down the long lane, brightly-clad women worked the fields, harvesting what looked like leaves from tall, bushy plants. Jane and Nick headed towards the small house in the distance. As they approached, they made out a figure sitting in the relative cool of one of the few shade trees. It was a teenage boy—maybe about fourteen years old.

"My turn to do something right for once and get us out of this. You know, when I was in Spain this winter, I found it to be a very patriarchal culture. Women were supposed to take a back seat. You had better let me do the talking."

Jane tried hard to keep her reactions to herself. After all, his intentions were good. While Nick had expected her to translate back at the grocery store when his language-skills proved inadequate, in reality he knew about fifty more words of Spanish than she did, which put him in the ballpark of a vocabulary of seventy-five words. For the trip he had honed very useful phrases, such as, "Dos cerveza, por favor", which Jane could recognize as "Two beers please". There was also his "¿Que esta tequila gusano?" which he told her meant "Does this tequila have a worm?" And then there was Nick's personal favorite, "¿hay caliente y picante?" which she had quickly and uncomfortably learned meant "Is this hot and spicy?" Occasionally Nick would say, "Es demasiado caro" when he wanted to bargain with the already impoverished natives.

"Hola!" Nick called out to the young fellow. "¿Habla usted Inglés, por favor?"

The boy, dressed in ragged jeans and a long-sleeved button-down plaid shirt, looked like he could have come from nearly any place in the United States. "No," he answered with a smile and made a vague wave of his hands in the direction of the house. "Vayan a la casa, por favor."

"Gracias," Nick said with a clearly British accent and nodded as he and Jane passed the boy. Another hundred feet brought them to a middle-aged version of the boy they had just met who might have been about forty, but then again, a lifetime spent under the hot sun could make age deceiving. This man was also lounging beneath a tall, shady tree. Despite the considerable heat, he wore a button-down, long-sleeved shirt, but with no pattern, and well-worn pants, not denim, Jane noticed. She wondered what the story was behind women working in the field while the only two men they had seen were resting under the trees, almost as if they were on some type of a lazy watch or guard duty. Then she wondered what they were harvesting. It wasn't like there were visible fruits or vegetables on those bushy shrubby trees that were more than half again as tall as the women tending them. What kind of trees did you harvest the leaves from? She couldn't imagine. Then she wondered if they grew tea here?

Three large dogs ran up to greet them, barking noisily and nipping at their heels. Jane felt her spine stiffen and her heart start to race. She wasn't sure if it was the barking, the drool, or the teeth. *No, honestly, it's the teeth,* she thought. *Don't show fear.* Summoning her courage, she said, "Ooooooh, look at you, big doggie! Aren't you the most beautiful big dog ever? You sure are big!" And then since the dog was already nearly upon her, she added, "C'mere boy! C'mere." Remembering what her childhood dogs responded to, she made sure that her voice hit a high register, speaking baby talk to the largest of the beasts. To her relief, the menacing bullmastiff immediately melted into a puddle of butt-wagging wiggles as it lapped up the affection it craved, but surely rarely received.

As she continued to coo at it and scratch it behind the ears, the canine, tall as her hip, happily leaned against her, both trying to bury it's head in her stomach and lean against her left side. Her ankle joint, still recovering from its ice-gymnastics performance of the previous March, started to hurt from the pressure. She grimaced and tried to push the dog aside. The bullmastiff growled. She scratched him harder behind the ear and cooed some more. The dog opened its huge jaws and gently closed down on Jane's forearm. "Ohhhh," she said as she breathed in deeply, wondering if like a shark in the water, the dog could sense her fear. "You want to hold my hand. You're a good boy! Please don't eat me! Don't eat me! I'm not a snack, you big love machine. You sure are a giant. Don't eat me!" The drool was now slipping down to her wrist and a glop of it dripped onto the ground.

Jane looked at Nick. He too had reached down to pet and quiet one of the huge canines, following her example. His dog excitedly licked his hand in response. She gave Nick a look of dismay. "Of course, you get kissed while I get checked out to see if I taste like chicken." She gave a heavy sigh and scratched the dog's ears again with her free hand.

"At least that should establish that we're friendly. We're friendly," she baby-talked, and added, "Dooooon't eat me!"

Nick gave an unempathetic smirk. As the dog still held Jane's arm in its mouth, Nick turned to the middle-aged gentleman and repeated his salutation. They proceeded to have exactly the same conversation as before, and the man pointed to the simple house at the end of the dusty drive.

"Right, darling. Off we go down the yellow brick road. Adventures away!" Nick was putting up a good front. If this situation was shaking him, she couldn't tell. It was possible that now when there was the light of rescue on the horizon, that he was actually a bit thrilled at the whole escapade. He took off at a clip, his canine companions trotting along at his heels.

Thrilled was not how she would quite describe her feelings. "They say opposites attract,", she said aloud to the dog grasping her arm in his jowls. She just wasn't feeling very attracted to Nick at this particular moment as she watched him jauntily step his way down the dusty road, but maybe that had something to do with him being slobber-free while her arm was dripping in goo. The bullmastiff loosed her arm so it could catch up with its companions following Nick as though he had called them to heel.

Another couple hundred feet and they arrived at a cinder block construction which seemed to be missing two important walls. Open to the air was an outdoor kitchen outfitted with appliances that looked like they were meant for a more traditional set-up—the kind that offered the usual amenities, like four walls, a roof, and not being subjected to rain and wind. Two doors led to the only enclosed part of the structure. One door was open a bit and Jane could see a small, sparse bed and a single, very dirty glass-paned window. The roof was some type of metal. She thought that must have sounded pleasant under the afternoon rain showers.

"¿Hola?" Nick called tentatively.

An elderly woman came out of the bedroom with the open door. She eyed them suspiciously. "Hola…"

Nick proceeded to rattle off Spanish that Jane could barely follow, but when she heard her name, it confirmed that he was introducing them. And then she heard the familiar question: "¿Por favor, habla usted Inglés?"

The woman shook her head and shuffled over to the other door and knocked gently on it. She waited patiently. She knocked again. And then a third time. Eventually an elderly man appeared. Jane thought the two of them looked like the Latin version of the American Gothic painting.

Jane quickly waved and said, "Hola!"

"Hola!" they said to her with a smile, introducing themselves as Isabel and Ramon. Nick proceeded to explain, in very broken Spanish, their predicament. After some minutes of confusion, which was obvious in any language, Ramon raised both his hands, palms facing the foreign couple, to get Nick to stop talking.

"Okay, okay, okay." He started to wave his hands as Nick prattled on in meaningless Spanish. "Let me understand," he said, in heavily-accented English that was clearly better than Nick's grasp of Spanish. "You want…" he searched for the word, "help. Your el barco is stuck on the playa. You need…" Then he made pushing motions with his hands.

Nick took a deep breath. "Si, Señor. We need help. But el barco? What is el barco? It's our lorry. Our car."

"Lorry? What is?" Ramon tried to reproduce the words Nick had said.

Jane was surprised. Of course, no one would know what a damn lorry was, she wasn't quite sure herself, but she thought "car" was an international word, like "credit card" or "Michael Jordan", or "Taylor Swift". Maybe it was because he pronounced it like "caaaa".

An elaborate game of charades followed, which only bred more confusion between the two men. *Nick was always pathetic at that game,* Jane thought. She noticed that Isabel had not spoken a word since

Ramon came out. She wondered if keeping quiet was as hard for the older woman as it was for Jane herself. And then she realized that keeping quiet, being in the middle, letting others go first—that was her way, wasn't it? What else did she ever do but support people from the background? She wasn't brave and assertive like Claudine, whom she was missing at this very moment. She wasn't artsy and quirky and proud like her sister, Summer. No, Jane got cups of tea and coffee for people. She waited to hear what they had to say. She gave her boss fabulous ideas and watched him take the credit while she smiled in the background. She told others how great they were—both at home and at work. She arranged fabulous honeymoon trips for them to enjoy and her to miss out on, and then caved in to their suggestions, even when she thought they were stupid. The moment was revelatory.

She looked at Isabel and realized that they had more in common than met the eye. Jane had the sudden epiphany that she didn't want to be the silent, subservient cheerleader of her male companion. She didn't want to be the model for American Gothic. She didn't want to be the wall decoration or the person who came in and cleaned up and made everything right after someone else left the mess. The brilliant, backstage idea-generator. She looked at the men, who were lost in translation, and she couldn't stand it any longer.

"Señor Ramon," she broke into their confusion. "It is not our el barco," she said, having no idea what that word meant. "It's our Jeep Grand Cherokee which is stuck in the, the..." She looked around her. She didn't know what playa meant either, and he obviously didn't know what sand meant. She bent down and picked up a handful of the dusty earth and let it fall through her fingers. "Sand?... playa? Por el grande agua."

"Ooooh!" he said excitedly, comprehension dawning on his face. "Your Jeep! Jeep Grand Cherokee! Jeeeeep! Si! Si! Beep! Beep! Four-wheel drive!"

Jane couldn't help but smile, her little marketer's heart feeling a sense of awe for those unknown colleagues from her profession who had created the commercials that impressed Señor Ramon so much that he was turning into a little boy again right in front of their eyes. Maybe he didn't know about Michael Jordan or Taylor Swift, but the powerful American car of his dreams brought out his inner child. Frail and elderly though he was, the gentleman was quite animated as he motioned, mimicking steering a car, shifting gears, and honking a horn while he made engine noises.

Of course, Nick had been doing just that motion repeatedly.

Nick turned to her. "Bugger! Why didn't he understand me?"

Jane ignored Nick and said again to Señor Ramon, with large arm motions, trying to get across the idea of the huge dune, hoping she was making sense. "Jeep Grand Cherokee in the playa! El grande playa!"

Señor Ramon's face fell. "Ohhhhh…" he said with dawning comprehension. "That is not good."

Jane nodded at Nick. "At least we're on the same page now."

Nick gave Jane a look of incredulity and it slowly dawned on her that she had just upstaged him again, as if everything that had happened so far was not enough. "I'm not having a very good day," Nick grumbled.

Jane started to reach out to put her hand on Nick's arm in an attempt to soothe and comfort him, to try to make it all better. Then she glanced at Isabel and shook her head. She wasn't going to be that girl anymore. "Again. On the same page. It's been quite the luna de miel," Jane said, repeating the Spanish word for honeymoon they had oft heard from the hotel staff, who congratulated them at every turn.

Suddenly Señor Ramon burst out laughing. Not only had he at last understood their predicament, but he'd also understood the larger situation. He laughed and laughed and then turned to his sister and spoke in a rapid-fire Spanish which neither Jane nor Nick could hope to follow. That was all right. They already knew the story.

Isabel looked at her brother wide-eyed and then she too burst out laughing. "Luna de miel?" she repeated astounded.

Jane smiled and tried to look innocent. Nick turned beet red and was shuffling his feet uncomfortably. When Isabel could finally catch her breath she stood, walked over to one of the shade trees by the house, and pulled on a short rope. A large bell hanging from the branches called out with a hollow *dong!* and before long all the women who had been working in the sun-bright fields made their way up to the tiny house. Joining them was the teenage boy and the man who had been lounging in the shade.

The group gathered around Señora Isabel, who, with that same smile on her face, simply turned and looked at Ramon. Jane counted nine women with the two men. Señor Ramon spoke slowly, and with great dignity, to the assembled group. No one laughed aloud as he explained the situation, but many of them hid surreptitious smiles, nonetheless.

After the Señor finished what Nick and Jane surmised was his explanation, no one moved or said a word. All was still for a long, uncomfortable moment. Jane wondered what was happening. Then Señor Ramon nodded and waved a hand. The group broke up and started to walk to the far side of the small cinder-block dwelling, breaking into groups, and whispering and giggling excitedly.

Señor Ramon turned to the young couple. "I am old man and not well. I cannot go." He pronounced every syllable of the English words carefully. "But they take you. They help you. Best luck." He smiled broadly. "Feliz luna de miel."

Jane and Nick thanked both him and Isabel, Jane with tears in her eyes, and then followed the crowd. As she rounded the corner, she pulled up short and Nick bumped into her from behind, nearly knocking her over.

"Oh my." She stared ahead. "You've got to be kidding me."

Chapter 22

"That's a relic," Nick said, staring ahead of them.

"I'm sure at one point in time, that was a truck. Yeah, a large truck." The rescue party just climbed in and perched carefully atop old tires and other dangerous looking, sharp metal debris which had been tossed in the bed. The hood was up. "Do you think it runs?" Jane whispered into Nick's ear as he helped her into the bed along with everyone else. After a moment's indecision, like everyone, she picked her way across the trash, rusted old metal, and tires, and wondered when she'd last had a tetanus shot. She figured if you couldn't even remember, that couldn't be good. "How many people spend time on their honeymoons thinking about tetanus shots?"

Nick gave a quiet little snort in return.

The middle-aged man was apparently the driver. He made several unsuccessful attempts to get the engine to turn over. Then he got out and started fiddling under the hood. Jane and Nick exchanged worried glances as they heard the clangs of metal on metal. "Is he pounding on the engine?" she whispered to Nick, who just shrugged in return. "Does that work?"

"What do I know about lorries?"

Jane tried to distract herself by striking up a conversation with the women. "So, what are you growing in the fields?" She gestured broadly.

Through a plastered-on smile and gritted teeth, Nick hissed, "Don't ask about the crops. Just. Don't. Ask."

Jane blinked a couple of times, and then pointed to herself and said "Jane. Me llamo Jane."

They gave her their names, which she found hard to understand with their strong accents.

"Hortense?" she asked, having gotten her first two attempts wrong. The woman nodded and smiled.

She tried another, finally getting a "Si! Si!" when she slowly repeated "Eee-seen-i-ah", but she had no idea of how to spell that or what that name might translate to in English. She turned to a third woman and raised her eyebrows in invitation, worried what the impossible-to-understand name might be.

"Maria."

"Maria! Yes, I can say that one!" Jane said excitedly and felt relieved. The banging and clanging from the engine compartment was now accompanied by loud exclamations from the middle-aged man. She leaned over to Nick. "What do you think he's saying?"

"Oh, Jane, cursing is unmistakable in any language!"

Before she could think of an answer, the truck's engine turned over, accompanied by shouts of triumph, which were also understandable in any language. The truck slowly pulled away from the little farmhouse, rumbling and bumping down the dusty driveway and onto the dirt lane. They truly were in the middle of nowhere without a proper road in sight. She thought that being this remote, they probably could grow any crops out here at all. That thought made her heart race as she suddenly understood Nick's directive to "just not ask".

The women continued to whisper to one another and giggle, surreptitiously stealing glances at Nick.

Jane leaned into Nick. "What do you think they're saying?"

"I'm sure they're having a good laugh about me." Suddenly he sounded very earnest and humble. "I'm dreadfully sorry, Jane. I really wish I'd heard you about those tracks." He looked at the women surrounding him. Every face had a smile on it. "But I'm sure they're remarking on what a total tosspot your brand-new husband is."

"Huh. How about that? I always heard that the women down here were very wise." She gave him a wink as he grimaced at her. Her old habits took over and she patted him on the arm in reassurance. But he was trying too now, and she appreciated that.

They passed the turn off where the Jeep had met its fate, and Nick leaned around to the driver's window, shouting, "Por favor, Señor, here! Here! Aqui! Aqui!"

The driver just smiled and waved and drove on.

Now Nick and Jane shared concerned looks. "Where's he taking us? What have we gotten ourselves into?"

A few bumps down the road, Nick mumbled, "Out of the frying pan...."

Jane looked at her new husband and the others in the truck bed, trying to hide the worry she felt with a friendly little smile, but her lip trembled. She wanted to seem confident and collected with these strangers, who she was now totally and completely dependent upon, but all she could focus on was remembering how to plead for her life in Spanish. The truck slowed down and came to a halt at a little shack next to the dusty dirt path. Another middle-aged man came out and spoke to the driver, who turned off the engine.

"Why did he turn the engine off?" Jane whispered. That tremor vibrated in her voice.

Nick whispered back, "Bloody hell! It would be a bloody miracle to get this heap running again!" Then he jumped over the side and walked up to the two men who were now conversing in rapid-fire Spanish. Nick did his best to communicate. The new man looked at him and said almost intelligibly, "My tractor... broke."

"Oh! Tractor!" Nick said with relief.

"No, broke." The man shook his head and turned to walk back in the house.

Jane was pretty sure that her heart and Nick's were in a dead-heat to see which one could sink the furthest, fastest.

A moment later, the new man came out bearing two shovels. He loaded them into the back, with the rest of the people and debris, and then climbed into the bed himself. Wondering why he hadn't climbed into the cab where there were proper seats, Jane turned around to look through the dirty rear window: the bullmastiff was staring lovingly back at her, drooling heavily.

"Hi, little buddy," she cooed at him, but the lack of enthusiasm was evident in her voice. "Remember, don't eat me. I don't taste like chicken."

Nick was sitting next to her again. He looked at the drooling dog and then back at his wife. "Oh, bloody hell. I'm afraid that to him, everything tastes like chicken. And you know, everyone likes to eat chicken."

Jane couldn't help the little shiver that went up her spine.

Somehow the driver managed to get the engine going again, and with some difficulty, he turned the relic around. This time on their journey, he turned up the lane Nick had anxiously pointed to and before long everyone could see the Jeep as it lay half-buried in the sand, looking like a modern, miniature Sphinx. Jane couldn't help the giggle that escaped her lips.

Nick looked at her expectantly. "What's so funny?"

She opened her mouth to speak and then just shook her head. "The stress is getting to me. I'm just losing my mind, that's all."

"Oh, I beat you to that!"

The driver wisely parked the truck on the mud flat at the base of the dune and again killed the engine. Everyone and the bullmastiff piled out. The dog took Jane's forearm in its mouth once again, drooling all over her arm in the process.

"Stay calm. Stay calm and carry on," Jane murmured and then started to baby-talk the dog again, which resulted in more back-end wiggles. She wished the happy wags didn't translate into the nips from the sharp teeth on her wrist. "Do dogs in Mexico get routine rabies shots like their American cousins?"

Nick just shrugged.

They all walked up to the Jeep where there was a fresh round of laughter. Nick beamed one of his most charismatic little boy smiles, but Jane could tell that he was faking it. The women certainly seemed to be moved by Nick's pouring on of the charm and Jane was amazed that he could still look so handsome after their ordeal. For her part, she was sure she looked a fright.

"Well, men, let's get to work!" Nick slapped his hands together and the two men and the teenager joined him at the half-visible jeep, digging with shovels or hands. The dog even relinquished its hold on Jane's arm, and as she wiped the slobber off on her shirt, the dog gave two loud, excited barks, and started to join in the efforts, huge paws moving mountains of sand that all just slid back into place.

After a few minutes of the women watching their efforts, Hortense rolled her eyes and clapped twice sharply. The crisp sounds breaking the air stilled the men's activity and even the massive bullmastiff stopped and sat down, ears perked up, looking at Hortense as though she were the Alpha.

Hortense started barking directions and the women encircled the stranded car, pushing the men out of the way. She motioned for Nick to climb in and for Jane to stand back. Then, on her signal, the women started to push the car. Hortense motioned again to Nick, who started the engine. The car started to rock with the efforts of the silent crew. The menfolk joined in, lending their strength and their many grunts and groans while the dog excitedly ran circles around the group, barking encouragement. The women laughed at them and pushed harder. Jane wished she had a camera, but her phone was still sitting in the glove box of the Jeep.

After rocking the vehicle back and forth several times, it burst forth from the sand as though it were being born of it. Everyone cheered, raising their hands and dancing in the joy of their victory. Jane felt her heart race as the once displaced wheels pulled back into their proper places, as if to answer Jane's unspoken prayer through the miracle of four-wheel independent suspension. Other than being suspiciously full of sand, no one could ever have guessed the adventure this particular Jeep Grand Cherokee had just been through. Jane promised herself that one day she would own one of these cars. Still cheering, the women all hugged each other, and then Jane. The men patted each other on the back, as if they had done all the work, and then they brought Nick into their circle and started patting him on the back as well. The bullmastiff barked in excitement and jumped around happily.

Jane felt unfettered joy. Joy and gratitude—emotions which required no translation at all. "Gracias! Gracias," was all Jane could say over and over again, tears streaming down her face as her calm exterior melted away. She had mustered bravery in the face of too many unknowns, and now she was spent. She had nothing left and all she wanted to do was cry tears of relief.

The locals piled back into their truck and, with many calls of "¡Buena suerte!" and "¡Feliz luna de miel!" drove off, the engine having magically turned over at the first try. Nick and Jane waved back and then just sat in the Jeep as their rescuers disappeared out of sight. It was all over so fast.

Nick sat in the driver's seat as the car was running. "Want to go to the beach? We could make another try for it?" Nick said, his voice full of determination, as he put the car into first gear.

"What!"

"Relax. I'm just kidding." He backed the jeep down the slope to the relative safety of the mud flat, and then killed the engine. "C'mon. After all we've been through, we really are a couple of jammy dodgers! We should at least see this beach. Let's take the beers. Mind how you go."

Jane was amazed that Nick seemed alive and excited for the first time in, well, months if she was being honest. As if all this adventure, now that it was behind them, had been some kind of exhilarating release for him. They packed up the beers they had purchased at the gas station where they had gotten their useless directions and headed over the dune—on foot this time—leaving the Jeep safely behind. The dune was tall and hot, but the blue of the ocean on the other side softened their traumatic experience just a bit. They sat on their shirts, lounging in the bathing suits they had worn under their clothes when they left the hotel that morning. They sat and sipped on bottles of very warm, very bad beer.

Wincing at the flavor in her mouth, Jane said, "In comparison to the rest of our day, this is a perfect moment." She looked up and down the beach. There was no one in sight. They sat next to one another, but Nick didn't answer her. Time passed and the silence grew deeper. Jane didn't know what to say. She didn't know what to think. She had been so happy, believing that in Claudine's coin toss of love she had flipped a solid "heads" in Nick. But now she wasn't so sure. If this was landing heads up, it wasn't turning out to be quite what she'd expected.

Nick stared out over the ocean as though he'd never seen one before: he was mesmerized. He seemed happy. She studied him. None of his recent behavior logically followed on from their years together. How could you know someone for so long… and then suddenly out pops a different side to them? She was utterly baffled. Exhaling a deep breath, she looked past him to the small mountain in the distance and was struck by the sheer beauty of the scene before her. It comforted her. The deserted beach made a crescent, cupping an ocean so blue it was hard to believe it could be real. To her right, beyond Nick in the distance, a couple of horseback riders were making their way up the beach, that lone large hill their scenic backdrop. She marveled how her day could have been such an epic disaster and then turnaround and leave them in this picturesque scene. Again, she wished she had a camera with her—in her mental exhaustion she had once again left her phone in the Jeep. So, she tried to commit all that beauty to memory. As the horses approached, they rode right up to Nick and Jane.

The woman said something excitedly in Spanish.

Her companion answered her and then turned to Jane. "Well, I didn't expect you until the end of the week! But I'm glad you came! You found us!"

Nick turned to her. "Do you know this bloke?" He looked confused.

Jane looked up, shielding her eyes from the sun. "Gregg? Wow! I can't believe you just rode up here. This is amazing! Nick, you remember Gregg from the plane? And you met his wife, Fabiola, at baggage claim."

"This day just gets weirder and weirder. Totally rum." Nick shook his head but stood up to shake Gregg's hand.

"We can get you some of that!" Gregg said with a laugh. Gregg and Fabiola insisted that Nick and Jane come back to the plantation with them, showing them how to drive around and find the real road to the house. Their coconut plantation was incredible. In anticipation of their visit, Gregg had filled the pool with the water from the underground cistern, explaining how they used the stored rainwater to fill the brick-lined pool, swim in it for a few days, and then open the gates, irrigating the coconut groves. "All this water is fresh as fresh. We just finished filling it last night, so your timing is perfect!"

He picked up coconuts from the ground, cut them open with a machete, and served them the freshest coconut Jane had ever tasted. Fabiola cooked up a wonderful meal that they heartily enjoyed, accompanied by ice cold beers. Good ones. Afterwards, they swam in the clear, cool rainwater-filled pool while Fabiola brought them her specialty rum drinks made with fresh coconut milk. She said something in Spanish to Gregg and he answered, "Si, si absolutamente!"

Jane swam over to Gregg and asked, "What did she say?"

"She said you two look like you're having the best honeymoon day ever!"

Jane and Nick both burst out laughing, but didn't recount their adventure.

As it turned out, Gregg specialized in sustainable building. He had been an early pioneer in California, but his recent health problems had set him back and made him less active in the field. Although he was just fifty-five, he was semi-retired to spend more time with Fabiola here in Baja, while he had the time to spend. Nick and Gregg had an endless conversation about green design, and Nick seemed to recover even more of his old self. As night fell, Fabiola drew them another map, one they could understand this time, and they drove the jeep back to their hotel without a problem, arriving a little after ten o'clock.

After a much-needed shower, Jane lay in bed that night unable to believe the bizarre day she had experienced. Nick snored heavily beside her. She got up on one elbow and looked at him. "Something is wrong. Something is wrong with you. Why won't you tell me?"

The only answer she got came in his snores.

Chapter 23

Jane raised her right hand, catching a bit of a breeze and signaled the waiter. It took a minute for him to cross the expanse of white sand. She waited, baking in the hot sun.

"Si, Señora?"

"Por Favor, uno Margarita. La mucho grande."

"Si, ensequida." The man smiled at her.

She knew the margarita would be excellent. Everything here was excellent.

Well, almost everything, she thought. She lay on the white beach chair, molded to accommodate the shape of a reclining beach-goer, and felt the hot sun on her skin, little patches of fire that moved around, jumping from one point of awareness to the next. First, she could feel the heat on her thighs, warm to burning hot. Then it would register on her face. The light of the sun reflected off her cheeks, which would slowly tan, then freckle, then burn if she stayed out here long enough. She didn't really care.

A drop of sweat slid slowly from behind her ear down her neck to her chest, between her breasts and finally lost itself someplace on her skin below. She could feel the sun searing her stomach. Every once in a while, a light breeze would kiss her skin, touch the fine hairs on her arms like a welcome caress. But the breezes on this tropical beach were few and far between today.

It wasn't supposed to be this way, kept ringing in her head like the endless Pacific waves upon the sand. *It wasn't supposed to be this way.* Inevitably followed by, *How could this have happened to me?*

This was the type of thing that happened to someone else. Not someone you actually knew. No, not that. But the cousin of a friend of a friend who you'd met once in a bar or at an airport or something. Or that you'd read about in a story online, with some third-party narrator recounting the O.P.'s point of view. But it never happened to people you knew. And certainly, it never happened to you.

You remained in the background. You didn't stand out. Your life didn't read like some horrible made-for-streaming movie. That was someone else's life.

But it did happen to me.

It is happening to me.

Why me? How? ran through her mind in some pathetic whining little voice that echoed the *shhhh* the sand made as the receding wave dragged it out to sea against its will. *Shhh ... Why me?... Silence... Crash!... Shhh... Why me?*

How could she silence that voice? *Might as well try to silence the sea,* she thought as she sat up, wondering where her margarita was. The effort made her heart race for a moment or two. Or maybe she was just over-hot and over-tired. Looking at the expanse of brilliant blue laid out before her, she tried to calm her mind. A decision. Maybe that was what had made her heart race. A decision. *I have to make a decision.*

She looked around for the waiter. Across the sandy expanse, he was walking towards her carrying her icy cold drink. It wasn't like in the pictures, though. No coat and tie, no tray held above his head in some grand balancing act. He was dressed in a shirt and baggy pants of loose white cotton, and he was not proper, but rather island-friendly. He was part of the tropical perfection of this place.

"Señora." He presented her the drink.

"Gracias." She accepted it with what she hoped was a smile. It was an effort.

Sweat had beaded up on the outside of the glass in the few short minutes the frozen liquid had resided there. Jane could feel the wetness of the hard surface as she held the giant goblet between her two hands and smelled its cool, sour, saltiness. It was excellent. Everything was. No mention of cost, no tipping, no questions—ever. Why was she alone? No one asked. She could drink herself to death here on this beach and no one would even so much as bat an eyelash.

Yes, everything here was excellent. Except for her. She was miserable. *It wasn't supposed to be this way...* She lay back on her chair careful not to spill her drink.

Regularly, like the waves on the shore, *why me,* floated across her mind, followed by: *I have to make a decision,* with the ocean echoing *shhh... shhh....*

Even in paradise, there was no escape.

She felt frozen, like the concoction trapped in ice-hard glass between her hands. Frozen in emotion while her body baked in the sun, sweat beading up on her surface. *It doesn't always end up like this. It didn't for Summer. Or Caroline. Or even Claudine. No. Their lives were different. Why?* Why had their lives turned out so different from her own? She had years and years invested in this. All her hopes and dreams. All her desires. Where had she gone so wrong? The moment was impossible to pinpoint.

"At least impossible this side of ten years in therapy". She grimaced and sighed, her chest falling, her exhale making her head spin for a moment. It was too much effort to time-trip over a lifetime. She had invested so much to believe in Nick. To believe in their love. That they were two sides of the same coin, two halves of a whole. They had said they would always find their way back to each other—and they had, time and time again. But there was some saying she'd read someplace, said by someone much wiser than she would ever be... something about in a pitched battle between perception and reality, perception always wins. She'd seen what she wanted to see. Believed what she'd wanted to believe. What troubled hopes and dreams had led her here to this beach in paradise where she was going to get stinking drunk on expensive margaritas and earn herself a truly impressive sunburn?

She looked at the drink balanced between her fingers, salt-rimmed and frozen just as she liked it. She took a sip of its cold sweet and sour taste. Sweet and sour. That was just like life, wasn't it? She had always joked that margaritas were the elixir of life, but this wasn't exactly what she'd meant. *I have to make a decision....*

Jane touched the rim of the giant glass and then rolled the crystals of salt between her fingertips, feeling their sharp rough edges, humming the tune to a sad song she couldn't quite remember.

Maybe I should have listened?

When something so powerful speaks to you, irrational though it may be, maybe you should listen? Chase had said, "Always go with your gut". She couldn't see it then, but now the stark reality bit at her hard.

"But I did listen. Or rather, I heard. I just didn't know what to do about it."

Just last night she had confronted Nick. She needed to know why he was drinking so much. Why he was chain smoking. Why that whole event with the Jeep had happened. As she looked in the mirror, brushing her hair before they were to go to dinner, she had stopped, brush in mid-stroke, frozen with realization. She had walked up to Nick. He was relaxing on the chaise on their balcony and texting someone, another scotch next to him and a cigarette in his mouth. She had walked up to him in her slinky little black dress. He had looked up at her, given her a once over and commented how very nice she looked, nearly dropping his burning cigarette onto his shirt. She had taken the phone from him. Apparently, he thought they were going to have a romantic moment, but instead she started to read it.

Very calmly, her voice quiet and unemotional she asked, "Nick, why did Astrid send you a text calling you a pig? That you broke her and Ashlyn up?"

Nick just stared at her, unable to speak. She went to the foot of his lounge chair and sat down. She handed him the phone, asking him the question she already knew the answer to.

"How long have you and Ashlyn been sleeping together?" She was amazed at the lack of anger in her voice. It was just out there. She felt a strange sense of total calm.

Nick stared at the ocean and took a long draw on his cigarette. "Since France. She showed up at the cabin four days into my stay there. Said I had to sign some contracts. Said I had to make some… business decisions. Stayed."

"Oh," Jane answered neutrally. "I see. She's been at your side a lot lately."

Nick nodded. "She's taking over my role when I leave. I've been training her."

"It's still going on?" Jane worked hard to keep her voice as unemotional as she could muster.

"No, it's over. I won't see her again. Greigh told me I should never let you know. I should just put it behind me. It's why he wouldn't be my best man. Or even come. None of them would. It's been eating me up, Jane, not telling you. It's been tearing me apart. But they all said I should never tell you."

"Tearing you apart. Yes, I can see that. I knew something was terribly wrong. I just couldn't figure out what." Jane took a slow breath, willing herself to stay calm.

"Well, I didn't want it to tear you apart too."

"It did, though. I just didn't understand what was happening to me."

Nick crushed out his cigarette. Eventually he turned to look at her. "I swear it's over, Jane. It will never happen again. I swear it. We're married now. It's just you and me."

"Nick, when was the last time you saw her?"

It took him longer to answer than she would have expected, given the relative ease and the lack of shouting or drama in this conversation. "Before I left England."

"How soon before?"

Again, a long pause. "Just," he finally said.

"Just. So, she saw you just before you left? She what? Drove you to the airport?" Jane wondered at her own voice. It was almost like she was making a joke.

"Well, yes," Nick said and downed the rest of the scotch in his glass.

"She drove you to the airport." Jane blinked a few times. "And she's been texting you constantly. Even at the wedding itself…." Her voice drifted off. "Nick, why did you go through with the wedding? Why did you marry me, if all this was going on?"

His face turned towards her so slowly that it looked strange. "I know in my heart that you and I are meant to be together. We will always find our way back to one another. Nothing can stop that. Two sides of the same coin. Of course I came back to you. I will always come back to you."

Jane sat back. It had sounded so romantic when he'd said that in years past. It crossed her mind that her accident on the ice pre-dated the start of his affair… so that little voice had been quite prescient. And then a horrible question popped into her head, almost like that voice was whispering to her again: "Was the honeymoon in France… Ashlyn's idea?"

The abashed look on his face was all the answer she needed.

The joke's on me. Haltingly, she said, "I think I'm going to go for a walk. I'll be back in a little while."

As she was about to head out the door he called out, "You know, you'll always come back to me too. It's our destiny to be together. We are two sides of the same coin. You'll get over this. We'll put it behind us."

Despite her discomfort with heights, she found herself sitting at the edge of a cliff overlooking the ocean as it crashed over rocks some sixty feet below. Her feet, still in her sexy black heels, dangled over the edge as she cried and cried until she felt numb. It would be so easy, so easy to simply fall off the cliff. So easy to stop feeling the tumult in her heart and instead feel it in the waves all around her. Siren-like, the breaking waves below called to her. As they crashed on the rocks, she kicked off her expensive heels, leaned forward and watched them disappear into the chaos of white foam and breaking waves. A little bit of the cliff edge crumbled underneath her left hand and her upper body slid forward, sending her off balance.

That jolted her.

Slowly, she pulled back and sat up, realizing that the exorcism of the tears was starting to calm her heartache enough to allow her sensible fear of heights to grab a hold of her again. Now she glanced down at the sharp rocks and saw only the certain death they held for the desperate or lovelorn, clumsy or unfortunate. Carefully, she leaned back and inched away from the unstable cliff edge until she felt she could stand without fear of accidentally falling off. Her heart was racing, pounding in her ears. She felt she had just narrowly escaped something, but whether it was the crumbling edge of the cliff, Nick, Ashlyn, or something else, she wasn't sure.

When she got back to the hotel room, her feet dirty and sore, her ankle aching, her dress a muddy mess, she found that Nick wasn't there. He was probably in the bar, but she didn't bother to go looking for him. He came in at two in the morning and she woke up as he bumbled around the room. He apologized again. He begged her to forgive him, getting down on his knees, tears streaming down his face. It broke her heart to see him like this. Almost against her will she held him as he sobbed into her stomach and she sobbed standing over him. She didn't speak a word. They made love, but it was slow and clumsy. It didn't feel like forgiveness or starting over or even goodbye—it was just going through the motions.

When she woke up in the morning, he was next to her, sleeping heavily. She got up and headed alone down to the beach. He never showed up, but that was okay. She didn't really want to see him. Her ticket home was for tomorrow. She certainly didn't have the ability to think clearly enough to do anything but drink margaritas and think about the cliffside. She'd let more than her shoes fall into the oblivion of the rocks and waves. She tried to sort out what part of her remained. What part of her survived the trial and had come back to testify about the experience. She listened intently, but that voice in her head was either silent or gone.

She lay on the lounge chair, ice cold margarita in hand and heavy realization in her heart. *I have to make a decision....*

The ocean was piercingly blue. There was no other way to describe it. Piercing. Jane heard a *tap, tap* next to her, and saw a few feet away a peacock starting to approach her palapa, looking for food. She had always thought of peacocks as blue and green, beautiful, but these were rather plain birds. Their cries were unnerving, like someone being murdered, suffering unendurable pain. "Snap! Know just what you mean," Jane said aloud to the bird. It looked at her, cocking its head. Then it turned and stretching its large wings, took to the air and flew off in the direction of the restaurant. Jane watched as it became smaller and smaller in the distance.

It was time. It was time to make a decision and move on. The bird was right. For all that its brain weighed a half an ounce, Jane thought it had more sense than she did. She'd flipped that stupid coin and now she had to be brave enough to look at it and make the call. Perception wasn't going to win this pitched battle. Reality was going to win. She was going to embrace reality here and now and forever more. Jane the dreamy wallflower had come on this trip. A different Jane was going back home. She didn't know quite who this woman was, but she was interested in finding out. She stood up, her head slightly clearer, and brushed the patches of sand from her body. Bending over to pick up her towel, she heard again the spine-chilling scream of a peacock in the distance. She slid her feet into her battered blue Birkenstocks and grabbed the brightly painted, hand-carved wooden tropical fish that served as a key chain for her room and started slowly across the sand to her villa. She had a phone call to make.

Chapter 24

Jane exited from the security gates with all the other passengers, home from holiday or starting a business trip. Beginnings or endings for each—and in her case, both at once. Charlie and Summer were there to meet her. Jane walked up to them. No one said anything for a while.

"Baggage claim?" Summer finally broke the tension.

Jane nodded. As they stood waiting for her single suitcase, Jane opened her mouth a couple of times, but nothing came out.

"Oh, Janie!" Charlie broke down and wrapped her arms around her sister.

Summer put a hand on each of them. "Janie, you don't have to talk about it. We're here. We'll do whatever you want."

Charlie nodded and took a step back, giving Jane some room. Jane nodded. "Oh, there's my bag." The requirements of the mundane tasks before them helped them navigate the awkwardness of the moment. While Summer and Charlie shared family news and talked about what had happened in the world in the last week, Jane didn't say anything else until they got her back to her condo.

They carried her luggage in for her and she took a deep breath and gave them each a hug. "Thanks guys. I'll talk to Mom and Dad. Maybe tomorrow. I'm not ready to face them yet. Or anyone."

"Do you want me to stay with you?" Charlie asked.

"Charlie, you're headed to Costa Rica in what? Days? You've got to get ready for your trip. You want to get into medical school, right?

This medical mission trip is important for you. You don't need to be distracted by me."

"Right now, you're more important. I don't have to go to Costa Rica." Charlie tried to give her an encouraging smile.

"Yes, you do!" Jane said. "Don't worry. I'm not suicidal or anything. If I were gonna do that, I would've thrown myself off that cliff. After all, that would've been pretty easy. I mean, it was crumbling beneath me as I sat there. It was actually harder to not fall."

Behind Jane's back Charlie and Summer exchanged shocked looks.

"I just need some time to think. I told Nick to find his own way home, back to England where he belongs. Not with me. I'm sure he's doing much worse than I am at present." She thought of his serious lack of coping skills. "I'll be okay. It's just going to take some time."

"Oh Janie…" Charlie's voice cracked.

Jane hugged her little sister. "Hey, you, get it together or you'll make me cry. I'm on a break from crying for at least twenty-four hours, or I'll dry up and blow away! Look, when you get back at the end of the summer, you won't even recognize me! I won't be this broken little girl I am now. I'm going to be all right—I promise you."

She felt some unnamable but welcome wave flow over her. It felt almost like… well, like peace. Like when she had heard that whisper and felt that awareness break across her mind of impending doom, only now she somehow knew that it was going to be okay. It might take a while, but in the end, everything was going to be all right. Maybe life could feel like a coin toss because no matter how much work you put into it, there was an element of luck or fate. It was beyond your control. And Jane had just flipped tails. That sucked, sure, but it wasn't the end. She'd get more chances to experience love and it wouldn't always land on tails. Jane was amazed that inside, deeper than the pain and heartbreak, was a somewhat profound sense of calm.

"Really, guys, you can go. Summer, I'm sure you need to nurse that baby in the worst way by now."

Summer laughed. "Yes, actually."

Jane heard a genuine laugh coming from her own voice. She felt herself relax and could see that her sisters started to relax as well. Charlie and Summer gave Jane another round of hugs.

"Lunch tomorrow?" Charlie asked.

"Sure, lunch tomorrow."

"You promise?"

Jane looked at her little sister and then gave her another hug. "Of course, I promise. I'll see you off before you go. Tomorrow."

After they left, Jane walked over to a picture of her and Nick, smiling and happy. She felt a pang of sadness. "It was never going to work out between us. Who knew?" She stared at the picture for a while thinking about the bizarre honeymoon trip and the even stranger six months before that.

Would she ever love someone with the abandon with which she had loved Nick? Her first love. In so many ways, he had become her identity. Her wallflower made visible by his light. The proof of her self-worth and lovability. At one time she had believed that no matter what, somehow, they would always find their way back to one another, just like he used to say.

"Find our way back to one another." The words hung heavily in the air. "Is that what I really want to come back to?"

She drifted over to the stack of mail awaiting her. Bills, advertisements, and a box with the necklace and a sealed envelope from the jeweler. "Apparently Mom's been here," she mumbled, "totally forgot about that."

Curious, she opened the envelope, pulling out a tri-folded, crisp, and surprisingly thick piece of paper. It had a very celebratory-looking border decorating it, fancy script in the title, and a picture of the necklace on the form. The description went on to read, ladies silver plate and blue-stoned necklace, imitation sapphire... She blinked and shook her head. Going to the bottom of the form, she saw, estimated value: $150.

"Were you duped, you stupid fool, or is this just another layer of lies?" Blowing out her breath, she picked up the picture of her and Nick, folded the appraisal form around it and dropped them both into the trash, frame and all, hearing the glass break as it landed. "You know what? I would rather be alone for the rest of my life than spend five more minutes with you. Goodbye Nick."

The rest of her life alone. She thought about that. It sounded like a long time. Was she sure about that? She was ready to be on her own for a while, but the rest of her life?

Eventually, someday, she would be ready to fall in love again. Surely. Surely, she would. And when she did, she hoped that it wasn't going be a lifetime of flipping tails.

"It'll be okay. I'm not the same girl I was."

Chapter 25
Ten Years Later

Jane walked down the street, looking at her phone. "Okay, you have to be around here somewhere." Her phone kept telling her she'd "arrived", but she couldn't see the restaurant where she was supposed to meet Claudine. A cheery *bing!* alerted her of a text message, but seeing the sender made her heart sink.

"Ugh. Not you again." Full of self-recrimination, she went back to her maps app as she muttered under her breath, "I'm in Rome, one of my favorite places in the world. You are not going to take that away from me." Speaking very firmly to herself, she said, "You are not the same girl you were. And you are *not* finding your way back there again."

One of her favorite sayings came to mind: In a pitched battle between perception and reality, perception always wins. Where had she heard that? She couldn't remember and made a mental note to look it up. After all, if you had a favorite saying, you really should know where it came from. However, at the moment, the truth of that particular axiom felt daunting.

"The trick is to avoid the battle. Don't let yourself fall for that. Don't set yourself up for it. Stay with reality."

Reality turned out be a bit of a challenge, however—particularly as the years rolled on by. Sometimes perception was so much more alluring. So much more abundant with hope and promise. Or longing. Or memory. Certainly more alluring than the loneliness she now lived with. Grimacing, she went back to texts and trashed the intruding message. She hoped that she was listening to her own sage advice because some things needed to be left in the past. She'd learned that the hard way, hadn't she? Even though the years rolled by slowly.

"Present moment," she told herself. "Time to be in the present moment. All those promotions you worked so hard for and now you get the Rome trips. Be in Rome."

Rome. She loved Rome. Everything about Italy, really. Italy was her favorite European country. Well, maybe she didn't love how the directions on the app never quite matched up with reality, or how roads always curved around and became something else. In Germany, all the lines were straight and all the names were accurate. Italians, however, had an apt reaction when they shrugged and said, "Eh?" as they smiled and happily moved on, unperturbed by the quirkiness of their homeland. That was life, si? And life was a little bit "ish", just like the map she was trying to follow. She looked away from her phone and towards the buildings around her. Evening was coming on, making it harder to find the signs Claudine told her to look for.

"Jane! Jane!" A heavy French accent caught her attention.

She turned around and there was Claudine, standing outside a nondescript door Jane had walked right past. Indeed, the place was a hole-in-the-wall and hard to spot. Maybe it was the flattering evening light, but Jane felt a sense of amazement at how Claudine never seemed to age even after knowing one another for almost fifteen years.

"Thank you for coming out and flagging me down! I never would have found it."

Claudine gave her a hug. "It's of no moment, my friend. Come, I have seats at the bar. It is, unfortunately, a bit crowded in there, so no table for us. But the bar seems very unpopular, which I think may because the bartender seems rather grouchy, so we shall have it to ourselves. A good place for us to talk and catch up!"

"I'm fine with the bar," Jane reassured Claudine. They went inside and took their seats at the line of empty tall chairs. Jane looked around, thinking how wonderful it was to be back in the land she loved so much. The smells of the food, the sounds of the street, the lively Italian chatter in the background. "So, Claudine, how have you been? You were so busy, things were so crazy, the last time we talked."

Claudine waved away the comment. "Ah! I am working, working, working all the time. But now and then I take the time to sneak out to meet you. And here we are, both in Roma. Is good, no? And it has been months and months since we have seen each other. Almost a year this time, oui?"

"Too long! I'm so glad we're here at the same time. How lucky for us. It's just great to be together again!"

A man wearing a shlumpy cowboy hat and boots clumped his way into the restaurant and seeing no open tables, stood at the bar. He chose a spot unfortunately close to Claudine, even though every other seat at the counter was unoccupied.

Claudine didn't seem to notice "Oui! We can now catch up on our lives, not on a video screen, and feel like we are constantly interrupting one another with the those awkward lags in transmission."

"But even when we're together in real life we constantly interrupt one another and finish each other's sentences!" Jane laughed, relishing in the warm feeling that came with having a friend so dear to her as Claudine.

"Some things never change."

The bartender brought the two of them menus and handed one to the Cowboy-in-Italy, mistaking him for one of their party. The girls ordered drinks, making a series of complicated special requests and alterations. The bartender looked at them blankly. "Are you sure you do not want to go to someplace like the Starbucks?" His heavy Italian accent failed to hide his sarcasm.

"They don't serve cocktails," Jane answered quite seriously and sounded puzzled. Claudine laughed and gave the man a wink. He sighed heavily and shuffled off to craft their special orders. The Cowboy-in-Italy seemed to find the whole exchange amusing and took the seat right behind Claudine.

Jane looked at her friend. "I see why the bar was not so popular!" She shot a glance at the unfriendly bartender.

Claudine nodded in agreement. Her voice was a bit tentative as she said, "So, how are things? You have also been working, working, working! Tonight is my treat, since we must celebrate your latest big promotion! This is what? The third promotion for you. Your career is fantastique!"

Jane smiled and blushed.

Claudine was all excitement. "You are rising high, no? Career woman. Successful. Independent. Good for you!"

"Thanks. The new job, like my last one, is likely to eat me alive. While I love it, it doesn't leave much time for me, unfortunately." She shrugged and then looked at her watch, which started to buzz.

"Anything important?" Claudine raised an eyebrow.

Jane rolled her eyes. "No, totally not important. My phone is sending me a memory."

"Oh! I love those! Pictures of the children, vacations, holidays, good times!"

Jane shook her head and showed Claudine the image on the tiny screen. Claudine just looked confused, not understanding what she was seeing.

"It's a PowerPoint slide. Of a spreadsheet. Their algorithm picks out what's important to me based on their data mining of all my pictures. Yours shows you your kids. Mine shows me the stuff I want to remember from meetings and presentations at work."

Claudine shook her head, this time to signify her disapproval, as she crossed her arms and gave a *tut, tut, tut* sound. "Well, we will celebrate your promotion anyway."

"I've been doing this job for well over a year already. While it's nice to get the title and salary that goes with it, my smart watch is telling me that I'm dumb at life!"

Claudine pursed her lips and paused a moment. "So, no love interest? No work and life balance? All work and no play could make my Jane an unhappy girl, no?"

"Well, eh, the price of success, I guess." She smiled pleasantly and then felt her eye twitch. Claudine gently laid her hand over Jane's. Jane let out a heavy breath, looked around the restaurant briefly, seeing all the happy couples, and blinking back a threatening tear. Claudine always went right to the heart with arrows that flew straight and true. She was the kind of friend who you could pour your soul out to—and you'd better be quick about it because she was someone you also couldn't hide anything from. She'd guess it before you'd get a chance to say it. Months and months could go by but when they finally saw one another again, it was like they were back in college having heart-to-hearts.

"He's hitting up my phone again," Jane admitted reluctantly.

"Oui? No! Merd! The rat bastard. It has been ten years, can he not move on? Why does he keep trying to pull back at you? What could he possibly have to say?"

"It's the 'I'm a different man now'. The 'You're always on my mind'. And the 'It's always been you. Always will be'. I'm paying the price for my mistake. Remember when I was in England and he was in England..." That was when her perception handily won the battle against reality... until it didn't.

"A year or so ago. Ancient history."

"Yeah, but I think my moment of weakness has given him perpetual hope that history will repeat itself. That no matter what, we will find our way back to each other."

Claudine snapped her fingers as she said, "A blip in time!"

Jane nodded. "Two weeks of madness. Then I came to my senses. I could see he hadn't changed. So now he reaches out, maybe every few months or so, but I'm sure it's only when he's in-between and needs someone to adore him and restore his ego." She shook her head. "I don't want to be an in-between… for anyone."

"So, what do you do when he tries to contact you? Have you changed your number?"

Jane shrugged. "It's too much disruption to change my number. Besides, it's easy to track me down and why should I be the one to have to change everything? It's just handing him a victory when he finds it. The whole process of me hiding gives him too much power."

Claudine clucked her tongue. "Well, just make sure his hope is a false hope."

Jane raised her hand. "Fool, that's me. I admit it." She breathed out sharply. "Nicky turned out to be a total tails. I'm not going there again." She held up her phone. "Delete, delete, delete. I am now looking for the other side of the coin. I want a totally different experience. A different feel. A different pace. Everything different. After all, I'm not the same girl I used to be. I want love and I want it to be nothing like being with Nick."

Claudine held back her smile. Jane didn't notice. "And how is that going?"

Jane looked at Claudine. She wasn't the kind of person you pretended to be brave with. She was a rock and could take whatever was thrown at her. "Dead end street. Turns out, I'm too successful. Can you believe it? My career completely intimidates the men I meet—who all seem to be looking for their personal cheerleader. And meanwhile I keep hearing this *bam! bam! bam!* sound ringing in my ears."

"Oh, my goodness! Jane, what is it?" Claudine's face was stricken with concern.

"Just my biological clock. I'm starting to think that I need to come to terms with the fact that I am more likely to become a CEO than I am a mother."

Claudine chuckled. "You should not scare me like that. And you never know, it could happen."

"I'm like one of those women you read about who disappear on some tropical island vacation. No permanent ties. No husband, no kids, not even a dog at home to miss me if I fell off the face of the earth."

"Now don't you say that! You have your family. Your sisters. Your Caroline—you two are very close. And don't forget me! I would come looking for you." Claudine sat back and looked seriously at Jane. "And your job. You know *they* would come looking for you. You are very important there, also with friends who love you. You have many, many ties."

"Thank you." Jane sniffed, hearing the truth in Claudine's words. "You're right. I'm not alone, but I'm also… well, alone. I'm really starting to get scared that I'm destined to be 'Just Jane'. Jane with a lot of acquaintances but not someone to spend her life with. Maybe there isn't anyone out there for me? Maybe it's all dating that goes no place and leaves you feeling emptied out." She let out a deep breath and said in almost a whisper, "I feel my time running out. I'm in my mid-thirties, Claudine. The statistics just aren't good for someone like me."

Claudine put her hand over Jane's, giving it a squeeze. "I re-read your email about Darren quite a few times. I am sorry."

"Old news that. Hardly left a scar at this point. Glad to be rid of him frankly. I'll just add him and Gage and Roman to that wall of disasters. Along with Nick, that is."

"Roman, that's a good name!"

"It's a good adjective maybe." Jane sighed heavily. "All the men I meet have serious flaws. And just like with Nick, it seems that my coin of love keeps landing with the wrong side up."

Claudine leaned forward. "Flaws like what?" Her eyebrows were raised, leaving Jane to feel as though she was about to be quizzed. Well, in the test of love, she certainly was not getting a passing grade. But the stories could be pretty entertaining… at least they could be if one could enjoy the schadenfreude of those experiences belonging to someone else. Just like her love affair with Nick, she was sure that would make an excellent dark comedy—and she would laugh at it, if only it wasn't her life up there on the screen.

"Well, let's see," Jane said, counting them off on her fingers. "Darren wanted a side game. Lived in that world once, not going there again."

Claudine nodded.

"Roman was really into putting everything about his life on TikTok and Instagram and some new platform that I don't even know. His new dance moves. Us. Stupid shit with milk crates." She shook her head. "The man could not resist a challenge of any sort. I couldn't have a relationship with him while he was already in a serious one with all the social media followers he aspired to have. I'm coming to the conclusion that the men who actually really want to commit are committed. At this point in my life, it's just the dregs left, I'm afraid."

"And Gage?"

Jane shook her head. "Gage had the small man problem." The Cowboy-in-Italy sitting behind Claudine caught Jane's eye. He was studying the drink menu but she had a growing suspicion that he might be listening in on their conversation.

The bartender brought them their drinks with a couple of little plates of extras.

"What's this?" Jane asked.

He still had that rather blank look on his face. "You wanted many changes to your cocktail. So, rather than me make something and you send it back five times, I bring you a little kit. You can dress up your cocktails just as you wish and be your own bartender." If he'd said it nicely, he would have won the bartender of the year award, but instead it came off as not wanting to be bothered by the audacity of their all-too-American special requests—so entitled!

Claudine's lip curled ever so slightly.

"This is fantastic!" Jane said excitedly, staring at the little plates holding a few spirals of lemon, lime and orange peel, a couple of citrus wedges, two tiny pickled onions, cherries, a few olives, sprigs of mint, and two stalks of celery. "It's like a charcuterie board for your drink. Making tapas of cocktails. Love it! And oh my God, I'm getting a whole new idea for my team's next marketing campaign." She quickly took out a notebook from her purse and began to scribble. Claudine laughed and the bartender did a slow eye roll and sauntered off. "This is great! I don't get to do the creative stuff so much anymore. It's all meetings and giving others the thumbs up or thumbs down at this point."

"You were saying the problem with Gage was that he was short?" Claudine brought Jane's attention back once she had completed her notes.

"No, he was tall actually. But he was intimidated by my success, like he felt castrated by the fact that I made more than he did. Way more. It was always competitive with him. He insisted that he didn't want a traditional relationship where he was the big provider. No, he was all for equality. But he also clearly didn't want any competition. I got burned-out on the subtle put-downs that came with that complicated landscape and jetted."

Claudine shook her head knowingly as she took a sip of her drink. "Men can be like that. They say one thing and want another. They say they don't want the pressure of providing for a whole family, but their egos can't let them follow either. They want a woman to commit to them, while they don't actually commit to her. Or they need so much attention, even from strangers."

Jane let out a deep breath. It felt good to talk about it with Claudine. Cathartic, even if it was depressing at the same time. "That describes my social life. Just once, I want the coin to land on heads. I deserve that, don't I? And until then, I guess I'm married to my career." She tasted her drink and then idly picked up one of the lemon zest spirals. She dropped it into the concoction sitting in her glass. "What I would give to meet a guy who was secure enough in himself that he'd be okay with my career." She stirred her cocktail around and was mesmerized by the swirling spiral. "He could let me do me, and he'd do him. If I was the more successful of the two of us, he could just, you know, like just enjoy it."

"Being able to just enjoy life is an important trait," Claudine replied, also playing with her drink, dropping in a slice of cucumber she picked up from the plate.

Jane tore up a bit of mint and sprinkled it in, feeling like she was making a potion, conjuring up the love of her dreams. She poured in a bit of grenadine, watching the liquid diffuse and turn her drink pink. "A guy who didn't want to be the center of attention all the time, or in the limelight."

Claudine dropped a pickled onion into her glass and watched it sink.

Jane picked up a cherry and did the same. "And someone who I could trust." She picked up a lime wedge and squeezed the juice into her glass. "Someone honest and faithful and fun."

Claudine sighed loudly as she stirred her drink. She took a sip. "Perfection! I am a surprisingly good bartender." It was a moment when she looked even more French than usual. Then she sat back and with great seriousness looked at Jane. "You will have to do a little witchcraft, you know? Changement your luck."

Jane laughed at how they were always on the same page, thinking the same thoughts, even when her friend's words were a mix of French and English. "Well then, I'll just take a little sip of my sweet, perfect potion here as the final step in my alchemy experiment and once I drink this, he'll magically pop into being!"

Claudine laughed again, a hearty sound, and then she got serious. "Men like that are a dream. I heard once that no one marries the 'right person' because no one can be perfect. I'm not sure they make those kinds of men anymore, the kind of man as you describe."

"Claudine, to you honesty and candor are just synonyms."

Claudine shook her head. "My English is imperfect, it is true. I do not understand what you mean?"

Jane sighed. "I guess what I was hoping for wasn't the truth of how I want something impossible." She smiled drily. "What I really wanted was the reassurance that someday my prince would come. But of course, not all fairy tales had happy endings, did they? And the modern interpretation of fairy tales is re-cast as all girl-power with finales that celebrate your liberated independence and singledom. Which doesn't sound like much of a fairy tale to me. Liberated independence is my reality and," she picked up her glass again, "here's to a little bit less of reality." She took a large sip, holding the liquid on her tongue and really tasting the flavors, her eyes closed. It was a strong drink and she could feel the burn as it slid down her throat. "I could use a real vacation from reality." *What I would give for another shot at a real love. An old-fashioned fairy tale.* Jane's mind had completely shut out the wisdom she'd been mulling over at the start of her evening. When she opened her eyes, Claudine was staring at her with a wry smile.

"And your conjuring? Did you say a little spell? He might just walk into your life. The future is hard to predict, no?" Then she gave her a wink. "Is that the candor you wanted? Or was that honesty? Because I think it was closer to merde."

Jane chortled despite a wave of sadness. "Maybe. Or it's the fabrication to feed my ego, but I'll take it!"

"You know, merde was a way of wishing you good luck. If the theater was full, the street, she would be full of 'horse's apples' because of all the carriages. It was a way of saying, 'have a good show with a good audience'. So, perhaps it fits candor, honesty, and fabrication—all at the same time."

Jane lifted her drink again and took a small sip. In her mid-thirties the chances of her finding love, of having her dreams fulfilled were, well, nearly nonexistent. "I look at a lot of statistics in my work. Those tell me that it's impossible to just keep flipping tails over and over again… but I do when it comes to relationships. So, I have to at least consider that I might have been gifted with a two-tailed coin when it comes to love."

"No!"

Jane held up her hand and shook her head. "My coin might say: In Love We Trust, but love is a dream. It's a fantasy. It might have happened for you. You and your perfect husband and those three adorable children, but my truth is that the spell I need to conjure up is my own happiness, liberated girl-power that is independent of whether I'm in a relationship or not. If love is a two-tailed coin for me, then I just need to flip other coins." *Damn, Jane. You sound so brave. So together! Your therapist would be so proud. What was her name again?* She liked that brave little voice in her head and quickly tried to shut down the other one, the wallflower voice, way in the back of her brain, that mocked her for it all just being an act.

Claudine gave her a small, sympathetic smile, but before she could speak the Cowboy-in-Italy interrupted. "Evening ladies," he said with a pleasant nod and an endearing smile. "Say, you sheilas wouldn't happen to be waiting for a couple of mates? I'm expecting a buddy of mine to pop on by and what do you say? We could make it a double?"

By the accent, Jane marked him for Australian, which accounted for why his look seemed a bit off and the hat didn't quite fit that classic John Wayne style.

Claudine turned around. "Your offer is so kind, to think that two women at a bar must be lonely and in need of rescuing." At first Jane worried the Aussie might be in for a verbal scorching at Claudine's hand, so she was glad when her friend took a gentler path. "But we must disappoint you. We are having a girls' night out and if you are not a girl, you are not welcome into our conversation. Shoo, now little boy. You go sit someplace else." She waved her hand as if to scoot him away. While Claudine's words were clear, her voice was playful and inviting. Not only would Claudine's admonishment fail to offend, Jane was pretty sure the man would feel welcomed to cozy up right next to them.

The scene caught Jane as funny and she burst out with a laugh. "You know, Claudine, you can be so bold. Bold like a chihuahua." Claudine answered with a playful bark and the stranger gave them a slow smile. It crossed Jane's mind that Claudine might actually be making a mistake. With that smile, she could probably sign him, adding him to the stable of male models she represented.

"Well, ladies, I meant no offense. But I think I'll keep parking my keister right here just the same. Italy's a free country still, right? You go on with your man-bashing and I'll just have a popper while I wait for my buddy." He gave them a roguish wink. "I have to say, it's nice to know that women are feisty in Europe. I thought I might have to go back Down Under to find a sheila worth going toe-to-toe with!"

Jane sighed but found she was smiling in spite of herself as he pulled out his phone and snickered at them.

"Just ignore him, little boy with the funny hat." Claudine scoffed, but she gave him a second look nonetheless and winked at Jane. After they had ordered dinner, she said, "There are advantages when you are working as a team and share a single goal. There are advantages. But we have struggled as well: when two people are each already married to their separate careers, it is hard for them to be in a real relationship together. It is a parallel life."

Jane marveled at how Claudine never phrased anything with an "I think" or "It seems to me". No, she stated her opinion free and clear as though it were known fact. She was so full of confidence.

"And while you may feel married to your career, at least your job is glamorous."

"My job? What do I do? I oversee a team marketing for Airbus. Airplanes to airlines." She picked up and shook her little idea notebook. "I make people want to buy something. And, okay, yeah, it's a something that's really, really big, but let's face it, it's a slightly manipulative way to make a living if you think about it. Marketing is not glamorous." Jane shook her head.

"Mon dieu! You travel to beautiful places. You stay in fabulous hotels. You fly first class. Oui! I think it is glamorous. And as you start to date again, I think you should be very careful of men who want you because of your fame and fortune." Claudine nodded wisely.

Jane burst out laughing. "Fame and fortune? I'm in the wrong world of marketing for that. I don't think my job is something that attracts men. I think it makes them run away."

"Run away?"

"Well, yeah. Guys want someone who's home for them. Someone to take care of them. Someone to walk the dog. Have dinner ready. Take care of everything while the man of the house is bringing home the bacon."

"Bringing home the bacon?"

"Oh, it's an American expression. Making money."

"Oh, oui, sure. So, men don't want a woman with bacon? I think bacon would be very nice."

"I make some good bacon, but no, I don't think modern men want a woman's bacon, at least not mine. The guys I meet seem to resent that I have to travel so much for work. Claudine, I'm on the road eighty percent of the time. When I'm home it's still constant meetings. And God forbid I'm more successful than they are. Ugh, that's a killer to a budding relationship. Once they see my car—or this watch you gave me…" Jane gestured to the Cartier on her wrist.

Claudine waved the comment away. "It is of no moment. I told you, it was free. They give us many trinkets in my business. I wanted you to have it. You never buy yourself anything nice. You have the money. What do you have to spend your money on besides yourself?"

Jane shook her head. She loved the watch and Claudine was right, she would never purchase something like this for herself.

"You should treat yourself."

"It's just not the way I was raised. I come from a simple family. I have simple needs. I'd like someone to make dinner at night. And walk the adorable dog I wish I was at home enough to actually have. And make a home for me."

Claudine held up her finger to quiet Jane and then turned around on her bar stool. "Excusez-moi, Monsieur cow-boy? Are you enjoying our conversation?"

The man sitting behind her slowly turned away from his phone. "Are you talking to me? Well, that's a nice change of pace. I'm waiting for my buddy but it would be way better to talk with a sheila as engaging as you." He flashed his brilliant smile at them again.

"Sorry about my friend. She's very protective," Jane said to the man.

He shrugged and winked at them. "No worries, ladies! I could enjoy having sheilas as beautiful as you walk all over me." He gave them another wink. "And your friend's cute. Cute like a chihuahua."

"Everyone tells me I remind them of a chihuahua. I think one day I will own one, so I can show them the difference." Claudine turned her back to the cowboy. "Jane, I think you should start dating again. I tell you something though—you should not date any more Americans. And never a Brit."

"No, certainly not. Never again."

"And never an Australian. You cannot trust an Australian." Claudine said it most pointedly, earning a snicker from the Aussie behind her.

Jane took the last sip of her cocktail. "So, my friend, you are seriously thinning down the available options. You just took three countries out of the running, all of which offer guys who speak English, which, in my world, is an asset."

Claudine waved her off again and then signaled the bartender to refresh their cocktail glasses. "Maybe a Canadian?"

Jane shook her head. "Nick was actually a Canadian masquerading as a Brit. No Canadians."

"It leaves you the rest of the world. You speak five languages."

"No, no—I don't speak five languages. I can speak in five languages. That does not make me fluent or conversant. So, I'm in Italy—maybe I should try an Italian guy?"

Claudine wrinkled her nose. "The truth is love gets us on the line and we are helpless, like a little fish. Italian, French, Hungarian… you cannot help who you fall in love with."

"Tell me about it," Jane said, but it was more to her empty glass than to her friend. Well, her little magic potion might have tasted wonderful and she definitely felt relaxed, but that was the extent of the power that particular elixir held.

Claudine sighed. "If I could control that, oh, the heartbreak I would have saved myself. And it can be impossible sometimes to really know who people are. Sometimes they present themselves to be someone else. Sometimes they have to." Claudine gave her a nod as she tossed back the remnants of her glass.

Jane looked at her best friend. "You make your life sound like some kind of spy thriller, just listen to you. 'Sometimes people have to present themselves like they're somebody else'," Jane said with a faux French accent. "Why would anyone have to do that? The key, Claudine, is to make sure you fall in love with the right person."

"Oh, oui! In the affairs of the heart the head must be in control? Now that sounds like my Jane!" Claudine raised her now empty glass in mock toast.

"Yeah. That's right. You know, with that French accent, everything you say sounds like you're the absolute authority on love. It's so easy to agree with you—all too easy. But I'm standing my ground. You can't let your heart run away with you. You have to be a good judge of character."

"And are you now a good judge of character?" Claudine looked at her, a mix of sympathy and curiosity on her face.

"Absolutely. After Nick, I'm the best judge of character. Just look at all the guys I've tossed since him. I'm not the girl I was." The two women looked at each other, serious for a moment, and then they both started to giggle.

Still talking on his phone as he sat behind Claudine, the cowboy started to laugh as well. The women could hear his buddy on the other end answer something like "Mate, you've sold me. It'll do."

The cowboy laughed and answered, "Crikey mate, any port in a storm." He threw some bills down on the bar and then stood up. Turning to Jane and Claudine, he said, "Well, ladies, as much fun as it would have been to double with you and my mate, it seems we're being called elsewhere. I hope you have wonderful lives and you, little lady," he gave Jane a slow motion, pretend little punch on the jaw, like a big brother might to an adored little sister, "I hope you find that man of your dreams!" And then with a laugh he clumped out of the restaurant and was gone.

Jane stared at him as he went out. "He was a bit weird. But I kind of miss him already."

"Oh, you have no taste in men. Clearly, he was a divo. I should have signed him. Oh! That smile!"

Before they finished their appetizers another couple came in and sat next to them, this time behind Jane. The woman attracted the attention of everyone in the room as the couple entered. Her outfit was obnoxiously flashy, yet she was just attractive enough to carry it off.

Jane mouthed to Claudine. "You should sign her."

Claudine waved off the idea. "You only say that because of the jewels. It is a distraction. She does not have the right bone structure. And her hair is too limp," Claudine whispered loudly and wrinkled her nose.

The couple ordered two glasses of wine. It seemed that nothing could please the woman. She tasted and refused each of the first three vintages served to her. She rolled her eyes at the appetizers when they arrived. Occasionally, Jane could hear the woman complaining—she didn't need perfect Italian to get it that nothing her poor date said was right and that the little restaurant was just a dumpy, unsuitable place. Her escort seemed to be plaintively explaining, his voice patient and kind, and then suddenly she stood up and yelled "Tennista professionista!", and other things at him that Jane couldn't quite translate, but she caught the gist that his beautiful date found him embarrassing to be with. Before she stormed out, the bejeweled woman picked up her wine glass and threw the contents in her date's face, partially hitting Jane as well.

The man sat quietly for a moment and then reached to pick up his napkin from the bar. Then he noticed that Jane was blotting her shoulder.

"Oh! Mi scusi! Mi scusi!" He stopped drying his own face and he started to blot the mess from her shoulder and the side of her face while he spoke gently in Italian.

"Not your fault. She threw the wine." Jane shook her head.

"Oh, you speak English." He stopped short. "Please forgive me. It is my fault. My fault for trying so hard to please Dominique."

"Dominique? What a beautiful name."

"A beautiful name for a beautiful woman. But only on the outside." He blotted Jane's hair. "This is my fault."

"It's not your fault." She thought he had gorgeous, kind eyes.

He shrugged in a most Italian way. As he spoke, he tenderly dabbed away at the little droplets of wine on her cheek, but he was looking into her eyes. "I tried to make her happy. But people, they need to be happy in their own hearts, no? No amount of pretty rocks on gold strings can fill the emptiness in our own hearts. We cannot choose happiness for another. We cannot make someone to be happy. The best we can do is to find someone who is kind and happy. I failed in that with Dominique, so you see, it is my fault, after all."

Jane was speechless.

"It is easy to get caught up in the beauty and not to see the real person," Claudine said sternly.

The man never broke his gaze with Jane. "Si, but it is more important to have beauty on the inside." He made sure she was as dry as she was going to get. "Again, my apologies. I am so sorry that my very bad evening has ruined your very good one."

Jane couldn't help but smile at this gentle Italian soul. "It's not ruined at all. It's just wine. It'll wash out." She took her own napkin and wiped some of the drops from his face and blotted his shoulder, although the chianti had soaked into his shirt already. She stole a glance over at Claudine, who looked surprised, maybe intrigued at the situation. Unconsciously, Jane pushed her chair back a few inches to be more inclusive of this stranger. "Are you okay? That was, well, dramatic. Was that your, uh, wife?"

"Wife? No." He shook his head. "I have not been so fortunate as to find a wife." He looked at the restaurant door. "But I think I have not been so unfortunate either. After all, I am not married to Dominique."

Jane looked at him curiously, feeling the small smile on her lips and suddenly she couldn't help herself: she started to giggle. Then to laugh. Then he started to laugh. The two of them couldn't stop, and for several minutes went through cycles of giggling then laughing then catching their breath and then giggling and starting the cycle all over again. Even with Claudine looking at the pair, amused curiosity in her eyes and probably a good measure of disbelief, Jane simply could not get a hold of herself. She felt happy.

Finally, Claudine interrupted. "Apparently you are to join us for a moment. I am Claudine and my best friend here is Jane."

"And you are French. You can always tell a French woman."

"And how is that?" Just the hint of suspicion rang in Claudine's voice.

"French women have a commanding presence. And you," he said turning to Jane, "are an American." He smiled at Jane. "It's the shoes. You can always tell Americans by their shoes."

Claudine gave an audible hrumpf! but she turned to the waiter and said, "Please replace this man's glass of wine. And put it on my bill." She turned back to the stranger. "Apparently you are going to have dinner with us."

"That is beyond kind. I do not want to intrude…"

"It's no intrusion!" Jane said it much more quickly and emphatically than she meant to. She could feel the blush rising to her cheeks.

The man gave a generous smile, as though he found her reaction endearing. "If I am not intruding, grazie. Let me introduce myself. My name is Giovanni. Giovanni Romano."

"Giovanni, how lovely. What a lovely name. It's so nice to meet you."

Chapter 26

Jane sighed as she swallowed a bite of the best tiramisu she'd ever eaten. She'd spent the day mesmerized by the canals and bridges connecting the lovely old-world architecture of the town of Treviso. Even the dessert echoed the low arches that decorated the city. Prosecco filled her glass and happiness filled her heart and she smiled at the man across the table from her.

"Did you know that Treviso is the birthplace of this lovely dessert?"

She adored his heavy Italian accent. "Somehow that doesn't surprise me. Tell me, did we make this pilgrimage to Treviso for a cake?"

He gave her an endearing smile. "Well, only in part. Mostly I wanted to show you my favorite town in Italy."

"Oh, Giovanni, they are all your favorite towns in Italy!" Her laugh was cut short by her cell phone ringing.

He gave her an admonishing look. "Do you really need to get that?"

"If it's work, I'll let it slide—I promise. Oh wait, it's Claudine! I've been not returning her calls. Let me just say hi, okay? After all, she is my best friend."

"Okay, but someday I hope to win that title away from her." He got up and left her with a kiss on her hand as he and their empty glasses made their way over to the bartender.

"Hi, Claudine! I wish I could have a long conversation. I have so much to tell you. But you called me—what's going on?"

"With me? Nothing of a moment. I just wanted to check on you. I have not heard from you—not an answer to my text or my email or my voice messages. I was starting to get concerned."

"Oh, did you email me at work?"

"Well, oui! That is where you usually are. You check your personal email only rarely. I finally called your secretary and they said that you were away. On a leave of absence! Jane, are you sick?"

Jane laughed, lighthearted and carefree. "No. I've never been better, actually. Claudine, I'm taking a vacation. An extended vacation."

"You are with that man from the bar! The man with the chianti stains all over his clothes! That man we met… two months ago!"

"Well, yes, I am. We actually got together for lunch the day after you and I had dinner," Jane said with a smile as she watched Giovanni chat happily with the bartender. He kept looking back at her with a warm smile. "And then we met the next day and he showed me churches all over Rome."

"Are you telling me you had a date with this man for three days after you met him?" Claudine sounded stunned.

"Actually, not a day has passed since I saw you that I haven't been with him."

"What?"

"Yeah. I realized that I'm working too hard. I called my boss and asked for, well, if I'm being honest," she said timidly, "I demanded a leave of absence. And I've been on vacation ever since."

Claudine was silent.

"You think I've lost my mind. You're going to tell me to come to my senses."

There was silence for a while. "I think you are a grown woman and you should do what makes you happy. Obviously, he is not going to kill you and steal your passport, or he would have done it already, so the worst of my fears are not going to come to pass."

Jane burst out laughing. "Oh, you do sound like a mother! No, but we've made good use of our passports. We've been everyplace. Six countries, and we've decided that Italy is our favorite. Oh, Claudine, I'm so happy. I've never had this much, well, what do I call it? Fun? Yeah, fun! I've never had this much fun."

"Then I am happy for you." But Claudine's voice still sounded a bit tentative.

"No, you're worried for me. I can hear it. Everything's okay. I swear it. I flipped heads, Claudine, I finally flipped heads."

After a pause, Claudine sighed. "Then I am glad for you. You and this man had a great chemistry. Usually, you and I finish one another's sentences, but I watched the two of you do that all the evening. I should not be surprised to hear this news. So, oui! I am happy for you."

"You know, he's just an ordinary guy, but even without a lot of schooling, he's still really knowledgeable."

"He plays tennis for a living?"

"Teaches tennis, yeah. Said he's worked some in retail. Some in restaurants. Bounced around."

"Hmmmm. I think there is more to this man than meets the eye."

"I know. You're right. He should seem kinda simple or something, but he's really smart and engaging. He's funny and…"

"All right! All right! You can stop there. You are infatuated. There is nothing I can say other than have a good time. And don't end up dead or in the papers, all right? I don't want to see you on the news."

"Don't be silly! I'm having the time of my life. Why did I wait so long to have the time of my life?"

"At some point you will need to go back to your life. While you make a good living you are not independently wealthy."

Jane nodded. There was truth to that. She would have to go back. But not today. Today she was happy. Today she was experiencing all she'd ever dreamed of. Even if this ended badly, the part of the journey that she was on now was worth any price at all. "I'll figure that out when I get there. Until then, just think of it as my fairy tale came true."

"But fairy tales… all 'girl-power and liberated independence'. That is what you told me."

"I'm going for the old school fairy tale this time." Her eyes were on Giovanni and her smile was all for him. He had their drinks refreshed and was making his way back to their table. "So, I'll call you soon. I promise. We'll catch up. I'll tell you everything. Bye!" She hung up the phone.

"And how is your best friend?"

A smile blossomed across Jane's face. "Oh, I think he's just about perfect."

Chapter 27

The room was dark. It was peaceful. The ceiling fan was on low, making a buzzy, drowsy sound that lulled Jane into a sleepy haze. It had been a full day and she was exhausted. Giovanni was deeply asleep, as always. He was a champion sleeper, whether it was on a plane or a couch or in their bed.

Sleep was elusive for Jane. Every time she lay down in bed it took only about ten minutes before work started spinning through her head: the data she'd reviewed, the decisions she had to make, the interpersonal workplace drama she had to figure out how to navigate. *He must sleep like a baby because the big drama in his life is what to make for dinner.* While that sounded uncharitable, to Jane it was a thought tinged with jealousy. What it must be like to live a life like that. And to sleep unplagued by the thoughts and regrets of the day.

Of course, he did dream. And vividly. They would be snuggled up asleep, Jane nestled in the crook of his arm, and Giovanni would twitch suddenly, jolting her out of the images in her own mind of spreadsheets and advertising layouts and meetings with her boss—nothing she minded being taken away from. She got enough of that during her waking hours. When she asked him, he always said he dreamed of tennis—reaching for a net shot or hitting a high lob seemed to be a common theme. And he would murmur, nothing that she could ever quite catch though. But it amused her how his sleeping voice always sounded like a different person.

Must be fun to have such an incredible dream life, she thought as she disentangled herself from his arms and gently slid a pillow into her place. His arms wrapped tightly around the pillow and she rolled over in search of sleep. Hours later, Jane was lost in her own dream of their time in Venice, riding in a gondola, when he'd first floated the idea that their extended date could evolve into an extended vacation... or perhaps a little bit more.

"Amore mio, I'm so glad you are enjoying seeing Italy through the eyes of a native. But Venice, ah, Venice is like a fantasy to me still. Every time I see it, it is as though it is the first time. Impossibility, that is Venice. How could such a jewel survive and remain so beautiful?"

"Yes. I've seen it before, but it never seemed as lovely to me as this trip. Thank you, Giovanni. I wish this could last forever." She looked around her at the lights glinting on the water as the sun started to set. Soon the gondolas would be docked for the night, lest they be rammed in the dark by the ever-present water taxis motoring their way down the canals and making the water choppy. "Unfortunately, my leave of absence is almost over. I'm going to have to go back to work."

"Jane." Giovanni's voice sounded tentative. "What if it could last a bit longer? What if we could find a way?"

She sighed as she looked at the beauty surrounding them, the soft-painted stucco facades of the buildings, the little white lights all starting to come on. "That's a dream." She took another deep breath. "As my friend Claudine reminded me recently, I'm not independently wealthy, so this life of leisure is not in the cards for me. Sadly, I have to live in a place called reality."

"You can make reality be what you want it to be, if you want it enough."

She pulled her eyes away from the beautiful buildings reflecting the last light of the sun and looked at Giovanni. That was okay. She preferred looking at him anyway, particularly framed by the rare beauty that was Venice. "Ah, Gio, we've spent more than two months now galivanting all over Europe. It's been wonderful, like seeing it for the first time. But this is a dream, and I have no choice. I have to go back to my real life before I don't have one to go back to." It was a sad realization, but it was true. If she didn't return from her leave of absence, they would give her job to someone else. It had been just enough time for the business to really miss her, to deeply understand how irreplaceable she was, but any more time and they would need to replace her.

Giovanni looked at her sympathetically. "I know you have to go back. You have a life. An important life. But my life, is not so important." He shrugged. "Eh, I play tennis. I have little jobs in shops. A little time in restaurants. Not so important."

Jane had never dated someone who wasn't rooted in a career, someone without an identity all tied up in work. She was embarrassed that she'd never thought much about the people who waited on her in restaurants or cashed out her purchases in retail stores. She just figured they had a life or whatever, which was really a dismissal of actually caring about them at all, a kind of erasure. But now that she was falling in love with Giovanni, she began to see that people could have just as strong a sense of self without that self being defined by a title or a head count or client lists—or even a salary. They had friends—outside of work friends. She had met many of his in whirlwind evenings out and by day in museum tours that somehow felt like the most fun interviews she'd ever been on—what a realization of just how much work owned her if meeting new people could only feel like "an interview". Obviously, Giovanni and his friends had hobbies and projects and relationships that filled them with the passion she got from work—but they were free. They could live wherever and could do anything. They could also leave anything. That was the difference. She couldn't leave her life. It was calling to her. She was missing it. She would miss him too, but this fantasy dream life wasn't hers. She couldn't live on vacation. Claudine was right.

"Your life is as important as mine. Absolutely as valid." She said it and she believed it, but she could see over the horizon of this conversation: this was the beginning of the end. The start of the long and painful breakup conversation. The moment when they would both say how they loved living this fantasy but admit that it was a dream. At best, didn't every dream end with daylight? Or at worst in the darkness with your heart beating in your ears and sweat on your brow while panic filled your confused mind, stuck in limbo, not having yet let go of that dream state nor yet fully grabbed back onto reality. Jane could feel the stab of pain, amazed at how emotions could become physical sensations even when that defied all logic. It was an emotion. It belonged to the mind. Then why did it create this painful stab in her chest?

Giovanni's voice interrupted the breakup rehearsal unraveling in her head. "But my life, such as it is, I can live it in Milan. Or here in Venice. Or, well, Jane, I could live it in… Charlotte."

She stopped thinking. She sat up straighter. "Live your life… where?"

"Well…" His face held a mixture of nervousness tinged with excitement. "Since people eat, dress, and play tennis in Charlotte, I could ply my trades there as well. With you. If you like. If you'd like to try… maybe see how it works?"

Just as Jane was about to lean forward to kiss Giovanni, the gondola rocked slightly. She grabbed the side for stability. Something dark and swift skimmed by them, too close and moving too fast. She couldn't see it in the dark. Then she heard a distinctly British-sounding voice shouting:

"Not this time, Sir Murray!"

She whipped her head around in time to see the ornately curved prow of an oncoming gondola materialize out of the growing darkness. Her boat rocked violently with the broadside impact of the other gondola. She clung to the sides of her boat, starting to cry out, knowing that they were going to be dumped into the cold Venetian water. Someplace in the back of her brain, she was struck with the idea that something was wrong. It hadn't happened this way, had it? Before she could sort that thought out, the boat capsized with Jane gulping in air before being plunged to the depths… and then she hit the hard bottom, opening her eyes into the darkness, tangled in the sheets with Giovanni leaping over her yelling something about "Murray" and "not today". Why did his voice sound so strange?

"Giovanni! Wake up! You're dreaming again! Wake up!"

Giovanni froze, his arm caught mid-stretch. Slowly he looked around, finally focusing on Jane. He seemed to shake himself, almost to come back into himself.

"You were dreaming. Oh my God, you leapt over me in your sleep and knocked me out of bed. Again! Gio, maybe we should take you to see someone? They're getting more vivid, aren't they?" She sighed. "And the dream you woke me up from was… was…"

"A nightmare?"

She looked at the scars on his chest and belly. A car accident that could do that would give anyone nightmares, no matter how far back in the past it had been. She could totally understand him asking that question. "Maybe yours was but not mine! Mine was divine. Probably the happiest I've ever been. I was dreaming of the gondola ride. The one where we decided to live together."

"Why do you get wonderful dreams of love and I get…" He sighed in disgust. "Si." He sounded sad as he helped her disentangle from the sheets and stand up again.

"Who is Murray?"

"Who?"

She sighed. "What were you dreaming about? You called out something about Sir Murray." Then she giggled. "And you sounded so funny. Not like you. More like, well, you almost sounded British!"

He paused for a moment, looking confused. "Ah, it was him, how you call it, my arch enemy, in my dream."

She stared at him, wondering what kind of nightmares plagued him.

"Si, my arch enemy in my dreams is Sir Andy Murray."

"Who?"

"He is a Scottish tennis player," he explained as he started to remake the bed. "I have this recurring dream that I am playing Wimbledon. And everyone is there. My mama, my nonna, even my papà. And he defeats me. I play badly. It is humiliating." He hung his head.

"You've had the dream before, haven't you?"

"Si, it is the same old dream."

"Maybe you should see someone about it? I mean, this is a recurring nightmare for you. It must be about something important. It's same dream over and over again."

"It is about something important." He reached over and stroked her cheek. "The dream is about humiliation."

"And it isn't changing."

He looked at her sadly. "No, it is changing. Now you are also there in the stands, watching me play, and I bear my defeat in front of your eyes." He stroked her cheek again. "I don't want to be a failure in your eyes."

She wrapped her arms around him tightly. "You are not a failure. I will never see you that way."

"But you are successful. You pay for our lives..."

She cut him off. "And you make my life worth living. No more talk of this. To me, you beat the pants off of this Murray guy, whoever he is."

"Ah, I only wish it were so. I fear that someday Murray will end it all for me."

"Wake up, Gio. That's just a dream."

They went back to bed and this time Jane fell asleep quickly. She was denied her lovely dream though, as her mind returned to spreadsheets and client lists. Giovanni, however, lay awake for long hours as he watched her sleep and listened to her breathing.

Chapter 28

Jane felt nervous. This felt very real. Sure, it was just a "bring the boyfriend home to meet the family", but when you hadn't seen your family for almost five months because even though you live in the same town, you haven't been in town in ages. And they thought that you'd maybe been kidnapped or brainwashed or joined a cult because there had never in your life been a stretch like that. And then they find out that it wasn't an extended work assignment, but that you'd met some foreign guy in a bar and you just never came home again. Until now. Until the moment of truth. They wanted to know if you'd lost your mind. Simple, right? Sure. No problem.

The truth was that her heart had been kidnapped. Her mind had been brainwashed. It had a total feel of unreality to it. It was the stuff of movies and books and girlhood dreams—if you overlooked the small inconveniences of love across international lines that made being together anything but simple. If you could navigate, then just maybe you could wring a happy ending out of this tale. But finding jobs was complicated. Not to mention the whole red-tape-wrapped challenge of taking up residence in another country. Most guys just had to meet the girl's parents, but Giovanni had to sacrifice his job, his friends, his culture: every facet of his life would get chopped up on that altar of love… and then he still faced the parent test to boot.

She chewed a nail as she thought about it.

"You seem nervous. What is bothering you, Amore?"

She took her finger out of her mouth and shook her head.

"Si, something is bothering you," he said with some concern. "Oh, you are worried that they won't find me... ah... suitable?"

She looked at him. "Suitable?"

"Si. Good enough for their little girl. I am not the high-powered executive they might expect. Or that they might want for you."

"Er, they don't want that. Really. They think I work too much. You being a... what did you call it? A high-powered executive, nah, that would just push me to work even more." She turned to look straight out the windshield and let out a big breath. "It's... it's... well, what if they find out what we've done?"

"Do you mean that I am sleeping with their daughter?"

Her breath came out in a chortle. "No." She turned to look at him. "But don't mention that anyway."

"Do you mean that I started sleeping with her by our third date?"

"Now stop that!" Jane punched Giovanni in the arm. "You wouldn't dare!"

He counted off on his fingers. "So, it is not underemployed. And it is not that I am making mad, passionate love to their daughter. It is not that I am a foreign agent? No? Then what is it that you are afraid of them knowing?"

"That we're married."

He looked puzzled. "Given number two on that list, I would think that being married would be something they would appreciate. A step in the right direction."

She chuckled. "Indeed. But we've known each other for less than five months. We've been back in Charlotte for nearly two months now and I know they think I've been avoiding them."

Giovanni raised one eyebrow. "And that would be true. They would be right."

"Uh, yeah, well. Okay, guilty on that count. But if they find out I got married... without telling them... without them ever meeting you… without time for us to know one another. Well, they'll think I've gone off my rocker!"

"What American expression is this? What is a… rocker?"

"Oh, sorry. Your English is so good it's easy for me to slip into slang. It means they'll think I've lost my mind. That I've done something dumb and desperate—that this isn't a legitimate relationship. They'll worry about me and wonder what's really going on."

Giovanni looked at her, mystified.

"I'm afraid that if they find out, they won't trust you. That they won't accept you because it's just too fast for them to understand. They don't see real people, well, sensible people who they've raised, making rash decisions like that. They'll worry about something weird." Her voice took on a sinister tone, "Like what you really want? They'll question your ulterior motive. Who you really are."

"Ohhhh, so they will think I am a foreign agent." He snickered. "That is amusing. No worries, mi Amore. When you are ready to tell them, we'll tell them."

"They wouldn't understand anyway. My father would have a million-and-one questions." Jane sighed again.

"Questions like how did you know that you loved me so quickly? A man who could only be a stranger to you?" He was funny in his overly dramatic delivery and made Jane chuckle.

"Oh no. He'll understand that totally. He fell for my mom in an instant. But my mother would give me the grilling of a lifetime over that one."

"And your father then? What would he ask about?"

"The INS."

Giovanni shook his head, confused.

"Oh, he'd want to know how in the world we convinced the INS that we're legit. Remember that the only thing he knows about people moving to the US is from an old movie called Green Card. They do everything and they can't convince the immigration service that their marriage is legit, so the guy is tossed back to France."

"Well, that would be because the man was French. I am not French. It is totally different for me. And besides, America is much more open now than it was many years ago when that old movie was made."

Jane looked at him, stunned. "What? What kind of world news have you been watching? We have huge fights over immigration. The US is a crazy hostile place to immigrants."

"Si, that may be true, but not to Italian ones. And I think it mattered who interviewed us. Our team seemed taken by our love story."

Jane couldn't help but giggle. No matter how serious a situation was, Giovanni always seemed unfazed by it. He always found the light side. She wished she had that talent, but she knew herself: she was a catastrophizer. "You know, now that you bring that up, I would've expected INS agents to be tough and mean even, but that old guy was actually crying over our story."

"He was a man of tender heart," Giovanni said with a smile and then added in a whisper, "I'm sure it made him think of his long-lost boyfriend." He nodded knowingly. "A poin-ge-nant memory for him."

"Poignant." She corrected him. "You pronounce it 'poin-yent.'" She sighed. "It just seemed. Well, it was almost too easy. You know, in my interview, I failed some of the questions. I don't know what kind of deodorant you use. My dad's an Old Spice guy, which is red and your thing is dark blue, but I couldn't remember the name of it. You do all the shopping anyway." Giovanni burst out laughing as Jane went on. "No, really, I thought we were going to need some high-powered attorneys. I was afraid I was going to lose you. Like in that Green Card movie. But it almost seemed, well, perfunctory. Like we were just going through the motions."

Giovanni's eyebrows knitted. "Per... per... fink... ach! I do not know this word? I won't even try to say it." He laughed, waving his hands.

"We were a, well, a pass through, I guess. It was just so easy. Just check the boxes."

"Si, we Italians are very popular. Everyone wants us. Do not fret, Amore. Your parents, they will love me." He held her hand. "Everything will be fine. And all your secrets will be safe with me." With his other hand he indicated zipping his lip. "I am very good at keeping secrets. You can always trust me to keep your truths you want to keep from everyone else."

Jane smiled at him. "I just feel so sneaky keeping this from them, but I'm not ready for the interrogation that we'll face when they find out."

They were interrupted by another car pulling up beside them.

"Who is, what? Oh lord. That's my sister Summer. And Hector. And the kids. Okay, so we'll not just be having dinner with my parents. It's a family party."

"Will your little sister show up as well?"

Jane shook her head. "Charlie? No. She's in California far as I know. Surgeon. Hard to get away from work. I think Summer will have my back but she's very perceptive. Very. Watch out. And her almost-tweenies, kind of a nightmare. Know no boundaries. Just like Summer."

"Apples... you know they fall close to the tree!"

They walked up to the house together, with Jane hoping to avoid facing the music.

* * *

As they sat down to dinner with eight people crowded around the table, Jane was actually glad for the welcome distraction that school-aged children brought to the evening. It was clear that her parents had their suspicions since the whole evening had offered a rotating cast of people cornering Giovanni to play a very personal version of twenty questions.

With basically no word from Jane for months, her nearly quitting her job, and then dragging a boyfriend home from her foreign travels, and rather than just staying at her condo, running off and buying a house together, well, any parents would be concerned, but Jane's parents were particularly protective after the whole debacle with Nicky. Sometimes she thought they had more trouble moving on from that than she had. After all, that was ancient history—and it finally, finally felt that way.

Audree was trying to make small talk and yet was obviously nervous about an inadvertent step on conversational thin ice that might prove to be embarrassing. Still, she plunged ahead into another round of twenty-question-style-parent-interrogation, but now Jane could tell that her mother was getting to what really mattered. In her lovely southern drawl, Audree asked, "So, tell us more about what you do, Giovanni. I think I heard that you were a banker?"

Jane and Giovanni looked at one another in surprise. "No, Audree. I am not a banker. While I think I am good with numbers, the game of money lending was not anything that ever appealed to me."

"I can understand that. I always thought that banking would be ridiculously boring," she cooed back at him in her very southern way.

"He'd make an awful banker, Grandee," ten-year old Echo explained. "Did you even see the advice he gave Stone when we were playing Speed Monopoly? Man, I so wiped the floor with you." She looked at Stone, lording her win over him.

Stone glared back at his big sister, still steaming from the loss. "I hate Monopoly," he said with a growl, and took another roll from the table.

"Stone, don't you even think about it." Summer's voice was sharp and swift.

Suddenly all innocence, Stone shrugged at the false accusation.

"You throw that, and your painted rock collection goes into the creek. I mean it this time."

Stone looked beyond her, an expression of curiosity resolving into shock registering on his face. All his adult relatives followed his gaze. While their heads were turned, Stone suddenly dealt his sister an evil look and then beaned the roll at her.

Giovanni's hand shot out and snatched the roll out of the air just before it would have hit Echo. He handed it to her gently and winked at Stone with a smile.

Turning his attention back to the table, Hector asked, "Uh, what just happened?" expressing the suspicion of the adults that they had just been had.

Giovanni laughed loudly. "It was funny. Stone made his point. But Audree, you were asking me a question I believe."

Audree stammered a moment and then said, "Why, why did you want to leave Italy?"

"Ah, it is a sad story. Very sad. You see, I committed a crime. It was no longer acceptable for me to be there. My family, they were in shock. Could not believe this could be true about me. And so, I must leave." He had the entire table in rapt attention, including Jane, who could nearly feel the room spin as her heart started to race.

"Cool!" Stone gasped.

"Yeah!" Echo turned to her brother. "We have an Italian crime lord as an uncle! We'll be the coolest kids in school!"

It was John who broke the silence among the adults. "So, son, tell us about this. Just what did you do?"

"I started to make pizza with pineapple." Giovanni shook his head sadly and then just looked at them.

Everyone exchanged confused looks.

"Si. Pizza. Pineapple. In Italy, that is considered a food crime. Italians have very strong feelings about how food is prepared and eaten. It is part of our cultural heritage. You are not considered Italian if you commit certain food crimes. Now, pineapple on pizza is not as bad as putting ketchup on pasta, which I admit I have never done!" He was Italian enough to shudder appropriately. "But the pineapple is one of the worst offenses you can make with Italian food."

"I love pineapple on pizza!" Echo said. "It's the best."

Giovanni gave her a playful, pretend punch in the shoulder. "And you are so right, right? It is so good. But if I am to eat pizza the way I love it, I must leave Italy. So, Jane, she saved me, you see? And here I am! In America. Where you have the freedom to eat your pizza any way you choose!"

Everyone burst out laughing, Audree and John looking like they were almost in tears with relief.

A little bit breathless, Audree asked, "So I take it that you like to cook?"

"I love to cook, even if it is contraband. I think that is one important thing that you and I have in common!" Giovanni's voice was filled with delight.

While staring her brother down, Echo took a taunting bite out of the dinner roll he had shot at her.

"Oh, then you're a chef?" Audree asked hopefully.

"No. The late nights at the restaurants are not to my liking. It leaves no time for family. I do not think that being a chef appeals to me. I am too spontaneous. Too inventive. Take the pineapple, for example." He winked at them. "And there is always the risk that people don't like your experiments."

Echo started to cough and then she grabbed for her water, drinking furiously. Giovanni picked up the roll she had dropped. "I see, like being creative and trying a jalapeno pepper sandwich. It might sound good," here he looked at Stone, "but the hot peppers exact their own revenge." He handed Echo a fresh roll while Stone gave his sister an evil grin.

Hector looked back and forth between his two children and then he laughed out loud. "This is a game, isn't it? It's like What's My Job?" He looked around the table. "Is this a game?"

Summer put her hand over Hector's. "Well, honey, I don't think it was official until this moment." She turned to Giovanni. "Jane might have told you that Hector is also a bit foreign. He grew up in the US, but he grew up Amish. They call our customs 'English', although they aren't English at all. Every once in a while, his upbringing shines through and illuminates some cultural differences between Amish and mainstream American life."

"I do not know this Amish." Giovanni nodded, "But I am happy to play the game. I love games."

"Good with numbers. An accountant?" John jumped in eagerly with the questions he'd been holding back.

"No, not an accountant."

"Are you good at fixing things?" Hector asked eagerly. "Are you a handyman?" He smiled broadly. "I'm a handyman."

"I have been known as a fixer. I can fix anything. Usually the impossible things. But I never thought of making a title out of it." Giovanni smiled coyly.

Summer gave him a sharp look. "Mafioso?" she asked jokingly, but everyone suddenly gave him another serious stare.

He shook his head slowly. "Despite my earlier attempt at humor, I must say that this is fascinating in America. I understand that there are… ah… many movies that, Jane, help me with the word, make it flashy?"

"Glamorize."

"Ah, si, that is it. Glamorize that life. But it is no joke in Italy. I am against everything that is related to the mafia. I take it most seriously."

Audree looked puzzled. "I was going to guess translator until you needed help with that word. Your English is just wonderful."

"Grazie, Audree. No, I am not a translator. And I know people who would tell me that I need to work on my Italian! My nonna, ah, that is grandmother, for one!"

Now it was Audree's turn to laugh. "I've told my Summer here many times that she needs to work on her English."

Summer rolled her eyes. "Mom can't stand that I say things like 'these dishes need washed' instead of 'these dishes need to be washed'", she twitted with a heavy drawl. "Some people are 'Team Oxford comma'. My mama is 'Team Infinitive'. And she's never gotten over that I didn't pick up her family accent."

"It's called a lovely Southern lilt." Audree gave her daughter an exasperated look.

Echo, having recovered from her brother's hot-pepper-stuffed revenge roll, suddenly burst out, "Zoo! You're a zookeeper! Do you take care of penguins? I love penguins!"

"Ah, now that is a profession I would have loved. And while penguins smell very bad, what a life, eh? And at times," he stopped and scratched his head, "I have felt like a zookeeper, as I'm sure your madre does as well?"

Echo and Stone both laughed loudly. Then Stone asked, "What's a madre?"

"Yeah, they're a real zoo all right. Are you a nurse?" Summer asked.

"A plumber?" Hector offered his suggestion in turn.

"Are you a teacher?" John asked.

"Oh, my lord, he's an actor!" Audree said, her voice deadpan, a look of horror on her face.

Hector turned to Summer and whispered, "He's starting to sound like he's independently wealthy."

The look of horror faded from Audree's face.

Giovanni melted into peals of laughter. "This is a fun little game. I am very good at patching up the wounded, but not a nurse. I know a great deal about getting things to go down the pipes, but alas I am not a plumber. Too many spiders." He shuddered. "I do teach people important skills while they are as you say, sweating bullets. And while they learn they also become better physically and mentally. It is grueling for them, but it's fun for me."

"You're a chess master!" Hector said with excitement.

Everyone turned from Hector to Giovanni, expectant looks on their faces.

"Ah, chess. Well, uh, no. I play tennis."

"You're a doctor!" Audree said excitedly, sharing her next guess. No one said anything. "Doctors play tennis." She looked a little defensive as she returned the stares from her family members.

"I am not a doctor, I'm afraid. I play tennis as more than a hobby."

"He's the tennis pro at my club," Jane said. "Well, Hector was the closest. Cheers, Hector." She raised her glass in toast and then took a swig of her wine. While it was at least out in the open, it was a real conversation stopper. No one seemed to be very interested in tennis.

Jane heard her mother whisper to her father, "You can make a living at playing tennis?"

Her father shrugged in return.

"So, uh, two months in Europe. Where'd you crazy kids go, anyway?" Summer asked as she prodded Stone to eat some of his vegetables. "Tell me again how you got that much time off work, Jane? I've hardly ever known you to take a vacation. Like ever. You're a classic workaholic."

Jane smiled. "We went everyplace. I've got eons of time off saved so getting a leave of absence wasn't hard, actually. Waking up to reality is what bites, though, since I had to go back eventually." Well, there was her first lie. She was totally refreshed when she went back and found that she'd missed it—the people, the pace, the creativity. Summer gave her a piercing look that deflated Jane.

"Si, but when you go back you are a new person. New perspective. It is refreshing, no?"

Summer nodded. "That sounds more like her. Giovanni, you sound more like my sister than my sister does. So, what'd you all see?"

"Like I said, everything. All over Italy. Rome, where we met. Milan, where Gio is from. Venice…"

"Where we fell in love!" Giovanni raised his glass and all the adults cheered and followed suit, clinking their crystal and toasting the new couple.

Jane could feel herself relaxing. While it could have been the wine, more likely it was that Giovanni had them eating out of the palm of his hand. He was unabashedly adoring of her, which they appreciated, and he delighted them with his stories about all the places they visited and their time together.

"Oh, honey," Audree said to her husband, "it just sounds amazing. John, now I want to go and see Europe for two months!"

"Yes, that would be nice, but my patients would have so many dental emergencies. I don't see how we can, Audree. These people all depend on me. How else would they be able to eat?"

Audree took another sip of her wine. "There goes my husband, saving the world, one mouth at a time. I suppose that is the life of a dentist."

Hector gave Jane a quizzical look. "Don't you go to a lot of those places for work, Jane? I thought your work had you trotting all over Europe and sometimes to the Middle East, sometimes China."

"Good memory, Hector. I have been to those places, some of them a dozen times or more. But this time it was like I was living the advertising campaigns that once upon a time I'd dreamed up to sell the airlines the new fleets. My time as a tourist has always been limited, so I mostly got to take in, well, let's see, the inside of boardrooms, countless elevators, some beautiful vistas from the top of high-rise office buildings, and a lot of private dining rooms in fabulous restaurants. But statues were seen strictly from taxis. And museums from scrolling through web pages on my phone. Mostly by the time I got back to my hotel room, it was so late that the only thing I could see was the pretty lights of the city. And while lovely, cities pretty much look the same when you get to the twinkly lights part."

"But together we floated on gondolas in Venice," said Giovanni. "We climbed the five-hundred and fifty-one stairs of St. Peter's

Basilica in Vatican City, and we even crawled through the catacombs underneath Roma!"

"Cool! Catacombs!" Echo and Stone said in unison. Then Stone added, "What's a catacomb?"

"Yeah, Gio here is way more adventuresome than I am. I could've given that last one a skip." Jane shuddered.

"No," said Summer. "That sounds utterly fascinating. How could you have missed that? Think of it, you could meet the Crypt Keeper of Rome! Doesn't that sound amazing, guys?" She turned to her children, who were now hanging on every word in the conversation, Stone still trying to figure out what a catacomb was and how the Crypt Keeper fit into the picture and if he actuallly combed cats.

"Giovanni," Jane said, "this is my sister who decorates gingerbread men at Christmas to look like scary, creepy clowns. And her kids' cookies, even more imaginative than that."

Audree didn't look so intrigued. "I'm with Janie on that one. No matter how your accent makes just everything sound like it can't be missed, Giovanni, I don't think even you would have been able to talk me into the underground catacomb cemetery tour."

"Ohhhhhh, coooool," Stone whispered, finally grasping what everyone older than he was so animated about. But he was surprised the adults were that into dead cats.

Giovanni turned to Audree. "Ah, my dear lady, it is you with the lovely accent that makes every word drip like poetry from your lips. If you had declined, I would have had no choice but to find something above ground that would delight you. The fountains of Roma, perhaps? The Trevi, with its horses stampeding in the water. Or the Fontana dei Quattro Fiumi—the Fountain of the Four Rivers."

"Oh, my word." Audree put a hand to her chest. "John, I don't think you can get out of taking me to Italy now."

"Indeed!" John smiled as he took another sip of his wine.

"So, what touristy kind of things have you done in Charlotte?" Summer asked brightly.

"Summer." Hector looked at her most seriously. "There are no touristy things to do in Charlotte. It's a residential city. A business city. I can't imagine them touring what? The university? A sports dome? Oh, sure, that would be… interesting. There's no Fountain of the Four Rivers here."

Giovanni looked a bit sheepish as he replied, "I must admit, we did struggle a bit to find things to look at and do at first."

"Well, certainly not after the descriptions we've heard of Rome!" Audree said somewhat breathlessly.

John burst out laughing. "Giovanni, I think you have captured the heart of my daughter and wife both!"

"I must warn you, John, I do not plan to return the heart of Jane." He lifted Jane's hand and kissed it while she blushed and smiled. "It is so nice to finally get to meet you all. We have been so busy with the new house, painting, fixing things, moving. Time has just gotten out of our fingers."

John looked puzzled for a moment, and Jane was worried that maybe Giovanni was laying it on a bit thickly. "So, what will you do when your ninety days are up?" John asked.

There was a general response of "What?" from all quarters of the table.

John looked around at everyone, surprised at the expressions on their faces. "Ninety days. Ninety-day visas. You can't stay in the country on a tourist visa for more than ninety days."

"Or I will become a contraband visitor?" Giovanni smiled.

"Actually, it's pretty serious," John answered. "You can get into real trouble with the government. You both seem very invested in this new house and I appreciate all the work you're putting into it, Giovanni. Every brush stroke you make is one I don't have to." John chuckled. "But you won't be able to stay in the country. You'll have to leave in, what, another four weeks? What then? What will the two of you do then?"

The silence hung heavily in the air.

Giovanni became serious. "Ah, you are worried that we will break the law. That I will break the law, perhaps, to stay? I agree with you, John. There is a name for it. It is called a 'visa-overstayer'. Jane and I already have a solution for that problem."

Jane's head snapped around to look at Giovanni and she tried to shake it in a *no* to him while making the movement imperceptible to everyone else at the table.

"Si! It seems that when you meet with immigration services, that there are categories in America that they need, that they cannot find enough of. And happily, I fit that category, so they welcomed me with open arms!"

John was leaning forward, his attention utterly captivated. "And what is it that we need in America that we can't get enough of?"

Giovanni puffed up proudly. "It seems that Americans are over fat. It seems that everything the country has tried, diet soda, non-fat cookies, vibrating rubber belts, milkshake diets, it has left them fatter than ever. And so, it turns out that I am most desperately needed here!"

"What did you say you do again?" Stone's question filled the sudden silence.

Giovanni surveyed the group with an air of confidence one might expect in a Pulitzer Prize winner or a Nobel Laurate: "I am a tennis professional!"

"And… and you can get a green card for that?" Audree said a bit awkwardly.

"You can today. America is such a place of opportunity. So, I will stay until my work is done. Until Americans are once again fit and healthy."

"One tennis game at a time…" Jane said as she took another large sip of her wine.

Chapter 29

The weeks rolled by and sure enough, Giovanni's paperwork came through with no hiccups. Green card in hand. Permanent resident.

"Well, that was... fast." Jane was amazed given that her company had struggled to get highly sought-after engineers granted the kind of work visas they needed, much less permanent residency, but Giovanni just shrugged it off with a smile.

"I told you, Americans love Italians. It is not just you who loves me—it is all of America."

"At least someone in INS loved you."

Giovanni stopped what he was doing and looked puzzled. "Maybe... maybe it's the pizza."

"The what? Pizza?"

"Si! Americans love their pizza, and me by... by... what is the word I'm looking for?" His hands were waving vigorously.

"Extension?" she offered. "Proxy? By fiat?"

"A Fiat is a car." Then his expression changed to a bit of a sneer. "An American car." He brightened again quickly. "Just like I told you your parents would love me. Love me like a pizza. Nothing to worry about." Then he started to sing, and surprisingly well:

"When the moon hits your eye, like a big pizza pie, that's amore!

When the world seems to shine like you've had too much wine, that's amore!"

Jane couldn't help but laugh and decided that he was right. They should count their blessings and enjoy them, rather than go looking for trouble.

As November came to a close, the weather started to get cooler. "So, you are now like a son to my father. My mother is practically taking cooking lessons from you. I can't believe we did an Italian-influenced Thanksgiving dinner last week."

"It was nice, no? A blending of traditions."

"Do you think maybe we should go back to Italy and possibly I should meet your family?" There. She'd said it. She'd been wanting to say it for months and months, but everything was so easy with Giovanni… she didn't want to break the magic spell that had kept her in this happy bubble.

"Oh, that would be so nice! You should meet mi Madre. And mi Nonna. Ah, if only." He crossed himself.

"What do you mean 'if only'?"

"To be honest, Jane, I am nervous. I am a bit scared."

"You mean… they won't like me?" She felt her bubble of happiness quivering dangerously.

"What? Of course, la mia famiglia would love you! No, I am afraid of leaving the country. I know I put up a good front with your father, who has asked me so many questions about INS that I have had to play the scene, like a movie, with him."

"Play the role? You mean roleplay? Act it out?"

"Si! Si! He has been so curious, and with good reason. We had to, what did you call it, role play, the interview. While I would not admit that to him, you are right, it has all been too easy. I am afraid that if I go running back and forth to Italy that our luck, our good fortune, might like smoke, eh…" He waved his hands around in the air, searching for the word.

"Evaporate?"

"Evap…evap…yes, that. To be totally honest, I am nervous that we could lose what we have."

"Then we'll stay here!"

"And I will celebrate my first Christmas in America!" He patted a box of ornaments that he'd dragged up from the basement. Then he walked over to Jane, putting his arms around her. "Someday you will meet mi madre. But only when we are sure that there is no risk to us being together."

Jane hugged him tightly. So he did share her concerns that the immigration and naturalization process had just been too easy. "Well, there's a simple solution to that—we'll keep a low profile. Although I am kinda sad that you can't come with me when I travel. I had hoped that we could make those trips together. Whatever will you do around here?"

Giovanni looked around. "You know, this house needs some updating. The kitchen, it is a nightmare. I think I will work on that while you are away. It will give me something to do." His wrist buzzed and he looked at his watch.

"Hey, I've been wondering what to get you for Christmas. How about I get you a smart watch? You could use an update. I mean, I don't even recognize that technology you're using there. You know, we could afford to get you whatever you want. You could get the very latest iWatch or a Galaxy if you'd like. Whatever you'd like. And update your weird phone while we're at it." She looked askance at the off-market, cobbled together, street vendor system he had.

He looked from her to his watch and back again. "Oh... no. This is Italian. I'm very attached to it."

"But it's so... um... off-brand. I mean, you can't even get support for that thing. You have to tinker with it all the time." Jane was amazed that he wouldn't want something with the latest technology to offer.

"Si! But that is the beauty of it! I have tinkered with it, as you say, and so, I make it my own. All my electronics talk to one another. It is my little hobby. And because it is so 'off-brand', as you call it, no one will ever hack it! There are no software loopholes that need updates and patches. It is not a target because no one knows about it. It is a one-of-a-kind!"

Jane sighed as she picked up and moved a box of Christmas ornaments. "Yes, yes, I know how you hate the hackers, you don't have to start that again. I gave up my Alexa because you were sure she was listening to everything we said and did. Now if I want to listen to my music I have to go and dig out a CD and pop it into the player. So old school! You won't even let me stream the songs." She turned to look at him. "You know, I think you have a little problem with tech. A little tech issue you never want to talk about. You seem just a little bit paranoid to me."

He came over with another box and set it down next to her. "I have my issues, I know, but don't we all have our, our little…" He waved his hands around in the air. "Help me, Jane."

"Try foibles. That's a good word to choose. I just thought you might like something easier than that clunky set up you have."

Giovanni burst out laughing. "I love my clunky set up. And to hear you make a recommendation to me about technology, that is amusing. I don't quite think of you and technology in the same sentence. You complain every time your firm has a technology update. Or have you turned over a new bush?"

"Turned over a new leaf. The saying is turned over a new leaf." She smiled. "You are more the gadget man than I am. And you're right—all that stuff is blah, blah, blah to me. It's not just the tech updates at the job—my team drives me crazy too. It's email, texting, GroupMe, Slack, Asana. They Tweet and Thread me. Teams messages fly across the bottom of my screen—if I'm lucky enough to even see them. Some Instagram me. What's up with that? Then there's some day-of-the-week thingy. Why don't people ever use the damn phone? Like what's wrong with an old-fashioned video conference? But no, I have to check fifteen different apps just so they can tell me they went off to get a latte and do I want anything? It drives me bananas!"

Giovanni raised an eyebrow. "I think someone needs to calm down a bit? No, I do not want more technology for Christmas. But a kitchen update? Now, if that sounds like something you'd like, I will take that for Christmas and my birthday and all the other pretend holidays you Americans celebrate."

"Like Valentine's Day."

"Si, whatever that is."

"Good to know. I'll make sure to send myself roses on February fourteenth and say they're from you!" She laughed.

"Ah! You mean la Festa Degli Innamorati! The Italians invented that day of celebration! We are lovers! So, a new kitchen from you to me for the Festa in February. That is, unless you're attached to the nineteen-nineties cucina? Do you like the pineapples and the 'American Country' motif?"

She had to admit, his expression looked a little bit queasy. She hadn't realized how much he didn't like the kitchen.

"Sure, I think a great present for the both of us would be a kitchen renovation. Do whatever you want." She couldn't decipher the look he was giving her.

"You know, Mrs. Romano, you are a very generous wife."

She wrapped her arms around him and kissed him. She hadn't changed her name, of course, but she loved it when he called her Mrs. Romano. "And you are a very loving husband. All I want for Christmas is to make you happier than you've ever been."

"Then my wish list is fulfilled."

Jane started unpacking the boxes that Giovanni had dragged up from the basement. Last night, they had gone out for hot chocolates at this little gourmet hole-in-the-wall that he had found and afterward picked out a fresh cut tree together. It was fun and she told herself that it should feel exciting because it was their first tree together, but that word *first* was the scary part. Sure, they were married but since they hadn't told anyone, there was a degree of unreality to it all, like it might only have been a beautiful dream that evaporated with the morning mist, leaving memories but no indelible trace in its wake. That kind of thin ice felt dangerous. To think that he was worried that his green card status could be revoked had given her a jolt.

She had wanted the other side of the coin. Not Nick. Someone totally opposite from him. And Giovanni had shown up in her life, materializing seemingly out of nowhere. In defiance of being controlled by the past, she decided to plunge in—and plunge in she had, even if no one in her family yet understood just how deeply she'd dived. She would do whatever it took to protect her relationship with Giovanni.

Giovanni interrupted her thoughts. "You know, I really like being married. And particularly being married at the holiday."

She smiled at him warmly. "And it felt very married to be figuring out how to get that tree to fit into the tree stand last night."

"Si! Maybe we should have looked more at the trunk before we selected our tree. Now it looks like the Leaning Tower of Christmas Pisa." He put his hand on his chin, studying the off-kilter fir that filled the corner of their living room and tilted precipitously into the space.

Jane stood by him, surveying the scene. "A precarious angle to be sure. We could have had our own sitcom just getting the lights on that thing."

"I could put in a wire to hold it up. Just by drilling an anchor in that wall…"

"No drilling holes in the walls of our new house just to keep a tree up! How about you pop down and bring up another box of decorations?" Jane sighed. He had enthusiastically hammered nails in the walls to hang art, and then afterwards decided it all needed to go in different places. Two rooms had needed patching and repainting already.

Giovanni brought up yet another box. "You have a lot of Christmas ornaments!" He laughed as he surveyed the plethora of tree trinkets she had laid about on the couch, table and available chairs. "It is so American… a sea of little…"

She cut him off before he said something that would annoy her. "Don't you decorate for Christmas in Italy?"

"Oh sure, Si," he answered, diverted. "But your Santa is our Babbo Natale, and he is mostly becoming popular because of the stores trying to sell trinkets to the children. They hang their stockings, eager for goodies, but it is La Befana, the old Christmas woman, who really is the spirit of the season. She is family. She is good food. She is the happiness of a life well lived. The popular decorations are the nativity scenes, which often have the live animals."

"I bet that's spectacular. I've never seen Italy at Christmas time." She turned back to the tree. "No live animals on this tree—I'm a bit worried about the decorations themselves toppling it over. I guess we'll have to live dangerously."

"What did you say?" Giovanni had stopped mid-step and turned to look at her.

"Huh? Oh, live dangerously. We'll have to live dangerously and see if the tree falls over or if it makes it. But I'm going to hang ornaments wisely! The more breakable ones will all go on the 'up-side' of the tree in case it goes timber in the middle of the night. Yeah, where would Balthazar hang this little beauty?"

Giovanni missed a couple of beats before he answered. "Si. When living dangerously it is always good to think like one of the three wise men." He came to her and looked at the ornament in her hand. "Your tree doesn't look like the one at the club."

She answered in an offhand manner, her focus on the project before her. "No, I don't suppose it would. The one at the club is pretty, but it's just that. It's only pretty. Just like all the ones you see in hotels and department stores. They don't mean anything. They don't tell a story. They have glitz but no soul."

"I have only seen American trees in stores. Or at the club. What do you mean by tell a story?"

Jane gave him a smile. "Well, the best trees all tell a story. You see, an ideal Christmas tree tells us who we are. Done right, it's a kaleidoscope of your life."

Giovanni laughed at her. "I know this kaleidoscope! I know what you are talking about. We have those in Italy, too! I had one as a child. I remember a time when it was a favorite toy." He looked at the tree dubiously, squinting at it. "But your tree doesn't look anything like that kind of colorful collage. I mean, it's colorful, si."

Jane started to feel quite animated. "The ornaments are all parts of a story, in this case, my story. All jumbled up of course, but they each symbolize some part of our lives. Like here, I bought these little things when we were in Italy. These were from the places when we were together. Remember in Rome when we saw the Sistine Chapel?"

He made a noncommittal grunt. "They eventually made us leave. Said we had to move on."

"Yes, every time I've been there that happens to me. They probably have my picture posted in some back room with the big bold print stamp over it screaming out 'OVER STAYER'. I bet they're on the lookout for me like I'm some criminally wanted woman!" Jane caught the funny look on Giovanni's face and quickly added, "I'm just kidding. I've never even gotten a traffic ticket. Don't worry, you haven't gone and gotten yourself involved with some underworld spy or anything." She playfully punched him in the arm and then did a swift spin and pointed a finger gun at him. Giovanni jumped. "You're pretty quick." She laughed and slowly blew pretend smoke from the end of her finger gun and then holstered it. "Look at you, so jumpy!"

"Well," he gave her a mischievous smile, "I'm glad to know you're not secretly some international cat burglar, a master of art thievery, or I might have to take you in."

She sidled up to him and with one finger slowly scratched him under the chin. "And just where would you take me? Hmmmm?"

"I could take you right now… in the living room," he said, giving her a wink.

* * *

An hour later, fresh from a shower, they returned to the task of decorating the tree.

Giovanni waltzed his way into the room with two glasses of cognac, handing one to Jane. He picked up one of the ornaments from their visit to the Vatican. "I feel a bit, how do you say? What is the word? Blasphemous to say this, holding this ornament in particular, but I have never enjoyed a Christmas tree so much." He gave her a kiss.

"Me either." She smiled back. Looking at the ornament in his hand, she exclaimed, "Oh! I remember this one. I bought this at that little shop at the top of Saint Peter's Basilica. Oh my God, I thought you were going to kill me with those stairs. I mean, I know you're an athlete for a living and all…"

"Hey, I'm just a club tennis pro. I wouldn't quite call myself an athlete."

"Believe me, I am also a bit stunned and amazed at the shape you are in given how you mostly stand around and shout instructions to women who are just biding their time until they can get to their mid-afternoon margarita. You nearly sprinted up those stairs… and there must have been a thousand of them to get to the top of the dome."

"No, there are only five-hundred-and-fifty-one steps. What? It was on the brochure. I remember reading it."

"Oh yeah, I guess I was so out of breath that I forgot how to read at that point."

"But you didn't forget how to shop…"

"Ha ha, very funny," she snickered at him. She took the ornament from his hand. "I do love this one. It's so special because it reminds me of that magical day. That was like our second date. Every year when I put this ornament on the tree, that day will come back to me. All those memories. And this one..." Jane picked up a tiny Venetian mask. "Remember when you showed me Venice? I bought this in one of those little shops."

"Si, and here's your tiny gondola for the tree. I remember when you bought this, right after our gondola ride where I asked you to marry me." He gave her a wink. "You know, I had this fear that I had fallen for some crazy American who overdoes Christmas."

"No, I think that would be my mother. Not me."

He gave a deep laugh. "That is the image we have of Americans in Europe—they overdo everything, especially in how they commercialize the holiday which is a holy day to so many."

Jane held up and studied the miniature gondola. "I wanted to forever capture that moment. To bring it back each year. To hold the memory in my hand."

He looked thoughtful for a moment. "And if you hadn't agreed to marry me? So that I could come to the U.S. and we could be together? Then what would you have done with these?" He held a couple of ornaments in his hand.

Jane looked at them and then took them from his grasp. Turning, she delicately placed the decorations on the branches, admiring how they looked. "I would be doing just what we are doing now. But they would bring back beautiful and sad memories rather than beautiful and happy ones."

"This one is interesting. What is it?"

"Oh. It's a cocoa pod. Huge isn't it? I went to Brazil, and you know how I love chocolate, so I picked up one of these to remember the trip by. You have to admit, it's better than picking up mementos and letting them gather dust on the shelf. Or sticking them in a box and never thinking of them again. This way, I revisit those wonderful memories every year."

"And what about these. What is this? It looks like, well, like macaroni. But painted gold."

"Bingo!"

"Bingo is an Italian game."

"Oh, sorry, I meant it as an expression." Jane corrected herself. "You're right: it is indeed macaroni. Echo and Stone made these for Auntie Jane when they were about, what? Four, I guess. Did them in preschool. Aren't they just darling?"

Giovanni did not look convinced.

"I will treasure them always." With a satisfied sigh, she put them on the tree.

He handed her a glass ball. "And this?"

"Sisters' trip to Asheville, up in the mountains. The three of us did a glass blowing excursion."

"You made this? It is incredible!"

"Oh, yeah, thanks. Uh, but I didn't make this one. Summer made it. She's the artist. We each blew a glass ornament in our class and fell in love with what we'd created. And then in this real Gift of the Magi moment, we gave them to each other. I gave mine to Charlie so she'd have a set, but she gave hers to Summer. And to my surprise, Summer gave her bulb to me, so I'd have a kind of a matched pair. It was a real sister moment." Jane smiled as she hung it on the tree. "And this little airplane is from one of our beach trips. We went to the Wright Brothers Memorial—that's the first flight people ever achieved, right here in North Carolina. It was a fun week. I think of it every time I hang this little plane on the tree."

"This is cute," Giovanni said as he picked up a bottle brush penguin.

"This one I got with my family when I was a kid. We were on a family vacation and we each got to pick out a special ornament. For years, this hung on my mother's tree and she always told me that when I grew up and started my own household, this ornament was mine and would hang on my tree. Then, the years rolled on by and I did get a place of my own. My mother came over with an early Christmas present one year—and it was this ornament. Now it's a part of my tree because it's a part of my story. Each object, each decoration, is linked to some part of my life." She pointed to different ornaments as she explained. "A trip. An event. A memory. So over time, this tree has become the story of my life. This dalmatian is a dog I loved when I was growing up. This," she laughed, "is from my ill-fated attempt to learn guitar. And here! This little beauty was my first car. The plane, the plane is of course an Airbus, who I work for. Right now, all these pieces really tell you about me. It's a kaleidoscope of my life. I like to think that a Christmas tree done right will tell you who you are. As you unpack the pieces you re-live your tale. It tells your story to anyone who you invite over and who sees your tree." She searched for the special trinkets, pointing to the ornaments from Italy. "This is where you come into the story. And here… and here…" She turned towards him again. "And in the future, this tree will become our story. Over time."

"Ahh, I see. This is why it feels like your tree has a soul. It isn't just pretty. It's living. It's a map of your life."

"My kaleidoscope. All the memories, in their colorful little bits, all jumbled up. No two trees ever look exactly the same year-to-year, just like a kaleidoscope never paints the same picture in its little tube."

"Ah, my Jane, you are a poet. I loved the Jane I knew before the tree." He stepped back and put his arm around his wife. "But I find I love her even more now."

Chapter 30

Jane woke up wrapped around Giovanni. He slept heavily and she both listened to and felt his breathing. It made her feel centered and safe. He was small for a guy, not much bigger than she was herself, but he had a way of making her feel as though they were on a private island. One of those all-inclusive ones where you felt special and every time you turned around there was something wonderful to enjoy. With three weeks of every four on the road for work, she relished her time with him. No matter how much of that she could get, it would never be enough.

"Wake up, sleepy head," he whispered, his Italian accent reinforcing her feeling that she was on an exotic holiday. "We need to get ready to go to the airport."

"Oh, that's right." She yawned. "For some stupid reason I agreed to travel for Christmas because I just don't get enough of planes and taxis and restaurant food in my day-to-day life. Right?"

"Don't be so glum. Seattle is supposed to be a lovely city. It will be fun. You will enjoy spending time with my cousin. And the food! They are all splendido cooks. My cousin owns a cooking store. It will be a traditional Italian feast, just like at home."

She sat up and looked at him. "And what did you always have at home?"

He stared at the ceiling, his face holding a look of rapture. "Imagine this: a Porchetta made with turkey wrapped in prosciutto. Lasagna, of course. Our family likes this crab and leek lasagna. I'm sure my cousin will make it since she knows how much I love it. A fresh caprese salad and hot roasted Italian vegetables, of course done in olive oil with rosemary, garlic and balsamic vinegar." He kissed the tips of his fingers. "I hope my cousin makes her famous chestnut cake. It is dripping with meringue and whipped cream and those candied chestnuts."

"I think I've only tried a chestnut once. It was a roasted one from a street vendor at the holidays. I can't even remember where I was."

"And was it che buono? Wonderful?" He gave her a generous smile as he mused on the memories of inspired dishes.

She grimaced. "I hate to disappoint you. I thought it tasted a lot like a barn floor."

"A floor of a barn? Like for animals?"

"Uh, yeah. But we filled our pockets with them and they did a great job of keeping our hands warm."

"Well, do not tell Sophia that her cake tastes like a barn floor or we will never be invited back!"

"I will eat it with a smile on my face," Jane promised solemnly.

* * *

Three days later saw them wined and dined in style in Seattle by Giovanni's cousin Sophia and her husband, Edoardo. Jane thought she would gain at least five pounds on the trip, the food was all delicious, plentiful, and heavy. No one here ate a salad for lunch. She decided that either Giovanni was prescient in his exact prediction of Christmas Eve dinner—or that his cousin never varied her menu, and thus his prediction was actually just reciting the courses from memory. At any rate, he'd nailed it down to the chestnut cake, which did not taste quite like a barn floor... but maybe one dusted with a lot of sugar. Jane ate her slice with a smile but politely refused seconds.

After dinner they gathered around the tree for a very American-style gift exchange. This tradition was made much more challenging by the fact that she had never previously met the recipients of her gifts, which made finding just the right thing like playing her own game of Magic Eight Ball. She'd reached into her closet full of goodies which held beautiful souvenirs from her travels—things she'd loved but had no idea what to do with once she got back home. So, she stacked them up on the shelves. A bad habit, she'd told herself, but now that the little shelf had come in so very handy, she knew she'd never be able to resist the temptation to pick up those oh-so-unique knick knacks in the future.

"Oh, mamma mia!" Sophia gushed at the Portuguese artisan necklace nestled in the box. "Jane, this is magnifico!"

"Yes, I l just loved it too. The husband makes and dyes the leather strap to match the wife's carved stone pendants, and she features his leather inside her carving. I thought the way they designed it was so clever, you just pull on these leather strings to adjust the pendant to the length you want and then the strings themselves become part of the necklace design. It's like a symbol of a perfect marriage."

"Si! Bellissima! I have always wanted one of their pieces since I saw them featured in a magazine. I can't imagine how you could know I wanted one of these?"

"You know… the artists?" Jane was shocked. She'd picked it up in a little shop in Portugal, maybe a street vendor even, in some city she couldn't remember the name of now. She remembered talking with the couple a bit about their creative collaboration.

"This is such a generous gift. Giovanni, you did even better than I thought in finding yourself a girlfriend." She gave her cousin a wink. "She is almost too good to be true, which makes me a bit suspicious."

There was a moment of awkward silence that Jane didn't know how to read or respond to. After a few beats, Giovanni burst out laughing. Then Sophia laughed. Then Edoardo. Lastly, Jane joined the chorus, but it was more confused than mirthful on her part. Still, the unique beauty, niche usefulness, or intriguing back stories she could share saved her embarrassment because the gifts her hosts gave in return were somewhat more extravagant. She wasn't sure what she was going to do with a cashmere duster living in Charlotte, where cold days were in rather short supply, but she appreciated the luxuriousness of it, nonetheless.

"And now, Giovanni, it is my turn," Edoardo announced as he hunted through the presents. Pulling a rather large package from under the back of the tree, he said, "Let me see if I can find something special. Ahhh, this one says it's for Giovanni!" Edoardo exuded the kind of gaiety of being the only person in the room who knows what the gift really is and expects it to be the most memorable of the evening. "Oh, it is heavy! I bet he is going to like this one!" Edoardo was playful as he hefted the gift over with a grunt. It filled Giovanni's lap.

Giovanni looked a bit dwarfed by the gaily wrapped package as he exclaimed, "Oh! You're not kidding—this is molto pesante, very heavy. I cannot imagine what you have gotten me!" He started to rip off the paper like a small child. The box beneath was emblazoned with Edoardo's Emporium, the cooking store he ran in downtown Seattle. Gio looked at Edoardo. "A beautiful box. And… with your own brand on it!"

Edoardo smiled shyly. "Just keeping up appearances, you know, But I do love all the details."

Giovanni smiled. "And because of that, I have always admired your work." The two men shared a warm, appreciative moment. Then Giovanni opened the box. "Mamma mia! Non ci credo! I cannot believe it. You didn't. Oh, you two are too generous. Look, Jane, they gave me a Dutch oven!"

"A Dutch what?" Jane came over to look at the very large pot in a jaunty red color. "Beautiful!" She wasn't sure what to say. It was cookware, after all.

Sophia and Edoardo were beaming with pride at their gift and Giovanni was obviously both impressed and thrilled. Jane wondered if perhaps Gio thought you could drive that thing, he was so excited, but she plastered a polite smile on her face. "Uh, neat! So, what kind of Dutch food do you make in it?"

There was silence for a moment and then Edoardo said, "You weren't kidding when you said that she cannot cook!" Giovanni and his cousins burst into laughter.

For her part, Jane was relieved that this was at least an authentic, relaxed laughter, even if it was at her expense.

"No, she can hardly make tea!" Giovanni was laughing so hard she thought he might need supplemental oxygen. "Oblivious. Oblivious to my cooking."

Jane was finding this whole charade to be less funny by the moment.

"Oh, that is good! She won't notice all your mistakes with Nonna's recipes." Sophia was fully into the act now, too, finding all this to be hilarious.

Giovanni suddenly got completely serious. "I never make a mistake with Nonna's recipes."

Jane would have described Gio as hurt. Maybe even a touch angry. All the mirthful laughter died instantly.

"Of course not. We meant no offence," Sophia added quickly.

Jane watched this exchange with bewilderment. She also had cousins who she hardly ever saw. They, too, had their awkward moments, but they never played for the audience. No, when she thought about it, the awkward silences in her extended family usually resolved with people disappearing for drinks or smokes after overly political discussions. She thought that could well explain why she hadn't seen those cousins in years.

"Jane," Giovanni said turning to his wife. "A Dutch oven is for many good dishes, but I will not use it to make Dutch food. I will make real North Carolina barbeque. And American pot roast. Beef stew. Macaroni and cheese. But no, not, ah, Dutch food." He turned to his cousins. "This is just beyond generous. Thank you so much. I will enjoy this."

With a smile of pride on her face, Sophia turned to Jane. "And I hope you will enjoy it too!"

"I'm sure I will. That looks like we're going to be eating a lot of rich and heavy food all winter! I can see that my New Year's resolution will be to take up running." She picked up the lid. "Wow. Or weightlifting. You know, I could get a workout just by picking up the pot. That thing's really heavy." Looking at Giovanni, she asked, "How will you get that home?"

"Oh," Sophia said stunned. "We hadn't thought of that."

"Maybe we can ship it to you," Edoardo offered.

"Nonsense! I will check my bag and take this as my carry-on luggage. No problemo."

"Oh sure," Jane said. "You'll get a workout as you walk through the airport. What could go wrong with that?"

*   *   *

Later that night as they snuggled in the guest room bed, Giovanni leaned close and whispered in Jane's ear, "So, mi amore, are you having a good time?"

Jane yawned, feeling sleepy, overfed and a little bit tipsy from the night's celebration. "Of course! You know, your cousin Sophia is pretty amazing. Did you notice that she recognized every one of the gifts we gave? She must be so well traveled. I picked those things up from, God, like, everyplace I've been and that's a bunch of damn miles. Either that girl travels a lot, or someplace she's got a stack of old Conde Nast magazines that she's addicted to."

Giovanni chuckled. "Sophia both loves to travel and she loves to read about travel on the internet. She has quite an imagination. You should see some of the trips she plans. I'm sure there are those who would call her, ah, a logistical genius. I'm sure she didn't know all of those wonderful gifts, but she is a very good actor. She can improvise quite well as she goes along."

"You know, your cousins are quite the foodies. Every meal is clearly meant to impress. Are you sure Sophia doesn't secretly YouTube her cooking or have some blog online?"

"Why would you say that?"

"Well, partly because it was so perfect. Like Martha Stewart meets Milan. I mean, real people just don't eat like that every day. It's been like, you know, textbook quintessential Italian. It was so funny because a couple of times I felt like there was a secret audience someplace. A hidden camera. I kept waiting for, I don't know, like the laugh track to kick in or some narrator's voice to provide context and closure to the evening. *Thank you for joining us for An Italian Christmas Holiday. The cookbook, signed by Sophia herself, is available at Edoardo's Emporium...*" Jane mimicked a deep-voiced narrator. *"Join us next time for Sophia's vision of Pasta Perfection of Pompeii."*

Giovanni laughed. "You are so American. I love it. Edoardo does own a cooking store. My cousins are indeed a foodie."

"They would be foodies. Plural. You are just a foodie. Singular. Remember when my parents called you a foodie?" They both laughed. "Sophia is great but it's almost like… like she's trying to prove to me that she's Italian. Like she thinks I'm not going to believe her or something?" Jane chortled. "Now that would be dysfunctional. I get it that she really, really wants to impress us, which I appreciate. It's obviously a lot of work."

"Well, she does like you. She told me to not lose you."

"Right, yeah, but she called me coperta. What's that? A blanket?"

A look of discomfort or perhaps concern flashed across Gio's face. "Your Italian is better than I thought. But do not be offended. She only meant that like a blanket, I am wrapped up in you, and that is good for me."

"You know, Gio, maybe we should just tell people that we got married? I mean, given it was the only way that you could stay in America you think they'd figure it out. That way Sophia wouldn't feel like she needs to win me over or something. She'd know I'm already in with both feet! For better or for worse. 'Til death do us part."

Gio was quiet for a bit. "She does want us to stay together. She thinks you are good for me." Then he seemed a bit awkward. "But I don't think we should share our little secret."

Jane felt her heart skip a beat. "Are you, maybe, um, well, regretting that we eloped?"

"Oh no! No, my Janie. Not at all." He stroked her cheek. Then he lay back down on the bed and looked at the ceiling. "It is just that in my family, we do not elope. We do big family weddings. I am not ready to hear from my mother how I have ruined her life by denying her that. Particularly if she hears it from my cousin. No, it must come from me, and it must be when I am with her. And then we both must be ready to have a big wedding all over again so that she can die a happy woman."

"And I thought women had a lot of pressure on them around getting married!"

"And Italian only children do as well. But I am fortunate. It would be worse if I had been her only daughter."

"It must be so intense to be Italian. I never realized."

"Concordato! Agreed. I find that being Italian is one of the more intense experiences of my life. But mia bella, I love it. And I love being wrapped up in you. My coperta."

Jane couldn't help but smile as she curled up with her husband. She thought it endlessly amusing how his translations would end up conveying something that was not quite what he actually meant. She hoped that adorable awkwardness would never go away even as his English continued to improve.

Chapter 31

On the twenty-seventh, Jane and Giovanni packed their bags and after many hugs and promises to celebrate another holiday together soon, the couple headed to the airport. Giovanni had his new favorite pot wrapped in tissue paper to prevent any scratches, all nestled in its original box, which was sitting in a sturdy forest green fabric shopping bag emblazoned with a gold "Edoardo's Emporium" on it.

"You're really taking that thing on the plane?"

"Of course! It would get damaged if I checked it. And maybe I would never see it again? You never know. And they say to never put anything valuable in your checked luggage."

"Honey, honestly, I don't think anyone is going to steal your cooking pot."

"Jane, do you know how much a Dutch oven like this can cost?"

Jane shrugged. It was pot. How much could it be?

Giovanni gave her a level look. "They can cost up to a thousand American dollars at the store."

Jane blinked. "That's crazy. Maybe we should give it a name and buy it a ticket for its own seat?"

"That's the spirit! I'm going to baby this thing until I can christen it in our own kitchen. Come to Papa!" He hugged the Edoardo's bag protectively in his lap. "I am very excited about my Christmas gift!"

Airport security was not as excited about Edoardo's generous gift, however.

A burly man in a too-tight TSA uniform shook his head. "Okay, who's the joker who put a huge metal pot through the x-ray machine, huh?" The TSA Official called out in an accent that indicated he was a recent transplant from his usual beat at JFK on the other coast. "Somebody goin' ta claim this metal pot?"

Jane prodded Gio. "Hey, it looks like we might have trouble. Look there."

Giovanni hopped over to the agent. "That would be mine, sir."

"Oh, you're a foreigner, huh? You from Switzerland or something?"

"Italy originally, but my wife's an American and I now live in North Carolina. And just where are you from?"

"No small talk," the agent answered gruffly. "Open the package."

Giovanni did as the agent requested.

"And please remove the lid, sir. Nice and slow there." While the security agent phrased his request politely, his tone was anything but. "No fast moves." He watched closely as Giovanni slowly removed the pot lid. The TSA official seemed disappointed that it was empty. "Eh. So, why did you think you could carry on a huge metal object, huh?"

"It's not a huge metal object. It's a cooking pot. And it wouldn't fit in my luggage, and my favorite cousin gave it to me as a holiday present. So, I have to bring it with me in my hands," Giovanni explained, holding his hands before him, as if to provide evidence.

"You can't. 'Gainst the rules."

"What? You can't bring cookware? I see nothing that lists cookware as a contraband." Giovanni pointed to the large video screen that showed a rolling list of the variety of prohibited items. "It's not a gun. It has no lithium battery. It's not an aerosol. It doesn't explode or light up. It doesn't provide small children with noisy entertainment…"

"Ain't you a comedian? It ain't cookware on a plane. Ya ain't cookin' on a plane. It's a weapon. It's contraband."

"A weapon?" Giovanni was stunned. "How could this be a weapon?"

From behind him another TSA guard walked up. "You could hit somebody with it. Yeah, Frank, you could do a lot of damage whacking them in the head with that."

A third agent, a woman with a badge that named her as Quetta joined them. She walked over to the pot and lifted the lid. Turning to the second agent, she said, "Sam, this thing weighs like a million pounds. Nobody could use this as a weapon. Not on a plane. You don't have the room."

Frank took the lid from her and held it like a shield, "Well, Quetta, you could if you did it like this." He demonstrated swinging the lid around in slow motion.

The agent named Sam offered a different suggestion. "Hey, you could frisbee it like Captain America did in that movie. Then that would be a weapon."

"Please don't do that! Please don't damage my new cookware!" Giovanni turned to Jane. "Janie, maybe you should just go ahead to the gate and I will meet you there. This may take a while."

Quetta took the lid from Sam and hefted it again. "No way you could make this fly like that in a tight space. I'd bet you a twelve pack that you couldn't do it even in an open field." She motioned like she was warming up to give it try, right there in security.

Jane shook her head. "Or you could sprain your back as you tried to do those things. You all be careful now, ya hear?" Turning to Gio she added, "I'll see you at the gate. Good luck." She gave him a quick kiss and headed off. A half an hour later, just as they were about to start the boarding process, Giovanni joined her.

"I see you have the green bag still!"

"Si! And it has my pot in there. I am allowed to carry it on." Giovanni was all smiles.

"And just how did you get them to agree that it isn't a weapon?"

"I started to join them in all the ways this pot could kill someone."

Jane was dumbfounded. "I... I can't believe that worked."

"Si. I said you can make the pot roast. And you can make the beef stew. And slow cooked American barbecue. Ahhh! And it makes a mac and cheese that will take ten years off of your life, but it would be worth it. And if you want to taste the best duck you have ever had, then you have to taste the bird baked in the Dutch oven."

Jane stared at him.

A slow smile grew on Giovanni's face. "Si, they started to understand how ridicolo, you would say ridiculous, they were being. And we all laughed at it and they let me through."

As they took their seats in row twenty-four, Jane lamented that they hadn't moved fast enough to upgrade to comfort plus. "It's going to be a long flight…"

Giovanni shrugged. "Neither of us are large people. We will fit just fine here. As long as my little baby fits under the seat."

"Why don't you put that thing up above?" Jane asked.

"No. I want to know it's here. I can touch it with my feet and I know it's real. I really have this beautiful Dutch oven."

"Giovanni, dude, you are way too into food."

Giovanni looked at her with such a sappy look it made her heart melt. "I know. Isn't it wonderful? I feel like I never got to be in my own life before. But now I have a life. An ordinary, perfect, happy life. I am really enjoying this."

It was such an odd comment, she found herself wondering if he had ever been homeless.

The flight was unremarkable with Giovanni sacking out in the first twenty minutes, just like always. She envied how he could sleep on a plane. It seemed unfair. She was the one who flew all the time and even after all these years, she still found it hard to sleep. She put her jealousy aside and got herself absorbed in a book until about halfway through their journey when some consternation started unfolding several rows in front of them in the coveted comfort-plus seats she had so envied. A man seemed to be arguing with a flight attendant. As they argued their voices got louder. At least his did.

"No, I will not. I don't have to. This is a free country!" The man's voice was now loud enough for her to hear clearly.

She couldn't quite hear the flight attendant, who still looked like she was staying calm and professional.

Now the man's voice was shouting. "I will not. This is tyranny. The constitution gives me rights, damn it! You can't take those from me."

Another flight attendant, the sole man on the team, now joined the discussion. He tried to reason with the customer.

"Oh no, this doesn't look good." She poked Giovanni. "Gio, wake up. Some guy is freaking out on the plane."

"Hmmmrumph?" Giovanni said groggily. "What's happening?"

Jane listened intently. "I think some guy up there is drunk and doesn't want to stop drinking or maybe doesn't want to wear his seat belt. Or maybe it's both. But he's being a real jerk about it. Oh my God! He's going off the rails!"

The man was now standing up and screaming about his rights and freedoms to the flight attendants, who were ordering him back to his seat. The man pushed the female flight attendant, causing her to fall over backwards, her head hitting the armrest of a seat as she fell. Flight attendants from the back of the plane rushed up the aisle to help her get up and supported her as they took her to the aft of the plane, her hand to her face covering an eye that was quickly swelling.

"You can't control me like I'm some animal. I live in a free country so fuck you! Your rules aren't my rules! I'm outta here. Where's the damn door?" He started towards an emergency exit.

Now the male flight attendant was shouting, barely managing to keep any cool he had remaining. "Sir, these are the airlines rules. I must ask you to take your seat."

"Fuck you! Take this." The man swung and landed a right cross on the unsuspecting flight attendant's jaw and he went down hard.

"Sit down!" passengers started shouting at the man, who simply flipped them off in return. A passenger three rows in back of the unruly man stood up; a large African American gentleman who looked to Jane like he regularly pressed two-hundred and was so tall he could barely stand in the plane. In a booming voice, he thundered, "You need to sit down now!"

The smaller belligerent man was undaunted. In fact, he seemed excited to have an adversary worth taking on. "And just who's gonna' make me? You?"

In his booming voice, the tall man said, "If I need to make you, I will."

The loudspeaker shattered what little peace was left, with the pilot saying, "Folks, we understand there's a little bit of excitement back there. For everyone's safety we're putting the fasten seat belt sign back on and we need you to take your seats, right away."

"Oh my God! This is insane." Jane was mesmerized by the scene, only barely noticing that Giovanni had ducked down, his head below the seat as if he didn't want to be a part of anything that was happening. *Oh well,* she thought, *he is just a tennis pro. And he's kind of a small guy.* Somehow, she couldn't tear herself away from the scene, even if he was too unnerved by it all to watch.

As a third flight attendant came rushing from the front of the plane, the pilot's voice came on so loudly from the overhead speakers that Jane had to cover her ears, as he announced that they were going to divert to the nearest airport and should be on the ground shortly. Jane felt the vibration of heavy footsteps pounding on the airplane floor. With her hands still over her ears, she turned to see a rather large man rushing up the aisle. His shirt was untucked over his generous belly and he looked scared to death… or perhaps he was over-excited since he shouted, "Air Marshal! Air Marshal!" as loud as he could, almost like he'd been waiting his whole life to shout those words with authority. Then everything started happening so fast that Jane wasn't sure what happened in what order. But somehow the belligerent man was now holding a knife. Not like a dinner knife but like the kind of object that the TSA should actually be looking for when they're worried about someone bringing a cooking pot on board. The large Black man was close to the unruly drunk and although several passengers screamed out, it was too late. The intoxicated passenger swung his arm and the knife went into the shoulder of the big man, who staggered backwards. A flight attendant from the front of the plane rushed in at that moment, and as she tried to help the bleeding passenger, the plane took a nosedive as it diverted for an emergency landing.

Then someone screamed, "Gun! He's got a gun!" Jane snapped her head around wondering who had a gun and how had she managed to get on this flight-from-hell and why was Giovanni still cowered down like that? She spotted the gun, which was in the waving hand of the over-excited Air Marshal. That gave her comfort for about three seconds, since as the plane dove, the Air Marshal lost his footing and fell forward, catching his bulk on one of the seats, bouncing, and landing his back on the upright part of the seat on the other side of the aisle. He thudded to the floor with a shudder that was felt all around and the gun went sliding from his hand up the aisle only to be stepped upon by the drunk, angry passenger. Looking down, surprised, the man picked up the gun and turned it in his hand a few times, a slow smile growing on his face.

Jane gasped. "Oh shit, the drunk dude's got the air marshal's gun!"

Giovanni's head popped up as he surveyed the situation. "He's not drunk. That's a meth trip. You stay here."

The tripped-out man was now laughing out loud, flashing the gun about. "Now, this will make you listen! Why do you people never listen until a gun is involved, huh? Guns are a constitutional right because they make us listen to one another. And now you're gonna listen to me. It's God's own law that men have guns. Yeah, you bunch of motherfuckers. Tell me to strap down like some animal on a leash."

Before she knew it, Giovanni was on his feet, but the aisle between him and the now doubly armed passenger was filled with the bodies of the groaning Air Marshal, who was calling out something like "My back! My back!", the bleeding, big, brave man who was calling out for Jesus and his mother up in Heaven, and the senior flight attendant who was trying to both put pressure on his wound and help the man back to his seat, all while the plane was nose diving towards the ground. The cabin lights dimmed suddenly, adding to the sense of confusion.

And then Giovanni was beyond them all and standing in front of the tripped-out man. Jane was about to scream, to tell Gio to get back to his seat before he got shot, but the oxygen masks fell from their compartments overhead, hitting her in the face. A mumble of "What the hell?" was all that came from her lips. She found it too hard to breathe, more from her fear for Gio than from anything else. And then she saw it in his hand. Bright red. He stood there before the meth-trippin' guy, looking a bit like Spiderman, and suddenly his arm snapped forward and he shot a blow to the passenger, lid to his Dutch oven in his grip. The man crumpled to the floor. The surrounding passengers cheered. Jane heard the random shout of "Chefs rule!" and then the screaming started up again as the plane maneuvered sharply into its emergency landing.

Giovanni stooped and picked up the gun. In a split second he had the ammunition removed and he shoved it all into his pocket. He hefted the now unconscious man and pushed him toward his seatmates. "Buckle in that piece of trash" he instructed them.

One of the flight attendants from the back of the plane rushed forward with duct tape. As she started strapping the man's hands together and taping him to his seat, she shot a guilty look over at Giovanni. "Just in case he wakes up."

"I thought you weren't supposed to tape the passengers anymore?" He raised an eyebrow at her.

She shrugged. "Well, that's true. But ever since those bizarre years during the pandemic when things got so crazy unruly, well, one of us just always brings a roll. For emergencies, you know."

Then Giovanni turned to the stabbed man and, disentangling him from the terrified and now bloodied flight attendant, he got the man back into his seat. Gio ripped off his own shirt and leaned into the big guy, applying pressure to the wound, holding the injured gentleman securely in his chair while the flight landed.

"You were so brave to take that man on!" Giovanni tried to make conversation, his patient visibly agitated.

"The blood. I can't take the blood—seeing the blood." The big man trembled.

Giovanni attended him like a professional. "The sight of blood bothers many people, the big and the small. You, my friend, are lucky. He missed the major arteries. That's right, close your eyes, breathe slowly." He whispered to comfort the man. "You are going to be just fine. But my friend, I think your suit... I'm afraid that your suit, it will need stitches." The man opened his eyes and then gave a slow smile.

"My suit."

"Yes. You and your suit both, perhaps." Giovanni gave the man a wink and the man started to visibly relax.

"And your shirt will need..."

"Don't look down," Giovanni coached him. "My shirt can be replaced. It is not nice like your suit." Giovanni stayed with him, using his balled-up shirt and the pot lid to focus the pressure until the flight had landed and the medics entered the plane. When Giovanni left the wounded man, the surrounding passengers all cheered him loudly.

Jane was frozen in her seat. Speechless, she stared at a now shirtless and blood-smeared Giovanni as he returned to take his seat beside her, pot lid in hand.

"Oh my God! How did you do that? I was so worried! Why did you do that?" Jane was stunned and felt like she was sputtering out the words.

Giovanni smiled in a way that was far too calm and reasonable for anyone who had just been in the middle of all that excitement: the hero of the day, who subdued a drugged-up and out-of-his-mind armed assailant.

"Of course, I had to do something! Jane, the TSA agents—they gave me the idea. My pot, it was a weapon after all. It was a shield just like that lady said. And it was an instrument to deliver a, what did he call it? A blunt blow? And so, how could I not? And I just went on instinct."

She shook her head in disbelief. "If that was instinct, I'd hate to see you with training! But how did you manage that, getting up the aisle? I kept thinking that you looked like you were, I don't know, Spiderman or something. You basically crawled up the backs of the seats."

"Well, the aisle was full of wounded people." He turned to look at the air marshal who was being taken out on a stretcher, having thrown his back out in his fall. They had already removed the stabbed passenger and the knocked-out flight attendant. "I could not step on them."

"But how could you do that? How would you know how to do that?"

Giovanni smiled at her warmly. "Hey, I do have training. Serious training. I am a tennis pro at the club. We do agility exercises so we can move and get the ball. Of course, I can spring up a few rows like that. Ah, my Janie, you should have seen me in my heyday. I was once so quick on the courts. You should have seen me at the net. This, this was nothing!"

"I don't think it was nothing! How did you know how to help that poor man who got stabbed?"

"Oh, playing the nurse? Eh, I used to play rugby in my youth. Rough game, rugby." He just shrugged.

"You play rugby with knives?" Jane didn't know what to think. "You're a hero. Oh my gosh, this will be all over the news. I bet you go viral. Giovanni, you're going to be famous after this."

Giovanni's smile was mysterious. "I bet you a good bottle of vino that it doesn't make the news at all. No! Too many crazy people on airlines these days. These events happen all the time. Just another story too boring for the news to bother to cover."

Much to her surprise, Giovanni was right. There was hardly a mention in the news at all and where it did get reported, the story was all wrong, crediting some random Australian dude with saving the day. Her hero of a secret husband never went viral at all. In fact, her family thought she was making it up when she told them. Of course, it didn't help that Giovanni wouldn't talk about it or support her version of events at all. He just didn't like the attention. The only thing he really wanted was to get cooking with his new pot.

Chapter 32

Jane was enjoying one of their rare weekends together. Work had kept her on overseas travel far too much lately and she'd been gone for the better part of the last seven weeks. All that wonderful time together at Christmas, but then the new year came rushing in, whisking her off to what felt like another life. A life filled with a lot of meetings but no Giovanni.

She was done. It had been too much. Now she was taking a full week off. No more meetings. No more phone calls. No texts. No excuses. That one Facetime talk had triggered it. She almost quit her job, threatened to walk out if they didn't give her some time to actually live her life. The sad thing was, she was so wrapped up in it all that she hadn't even noticed. Until that call. It was that last damn promotion. They'd bumped her up again right after New Year's.

"It's not like you have to fly the plane." Giovanni's face looked so sad on that small screen during their Facetime call. About six months into their marriage and Facetime and texting were the only times they were together. "Your job is marketing the plane. I'm sure they can learn to live without you while we spend just a week finding each other again. That's all I ask for. Just a week."

Finding each other again. That hit her hard. In his own head, he probably phrased that as a romantic sentiment, but it made her worry that she could lose the love of her life before their first anniversary. That was her greatest fear and here it was actually starting to happen.

Newlyweds, even secret ones, should have time together. She took the leave and refused to go anyplace. If she was taking time off, she was going to stay in her own home. *In our own home,* she corrected herself. *In our own home.*

She was trying to think of something to say. Like one of those clever little things they used to laugh themselves into tears over when they'd first gotten together. When their love was fresh and new and before her latest promotion had reinforced just how much she was married to her job. She watched him carefully put all the vegetables he'd been cutting so meticulously into the pan on the stove. Then he walked over to the new double oven and peeked inside, releasing the most wonderful aromas into the kitchen. *He may be just a part-time tennis pro at the club, but the man can cook,* she thought. She'd had a lot of good food on the road, but nothing tasted like his home cooking. He always talked about how his Nonna had made this entrée or that particular dessert. She marveled that real old-world Italian cooking was so much more than pasta. God bless those women in his life who had taken their unambitious little boy under their wing and taught him how to master the cucina.

Giovanni was unpretentious. That was a good description and certainly not a surprise. He'd been exactly that when she'd met him. He was relaxed. Happy.

"Giovanni, what's your goal in life?"

"What's my goal in life? Eh, just to stay alive. To have enough. Not too much. Just enough for no worries." He laughed with dramatic flair as he pulled down two wine glasses. "I do not need to be famous. In fact, I rather like it that no one knows me. I am hidden from the world here in Charlotte. To simply exist and love my life… my life with you, now that you are back again… that is my greatest dream. That is true freedom." Giovanni sighed deeply with contentment as he opened up a bottle of wine and Jane felt shivers down her spine. He could blow her away with the most romantic comments. While his words could stop her in her tracks, evoking a tide of emotions that surrounded her and stranded her on her little island of logic and objectivity, he seemed as comfortable as if he were commenting on the weather. These beautiful sentiments were just natural to him. Jane couldn't have mustered those touchy-feely statements even with a day's worth of concentrated effort. Well, maybe that's why she marketed Airbus and not Hallmark.

She might not be able to author them, but she loved the effect they had on her. At least she told herself she did. In truth she wasn't always sure how to manage the flow of emotions they brought about. She'd always been cast as the lover rather than the beloved. The one doing all the nice and thoughtful things. The running. The chasing. The hungering for the love you hoped to get back. And, if she were being honest, the starving and eventually the utter exhaustion at the end of the relationship road. This was a new dance and she realized she felt clumsy and unskilled, unsure of her next move. She wasn't used to playing the lead.

But since Nick, she'd never loved anyone like she did now. Not since Nick had she felt this all-consuming-I-would-do-anything-for-you kind of feeling. After loving and losing, loving deeply again was strange territory. She knew she should tread lightly on the permafrost of her heart lest she damage that tender ground. The vulnerability of being in love had been hard enough the first time around. The second time, well, she realized just how much she had to lose. With Nicky it was easy at first but eventually became a boulder she was pushing up a hill. You kept at it because that's what you did. And you loved it, right? Love was work, wasn't it? But it hadn't been obvious when it became too much of a burden, too much of a chore. Then that boulder started to roll backwards and run her over, and she didn't realize what was happening until she'd been flattened.

But the second time around you saw love for what it was—a dangerous journey. And you didn't gloss over the difficult bits – you knew it was a weighty mass that had to be moved along with commitment and risk and patience and work. She found the situation to be crystal clear—at least the second time around. But now the roles were reversed and she was the beloved. Maybe she was the boulder?

Jane glanced at the bottle label. This was one of the expensive ones. But they were all expensive ones. Giovanni seemed deceptively simple to her friends and family, but in reality he had excellent taste and nothing came cheaply. Nothing he picked out anyway. She glanced down and saw that he was once again in tennis shorts, no matter that it was February and the high today hadn't made it to forty degrees. While he nearly lived in tennis shorts, they were top quality and always new.

"Is it better to have so much money that you never needed to worry? I mean, you could do whatever you wanted and not have to give it a second thought… I wonder what would that be like?"

"It would be fantastico!" Giovanni was characteristically enthusiastic. She thought he would break the wine glass if he didn't stop speaking with his hands like that.

"Fantastic? This is going to sound strange, but I don't know. I see people who live like that, and they have all this freedom but not success. They never accomplish anything worth accomplishing. There's nothing to show for the fact that they lived. I once knew this guy who had a trust fund and all he did was ski."

Giovanni gave her a dumbfounded look. "That sounds like a wonderful life."

"He died in a back country avalanche. He might have accomplished the perfect black diamond run, but no one'll ever know it."

Giovanni started to pour the wine into the glasses. The glass was beautiful. From Venice, just a few hours from his hometown. He'd had these glasses blown by hand just for her by artisans who, for generations, had been making art of melted sand blended with raw metals. "I think it would be fantastico to have endless money. Money and no worries. In Italy no one has any money. No one outside of the mafia, but then, they all have to live down in the south. Eh." He shrugged dismissively. "But the north is so expensive… Milan? Forget it. Venice? Impossible! I'm glad to live here. Here you can live with no money."

"Well, thanks a lot. I rather thought I made a decent living until just this moment." The annoyance rankled more than she liked to admit. This was part of the boulder, wasn't it? She provided the living and he made the life worth living. Wasn't that what she wanted? Someone who didn't resent her success? Someone who could just enjoy it? After all, that's what she'd conjured up in her little cocktail glass the night they met. And wasn't that the deal her parents had, only in reverse? It worked, didn't it? She wondered if her father had ever resented the arrangement. If he had, he'd hidden it well. Of course, her mother's resentment at never having had a career was kept barely under the surface. Her frustrated ambitions leaked out as she posted her culinary creations on Pinterest and Facebook—man, what that woman could do with a blow torch and a cake! A little meringue, a little isomalt and she was like a food wizard. Her online world with strangers was her form of professional recognition.

Giovanni looked at Jane, his expression morphing into contrition. "You do. You're a great provider. I wasn't thinking about you, actually. I was thinking about me. What do I do? I teach tennis? Tennis professionista. You galivant all around the world with your glamorous job while I do the laundry and have dinner waiting for you when the plane brings you home. Let's face it, in this relationship… you're the boss. I'm just, just the window dressing. Madre Maria di Gesù! If my poor Papà could see this, he'd be so ashamed."

Jane could feel her annoyance melt away instantly. She moved over to Giovanni and wrapped her arms around him. "Mother Mary of Jesus! Maybe your dear mama would be happy that her son ended up with the kind of life where he got to follow his bliss, even if that bliss is on the tennis court."

"I take my failure out on the little yellow balls." He gave her a weak smile. "Mi Madre, she would be happy I found a warm blanket to keep me safe, you know?" He shook his head sadly. "Papà would not be surprised, I think. He always said my cousin was the great hope of the family. He didn't seem to have much faith in me, the spoiled only child."

Jane rubbed his shoulder and tried to think of something to say. She drew a blank. She should be able to relate to this. Summer overshadowed everyone in the family with her wild ways and crazy art. She'd made a name for herself. And her younger sister the successful surgeon. Of course, Charlie was so busy they never heard from her these days. Jane had always felt overshadowed. A decade ago she was a minor marketing executive with a very failed marriage that never even got out of the gate. Probably why she'd poured herself into that job. And now she was successful in her own right. She loved her career. Okay, it was a love/hate relationship, but only because she loved it too much. Now that Giovanni was in it, she loved her life. She'd never loved her life before, which was why she'd been married to the job. Truth be told, she appreciated it that Gio wanted to stay home and keep things running and have dinner waiting when the winds brought her back. Yes, she loved it, but also resented it. It was so complex. How could it be so complex? It was wrong to say you couldn't have it both ways. It seems life came at you from a million directions at once. You had no choice but to have it both ways.

"You are lucky. You have a kind of drive I never had." He looked sad for a moment but then he took a big drink of his wine and perked up, happy again. "Ah, you are so serious, amore mio, my Janie, and now for some reason I am being serious." He gave her a wink. "We are such a good match, you know? I think you need me to help balance you out."

"To help me deal with the monkey on my back?"

He looked at her, concern playing across his face. "You have a... a monkey on your back?" He playfully looked over her shoulder, but his concern was evident.

"Oh, you wouldn't know what that's like, lucky you! You're a tennis pro. Living with the monkey is something I've done all my life."

He sounded very gentle, almost a little bit afraid as he probed, "Tell me about your... your monkey."

Jane took a sip of her wine. It deserved to be served in a glass like this. Once again, he'd picked a great one. The wine and the glass—works of art. She picked up a little slice of cheese from the plate he'd set out. Delicious. A perfect pairing. Probably wickedly expensive. Cave-aged cheese. Smooth flavor contrasting nicely with the little crystals of calcium in there.

"My monkey. Hmmm. I named him George, like the children's story. I've just about always had my monkey."

"Go on."

"Once you have a monkey, it sticks with you, through thick and thin. It's always there. It rides your shoulders and it loves to whip you, when you're down, when you're up—doesn't matter. It always wants more and more and more. And you have to feed that monkey. Damn thing's ravenous."

"Ravenous. That sounds... ah... dreadful."

"Here's what's funny: it actually isn't."

"So, you like having this monkey on your back?"

She gave him a joking smile. "Well, let me see if I can explain it. I mean, I don't know if you're going to understand."

"Give me a try, my Jane."

"Okay. Well, I know you're frustrated with how much time I spend at work. I love my work. And my monkey loves my work. When you have a monkey, it rides your back. It whips you forward, and then you push harder and harder. It isn't about just getting the job done. It isn't about just getting the job right. It's about getting the job done faster and better than it's ever been done before. It's not about meeting the expectation of the boss or the customer or whoever. It's about blowing them away, shooting so far beyond their expectations that it redefines what they want, what they need. It's about changing them in ways they never knew they could change. It's about creating something that, not only did no one ever really think about before, but creating something that couldn't exist until you made it happen. When you do that it's awesome. Then you go to bed at night with this sense that the whole universe is within your reach. And that monkey lies right down with you and it's happy. And when it's happy, you're happy. You feed the monkey and it's this huge sea of contentment. That's living your bliss."

Giovanni stared at her for a moment. "Okay, Jane. Your monkey… you are saying that your monkey makes you, makes you work harder?"

"Okay, that's one way to put it. The monkey makes you chase your bliss through work. People who don't have that drive, who can just enjoy life and play tennis and walk the dog and take their time picking out great wine… they don't have to deal with a monkey on their back. That's the difference between the two of us. You don't live with a monkey."

"Eh, Jane, do you, eh, talk about the monkey to other people? Like at work?"

"What? No. Of course not! They'd think I was crazy. Oh my God, now you think I'm crazy, don't you?" She started to pace around. "Here I was worried that you might not love me anymore because I'm a workaholic and now I'm worried that you think I'm crazy!"

"Crazy? No. Totally obsessed with work and a little bit, eh, what do you American's call it? Anal? Si. Yes. But I knew that about you before I decided to move to America to be with you. As we traveled around Europe last summer, you really did talk about your work quite a bit. Amore mio, did you know, were you aware, that having a 'monkey on your back' means you're dealing with an addiction?"

"Well, I sort of do have an addiction to work. You tease me about that all the time."

"Yes, if you were an attorney, I'm sure you'd bill more than twenty-four hundred hours."

"I think that's a compliment?"

"Only if you grew up with an imaginary monkey named George. But this kind of addiction is different. Most people who have a 'monkey on their back', well, let's just say that George sticks them with a little syringe."

Jane looked at him, non-comprehending.

"It's a heroin addiction."

"Oh, I don't have that!"

"I'm glad to hear it," he laughed. "Si, obviously not. People with that problem aren't usually obsessed with being the best in their field. Even when that field is marketing great big airplanes."

"I guess everyone has their drug." She laughed a little bit nervously. "At least mine isn't something you shoot up with. Or, uh, smoke. Or bake into brownies. Or um, whatever people do with heroin." She felt like an idiot. She'd heard of heroin. Everyone had heard of heroin. But she didn't know precisely what people did with it or what exactly it did to them. Jane wanted to change the subject. She gestured at the kitchen renovation Giovanni had just completed. "And the monkey has benefits!"

"Benefits? It looks to me like a lot of travel and meetings. Even on the weekends you're home, you're really always at work."

"There's this." She toasted him with the wine glass. "And that." She pointed to the new double ovens. "And someplace around here is a sub-zero freezer that is magically concealed behind a panel that looks just like one of the walls. I remember you sent me a picture of it, so I'm sure it's here."

He walked over and pushed on a wood covered section of wall. "Ecco! I did not lie."

"So, without the monkey, I'd be helping you teach tennis and we might have a camping cooler, or something like that. The monkey is responsible for the bonuses, the raises, the promotions. George is responsible for me being obsessed with my job."

"Okay, so Giorgio, he is both our best friend. I love the kitchen renovation." He grinned. "Viva la monkey!" He tipped his wine glass towards her and took a sip.

"Viva la monkey." As she felt the wine slide down her throat she realized just how much she valued his good opinion of her. It meant everything. She had felt so proud that she could afford to give him whatever he wanted in the house that he'd picked out for them. Like the kitchen renovation that he'd designed and managed and had somehow magically completed during her last long trip. With his stupid expensive shorts and bottles of wine. She wanted Giovanni to love her. She needed him to love her. And he needed to love the monkey too.

Chapter 33

June rolled in with record temperatures, the year in a rush to get the hot months going. Jane spent a good bit of time overseas on trips, missing Giovanni and missing home. She'd never really missed home before because, while it was a place to relax and catch up on both her mail and sleep, it wasn't actually home. Her old condo had always felt like another hotel room in a way, probably because she spent so little time there. But now she and Gio had a house—a real home. Someplace to come home to, and yet....

She thought of the Christmas tree and how that was all her, her history. It seemed that Giovanni had taken that to heart, and he had inserted himself into the fabric of the house. She would come home from a trip, and he'd have redecorated a room or changed the color of their bedroom. He had great taste even if it was a bit minimalist with color being used as an accent piece. The house had a completely "male" feel to it and while it was nice to come home to, she often felt like she was visiting Giovanni in his home.

She couldn't find the words to explain it to him. Once she tried and offended him after he'd put all that work into nesting, so she decided to simply appreciate his efforts. After all, he paid the bills, did all the shopping, kept her fed, even bought her clothes. He addressed every maintenance need and kept the place clean. She lived there twenty-five percent of the time and he lived there one-hundred percent of the time. She let it go, feeling she didn't have a leg to stand on. But he could pick up that she was glum. Things weren't quite right.

"You seem a bit distracted, Amore mio. When was the last time you got together with your sister?"

"She's on one of those Fulbright thingy's. You know, college professor. She's living in Romania for the next three months."

Giovanni looked pensive. "How about friends? You need a girl's night out perhaps?"

She thought about that. She hadn't seen some of her girlfriends in ages. "Maybe that's just what I need. Some girl-time. That's a great idea. Thanks, Giovanni. I'll reach out to some of my friends and set something up."

She sent some emails and made some calls and quickly had a group of girlfriends scheduled to hit a cute little craft cocktail place for the coming weekend. As the date approached, she started to feel excited about the get-together, something she hadn't felt in longer than she could remember. But then again, because of her travel schedule over the winter, she hadn't been able to see these friends in months and months and months.

As Saturday afternoon came to a close and she hit save for her latest spreadsheet, Giovanni came into her home office.

"Are you excited? Tonight is your big night out!"

She spun around slowly. "Actually, I'm feeling a little bit guilty."

"Guilty? Because you are cheating on me with your girlfriends? No, no, no, no, no, no, no."

"But it's Saturday night and I'm hardly ever home. And now I'm heading out with a bunch of other women who I hardly ever see—and who, frankly, might have kind of forgotten me."

"I want to spend time with you, si. But you need friends, too. Go, have a good time. And tomorrow we will take the whole day together with no spreadsheets and no last-minute meetings and no emergencies, eh?"

She nodded.

"And, because this is a special night, I have a little present for you."

From behind his back he pulled out a gift bag. Inside she found a new shirt, bright colors, a drapey cut of layered diaphanous cloth—just perfect for the occasion. How he could always manage to pick out exactly the right thing for her, she couldn't imagine. They were just so connected. Of course, she was glad he didn't try to dress her like the house or her whole wardrobe would be beige or ecru paired with red accent jewelry. She changed her clothes and felt supercharged for her evening.

"You have a good time. Go be a girl for a night and not a high-powered executive." He gave her a kiss as she left the house.

* * *

Jane came back from her girl's night out, but she wasn't in the high spirits she'd expected to be. Somehow, after three hours with friends, she just felt empty. She tossed her bag down on the table inside the door. Gio came from the other room and leaned on the doorframe. He looked at the handbag lying on its side, car keys and a lipstick spilling out of the top.

"And how was your ciao bello evening with your friends?"

Jane didn't answer for a while as she puttered around a bit.

He asked again, "And your evening?"

She looked up at him, as if hearing him for the first time. "Meh. I would say it was... meh."

"Amore mio, what is wrong? Why do you seem so sad? Did you have a fight with your friends?" Giovanni tenderly brushed Jane's hair back and out of her face, tucking the lock behind her ear. Gently, he put two fingers under her chin and gave her two quick strokes, making her smile, but she also turned her head away.

"It's silly. I'm being silly."

He gave her a serious look. "My Nonna, may her spirit always guide us and lookout for us," he crossed himself quickly, "my Nonna always said that if it gives you passion, it is not silly. It is real. When emotion is blowing through you like a storm, it is real. Storms are not silly things. I can see the storm clouds in your eyes. Come, sit down. Tell me, mio Jane, what is going on?" He led her to the living room, where they sat on the loveseat, facing one another.

He was right. It did feel like storm clouds. Like silly, little girl storm clouds. The kind that middle-schoolers lost sleep over. She was embarrassed to tell him, lest he see her for who she really was deep down: so goddamn insecure that he wouldn't want to waste time on her. The old scars may have healed but they were still there. After all these years. How could they still be there after all this time? How could she be so goddamn successful and still feel like an imposter? After all, Nicky didn't want to waste time on her, at least at some level, or he wouldn't have cheated on her like he did.

Don't do that to yourself! she told herself firmly. *Gio is not Nick. And Nick did want to spend time with you. He married you. He just also… lied. A shitload. That was about him. Not about you.*

"It's a little silly. I got my feelings hurt. We went to this specialty bar, very cool with amazing craft cocktails. As they had their second drinks, which I couldn't do because they just were too strong for me, they all got pretty tipsy. So much talk about their kids. And then they started talking and laughing about all the things they did together over the past two years. Like girls' trips to the beach, the movies, meeting at cute little cafes, backyard bonfires. They did a 'tough mudder' race together, as a team."

Gio nodded. "Those things sound like fun."

"Yeah, they sounded like fun to me too. I would have loved to have been invited, but I wasn't. Even if I couldn't have gone, I would have liked it if they had just thought of me. And they seemed to forget that I hadn't been there and didn't know anything about those great times. A huge topic of conversation was about how cute or frustrating or mystifying their children are. It left me with this sudden revelation that I'm not actually a part of the group—I'm not a mother or a mudder.

I'm not around. I'm just a sometimes part of the group. And then one of them turned to me and said, 'We have such a special friendship'."

"That sounds like a nice thing to say to you."

Jane shook her head. "She didn't mean me. She meant them. The 'we' was them. Not me. I felt like a fifth wheel. After that, I didn't even say anything."

"Oh, like you didn't fit."

"Like I'd been invited along tonight because when I reached out, I found out about the plans they already had in place. And Hannah was just too embarrassed to not invite me. The others seemed surprised that I showed up. I wasn't even counted in the reservation. So, it struck me that I'm actually just an interloper on their good time. It felt like the topic of conversation was, in fact, meant to set me straight."

"No, surely…"

Jane sighed. "You're right. I know that can't be true. I've already told myself a dozen times tonight that I'm being silly. That I'm over-reacting. There's a logical explanation. But mostly I just felt pretty stupid. Here I'd thought that these girls were my friends, like my good friends. I could call on them and count on them. I know I travel a lot. I know I'm not around to be with them like they are with each other. I know I don't share their mom experience. But then, all of a sudden, it became so much clearer to me that *they* are really good friends. I mean with each other. And they like me, sure, but I'm a second stringer. Convenient when they have extra room. Good to fill the empty spot but I'm the first to be cut off the list when they need to winnow it down. I'm definitely not on their A-team."

"Do you want to be on their A-team? Do you need to be a first-string player with them?"

She thought about that. "I don't know, actually. It's more that I thought I was on the team and because I assumed it, I never actually thought about it. It was just 'these are my friends'. And I accepted them with all their wrinkles and foibles, just like I thought they accepted me with mine. But in one stroke of lightning, I had the realization that they're a clique and I'm on the B-team. And it made me wonder if I'm a… a hanger-on? If they maybe, I don't know, take a deep breath before I show up? Or maybe when they're creating the list of who's invited, they think twice before adding my name to the roster?"

He looked at her, eyebrows raised.

"Gio, this is hard to… to… find the words. I'm hurt, yes, of course I am, but it's also something else. I had one idea, one vision of myself, of being a friend and having friends. And then all of a sudden, I get this reflection in the mirror that I'm the fifth wheel, the little sibling that no one really wants to come along, but mama says 'you can't go if you don't take your little sister. And I'll find out if you're not nice to her!' Nobody wants to play that role, I mean not as an adult. You know, I've brought them all these gifts from my travels, because they were my friends, and then I got this creepy feeling like all this time I'd just been bribing them to like me. And I went from one instant of believing 'these are my good friends' to the next instant, 'Well, shit… I'm the uninvited guest. I'm horning in on their good time, better have a good gift.' I've just never had that view of myself."

Of course, Jane knew that she had indeed had that experience before. That she'd had one idea of herself: as the lover, the beloved, the cherished. And then in one stroke of lightning she found she was the uninvited wife, the interloper, and definitely a third wheel on Nick's bicycle-built-for-two that he was actually riding with Ashlyn. What she'd felt tonight, rejection, was a small thing, but what had resurfaced from the deep recesses of her locked vault of emotions was rocking her in ways she wasn't sure how to navigate. Was she never going to let go of that baggage? Was she going to be forever haunted by the scars of her past? Did it come up because she felt a bit like a stranger in her own home? Was that the trigger?

She was afraid to look at Gio, afraid to see an answer she didn't want to see in his eyes, so she looked away. "I'm not that person… or am I? Am I that person?" She knew there was no way he could understand the many layers underneath that question. And there were conversations she just didn't feel ready to have with him.

"Hmmmm. This is complicated." He sat back and stroked his chin. "I do not see you as an in-ter-loper. Did I say that word right? Buono! Good. I do not have experience of you inviting yourself or imposing yourself in situations. But it is true that you are not around like they are. Your work has you all over the world. But I think, if Nonna were here, that she would say you have a very different problem."

Jane could feel herself stiffen up, waiting for the other shoe to drop: his judgement, perhaps his censure of her inner drama queen, who was, apparently, demanding to be everyone's center of attention at the moment. Perhaps she shouldn't have told him? There was always a danger when confiding in people. Some of them would guess what you really thought deep down. Some of them would see through you. Some of them would hold it against you. She steeled herself by taking a deep breath.

"I think you have a circle problem."

All of Jane's self-recriminating thoughts stopped suddenly. "A what?"

"A circle problem. Let me show you. I learned this from my Nonna." He retrieved a pen, a pencil, and piece of paper, drawing three concentric circles in the black pen. "Here you are in the center." He drew a lovely script J in the middle of the inner circle. "And here, if I may take the liberty, is my circle right next to you." He drew a circle with a script G in it next to hers, then lifted her hand and kissed it. She smiled at him. "Ah, that is a good sign. I love to see your smile." He handed her the pencil. "Draw in the circles of where you thought these friends of yours were. Where would their circles fall?"

Jane drew in the three circles in the middle ring, not as close in as his circle, though.

Gio looked at it and nodded. "And now draw in the circles where you think they would put themselves on your picture."

Jane winced. She picked up the pencil again and drew them in along the edge of the outermost circle. "That's where I think they want to be." She looked at it and made a face. "Or maybe here," she said as she penciled in circles towards the edge of the page.

"I see. So, you have a circle problem. Where you think their circles fall is maybe not where they really are. It may not be where their lives give them the freedom to be, even if they might want to be there. Tell you what, Janie, draw in the circles of your parents and sisters." He handed her the pen this time.

In ink, she drew circles for her parents, Claudine, Summer, Charlie and Caroline. "Claudine is as close as a sister to me. So is Caroline."

Giovanni looked thoughtfully at her drawing. "Nonna told me that some people are in your life for a reason. That is my circle. And I would guess that is your friend Claudine and your family. And you are not so alone. Other people are in your life for… well, a season." He pointed to the penciled-in circles. "It is not that they fail to be important or dear to you, but they are like balloons drifting on the breeze. They float in, bringing bright colors and a smile to your face, but they have their season and you have to let them drift. It is their nature. It is the nature of people themselves. If you try to tie them down, they will pop." He mimicked the popping with his hands. "And it is better to have the bright balloon still floating out of reach than it is to have a popped and ruined piece of garbage in your hand, is it not?"

"Wow. That is so poetic… and makes me feel… horrible, I have to say."

Giovanni burst out laughing. "You are not the broken balloon. The relationship, stretched to be what it is not, forced out of its natural shape, that is the broken balloon. You need to let people come into your life for the reason they need to be there, and for the season they can be there. Then you have to let them go."

She looked at him. "What if there is one very special balloon that you don't want for only a season? One that you want for all the seasons to come? How do you just let it be? How do you sleep when you are worried that it will drift away?"

He picked up her hand again. "I believe that some balloons will tie themselves down. They give themselves an anchor because they don't want to blow away."

"I like that theory."

"And Jane, there is always the wind for each of us. We don't control the wind."

"That's what I'm afraid of. Like with my friends, these women, um, gosh I don't quite know what to call them all of a sudden."

"I think 'friends' works." He shrugged. "It is a wide term, like the highway around Charlotte with all the many lanes. There are a lot of lanes to drive in."

She couldn't help but smile. "Friends then. I was surprised that the breeze had moved their balloons along and I felt stupid because I missed that. I misjudged the whole thing. And if I could have missed that, am I going to miss something about us?"

There. She'd said it. She'd certainly missed all the signs with Nicky and his balloon didn't blow away—it had popped suddenly, explosively, dramatically, leaving discarded garbage in its wake and she'd been left holding the pieces. All of a sudden, she reeled. It was like she could hear the clicking of pieces falling into place. She wasn't so hurt because of these girlfriends. She liked them, sure, and her feelings were hurt, admittedly. But that wasn't the real issue. They were a safer proxy for her feelings, for her sheer terror, that she was going to re-live the experience of Nick with Gio. That she would love Gio and open herself to him, trust him, allow him into her most vulnerable self, and that he wouldn't turn out to be the other side of the coin at all: he would be the same damn coin and she'd live the same damn nightmare all over again.

"Oh shit, I don't want to do this again!" She got up and started pacing. She looked at Gio, a bit wide-eyed. She couldn't tell him. She couldn't draw this out as a simple diagram. This wasn't simple. This was twisted and sad and impossibly rooted in a past she thought was long behind her, but the tendrils of that trauma were winding their way through time to ensnare her still. "Am I ever going to fucking heal?"

"Oh," Giovanni said slowly. "This is about Nicky."

She looked at him as though she were a deer caught in headlights. She felt transparent. She'd somehow been chewing on those bitter memories from the past and now it was threatening the present. She'd met people who liked to find something bitter and then to chew on it. She didn't want to be one of them. This had snuck up on her. She'd told herself she wasn't holding onto it, but it sure was holding onto her and silently fucking with her mind.

"Si! I can see that this is about Nick. So, Jane, the answer to that question is both yes and it is no."

She shook her head, confused.

"It is yes. You have healed. And you will continue to heal." He pulled up his shirt, showing the long lines that ran down his chest and belly. She didn't want to imagine that ages old car accident that had left those marks on him. He was lucky to be alive. "But scars don't go away, do they? They stay because they are our stories. A mark of our history. My Nonna was both mad at my Papà until the day she died and she was also a happy and a fulfilled person. She would be fine for a long time and then the anger and pain would pop up. But she would deal with it and move on to be happy again."

"I don't want to keep living with the pain. I want to lose that old baggage! I don't want the pain of the past to define me or my future. Or us."

"So don't let it. You have trauma. It is natural. Everyone has trauma. Don't try to pretend that it didn't happen. Live with your scars, but don't live from your wounds. If you ignored what you learned from your relationship with Nick, then you might have picked someone just like him and lived that story all over again."

Jane shuddered.

"Jane, it looks to me like you live quite well with those scars and you picked someone very different from what was his name? Nicholas David Delta Tango Lambda Ashworth? No! You picked me!"

Jane flew into Giovanni's arms and hugged him tightly. "You make me brave."

"Amore mio, you are brave. I just give you motivation to allow yourself to be who you are."

As Jane fell asleep that night she wondered how, on top of everything else Giovanni was to her, could he also be part therapist? Did he sit around and read libraries full of self-help books while she was gone? Did he end up spending as much time counseling the middle-aged women at the club as he did trying to help them with their backswing? She would have asked him, but he was, characteristically, solidly asleep while she was left to her thoughts. There was so much to Giovanni. It would take her a lifetime to unpack and understand who he was as a person. She sighed. It was a lifetime she was looking forward to. She snuggled up against him and settled in for a night of his dreams of an epic tennis battle with someone named Murray.

Chapter 34

The summer wore on and Jane was able to wrangle a bit less travel out of her work. Summers were easier. So many of her European counterparts were on vacation in August that traveling for work was a useless exercise anyway. She was enjoying being home for the whole month—and it gave her time to catch up, doing some deep dives into the business that she just couldn't manage when she was on the road.

Jane was in concentrated thought, buried in a detailed report, when her phone pinged. Then pinged again. Then a third time. She growled, wondering if she should turn off the sound or break her concentration and answer? Realizing her concentration was already shot, she picked up the phone. It was a text from Claudine.

> You haven't answered my last twelve emails. Are you mad at me? Or are you dead?

She smiled.

> **Sorry, up to my ears in work.**

> I think I am losing my friend Jane to the workaholic Jane!

Claudine pegged her. Man, that woman could read people like sharks read a poker table. It was great, and really hard, when you had a friend there was no hiding from.

> Tell me: it is hard to be right all the time?

> > Eh, you get used to it. Let's play tennis this weekend. I am here from France and would like to see you. Time to catch up.

While that sounded like an invitation, it was also an order. Claudine was very direct, highly efficient. If she wanted to get together with Jane to play tennis, there was a reason. Jane was awful at tennis. This wasn't about exercise. It was just a cover. Either Claudine needed to talk or she needed to intervene. Missing her chance to steer Jane straight about Nick seemed to rankle Claudine and she was determined to make sure that her friend was firmly on the path to happiness. Claudine had liked Giovanni from the start, but she also seemed to be continually curious about him. Awfully curious. With some trepidation, Jane replied:

> Tennis sounds great. How about ten on Saturday? I'll meet you at my club. I'll make a reservation.

> > Sounds perfect! See you then!

Of course, every good cover needed props. She would have to find her racquet. And tennis balls. And she wondered if she still owned a tennis skirt? Oh well, she could worry about that later. Right now, she had a mire of spreadsheets she needed to get back to.

* * *

Saturday morning arrived in a blink. While Jane finished her calculations and the report she was working on, she hadn't given her tennis date with Claudine a second thought.

"Oh damn, damn, damn!" Jane ran around the house pulling on a hot pink pair of shorts and throwing a white shirt over it. The shirt was long and looked a bit awkward, but it covered a lot of the shorts, which was a good thing because that pink swath on her butt would be rather a glare on the courts where nearly everyone wore all white. She really didn't need anything else to highlight her lack of game. You could wear stuff like that, but only if you could serve an ace that would leave the bystanders awed and maybe create a little breeze that became a hurricane in a far-off land.

"Where is my damn tennis racquet? Where the hell could he have put it?" After hunting through four closets, she finally located her racquet case in a dingy old basement chest she didn't even know they owned. While that was annoying, she had to accept the fact the Giovanni ran a tight ship—the house fell under his domain. He kept it spotless and uncluttered. She hadn't picked up her racquet in over a year, maybe more, so it probably deserved to be buried away like that. She was running seriously late, so she just grabbed the case and ran. She could feel the lumps of a can of tennis balls in there. "Hopefully they're not dead. Please don't be dead," she said aloud to herself as she got in the car and looked at the clock on the display. "It's okay, it's okay. You can always buy new ones at the club."

Twenty minutes later she pulled in and parked. "Only eleven minutes late," she said, trying to sound cheery to Claudine, who had arrived ten minutes early.

"It is of no moment!" Claudine gave her a hug. "I used the time to do some stretching. I find as I get older, I do not want to get an injury. Come, let us both stretch some before we take our place on the court."

Jane laughed. "Like I could ever hit a ball that would cause you to injure yourself! You're as close to a pro as I'm likely to get."

"I don't know about that. I would guess that you quite often get very close to Giovanni." She winked and laughed back.

"Yes, I suppose I do, but not on the courts. We try to do things together where we're more closely matched."

"Which is?"

Jane thought about that. "Well, he likes to cook and I like to eat, so that's a pretty good match. And we like to read together. And rail at the news."

"So not so different from my own life. And I am very content."

They checked in at the club and got their court assignment, catching up with small talk. Claudine gave Jane pointers on how to stretch out properly.

"Tell me, Jane—are you happy? Are you content?"

Jane thought about that question. Once upon a time it would have been superficial. Easy to answer. The image of that boulder came to mind. She heard her voice reply an unsteady, "Yes."

Claudine gave her a searching look. "Love is complicated, no? It is not a child's game. There is darkness and there is light. Hopefully more light!"

Jane exhaled deeply. "I am happy," she said more confidently. "I've been having these weird memories of Nick. Like he's jumping out of my subconscious."

"Is he hitting up your phone again?" Claudine looked incredulous. "Trying to romance you with those ridiculous statements?"

"Oh no! When I told Giovanni that I'd heard from Nicky on the very night that Gio and I met, he became rather curious about that pattern old Nick had of reaching out."

"He was curious? I wonder why he would care? Tell me more…"

"He could see that it bothered me. Kept bringing back bad memories. And after Gio and I had been together about a month, Nick texted me a couple of times. It really upset me. And Giovanni promised that Nick would never contact me again."

"That is a stupid thing to promise!" Claudine stamped her foot on the ground. "What could he do about it anyway?"

Jane laughed. "We were at one of those famous fountains in Rome. Oh my, there are so many, I don't even remember which one. But he took a coin out of his pocket, and in that adorable Italian accent he said, 'Nicholas will never bother you again. I promise.' And then he tossed it in. He threw it in the fountain. You know, like to make a wish."

"And you have not heard from Nick, the rat bastard, since?"

Jane shook her head. "Gio was making a joke. It was a hopeful wish for someone he cared about. Nick will continue to be old faithful and ping my phone again someday, sure as Kansas gets hit with tornadoes. But no, not yet. I haven't heard from him. There's no blame on Gio for my little funk; it's something with me. I'm dealing with my own fear of screwing it up with Giovanni. Maybe because I'm gone all the time. Or maybe because I'm not super fit like he is. Or maybe because we'll grow apart. Or maybe because we jumped into this before we ever really got to know one another. I don't know. I just worry."

Claudine crossed her arms and looked at Jane. "You spent many years with Nick, getting to know him before you wed. And what did you learn? That the poor spoiled rich boy could never live up to his parents' expectations. Hrumph! We all must grow up someday and stop living for our parents' expectations. It is our life. My father never approved of my lack of success, but that is his problem. He should have been more successful if it meant that much to him, and not asked me to make up for his failures."

"Giovanni said his father would see him as a failure, but it doesn't seem to rankle him. He laments it with passion… and the next second, he's moved on and forgotten about it. He seems simplistically happy.

He is so fond of his past, his mother and his Nonna, but somehow he's also not that attached to the past." Jane thought of the circles he had made her draw out. "You know, he told me he once had a job that made it hard for him to have friends. That he'd felt isolated and lonely, and my job does that to me. It eats me alive." She sighed heavily. "So, he understands. But he said that he's soooo very content now. He loves his life." She felt a sense of thrill as that sentiment reverberated within her. She also loved their life and like Giovanni, she was very content.

"You know, I like Giovanni, even though he is, if anything, a little bit too perfect. I have now met him several times and he seems to be at peace. I am happy for you, Jane. I hope you do not think you need someone with a big job and a big title to keep you happy. Are you embarrassed about your lover?"

Jane blushed.

Claudine gave her a gentle smile. "All too often, life requires married people to work so much that they only pretend to be married to each other. But really, they are just married to their two different jobs. You are both keeping life moving, and that is a privilege, is it not? You are functioning as a couple. He seems to be dedicated to you. Or does it feel like a burden on your shoulders, your responsibilities? Because I always thought you were pretty happy at your big job."

Without hesitation Jane answered, "I love my job. It's fun. It's exciting. It pays well."

"Then you are keeping the ship afloat, and that is a good thing, no? Every captain needs a crew to support their efforts. It seems to me that your Giovanni does a good job at taking care of you when you let him." Claudine put her hand over Jane's. "I think you should relax and let him. Enjoy your life."

Jane felt uncomfortable with how Claudine had once again reached into her world and seen her deeper fears. "He teaches tennis a few hours a week here at the club. He's mastering the art of cooking. He walks the neighbor's dogs. I see him when I can finally get home. I can't imagine what he does with all his time."

"Is he happy?"

"He says he is fantastico. I would die of boredom if our roles were switched."

Claudine changed positions to stretch her left calf and ankle. "You know Jane, it was very hard for me to find love. What I learned about myself is that when I did find love, real love, there was nothing I would not do for it. No sacrifice that I wouldn't make. No challenge I would not face down. We are lucky to have real love, for however long it may grace our lives. Real love is forever love."

Jane blinked away a tear she was afraid would escape her eye.

Claudine smiled warmly. "And it seems to me that you and Giovanni are the real thing. I am so happy for you. Is there anything you would not do for that man?"

"You mean, like support him so that he can pretend to be a tennis pro at my club and fill my shelves at home with fancy, expensive wine?"

"You make it sound like such a burden! And you would rather come home to a tired, paunchy man, exhausted from business travel, too wrapped in work to care about you, while you both live in a house that no one has attended to, because you were both too busy? I remember when, without Giovanni, you were well known for having only three oranges in your refrigerator!"

Jane laughed. "Okay. So, okay. You're right. It's a wonderful life. It's just the role reversal from my parents' generation to mine that I'm having trouble with. Some days I can't tell if I'm a success or if I actually got the consolation prize." She shook her head. "And there's guilt either way."

"Guilt was always a recreational pastime with you."

"And still like an old addiction that's hard to completely leave behind." Jane smiled back. Something in her snapped. It was so good to have someone to talk about these things with. She felt a flood of relief. "You know, you're right. I do love Giovanni. And I love that he supports my career, even if I sometimes get snide comments about him mooching off of me... even from my own family. He no more does that than my mother mooches off my father. We're a team. And yes, I would do anything for him. Anything at all." There. She had said it. And hearing it, she knew it was true. He never needed to earn a dime and she couldn't care less. She earned enough dimes to keep them quite well.

"Good! I am glad to hear it. I hope you marry him. He is just the right man for you!"

"Well, with your blessing, maybe I will." Jane smiled broadly, amazed that they had kept their secret so well hidden even from Claudine's perceptive eye. "I would do anything for him."

A knot deep in her psyche started to undo itself. A relieved relaxation began to flow through her. She bounced up and down on her toes and smiled. *Role reversal is fine. It's feminist. It's awesome.* She felt great, like winning. Well, maybe not against Claudine, but winning in general.

"You seem energetic, Jane! And I see our court is free." They moved over to the bench by their assigned area as the sweaty pair who'd just completed their set headed to the locker room, laughing and talking about their game. Another couple of players were a few feet down the bench. "Let us play. I hope you brought the balls? I had no success finding any at our house that were not completely flat."

Jane grabbed her tennis bag and set it on the bench. "Yes, and I'm quite sure that while the can is old, at least it's never been opened. Because I haven't opened this tennis bag in a couple of years."

She unzipped her bag and the two women stared. Those lumpy things were not cans of balls. The straight rod was not the handle of her racquet. The bag was full of guns and rounds of ammunition, and she thought maybe some type of explosive?

"Oh my God." Jane stared at the weapons.

Claudine reached over and quietly zipped the bag closed. "Mon Dieu!" She gave Jane a level look. "I think we do not play today?"

Jane began to shake.

Claudine looked around them quickly in case they had drawn any attention. "Ouch! Mon Dieu, Jane, I think my foot has not yet recovered enough for us to play today. I am so sorry."

Jane tried to get a hold of herself and managed to do better when she got a soft whack in the arm from Claudine. "Oh, yeah. I'm so sorry to hear that. We'll have to give up our court."

They made their way back outside not saying anything. When they got to Jane's car Claudine asked, "So, are we headed for a coffee shop or a bar? Surely there is a bar open this early in the morning." She looked around as if one might have magically materialized in the parking lot.

"I can't... I can't believe it." Jane put the bag into her trunk gently, like it might explode.

"Jane, there is a logical explanation for everything. I'm sure Giovanni can help you understand why your, your tennis bag, is ready for a bank heist. Oh my!"

"More like oh shit." She could really feel that boulder now. She wondered just what she would do if it crushed her all over again. "Oh yeah, oh shit. I've, uh, I've got to get home."

"You call me later?"

"Yeah. Sure. See ya." Jane got into her car. She didn't notice the drive home at all. The lights, the turns, were all automatic pilot to her. All she could think about was what she had just told Claudine:

I'd do anything for him.

But where was that line in the sand? Did anything mean *anything?* Could you just stop loving someone if they turned out to be someone or something else? What was he? She pulled into the driveway, not sure what to do next.

Chapter 35

Carrying the bag like it was full of the plague, Jane carefully restored it to the trunk in the basement. Dully, she wondered what had actually happened to her tennis racquet. It was an excellent place to hide the guns. She never played tennis. She rarely went into the basement and she didn't even know that trunk was down there until she tore the place apart so she could spend some time with Claudine at the club. She knew she needed to bring this up with Giovanni but decided to wait until after dinner. Or maybe until tomorrow. What she really wanted was to pretend it never happened. "But can you sleep under the same roof as he does knowing those guns are in the house and not knowing why? Maybe even knowing why?"

She had the whole day to wonder, and ponder, and let her imagination run away with her. Giovanni was gone and didn't come home until nearly dinnertime. She realized that he was gone frequently and she had no idea where he went. Even when she was home, she'd be in the office and he would be out running errands, or at the club, or going to the library, always someplace, but she never quite knew where he was or what he did there. She could feel her heart race. She decided to take a hot bath, try to force herself to relax, and found that she had to lock the bathroom door just so she could calm down enough to get into the tub. As she soaked, she realized that a locked door would mean nothing to a man who had that many guns—a thought that undid all her forced relaxation.

As the afternoon wound down, she at last heard the front door close and Giovanni's voice singing an Italian folk song as he made his way through the house.

"Amore mio! You are not connected to a computer! And you look so fresh."

"I uh, I took a hot bath."

"Oh, are we going out tonight?" He looked surprised.

She felt her anxiety abate. "Yes! Yes, we are. We're going out for cocktails and dinner," she said brightly. She wanted to be around people. She needed to have this conversation but not in this big, empty house alone with a man she wasn't sure she knew. A man who now suddenly owned a shitload of weapons. No, she wanted to have this conversation quietly but someplace that was crowded.

As they sat in their comfy chairs at the Krunkleton bar, enjoying the made-for-TV British pub atmosphere, their conversation was stilted.

"Amore mio, what is on your mind?" He looked at her with such, well, she would have to call it adoration. And a little bit of concern. True, she'd struggled to string two sentences together the entire evening.

You love him. You love him. Trust him. He's not going to kill you... in your sleep kept running through her mind. She screwed up her courage. "Gio, today I went to the club. Your club. I met Claudine to play tennis."

"Oh! That is fantastico! You playing tennis again. Maybe someday you'll play with me."

This was not the response she had expected.

Then he looked at her slyly. Expectantly. "Tell me, what did you think when you opened the racquet case?"

"The racquet case?" She could hear a tremor in her voice. She didn't want to say what she thought. She was afraid of what she thought.

"Si, it is bellissima, is it not?"

"Bellissima?"

Then, he seemed distracted. *He knows. He knows what I found.* She could feel her heart starting to race. She pressed her hands against the table so they wouldn't visibly shake. She was very glad she had chosen a public place, but she had no idea what her next move was.

A serious look grew on his face. "Wait a minute, tell me... tell me..."

"Tell you what?"

His eyebrows furrowed and he leaned over toward her, saying in a quiet voice, "Did they give you... the discount?"

She shook her head slightly, hardly able to process what he had just said. "Huh?" She wondered if this was some type of code word?

"They are supposed to give you a discount on the court time because I work there. The employee discount." He shook his head. "Ah, they are nice people but have such poor training. I have you listed as my family member and you are entitled to the employee discount." He became more animated. "Especially in the pro shop, so if you need to buy new balls, make sure you use my name."

"The employee discount... oh, okay. Yeah, that's, uh, good to know." Here she was thinking about life and death and whether he was going to murder her in her sleep and he was worried whether she got ten percent off a new can of Wilson Championships? She blinked a couple of times, not knowing what to say.

"Oh, I see the look on your face. No discount, huh?" He shrugged. "Don't worry about it. Next time. Now you know. And I'll make sure they know who you are. Si, next time." He smiled and picked up his wine glass.

"We never got to play tennis because I had no racquet."

"Of course, you have a racquet! On the sports shelf in the garage. I bought you a new racquet and case—and I got the employee discount! It is bellissmia! A beautiful racquet."

"Oh. I never thought to look in the garage. I went through the hall closet. The upstairs junk closet. The spare room closet and the attic. And finally, I looked in the basement. Somehow my old racquet case was in some weird trunk in the basement." Then she stopped for a moment. "You bought me a new racquet?"

"Si! Yes, I told you six months ago." He shrugged. "I thought maybe your ankle was hurting again and you did not want to test it out on tennis just yet. So, I put your beautiful new racquet in the garage. On my sports shelf." He gave her a searching look. "Jane, are you going to tell me that you are so wrapped up in your work that you never even looked at my gift for you?"

She shook her head. "I never even heard you mention it. I'm so sorry, Gio. Here you bought me this beautiful gift and I never even registered it."

"Ah, Jane. You really must do something about that monkey on your back! Here, have more of your cocktail. You look absolutely distressed. It is all right. I do not love you less." He smiled at her and then began to chide her. "But from now on when I get you a present, I am going to make a big deal about it with big gift wrap and huge bows so you cannot be so blinded."

She stared into his eyes. *I love this man.* She took a deep breath. "I found a case full of guns and, uh, other stuff… I couldn't quite figure out what it was, in my old tennis case. In the basement. In the trunk." She realized she had put her phone on the seat next to her. Right by her thigh so she could grab it in a moment. *And do what with it?* She wasn't sure about that answer. But it was out. The truth was out.

Giovanni became very still. Then he leaned back into his chair. "I see. And what did you think?"

"It's not what I thought. It's what I didn't want to think. That you are planning a bank robbery. Or that you're a gangster. Or a I don't know what. Or… or… Gio, can you tell me why there are guns in our house? Hidden in a tennis bag? Hidden in a skanky old trunk?"

He looked at her seriously and then his face started to twist and suddenly he broke out in laughter. A deep, rib shaking laughter. He couldn't talk until he could catch his breath. "You thought… you thought…" He was wiping tears of laughter from his eyes.

Suddenly she started to laugh too, as uncontrollably as he was. She felt a rush of relief as she detached herself from her suspicions about this gentle soul in front of her. The relief of the laughter, the release of the pent-up fears as tears streamed down her cheeks put a distance between her and all those crazy thoughts she had been harboring.

"Oh, Jane, Jane. My Janie, let me tell you about my stash. My cache. My minuscolo little horde. This is a good story! And I should have told you before, because guns have made me who I am. But honestly, I had forgotten about them."

"How could you forget about… that?"

"So, when you and I met back in Roma, we fell in love so fast. So very fast. And your job was taking you away on another assignment. You were not coming back to Italy. I was going to lose you. I could not bear to lose you. And so, we decided to come here, to America. And I would live with you. We got married, quickly, so I could come, and in secret, because you could not bear to tell your family that you married someone you had just met. And I left my life in Italy. But America is not like Italy. America is a dangerous place. And you were so often gone, and I was here alone. And I had little to do, other than to watch TV. And I learned what a wild place America is. I mean, Europeans know this, but knowing it from Europe and knowing it from right here in the U.S. is quite different."

"And just what did you watch? Old westerns?"

"No. I think I would have enjoyed that." He smiled. "But what I did watch is the news. Did you know that Americans threaten others with guns when their order for Kentucky Fried Chicken takes too long at the pick-up window? Or they threaten to shoot the clerk at McDonald's because they don't like the amount of salt on their fries? Or they actually fire shots at the fast-food store because their take-out was wrong? And don't get me started on what you call road rage here. Or if someone is going to get fired, even for a good reason, they think they have no other solution but to kill all of their co-workers. This really happens in America! It is full of crazy people. Crazy, violent people… with firearms!"

"Wow. That shit really happened? I mean not that last one. I have heard about that, and more than once, come to think of it. Yeah."

Giovanni nodded, eyes wide. "And your newscasters, they report this like it is as ordinary as the weather. So, I decided that if I am going to live here, I need to protect myself like Americans do."

"Like Americans do? I mean we have, like doorbell cameras and our houses all automated on our phones. What do you mean like Americans do?"

"Americans have more guns than cocaine farmers in the jungle. And I thought, sitting in this big empty house without you, that I would need to defend us, our home. Protect you when you are here. So, I got a permit and I took lessons. I went to a shooting range and got an instructor. A firearms teacher. I met a lot of Southern, what would you call them? Good old boys. You remember, I told you about them. Billy Ray, Billy Joe, Billy Bob…"

"Wait, those were different people? I thought that was one guy."

He smiled broadly. "In a way, they were. For a while, I had these friends. I got into the good old boy club. But there is no employee discount with them. And, as I got to know them, I came to the conclusion that they are like those boys in Southern Italy who only know who they are by the power those guns make them feel. Like big shots. And it struck me, I am my Nonna's boy. A North Italy boy. And Charlotte is not a dangerous town. It is a big sleepy town. It does not even have a metro or a subway or even a good bus system. Where we live in the suburbs is as quiet as rural Italy. And I realized that while all those crazy stories do happen in America, they don't happen in Charlotte, North Carolina. So, I packed up all the guns and shoved them in a bag and put them away. And you know what I did next?"

She shook her head.

"I took up cooking. It was a much more fun preoccupation than shooting off guns. And it was much quieter. But of course, then I really had to take up tennis because I was getting fat from all the cooking! And so you see, that my brief love affair with guns brought me to my love affair with food and wine and that brought me back to my love affair with tennis. And so, guns are important because they helped me find out who I am. And who I am not. I am not a Billy Bob Giovanni."

She liked this story. She wanted to believe his version of reality. "But guns… need to be in a… a… gun safe."

"Si. That is a good thing. That was on my permit test!" He pointed excitedly. "I got that one right! But, eh, it was another piece of furniture. And so brutto, so ugly furniture at that. It was money I did not have and did not want to spend your money on. After all, I'd already spent so much of your money on all the guns." He looked sheepish.

"Our money. Not my money. Our money. We're married."

He smiled warmly. "I know. And besides my issues with ugly furniture, I thought we could worry about that when we have children. But if you don't yet have bambinos, then maybe an out-of-sight old bag in an old chest in an old basement, eh!" He shrugged. "Maybe it can do just as well?"

"Children?"

"Si. I was, well, to be honest, a bit afraid to bring it up. Did not want to pressure you. And I thought that maybe, well, maybe we should start with a… a dog. A dog of our own. Or maybe two. What would you say to a dog, Jane?"

"A dog? A fur baby?"

"What is a fur baby?"

"It's the, uh, dog or cat that people have, who don't have kids. But they love them like kids. A fur baby."

He shook his head. "No self-respecting man could ever call them that. But I understand what you mean. The pet that is the child."

"Children…"

"Si, eh, bambinos."

Chapter 36

Jane walked through the Charlotte airport, following the signs to baggage claim. She pulled out her cell phone and called Giovanni.

"Hey! I'm here. On my way to get my bag."

"I am in the cell phone lot. Send me a text when I can pick you up."

"Sure. You know, it was so sweet of you to come and get me. I could have just taken an Uber or a Lyft or something."

"No, it is special that you're home. It is right that I come and get you. Besides, it means I don't have to wait so long to see you."

"I love you too." *Damn, that man just never stops being wonderful.* "Well, I'm afraid you're going to spend two days watching me sleep as I try to recover from my trip. Won't that be romantic?"

Twenty minutes later she was zooming down I-85 as Giovanni was telling her all about the club and how he was trying to get management to allow him to start a special tennis program for underprivileged kids, but they weren't buying it.

"Can you believe it? They think it will hurt business, not help it! It will help these kids be healthy. It will help them have things to do so they stay out of trouble, make friends. Not street friends but sport friends, like you and I had when we were little."

"I didn't ever have sport friends as a kid. Not very, uh, sporty," Jane could hear the exhaustion in her voice, but Giovanni didn't seem to notice.

"And management says it will hurt business to have these kids around. I told him we could have them come at the unpopular times, but no! It was not good for business. Can you believe that?" Giovanni was fuming.

"Uh, yeah. This is America. This is the American South. This is Charlotte. I'm sorry to hear it, sure." She couldn't stifle a yawn. "But am I surprised? Not at all. Most people are only high-minded when they are giving away something that they never needed and weren't using anyway, not something important like time. In this case, court time."

"You're so right. And it is the kind of court time these kids need." He drove for a few minutes in silence. "Anyway, grazie for listening to my ranting. I think I must be starting to sound like my father." He grimaced. "You must be tired. Coming back from Southeast Asia is a long trip, no? Did you bring me something nice?"

Jane started up from her sleepy reverie, surprised she had been dozing in the car. She kind of hoped he would have gone on about his frustration with the club management all the way home so she could have pretended to listen while she snoozed. But it seemed he wanted to make actual conversation. That might be hard given how thinly stretched she felt at the moment. It had been a rough flight back with cancellations and re-bookings and far less sleep than she'd hoped for.

"Oh yes. I brought you all kinds of goodies." Luckily her local hosts and clients had showered her with gifts, many things she was sure Giovanni and her family and friends would love. Gift cultures were charming in their own way, but it always did mean taking an extra suitcase of things you picked out blindly and just hoped the recipients would like instead of you making some horrible blunder and inadvertently terribly offending them. Cultural elasticity was a great ideal, but no rubber band could guarantee to be unbreakable.

"So, you are home four days earlier than your original travel plans."

"Uh huh." She yawned again. "That's okay with you, isn't it?"

"Si! Si! You know I love it when you are back home. After all, you are the one I was looking for all my life. I was just surprised. A little bit worried, to be honest, that something on the trip went wrong?" He shot her a quick look while he navigated traffic. When she didn't answer, he added, "Or maybe it went so right that you could come home early?"

"Oh, that. It was fine. I had to come back home…" She yawned. "Excuse me. For you."

"For me?" He drove for a bit. "You missed me that much?"

She gave a tired little laugh. "Sure. As always. But I had to change my schedule because my app says I ovulate in four days. And it's not that exact of a science. And I know I'll probably sleep my first two days here. So, get ready, buddy, because I have a lot of sex on your to-do list!"

"Oh! So, this is a romantic kind of come home early. So romantic! With lots of 'Hurry up, honey, we have to have sex right now!' kind of couple's time." He laughed.

Jane giggled. "I suppose it has been kind of like that. You know, I can't tell them at work why I just won't travel some weeks and like on this trip, I just announced that I had to get home. Oh my God, everyone thought my dad had a heart attack or something."

"Did you straighten that out with them?"

Jane looked guilty. "Uh. No. I just let their imaginations run wild. They're pretty used to me being a private person, so they didn't ask and I didn't tell. But at least I got no push back when I announced I had to get home."

"Oh, that's bad!"

"Well, I wasn't going to tell them I had to change all my flights and shoot outta there early because I had to go and have emergency sex since I don't ever seem to ovulate on the highly predictable schedule of every other woman on the planet."

Giovanni clucked his tongue at her. "Now you sound frustrated. And if anything should be fun, it should be emergency sex. Particularly when your work mates think you are off handling a family crisis."

She chuffed but didn't say anything.

They pulled up into the driveway and Giovanni carried her bags into the house. "Let me get you a little glass of vino. Then you can go and lie down and start to get back on this time zone."

She gratefully accepted his offer and went to stretch out on the couch. It was at moments like this she wished they had a cat or a dog or a parrot or something. Some little animal that would be so glad to see you and come over and cuddle with you while you just sat there and thought nothing, your only movement being to stroke the soft fur of that pet. Okay, so maybe that wasn't what you did with parrots. She wasn't sure.

Giovanni came in with a little tray carrying two glasses of wine, some dried fruit, warm nuts, and a few olives. He loved olives. She picked up a dried apricot.

"Thank you. This is lovely. There is nothing so wonderful in this world as coming home to you." She looked at him gratefully and wondered if her eye makeup was smudged and whether she looked as frightful as she felt.

"Jane. Let me say something to you. If this is too much pressure, this trying to have a baby, maybe we should, well, not chase it so hard. If it is stressing you, then that is no good."

"No! We definitely should keep trying!" She set her glass back down. "I'm sorry. Let me take a step back. Yes, it is a lot. Balancing my job with trying to conceive. If this is hard, think of what it will be like to actually have a kid. I mean… I'll never be here."

"I think our child will understand that they have a traveling madre. Some have traveling papàs. Others have traveling madres."

Giovanni looked so calm, like this was purely rational. He could have been talking about vacation plans or the weather. No, if it were vacation plans, he would have been more animated.

She wasn't calm. She had the animation borne of travel exhaustion and sleep deprivation. It all came spilling out of her at once. "I want to have a child, but this just feels… impossible. Four months of tracking and recording and running back home. And that line, that little pink line that never turns into a plus sign. I mean, I love my job, but I don't want to miss out on having a family. And all this time my biological clock is slamming in my ears and I had just been coming to the conclusion that it would never happen for me and then you came along and I thought I was going to get a second shot at life, at the whole thing, a family… and now I feel I'm running out of time again." She burst into tears. "I just can't do it all."

Jane melted into Giovanni's embrace as he stroked her hair and shushed her tears. "Oh Janie, amore mio. I never meant to put any pressure on you. We are a family whether we have children or no. Sex should not feel like a chore… or a goal that always holds disappointment. You do not have that pressure on you from me."

Jane started to catch her breath and sniffled as he held her. "I'm sorry."

"You have nothing to be sorry about, amore mio. Neither of us has anything to be sorry about. We have a good life. If it happens, it happens. We have each other, and really, that is all that matters."

Jane nodded. She couldn't speak. They were lovely words, but unfortunately now that she had been so focused on conceiving that baby, she really wanted one. She didn't want the future that was looming in front of her of endless board meetings and a trail of promotions that would just continue to siphon off any semblance of a personal life. She didn't want the title of CEO. She wanted to try something different.

Giovanni held her for a long time and then took her up to bed, where she slept long and hard, exhausted in every definition of the word.

* * *

Two days later Giovanni was taking her on a surprise outing. "You'll like this. And besides, we can't only eat, shower and have sex while you are home. We should also go out of the house from time to time." He shot her a sly wink.

"But where are you taking me?" She laughed, glad that she'd recovered from whatever that strange breakdown had been when she'd returned two days ago.

"It's a surprise!" He wouldn't reveal even a clue, so they talked about her recent trip and in another half an hour they came to a small farm in the middle of nowhere. "And here we are!"

"A farm? Are we going to pet baby goats or something?" She thought this was a strange way of trying to cheer her up after her embarrassing meltdown.

"No, it is November. Baby goats come in February."

"Oh, they do? Hey, wait a minute, how do you know about when baby goats are born?"

Before he could do anything but give her a mischievous smile, he parked the car and hopped out. Jane joined him, looking around at the rather unkempt grass, a small ranch house hugged by similarly unattended bushes, a few outbuildings that looked like they were trying to be barns. She vaguely wondered if they were on some type of property hunt and maybe his solution to the complexity of her life was a quiet, rural settled down life? Not a chance. Then she saw the sign: Daisy Hill Puppy Farm.

"We're getting a dog?"

"Si! A fur baby is just what we need."

"A fur baby?"

"Si! Can you believe I said those words?" He burst out in peals of laughter. "You will have someone to cuddle while I make dinner for you," he said, giving her a pinch on the butt while he walked by her and towards one of the wannabe-barns.

"Just what kind of dogs do they have here?"

A robust man in his late fifties approached them, having appeared from around the side of the house. "Hello! You must be the Romanos! My name is John Darling. Welcome to the Daisy Hill Puppy Farm!" He was waving so heartily, Jane thought he could be part Italian himself. "My wife is going to join us in a moment. She's with the mom and the new litter."

"A new litter? How cute! What kind of puppies?" Jane asked again. "Beagles?"

"You know, it's funny how often I get asked that question." John Darling scratched his head. "And I can't imagine why. I guess beagles are popular these days. Everybody loves beagles. But no, we have a dalmatian bitch that is the pride and joy of my wife and we have two dachshunds at stud and two bitches. We're a small operation, but I love my dogs. C'mon! Let me introduce you!"

The man was certainly enthusiastic, and they followed him to the outbuilding.

"What are those?" Jane asked as she pointed to structures that looked somewhat like small doghouses with cages.

"Oh them, those are rabbits. Our daughter raises those. She'd be happy to show you. She just loves rabbits! Hey, Annie!" he called loudly. "Annie, where're ya?"

A woman a decade or so younger than Jane came bounding out of the house with the same enthusiasm as her father. "Yeah, Dad?" As Jane looked at her, she realized the woman had Down's syndrome. The woman was energetic and cheerful, introducing herself as "Annie, the grandmother of bunnies." Her laugh was infectious, leaving Jane and Giovanni all smiles as she explained about her bunnies. They were huge creatures for rabbits, much larger than many small dogs Jane had seen. "These are Flemish Giants."

"How big is that rabbit?" Giovanni asked.

Annie gave him a funny look. "It's that big. You can see it right there."

John Darling burst out laughing. "Annie is a stickler for asking the right question, aren't you, Annie?" He turned to his visitors. "Maybe you should ask how much it weighs?"

Before anyone could ask the question, Annie jumped in, "That one weighs just over fifteen pounds. And that one," she pointed to another hutch, "is thirteen pounds. And that one is fourteen pounds."

Jane jumped in before they got the run-down of every rabbit in the yard. "Oh, so the size of small dogs! I would have guessed they were even heavier than that!"

Giovanni whispered to her, "I think that's the fur."

"My rabbits are champion bunny makers!" Annie grabbed Jane's hand and pulled her over to a hutch. "This one is Matilda. She's my favorite. And this one is Glenda. Glenda is really good at having baby bunnies!"

"Yes," her father agreed. "If we could only get people to eat lapin, there would be no hunger in the world at all!"

"Lapin?" Giovanni repeated. "French? For rabbit?"

"Yeah," Annie jumped in, giving Giovanni a serious look. "Are you French?"

Giovanni shook his head and laughed. "I'm sorry if I disappoint, but no. I am Italian."

Annie looked around her conspiratorially and said in a loud whisper, "Well, don't speak in that language. We know they don't understand French, so when we talk about," she looked around her again, "you know what, we use the French word."

"That's right! We're sure those rabbits know English, so we have to be extra careful around them." John added. He smiled lovingly at his daughter. "They might speak Italian. You never know."

"No, Dad. We don't want to frighten the rabbits." Annie nodded seriously as she agreed with him.

Giovanni looked from father to daughter. "But do the dogs not scare the rabbits?"

"Nah!" John said. "We introduce them early, so they get used to other animals. And the bunnies are so darned big. Really, the dogs are more afraid of them. Aw, they weigh about the same, but the dogs have such short hair that they're tiny by comparison."

"Speaking of dogs, maybe we should go and meet these puppies my husband wanted me to see," Jane said with a smile. "We are potential adoptive parents."

They resumed their walk to the barn. Inside Jane could see that this was John Darling's version of a 'She Shed'. He had poured all the creative energy he didn't seem to invest in his yard into this twenty-by-twenty backyard structure. Along the wall set up at chest height were a series of comfortably appointed cages, several for the dogs in different stages of need.

"You see, I keep the pairs in here when they're a breedin'."

Jane noticed that the walls above were decorated with moons and stars. She had never considered a romantic atmosphere as important for breeding dogs.

"And these are for the bitches once they're pregnant. I play them classical music. They like that. Makes for smart dogs."

"Don't the dogs like to get out and run around?" Jane asked.

"Sure! And they get out every day." He pointed to the large play space in the middle of the floor.

Jane turned and noticed his elaborate setup, suddenly sure this man must have his own YouTube or TikTok channel which shared his intending-to-be-hilarious puppy videos with the world. But of course, that was probably how Giovanni found the man, she realized.

"I take the dogs out for walks every day the weather's good. And they play in here. But dachshunds like to rest. They sleep a lot. So, I know they're safe and warm in their little rooms here." He gestured towards the cages.

"Oh. okay. Why are they up so high? They can't jump up or down from that height, surely?" She looked at the stubby legs of the hounds, doubtful they could even jump up onto a couch.

"Oh that. Yeah, I used to have their cages on the ground. But drafty, that. And then my back. It was easier to just build the cages up to this height—and it gave me all that storage below. Plus, all my dogs are good at walking down the ramp, so that's good for the owners who want the pups to reach their bed for a little bit of snugglin'!"

"Little puppies use that ramp?" Jane was astonished that he had any puppies surviving to sell. It was quite a drop off down the sides of the ramp extending from their caged bedrooms, about waist high. She tried to imagine them making their way to the play floor—a bit like a dog walking the plank.

"Oh naw! Ain't you a funny one! New mammas, like Ginger there, and her litter will stay down on the floor for a few weeks until the puppies get a bit older. They have all those little ramps in their play space to practice on. Any that are still with me at four months are good on the ramps, though. These are smart dogs. They learn fast."

Giovanni looked serious. "I imagine they would. How old are Ginger's puppies?"

John looked as proud of the litter as if they were his own children. "Six weeks. Hop in there with 'em. They're about to wake up. Just go in and sit down. They'll find ya!"

Sure enough, in a few minutes the sacked-out puppies started to rouse and soon were jumping playfully, climbing over each other, Jane, Giovanni, and the play structures that surrounded them in the large circular pen.

John Darling was laughing loudly. "Aren't they a bunch of little clowns? And the sides here are tall enough that they can't get out," he said, pointing out the obvious.

"Oh my gosh, they're tiny. And adorable," Jane gushed. "And their noses. They look like little Labradors." She looked up at John.

"Oh, they'll grow their noses, don't you worry. Now those two, the red and the golden, are spoken for. And I've got a little girl coming today to pick out one for her birthday. So, these black and tan with the spots and the pure black and tan are available."

The two dachshund puppies with the spots were all over Jane and Giovanni. One found Jane's purse and quickly chewed a hole in it while she was distracted by the golden. He was pulling her wallet out by the time she noticed. "Oh, my goodness, look what you've done!" She picked up the pup and held him in front of her. "You're a regular pickpocket, aren't you? Just a bad little boy. But so cute."

The puppy peed all over her leg.

"Oh, you've got to be kidding." Jane sighed, looking at the mess on her pants.

Giovanni was laughing until tears were running down his cheeks. "That one just claimed you as his own." He pointed to her leg. The other dark pup with spots was chewing on his shirt and managed to put a tear in it.

"And I think you've just been similarly marked by that little criminal."

Giovanni looked up at John Darling. "We'll take these two! How much?"

Jane's head whipped around. "What? Two of them? I didn't even know dogs were on the list today and we're signing up for two of them?"

"Sure! We'll call them Horace and Jasper! Perfetti names." He looked up at John. "When will they be ready for their new home?"

"When they're eight weeks old you can take them. They'll be all up to date with the vet. We'll give you a list of what you need on hand, what their next vet visits should entail. A whole puppy parenting guide."

"We have two weeks to get ready." Jane looked a little wide-eyed and bewildered.

"Yes, Madre. We have two weeks to get ready for our fur babies. And look at it this way: it will be good practice in case we have twins!"

Horace and Jasper turned out to be perfect names for the pups, which were destructive beyond anything that Jane could have dreamed, given how small they were. When they played with them in the living room, their little boys would run under the couch and look like they'd become all teeth, playfully growling from the darkness.

"Until they get older, I think we need a play space for them. Someplace safe. Someplace they can't destroy."

"I could do something with the guest room," Giovanni suggested.

"Yeah, well, how about the basement?"

"The basement! Put them in the basement?" Giovanni seemed horrified.

"It's only for a few weeks. And it's not like we won't be bringing them up the stairs all the time and playing with them. And taking them out in the yard to play. But they can have their food and water there. You have to agree that the basement floor is so much easier to clean up."

Giovanni nodded. "I am a bit tired of using the wet carpet vacuum we had to buy."

"Hah! I'd be amazed if we didn't have to put down new carpet in the living room. Maybe we can just use this as the opportunity to move to hardwood floors."

"Or tile..." Giovanni said absentmindedly.

Jane looked at him. "Tile? In the living room?"

"Oh, si, not Italy." He sighed. "Okay, the basement. But just for a short while!" He nuzzled Horace. "It's only for a tiny little bit, until you grow a little more. I'll put your big bed down there and make a play space for you, my little boys."

As Jane watched him with the puppies, she fervently wished that she would get pregnant. It was clear that he would make a great father, that he wanted to be a father. She had to admit that his idea of getting the dogs was a good one. While it was stressful in its own way, it completely distracted her from that different stress of trying to conceive. Lovemaking was starting to be fun again, now that she wasn't quite so focused on the why of it all, the purpose behind all that rolling around between the sheets together.

"You'll have to child-proof your doomsday pantry."

He scoffed.

"No, I'm serious. If they get into that… Oh! What a mess that would be. And where would you be without seven years of instant mashed potatoes and fifty-two weeks' worth of canned tuna?"

He looked at her, incredulous. "It's not a doomsday pantry."

"Then what is it?"

"I just have a love affair… with Costco."

She looked at him and crossed her arms. "If I didn't know you better, I'd say you were secretly a prepper."

He shook his head emphatically. "We don't have anything like this in Italy! I get so excited when I go to Costco. And you can't just buy one of anything. They all come in the big packs. And sometimes I forget what we already have…"

"Like tuna fish. Or tomato sauce. Or entire flats of beans. Or fifty pounds of rice. My God, man, you even bought survival rations in a bucket! Two of them!"

"Oh, you can't tease me over that one. The governor said that in North Carolina every house should be able to go two weeks before getting help after a hurricane. I have batteries and emergency lights. I'm just following orders." He gave her his most innocent look. "There is a whole set of YouTube videos about it. They call it 'getting ready for the zombie apocalypse.'"

"Yeah, for Bald Head Island maybe. But hurricanes don't hit Charlotte. This is where people come to get away from the hurricanes."

"Ice storms?"

"Once every twenty years."

"Sorry?"

"That works."

Giovanni laughed. "I will set up a play space for our little boys down there, and I'll puppy-proof the basement too. They will be fine. And in no time, they will be up here all the time entertaining us with their corrupt but cute little ways."

"What else could we expect after christening those little criminals Jasper and Horace?" She sighed heavily. "You know, we could have gotten some of those Flemish Giants. We could have had rabbits instead."

"Oh no! No rabbits. They would eat the baseboards," Giovanni said in an aside as he played with the pups. "They would be so much more destructive than our little angels here."

"Rabbits eat baseboards? How do you know that?"

"Oh, si! Rabbits can be very hard on a house. I saw it on a YouTube video. I may not be an expert, but I learn a lot watching YouTube videos!"

Chapter 37

"I am never going to get this done in time!" Jane tried to blow her bangs out of her eyes. No time for a haircut. No time for getting the place straightened up. And now she had no time to get this sauce going before Giovanni got back from the store. She'd thought she could squeeze in that last check of the report… and then she'd found the error her project manager had made and of course that had to be fixed, which meant going back into the spreadsheets and re-checking the formulas. By the time she'd ironed that out, she was hugely behind. She'd promised Gio that she'd follow Nonna's recipe and get that sauce started so it could simmer on a slow heat and meld the flavors… or something like that. She looked at the huge pile of vegetables he wanted her to wash and chop. Some got sauteed in wine and others pan fried with the pancetta. Eventually everything went into the big pot of sauce. "This is never going to work." She glanced at the clock on the wall in frustration. She took a deep breath and looked up at the ceiling as if for inspiration. "Nonna, help me." She knew what she had to do.

She went down to the basement and opened Giovanni's doomsday pantry.

"Maybe he won't notice. Ha! Fat chance of that." But she decided to risk it. Reaching into the back of the shelf she pulled out three jars of pasta sauce. "So, what do you think?" she asked the two dachshund puppies sacked out on their way-too-big dog bed. Another Costco purchase. "Can alfredo sauce be mixed with these tomato-based ones?"

She looked at the label. "Probably a risk. Better match colors." She put the alfredo back. The puppies sighed deeply but didn't so much as bat an eyelash at her intrusion into their nap time. "Yeah, I should probably stick as close to Nonna's recipe as possible. Close enough for cheating anyway." She ran upstairs, twisted open the lids with a satisfying *pop!* and emptied the two jars into the pot and started to simmer it on the stove. She hid the empty jars in the very bottom of the recycling, hoping he wouldn't see them. She looked at the vegetables and meats on the counter and felt a bit like a mad scientist. "Now to chop you guys up and stew you in the pot."

As she was madly slicing and dicing, the phone rang in her ear and Jane looked at her cell lying on the counter on the other side of the room. Of course, she'd never taken the earpiece out after her last meeting. She could hardly notice the thing anymore, she wore it so much, it was practically growing into her head. She tapped the button to pick up the call, feeling for a moment like she was a secret agent. Touch your ear, talk to someone. When she was a kid, this stuff was futuristic, but now it was simply compulsory. She could talk through her watch. She could talk through her earpiece. The only problem with not seeing the phone was she didn't know who was calling. That meant using her professional voice. If she was sure it was Giovanni calling, she knew she'd sound different.

"Hello, Jane Donahue here."

"Wow, I have to say it—that sounds like fake cheeriness. Is this you, or is this your voice mail?"

"Oh, hey, Summer. You got the real thing here. I just didn't know it was you, or I'd have used my little sister voice."

Summer laughed. "Well, I'm glad I got you, even though you sounded like you thought I was your boss calling. Hector and I want to know if you guys might be interested in coming over next weekend? We thought we'd make a little dinner, dine out on the new patio, tell you all about Romania."

"Sounds fun… but hey, wait a minute. You guys aren't into any new weird food fads, are you? Before I commit us, I just want to make sure we aren't guinea pigs for some bizarre trendy thing you got into over there."

"What do you mean, 'new weird fads?' I can't imagine what you're talking about." The innocence dripped all too conspicuously from Summer's voice.

Jane rolled her eyes, but she had a smile on her face. "Well, you did go through your 'off the grid' phase where you didn't have a refrigerator… I remember that antique ice chest you had. I have to admit, I had nightmares about food poisoning."

"Hey, it was an attempt to cut down on our carbon footprint. Do you know what an environmental disaster refrigerators are?"

"True. But unless you're cutting the ice out of the great frozen lake and toting it home with your sled dogs, I don't think you can call it even with custom ice blocks delivered to your door. Someone's still using refrigerant. And gasoline."

"Touché. Best laid plans and all that."

"What finally killed that one?"

"Truth be told… it was done in by the serious lack of ice cream. And maybe a little bit of food poisoning."

"And then you did the 'no white foods' thing."

"Oh yeah that… it does cut down on a lot of sugar."

"But it was also done in by a serious lack of ice cream, as I remember," Jane said.

"True, true."

"The fish-only thing was an interesting take. Really took pechepalo to a whole new level. I mean geez, Summer, breakfast must've been so weird."

"Yeah, yeah, okay, I get it. We did drop those pesky pounds we'd gained as new parents."

"Uh huh, I can see why."

"Anyway, we're between experiments at the moment, so it'll be normal, regular food. Maybe a little Romanian inspired! We discovered these amazing cabbage rolls and a to-die-for garlic-loaded pork goulash."

Moments passed.

"Oh. I hear a lot of silence from you. Well, we could always grill out. You know, something bland. Uninteresting. Uninspired. Non-artistic stuff like chicken breasts and vegetables thrown on a grill."

"Nothing artistic and experimental? Nothing that sounds like it was designed to keep away vampires? Great! Count us in for nothing experimental. Besides, I've got my own experiment going on here."

"You mean with the pregnancy?"

"Let's more accurately call it 'the hopeful pregnancy.' No change on that front. No luck yet. I can't believe we're trying."

"I can't believe you're trying when you're not married. I mean, that's so me, but that's just not so you. When you get there, and I believe you'll get there, Mom and Dad will just fall over."

Jane could hear the teasing tone in Summer's voice. Honestly, she thought her parents would be thrilled at having more grandchildren, whether they came in the proper sequence or not. After Jane's tangled past with love, they'd just be happy for her as a mother. But she did worry that they'd be even more surprised to find out that their daughter had been married for over a year and had just never told anyone. So much time had gone by now, she wasn't sure how to tell her family that she and Giovanni had checked that particular box. She realized it was easy to break the news that you'd just eloped. That was a cause for a celebration. But that you'd eloped more than a year ago when you'd only known each other a couple of months? And you never told anybody? That was more likely to result in a full-blown parental inquiry. Why the secrets? Why the subterfuge? What were you really hiding? She didn't want to face that particular look in her mother's eye when she asked if Jane kept it a secret because she was just trying it out and wasn't sure it would be different from the last time.

"I guess we're just one of those crazy unpredictable couples."

This response resulted in peels of laugher from her sister. "Yeah, right."

Jane looked down at her vegetables. She'd been paying more attention to the conversation than the vegetables and apparently had been chopping away. The array of produce lay before her in veritable shreds. "Yes, yes, very funny," she said to her sister as she shrugged and dumped all the bits into the now bubbling sauce. "Hey Summer, do you have to cook pancetta before you put it into pasta sauce? Or can I just dump it in there?"

"Oh yeah, you're my 'I only have three oranges in my fridge' sister, so coming from you, that question makes sense. If you don't cook it first, you'll have a lot of grease in your sauce. Bacon, sausage, stuff like that, you cook first to get the fat out of it and then you add it your dish. Without the fat."

"Okay, thanks." Jane tossed the pancetta back in the fridge and pulled a box of veggie sausage patties out of the freezer. This needed no special care. She dumped the whole bag into the sauce and stirred it up. It also might not taste like much but there was a lot already happening in that pot, so maybe no one would notice?

"What are you making?"

"Uh, Giovanni's grandmother's pasta sauce. On special request. But I think the task is beyond me. I'm improvising."

"Good news then: you can't miss with pasta sauce. I mean, hey, people, like, stick it in jars and sell it. It's just not hard."

"Thanks. I'll remember that."

"So next weekend for dinner?"

"Sounds good. I'll double check it with Giovanni and text you tomorrow."

They said their goodbyes and Jane absentmindedly stirred the sauce.

A baby. The last little line hadn't turned into a plus sign. It was that sad blue negative. Was it sad, though? Was she ready for this step?

Was he ready? It seemed like there was so much she didn't know about him. She'd still never met any of his family back in Italy. She liked his cousins on the West Coast, even heard from them once in a while through cards in the mail or a random text. She wondered if Gio's family in the homeland even knew Giovanni was married and what they would think of her? Did she want to show up on his mother's doorstep with a babe in arms? An American baby? He made it sound like his family was pretty dead set that he marry a Northern Italian girl. She wondered how well that would go? Maybe as well as telling her mother that she'd eloped. An eternity ago.

She heard the garage door open—he was home. She looked around, wanting to make sure that she'd hidden any evidence of her cheating on Nonna's heralded secret family recipe. She threw a bunch of perfectly clean pans she should have used into the sink full of soapy water. "At least they'll be easy to wash up," she said to herself. The garage door ground again, signifying that it was now closed. She quickly stirred the pot, realizing that she needed to break up the sizable discs of the veggie sausage. That would be a dead giveaway. Then it struck her that her sausage and pancetta were really nothing at all alike. She worked harder at breaking up the patties.

The door to the garage opened, and in waltzed Giovanni. "Ah, my love, mia bella. I am home from the hunt!" He pushed the door closed with his foot and set down the three bags of groceries he had in his arms. "I was able to find the freshest of pasta! You can never find it quite right in America, but I found this little Italian store and Nonna would've been proud." He came over to her and kissed her warmly. "How was your day, mia bella Jane?"

She melted into his kiss and felt that this was just the man she wanted to have a baby with. "It was great. Once I fixed Harold's ongoing problem with Excel spreadsheets." She saw the glaze in his eye that always happened when she talked about work. "Aaaand…. I have been working to perfect Nonna's recipe. Not that I think she'd approve if she were here." Thinking fast she added, "That's a really complicated recipe."

"Let me put away the groceries I bought and then I'll give it a try and let you know what Nonna would say. I'm sure you did it perfetto. Just like mia Nonna."

As he busied himself with putting things away, Jane tried to look casual while she worked feverishly to break up all the fake sausage patties. She'd done a pretty good job by the time he came over to stand by her and raised his eyebrows—his way of asking for the spoon. She took a quick breath and handed it to him, stepping back to allow him command of the stove. While he tasted, she winced, worried that she'd be found out. *Is it a trust breaker to cheat on a recipe? To ruin his favorite dish? Will he even want to have a baby with me if he finds out he can't trust me to carry out the family tradition?*

She watched him slowly taste the sauce. Then he dipped the wooden spoon back into the pot and tried it again. He turned around and looked at her.

Here it comes. She steeled herself.

"What have you done? I am... speechless."

"I can explain..." she said, while her rebellious side wondered why a stupid pasta sauce should even matter. *Oh yeah, it's him missing his home. Him leaving his country to be with me and I've ruined the taste of home.*

"Mia Bella! It is just like Nonna used to make. I am like a little boy again, tasting her cooking. Takes me back. Grazie mille, amore mio. Si, perfetto!"

Jane felt an instant flush of thrill at her accomplishment, quickly followed by the guilt of the lie. "Tell me something, your Nonna, her last name wasn't anything like, uh, Progresso, was it?"

"No, she was a Romano. Your sauce is a masterpiece. It is so good, you could sell it! I'll get the pasta started."

"How about you let me get the pasta started and you go grab a shower." She winked at him and he grinned at her, a goofy wide-eyed look on his face.

"You mean, I smell like victory!" Dramatically he threw up one arm and took a big whiff of his armpit. Then he coughed. "Ah, yes. I see you are right, and I do. Si, a shower it is for me."

She laughed as he headed upstairs to freshen up, then busied herself with making the rest of dinner.

As she set the table, washed up already clean pots and pans, and got the water going for the pasta, she started to smell something weird. Something acrid. She looked around. Nothing was burning on the stove. She opened the oven. It was hot, ready for the "not at all like real Italian" garlic bread to go in, but the bad smell wasn't emanating from there. And it was getting worse. She went to the bottom of the stairs and called up to Giovanni:

"Honey, I think something must be wrong with the furnace. I'm smelling something horrible down here. Can you come check it out?"

Fresh and clean, he bopped down the stairs, stopping immediately as he sniffed it too. They both went into the kitchen. He went to the door to the basement and opened it.

"Nothing here."

Jane walked over to the garage door that he had waltzed through less than half an hour before and opened it. "Oh, holy shit!" It was filled with black, acrid smoke.

"Oh no!" Giovanni cried out and before she could close the door, he shot through it.

"What are you doing? We have to call 9-1-1! You don't run into the smoke!"

But he was gone. She peered through the dingy blackness. Someplace in that inky mess, his truck was sitting in the garage and it was on fire. She could see the glow of the flames. The tires were melting already. She was astounded. Giovanni was in the cab, frantically rustling around, seemingly desperate to find whatever it was that made him lose all his good sense.

"Get out of there!" she screamed. "The car is on fire. You have to get out of there!" She knew she should be calling in the emergency, getting a dispatcher to send help, but she wanted him out of the truck. There was no way this could turn out well.

Suddenly the fire alarms in the kitchen went off, strong male voices shouting "Fire! Abandon the structure! Run! Get out! Fire! Abandon the structure! Run! Get out!" in rapid succession. She heard them start to tick off in other rooms, other voices shouting words of alarm that she couldn't understand but well knew the meaning of. The house felt alive with the voices of computerized strangers shouting and black smoke billowing and flames rising. She took a deep breath of the best air she could manage to get and plunged into the inky garage. The clouds were billowing into the kitchen. By some miracle she found Gio, mostly by feel, and pulled on his arm. Spluttering and coughing they made their way back into the kitchen and closed the garage door.

"We've got to call 9-1-1!" she managed to gasp out.

He shook his head emphatically and started to move through the kitchen, grabbing her roughly by the arm, pulling her through the house to the front door. She noticed he grabbed electronics as they went: his phone, a small device he often carried on him but she'd never bothered to figure out what it was, his wallet, and an earpiece. Once outside, where they could both breathe the air, he pulled her down to the edge of the driveway.

"We've got to call the fire department!" she spluttered at him.

"No time," he managed to gasp. He didn't sound at all like himself, halfway bent over and gasping for air as he stared at the house. "It's Murray! It's going to blow..." He tried to pull her further away and push her down.

She resisted his push. "It's just a car fire, we need to call the..." but she never got the chance to finish her sentence. As he forcefully pushed her down and lay on top of her, the garage exploded in a spectacular display of red and orange flames and black smoke, which was quickly followed by an onslaught of wooden bits raining down on them.

"Crikey! Are you alright? Are you okay?" He rolled off of her, helping her to sit up once the shower of debris ended.

She could hear him but her ears were all fuzzy and nothing sounded normal. Particularly his voice. She turned to their house. The garage was gone along with the right edge of the building. What remained was starting to burn. The driveway was scarred black, dotted with a couple of the pots she'd dumped in the kitchen sink. The trees that overhung the house had been sheared away by the blast and two of them were now burning as well. She reached down and ran her hands over her body. They came back red and bloody but she didn't feel anything. "I'm, I'm… okay, I guess. Some cuts. Nothing broken." She looked down at the considerable blood on her hand. Her hair was matted with it. She turned to look at him. "How did that happen?" She pointed to the house with her bloody hand.

He stood up and looked at the house for a moment, and then he started to pace. "Oh crikey… damn you, Murray! The blighters have found me. I'll have to bail back to the bush. I'm devo. They bloody found me." He continued to talk to himself as his arms briskly slapped the opposite triceps, as though to wake himself up or keep himself out of shock. "I've got no choice. Don't be a drongo, mate." He continued to talk to himself and then turned to look at Jane.

Slowly she stood up, the world spinning as she did so. Staring at Gio, she turned from him to their burning house and once again back to him. "How…" she looked at the house. Then "Why…" she looked at him.

"Jane, I think they found me. Murray. The cartel." He looked around, a wild look in his eye she hadn't seen before. He had blood running down the side of his face, too.

"What? Cartel? Murray's a tennis player! What? And why… why are you speaking with an Australian accent?" She wondered just how hard he'd been hit by the contents of the garage that had rained down on them and now littered the yard. Looking around she saw balls and broken tennis racquets, twisted golf clubs, and a mangled bike that lay among the less recognizable junk in the debris field. Closer to the house, a smoldering pile looked a bit like their double oven, only mangled and twisted. She suddenly felt very lucky at what hadn't landed on them.

He grabbed her by her arms, and in a strong Aussie accent said slowly and clearly, "Jane, listen to me. My name's not Giovanni. I'm a True Blue undercover agent working with the American DEA. My cover is the Italian Giovanni Romano, and I never, ever dreamed that Murray would find me here." He paused for a moment. "Well, let me say that again. It was the stuff of my nightmares, but I swear, Jane, I never thought I'd endanger you." He looked at the house. "I managed to hit the panic button. The team'll arrive any minute." He breathed out heavily. "I've got to disappear."

Another small explosion made them both turn towards the house.

Jane swallowed hard. "The puppies! Oh my God, those poor puppies."

The man she had known as Giovanni slowly turned back to her. "Listen closely. Jane, I love you more than life itself. The time since we first met has been the best I've ever known. But it's time for me to move on or you'll be in danger. In fact, I've got to die in this explosion in order for you to be safe. It's me that Murray wants. Not you. And if I'm dead, then he has no reason to want to hurt you."

"What? But no, you're here. You're safe with me." She clutched onto him.

"But not for long. That car shouldn't have exploded. It's classic Murray and they'll know soon they missed me. So, they can't have missed me, you understand? Or they'll be back and there'll be no running from them. I'm going to go back into that house. You tell them that: that I went back into the burning house. Yeah, to find the dogs, right, Mate?"

"You can't go into a burning house! It's too dangerous!" Jane wasn't sure if she was even breathing anymore. She felt outside of her body. This was all too much to take in.

"Jane, this is what I do for a living. In fact, for me, this is tame." He gave a sideways nod to the house. "And that blighter is not getting our babies. But time is shy, so you'll know that I'm on the other side if you find the dogs in the backyard. But remember. I have to die in this fire, no matter where the dogs end up. Right? You've got that? This is where I die."

She nodded.

"I love you. And when I'm gone the cartel won't be chasing you. They'll have done their work. Take care of our babies."

And then he was gone. She stared dumbfounded as he ran into the burning building. Within five minutes the sirens were screaming up her street and then she was surrounded by firefighters. Police cars pulled up along with a few unmarked black cars. An EMT wanted to put her into an ambulance but she resisted, screaming out, "He went into the house! He went back into the house!"

"Are you saying there's a man in there?"

She nodded. "He wanted to save the dogs."

The firefighter had a grim look on her face. "We'll do everything we can." Then she went to tell her colleagues the news that there was someone in the flaming structure. The team was efficient and fast, but the house was burning in earnest now. Jane felt faint and wobbled. Someone from behind caught her by the arm and escorted her to one of the ambulances. She was dazed and confused, but noticed that as the EMT was treating her, they were surrounded by several serious-looking men in black suits and sunglasses. The EMT kept calling her Mrs. Romano. Had Jane given her name to him? She didn't remember doing so.

"My husband. Is there any news of my husband?" she kept asking, but they only answered with the questions they continued to pepper her with. Things about her name, the day, who was the president.

Questions about did this hurt and could she see how many fingers they were holding up. She told them she didn't want to see their fingers. She wanted to see Giovanni. Had they gotten him out of the house yet?

She didn't know how many minutes went by, but the house was fully aflame now. Parts of the second story were caving in, crashing down on the first floor. Now she hoped none of the firefighters had gone in after Gio, or more than his life would be lost today. For the first time she noticed that tears were streaming down her face.

A dark-suited man approached her from the side. Slowly, in shock, she turned to him.

"Mrs. Romano. I believe these little ones are yours?"

She looked up into his eyes and then saw two similarly-clad men standing behind him. Each took a step forward and one after the other handed her a small, terrified, dachshund puppy. One of them had a serious burn.

"Oh my God, oh my God, you two are all right. I thought there was no way…" She held and kissed the pups and then looked up at the house. "He made it."

The dark-suited man standing in front of her got down on one knee so that he'd be closer to eye level with her. "Mrs. Romano, I don't know how to tell you this, but the fire team said they couldn't get inside to rescue your husband. I'm so sorry. They did all they could."

"Ma'am," the EMT interrupted, but his tone was very gentle. "We need to take you to the hospital. You need to be checked out for smoke inhalation and some of these cuts are going to need stitches. We can't do that here. We need to take you in. You've had a blow to the head. You've lost quite a bit of blood."

She felt confused and fuzzy still. "He was Australian?" She felt the world slip around her, and a moment of blackness numbed her mind. Suddenly her arms were empty and she was looking up at a world filled with black, billowing smoke against a crystal blue North Carolina sky.

It reminded her of when she'd slipped on the ice more than a decade ago. She felt an eerie chill.

The dark-suited man turned to the EMT. "We'll keep the dogs safe until she's released from the hospital. She's showing signs of concussion. Go ahead and take her now." Turning to Jane, he leaned down to be close to her face. "Giovanni was a good man. You won't be alone. We'll take good care of these little guys and they'll get checked out by a veterinarian. This little one's got a bit of a burn here. They'll be fine and they'll be back with you soon. You're going to go to the hospital now. Your family has already been notified and they'll meet you there."

She tried to reach out for the dogs but wasn't sure if her arms moved or not. They were going to the doctor's. But where was Giovanni?

Chapter 38

Jane wasn't sure when she woke up. She didn't know she had fallen asleep. Everything was fuzzy, like she'd had some awful nightmare that she couldn't quite remember. But she couldn't fully wake up and she was stuck hovering in the twilight between being able to interact with the world around her and then feeling it so far removed, it was as though it didn't exist.

"Honey, she's opening her eyes! Look! Jane, my dear, Jane, can you hear me?"

She wondered why she was dreaming about her mother's voice. It was insistent. Just like when she was a child, and her mother would nag her to clean up her room. But she was sure she'd straightened it up. She wasn't Summer; my God, she wasn't Summer. It was amazing you could even find Summer in that mess that was her room. But no… she had left her room a mess, hadn't she? She struggled to walk toward the door to her bedroom, moving through the molasses of her mind, pushing against it until she could reach the knob. She grabbed the knob that was surprisingly warm to the touch. Turning it, she pushed the door open in that misty darkness and peered in. Dumbstruck, she stared. It was blackened, roofless, the furniture turned to ash, the skeletons of bedposts standing sentinel like darkened gravestones: the smoldering remains of her life. Her eyes flew open, ending the dream.

"Jane, Jane, can you hear me?"

Her mother's face was hovering over her. Then her father's was there as well. She tried to speak but only scratchy sounds came out.

"Don't try to talk, Jane," her father said. "It's the smoke. You inhaled a lot of smoke. You'll get your voice back, but it will take a bit of time."

Yes, there had been a lot of smoke.

Then her mother's face came back into focus. "Honey, there was a fire. You're okay. You're okay…" Jane knew her mother was crying. "Thank God you're okay." Then the real sobbing started. "She's going to be okay, John. She's going to be okay."

"Of course, she is." And then she felt her father's hand grasp her own. "Of course, you'll be okay, Janie. You are strong. You are determined, probably the most determined of my girls. You're going to be just fine." Audree and John kept repeating their words in the way people do when they're trying hard to convince themselves of what they're saying.

Jane could feel her eyes blinking, but there was this weird numbness, like everything was happening to someone else's body; like a drone pilot controlling the altitude and speed with the camera on the apparatus recording on autopilot. She took in a deep and sharp inhale, which did a good job clearing her head, and she blinked again.

"Mom?"

"Yes, honey, I'm here. I'm right here. I'm not going anywhere. Daddy is right here with me."

"Are the puppies alive?"

She could see Audree shoot a concerned look at John and then turn back to Jane. "I… I don't know, honey. I think you were lucky to get out alive. The house… exploded."

"It was a hit."

"Yes, you were hit by some of the flying debris. You had surgery. You were hit in the head. And on the back of your leg." Her father's voice was kind and patient, speaking slowly so his daughter could digest the information.

"Giovanni... he's... gone."

Jane could see her parents exchange worried glances. Her mother bit her lip. "Yes, dear. He's gone."

"He left. Ran away. My husband."

"Damn fool ran into the house to save the dogs." Her father was struggling to say the words. "To save the puppies. Damn brave... Italian... fool." Then he started to sob.

"He's not who you think he is."

Her mother's voice sounded conciliatory. "He wasn't a fool. Giovanni was a good man. An excellent man. But I wish, I wish your boyfriend hadn't tried to save the dogs." Her voice broke as she said it.

"No. Husband. Not Italian. Aussie. Dogs... fine." She wondered if they could hear her, her voice was so weak. "Sunglasses took them. Suits. Don't know. Get my dogs."

Then she heard another voice. Someone not wracked by emotions. Someone calm and rational, saying that she needed to rest and that she shouldn't be trying to talk. There would be time for that.

"Doctor, she doesn't know. She thinks..."

"That's okay for now. There'll be plenty of time after she's recovered a bit more. She has a lot of healing to do. She might tell you some things that you don't understand. She might believe things that aren't true, at least for a while. That's normal, too, after injuries like hers. Try not to upset her. Just let her rest and heal."

Injuries like hers? She wondered what had happened, but mostly she wondered who had taken her dogs? Then, as the medical attendant put something into that tube that ran into her arm, everything went fuzzy again and she felt herself sinking down into a numb grayness, thankful that it was just quiet and not full of the dreams of her burned-out bedroom.

* * *

Jane was sitting up in the hospital bed, trying to eat the tasteless food on her tray. She wasn't sure if it was the meal or if she was just so depressed that food no longer held any interest for her. She dropped her fork, feeling like the bite in her mouth had turned to ash. Everything was ash. Her blackened bedroom had not been a dream. Her home was ash. Her marriage. Her life. Nothing was left. She'd seen the clip on the news a dozen times at least. Phones were good for that—you could watch the news clip over and over again as you read the story, trying to wrap your mind around those words on the screen. They might stand out in black and white but reconciling their meaning into your life was the hard part. Of course, you had time for that. Long after the live-broadcast world had moved on to the next tragedy du jour, you could stay rooted in that moment because the internet was forever.

House explosion in Charlotte suburb. A rare gas line leak, they reported. Whole house destroyed. One occupant—her—miraculously survived. The other occupant—a man—tragically dead. She'd seen the body bag being carried out of the blackened shambles. The reporter went on and on about leaving the rescuing to the professionals, warned others about the dangers of going back into a burning structure to get your beloved pets. It was too dangerous and had cost this unfortunate man his life.

No one wanted to hear her insist that Giovanni was alive. Or that his name wasn't Giovanni. Or that he wasn't Italian and never had been. Or that he wasn't her boyfriend, he was her husband. Or that he had saved the dogs and that's how she knew he was alive. They just turned away with sad looks on their faces and no words to dispel her comforting delusion. She began to wonder if any of it had been real. Of course, none of it was real, because nothing about him was real. If she didn't have the pictures to look at on her parent's phone, she might have wondered if she had simply conjured him up from the endless loneliness after her broken heart with Nick.

It was decided, she wasn't sure by whom, that she would move into her parent's house for a while to heal. When she was ready, she could live in her old condo, which she'd been renting out. From there, she would start to put her life back together again. Decide about when she wanted to start back to work. Decide how she wanted to resume her life. She thought that should include a discussion of whether she wanted to resume her life, but she knew better than to utter any of those thoughts aloud. Saying that would just result in more little bottles of pills lining up beside her bed.

A few weeks after her discharge, Jane was sitting alone in her childhood bedroom. Summer and Charlie had just left, Charlie having flown all the way across the country for an extended visit. Jane had been careful to say all the right things. To show her doctor sister, in particular, that she was on the path to getting better. That she was living in reality.

There was a soft knock at the door, but Jane continued to stare out the window at nothing. She took a deep breath. It felt like a tremendous effort to speak. "Come in."

"Oui, I would like to. But I am not sure if you actually want the company?" Claudine's lovely accent and commanding tone caught Jane by surprise. Everyone else walked around her like they were on eggshells, either overly serious or artificially cheery. No one seemed to know how to be themselves with Jane after all that had happened.

Jane turned her head. "The company would be fine."

Claudine popped her face around the open door. "Oui, that is good, because I was going to come in anyway." She waltzed in with her usual aplomb, commanding the room in a surprising way for such a small woman, and she sat down next to Jane. "After all, I flew all the way from Paris to see you, so I was not prepared to take 'no' for an answer."

Jane couldn't help but smile. "I'm glad to see you."

"And I am here." Claudine took Jane's hand. "How are you? I mean actually?"

Jane stared out the window again and struggled to speak her truth even though she knew Claudine was the safest person to confide in. "I feel exhausted and sick all the time. I can hardly get out of bed. I could throw up at any minute. Without him, I'm just truly lost." Jane looked at Claudine. "What do I do from here? I don't think I know how to live without him. I'm not sure I want to live without him."

Claudine patted Jane's hand a couple of times. After a heavy sigh, she said, "But you will go on."

"He was my compass. He was my home. Now I'm aimless. Meaningless. I'm, I'm so confused." Jane wiped a tear from her eye.

"I am so, so very sorry for your loss and grief. Well, not so much for your grief, my friend, since that is the other side of the coin of love, is it not? The beauty of the one brings that breath-taking pain of the other. Two halves of a whole, like you and Giovanni, sun and moon, dark and light. Your experience of love was so full that your cup is overflowing, which, while overwhelming, is not a cup half-empty. To be overflowing with that love, that is a blessing, my friend. My heart breaks for you, to see you like this, and yet at the same time, it sings for you that you got that hard, um, the hard to grab hold of? What is that word?" Claudine made grasping motions in the air.

"Elusive?"

"Oui, I think that is it! That elusive chance to live fully, love fully, really embrace what it means for two hearts to beat as one."

"We did beat as one." Jane clutched at the pain in her chest and swooned a moment from the nausea that intermittently wracked her, whether it was caused by her grief or the little pills they made her take, she wasn't sure.

"Great love comes with a very high price tag, which I'm afraid you are paying now." Claudine shook her head and then picked up a comb on the bedside table and started to gently run it through Jane's limp and unwashed hair.

"I should have been able to save him. To stop him from running into the burning house. From leaving me. From running away. I'm in this no-man's land of grief. He's gone, but he's not. I keep thinking I'll see him again." Then Jane said in a whisper, "They think I've lost my mind."

Claudine stopped fussing with Jane's hair. She looked thoughtful. "Oui. They think you are dreaming, wishing for an outcome that is different from that which we all know."

"But the outcome is different than that which we all know." Jane was very serious. "I saw the dogs. I know he's alive."

Claudine nodded. "Your family has told me." She looked over at the prescription bottles on the table next to Jane's chair. "And do you take those little pills? Or those? Or the other ones?"

Jane turned slowly to look at them. "They want me to. Every day. They say it will help me 'cope'. Until I can handle reality, because, you know, it's all been a huge shock."

Claudine laughed. "Oui. I would assume that it was a most amazing shock. When people turn out to be someone other than we think they are, they are living a double-life, it is a very big shock indeed."

Jane did a double take. "What did you say?"

Claudine's face broke in a small, slow grin. "I said that when the world is not what we thought it was, it can turn us upside down. Oh, and, oui! Having your house suddenly explode, being hit by wreckage flying through the air, ending up in the hospital, are also, as you Americans say, some rather nasty business."

"You believe me about Giovanni." It wasn't a question. Jane thought of her long phone calls with Claudine since the accident. "You believe me. You believe everything I told you, about what he said? About what happened?"

Claudine shrugged. "To be honest, I do not know any truths. What I do know is that Giovanni was too perfect to be true. He was too quintessentially Italian. There was no flaw in him. It was like he'd studied it."

"Yes, that's so… right. Textbook!"

"And then there was that tennis bag."

Jane nodded. "All those guns."

Claudine nodded back at Jane. "And the flimsy excuse he gave you. So pathetic."

"Hey, I believed him!"

"Oui! But you were in love with him and I was not." Claudine gave Jane a wink. "You know, given the choice between perception and reality, perception, even when foolish, wins every time. And love, she makes fools of us all, does she not? But I was not a fool and from that moment on, I started to wonder who was this man we all knew as the beyond perfect Giovanni."

"Why didn't you tell me you suspected him?"

Claudine shrugged. "And what good would that have done? You were already married. Oui, of course I figured that out." She waved off the look of surprise on Jane's face. "You were happier than I had ever seen you. And he was very good to you. Again, almost too perfect. I did not fear for you, although I did wonder if he was having a good time while you provided a comfortable life for him. Remember, I did press you about keeping your finances separate. At least your investments."

Jane snorted. "Well, you needn't have worried about that. Look at what I got in the mail yesterday. I haven't told my parents." She got up and walked with only a slight limp over to the desk on the far side of the room. Opening the drawer, she pulled out a book and carefully carried it back with her. When she sat down, she stroked the cover gently.

"Is that a special book?"

"No. I'm not even sure what it's about. It's just a convenient hiding place." Opening the cover, Jane slid a letter out from the pages. She handed it to Claudine.

Claudine looked surprised, but took the paper, unfolded it and read it slowly. "Mon dieu!" she said in almost a whisper. "Jane, this is… this is…"

"I know."

"His life insurance policy…"

"Yes. He had life insurance. I never knew. And he made sure to take care of me."

"You will never need to work again." Claudine looked at her friend and blinked a couple of times in astonishment. "In fact, you can live most comfortably for… many lifetimes. Eh!"

Jane nodded. "He knew something could happen. Thought it might. The guns. All the little electronic devices, those 'experimental gadgets' he had about. You know, he retrieved… well, I don't know what… from the burning truck. And he grabbed his things as we ran from the house. And he was prepared for his exit by making sure all my needs would be cared for."

Claudine was still astonished. "He was a loving, generous husband. He cared for you very much. And he tried to prepare for everything."

Jane nodded and then felt the tears welling up. "Except for how much I am going to miss him." She started to cry and then ended up sobbing in Claudine's arms. After the torrent loosened its grip on her, she wiped her eyes and blew her nose. "Sorry about that. It happens sometimes. Well, most of the time."

"Of course it does. You have just lost your husband."

"I know he's alive."

Claudine took Jane's hand again. "And if what you say is true, then you must do as he asked. You must trust him. You must let the world know he is dead. You must be the grieving wife, most publicly." Claudine shook her head sadly and gazed out the window. "I remember telling you I never wanted to read about you in the papers or hear about this relationship in the news." She let out a heavy sigh and gave Jane a hard look. "You know some of my darkest days. You know the kinds of people I have had to tangle with. Those underground operators are not people you want to mess with you. If Giovanni was, well, someone else, then you need to let him die so that he can live. Do you understand me? You cannot be telling the world there is another story. You need to tell the story he is asking of you. And it needs to be in the papers and on the news."

"You mean, just pretend that everything I loved died in that fire?"

"He cannot come back to you as Giovanni. He made that clear. Everything you did love died in that fire. If you love him, you can help protect him. Like he protected you." Claudine picked up the check again, slid it back into the book, and handed the book back to Jane.

Jane stared at the book in her hands and then turned to look out the window again. The sunlight reflected off the leaves and she could hear birds singing in the distance. She took a deep breath and felt like her lungs were filling up for the first time in a long time. She picked up the prescription bottles from the table and looked at the labels. "You know, I didn't want to take these anyway, but now I think I'm done with them." She handed the bottles to Claudine. "Can you make these conveniently disappear?"

"Certainement! For you, my Janie, anything." Claudine slipped them into her handbag. "You seem… lighter all of a sudden."

"Well, that's ironic, because I feel like I've been a balloon battered about by the wind since the explosion. The fire turned all my purpose to ashes. But Claudine, you've helped me see that I do have a purpose still. And now it feels like a million pounds on my shoulders." She exhaled sharply. "But that's better than drifting with no reason to exist."

"And what, mon ami, is that?"

"I might be suffering every day, missing him, but I can protect him. I think you're right. I can't let my aching for Gio endanger him. Clearly, these people are serious when it comes to revenge. I need to somehow embrace my grieving and let him be safe."

* * *

Jane wasn't sure how she did it, but she worked with her mother to plan the funeral. It was easier, in a macabre way, to finally have something to do. They held it seven weeks after 'the accident', as they called it now. At least she wasn't sitting around, drowning in her anguish, while everyone thought she was delusional with grief, conveniently living a reality much more to her liking. Giving into their illusion of the truth was only possible now that a noble purpose had found her: she was going to save Giovanni, or whatever his name was. And she was going to play the role as well as he had played his role for her. She planned a funeral, ordered his gravestone, and had her name carved into it for good measure. Might as well go all the way—and they were a married couple after all. At least she thought they were. She wasn't sure what was true anymore. She dressed in black and cried at the service and again at the burial. She was solemn and quiet at the reception, accepting hugs and brief presses of cheek-on-cheek that were meant to be substitute kisses from women who wanted to comfort her but didn't want to smudge their lipstick. She released a statement to a very hungry press explaining that while she greatly appreciated the outpouring of love and support, she was also kindly requesting some privacy because she needed to grieve. In the near future, she would set up a foundation for tennis opportunities for underprivileged youth in his name. And after it all, she went back to her old condo from a former life, now filled with new furniture and feeling like it was someone else's home.

Two days later there was a knock on the door. A man in a dark suit asked if he could come in. There was something vaguely familiar about him, but she couldn't quite place it. That neither surprised nor alarmed her. So much of the past couple of months was completely fuzzy as she'd been wading through her emotional and physical exhaustion.

"Mrs. Romano, you've done a lovely job creating your new home. It's quite striking," the man said as he looked around from behind his dark sunglasses. "It would seem that you are putting the life insurance policy to good use."

"Um… thank you?" He certainly seemed to be aware of some facts about her situation that were not public, which unnerved Jane. She stumbled over what to say, hearing herself mumble, "Actually my mother and Mimi did all this... wait a minute!" She perked up suddenly. "I think I know who you are." She felt both excited and as if her breath had suddenly rushed out of her body.

"We just wanted to say how much we appreciated the funeral for Mr. Romano. Very dignified."

"Thank you. It was all over the news, I noticed." Jane blinked back the wetness in her eyes.

"Yes. Friends and family there. The grieving spouse. Had a real air of, well, finality, to it, didn't it? Closing of a chapter. A good 'the end' to a fine tale. And closure is such a good thing, don't you think?" He removed his sunglasses and looked at her sharply.

"Yeeesss," came out sounding tentative. She wasn't sure what to say. She still ached with the empty hole in her heart where Giovanni, or whatever the hell his name was, should be, but she heard the song beneath the man's words. She'd helped the world see Giovanni Romano as dead, and that was just what those sunglassed-strangers wanted.

"There are just a couple more loose strings, I'm afraid. We'll have to tie those up."

For a moment Jane had a flash of fear that he was going to kill her. Then she wondered if she would need to go into some kind of witness protection and never see her family again. She pictured another fake funeral, this time with the fake dates of her life carved into that headstone. She took a deep breath to steel herself.

"If I might call in a couple of my associates?"

She nodded.

The man touched his ear and quietly said, "All clear."

Within seconds, two matching black-suited agents came in through her front door each carrying a transport container. They didn't remove their dark sunglasses as they came over to her and set the containers down by her feet, then stepped back, framing their leader.

"We have the matter of these two small dogs which need a home. Their veterinary bills have been taken care of by an anonymous donor.

We've also had to put them through, well, a hell of a lot of behavioral training. We wondered if you might be able to provide care for them from here on out?" He had the smallest of smiles on his face.

Jane fell to her knees and opened each of the crates. The puppies, now quite a bit bigger, bounded out and jumped on her, licking her face. Jasper had a nasty burn scar on his back. He peed all over her leg in his excitement. Jane was crying and laughing at the same time, trying to gather the dogs up and hug them, as they squirmed and yapped in typical puppy fashion.

"Thank you, thank you." She turned towards the agents, but she was alone. They hadn't even left footprints in the carpet. It was as if they had never been there.

Chapter 39

Jane walked down the dark alley, her heart thumping in her ears. She wondered if someone was going to jump out of the shadows.

No need to try to sneak up on me. They could march up playing a bass drum and I would never hear them over the pounding in my own chest.

Usually, logical objectivity calmed her down, however that acknowledgement of the truth only served to heighten her fear.

"What am I doing here? Why did I say I would come?" she muttered under her breath.

"Ma'am?" A man's voice called out.

She jumped. "Who's there?" she said to the beat of her heart slamming in her chest.

"Sharks swim silently in shallow water."

What was she supposed to say back? She tried to remember. "And on the, um, er, the Great Barrier Reef they roam in... um... vast numbers?" He hoped she got that right.

"Close enough. Right this way, ma'am." He stepped out of the shadows and gestured for her to follow him. He looked vaguely familiar, but she couldn't place him. They went through three more alleys and past two doors where he said something nonsensical and received a similar reply. Passwords, she guessed, but they must've worked because she and her escort gained entrance. It felt very "secret agent" but in kind of a kitschy way. She followed him up three flights in a dim stairwell to a large tent on a roof. "Head right in. He's waiting." The man gave her a brilliant smile and she was hit with the recognition: the cowboy in Italy.

The rooftop was derelict. Dirty. Even in the dark she could see that much and she had to pick her way over to the tent. She nodded mutely at her escort, turned, and walked in through the flap that served as a doorway. Inside, by comparison, was bright and she blinked as her eyes adjusted to the new scene. Before her was a garden café, with soft lighting on each of the three tables, a bar to the side and a dozen big, flowering plants. A neon sign on the front of the bar said, "No Place Like Home". An oasis of their own for the undercover agents.

"I'm so glad you decided to come." Giovanni's soft voice came out of the shadows, followed by him stepping out from behind a screen of green espalier vines. She ran over to him, nearly leaping into his open arms.

"Oh my God, you're alive! You're alive! Let me touch you. Let me look at you." She gazed into his eyes for a moment and then kissed him hard, so glad he returned the kiss with his usual passion.

He put his hands to her face and said tenderly, "Of course I'm alive. I told you if the pups were out back, that meant I would be fine. How are they, Jasper and Horace? How are they doing?"

"I can't even tell you how totally weird it is to hear that Australian accent coming out of your mouth. Gio… oh…" She had to stop with the sudden realization. "That's not really your name, is it?"

"Let's sit down. I can't tell you a lot, but I can fill you in on some basics." He led her over to a table. "Let me get us something to drink." He went over to the bar and in short order returned with two wine glasses and one of their favorite bottles. He pulled a corkscrew out of his pocket and proceeded to open the wine. "While we don't exist high on the hog in this 'hereafter', we also don't need to suffer."

"Giovanni, or whoever you are…"

"You can call me Giovanni. Of the many I've had, I rather like that name."

"I can't know your real name?"

He shook his head.

"What is true? And what was a lie, just a cover?"

He poured out two glasses. "Again, I can only tell you so much." He gave her a wink. "Or I'd have to kill you."

She froze for a moment and then let out her breath and slowly started to smile. "I came close enough to that when the house blew up. If that was your objective, then you missed your big chance. I think we can check that one off the list." She picked up her glass, raising it to him and smiling at him over the rim as she took a sip.

He laughed. She missed that laugh. She dreamed of that laugh. Of course, now it did sound a little different. She hadn't realized that you could laugh like an Italian or you could laugh like an Australian… and now he laughed like an Australian.

"Oh, when it comes to sheilas, my Janie, you're one of a kind. As I said, probably in shock, I shouldn't have told you, I was under cover, in hiding, my lovely life in Charlotte a decoy to keep the cartels off my trail. I really thought that damn Murray had found me. If he and his cartel had, you and I could never have met again. You'd be in danger as long as you believed I was alive."

"Sir Murray, the Scottish tennis player? Is a cartel drug lord?" Jane was in disbelief.

"What? No? That would be ridiculous. Murray's just a code name we had for a particular cartel leader we thought we'd neutralized."

"So, the whole arch enemy thing—it wasn't the famous Scottish guy?" She realized that she was just at the start of the journey, figuring out what was real and what was deception. She got it that on a high level he wasn't who he said he was, but was everything, everything he'd said a lie?

"Nah! Don't know two hoots about him actually. Just seen a clip of him on ESPN. But when I talked about Murray in my sleep, well that was a real problem. I had to think of something fast. I always was way too deep of a sleeper. My greatest fault in my line of work."

"Okay, just so you know, you never said anything so weird in your sleep that I got tipped off, so you don't need to kill me." She said it with a straight face, which made him burst into peals of laughter. She found she could smile at that one, too. If she could make a joke, surely she was going to be okay. "But if you do kill me, make sure I die in your arms. No place I'd rather be."

He had to catch his breath with that one. "Oh Janie, if only things could've been different. I do love you so."

She swallowed hard. "And they haven't found you? The cartel didn't find you after all?" She wanted to ask, *So, can you come back then? Can we pick up someplace else?*

"Nah. The forensics said it was the car itself that caught fire. A recall notice I'd missed because I bought the damn thing second hand. So, it'd never been fixed." He shrugged. "Or maybe the notice came when I was undercover infiltrating radical paramilitary organizations in western North Carolina. Yeah, that was a busy time. I remember trying to get the testimony wrapped up before you got back. We put those boys in jail, felonies every one of them. Poor dorbas can't ever own guns again. That'll break their little hearts." He smiled unempathetically as he took a sip.

"Wait a minute… you mean all those… Billy people?"

He gave her a mischievous smile.

"So, the guns were yours. And the story about taking lessons?"

"Well, I did take a lot of firearms lessons, but that was like a million years ago." He looked so innocent.

"So… the old tennis case…"

"Tools of the trade, love."

Her lips pressed tightly together; she managed a terse half-smile as she tried to keep the wetness in her eyes from betraying her. "Love." She said it with an almost sarcastic laugh. "You cased me, didn't you? Back in Italy. With that cowboy out there." She nodded towards the tent entrance where her escort had left her. "Dated me to reel me in.

Married me for cover." It wasn't a question. She had already reasoned that one out on her own.

He leaned over and took her hand. "Now, Jane, I had them bring you here for one purpose, and one purpose only. I had to beg for this opportunity, this chance to see you one last time. I have something to tell you. To confess because I love you and you're my missus. And I can only do so because we don't think it will endanger you. But it also doesn't change anything."

She looked at him, raising one eyebrow.

"It's true, my buddy pegged you as a likely target in the bar. He deduced that you might go for an Italian, and since I was fluent, they sent me for the job."

"Whoa, bummer for you. That's a hard lot to draw. See if you can rope a complete stranger into falling for you enough to create a cover." She didn't say it very nicely.

"Can be. But when I got my first look at you, I thought I'd gotten the lucky end of the deal. Poor you were gonna get stuck with stringy ole' me."

"You fake a really convincing Italian."

Giovanni's watch buzzed. He looked at it, turned the outer ring a bit and hit a few buttons, then looked back at her.

She put her hand to her forehead. "So, when I offered you a swanky new smart watch for Christmas… that's not an off-brand, street-vendor knock off, is it?"

Giovanni chuckled. "Oh, I don't know. I think you hit that nail on the head, actually. It's about as off-brand as you can get and nigh un-hackable. It was a blessing that you weren't at all interested in tech. The millions of dollars' worth of materials I could leave round… and I knew they'd never be touched. You had to ask me how to work the cable remote every time you watched anything on TV."

She had to nod. "Gadgets are not my thing. True. Hey, wait a minute… all those friends of yours I met when we first started dating. You don't have real friends, do you?"

"Oh, you're a bright one. Those were, I hate to say this: interviews. My colleagues had to approve you before we could go forward. You got checked out by US and Australian government officials. Damn, they might try to recruit you after this. Found you to be the most trustworthy level of person they measure. Of course, you're so trusting that you'll never actually get the call from them." He snickered.

"Ah! They felt like interviews. I told myself I was crazy to think that, but they felt like interviews."

"Well, you impressed the hell out of them, I'll tell you that." Giovanni actually looked so proud.

"Wait a minute!" She gave him a stern look. "You and I were already sleeping together long before you put me through those interviews…" Jane could feel the blush rising in her cheeks. It was weird to feel embarrassed about having sex with Giovanni at this point. He was her husband, after all.

He looked a bit flushed for a moment, but a wicked grin also crossed his face. "That's fair. Since we're being at least somewhat honest here, I'll confess that I also wanted to know what I was in for, if you being my missus was in the cards. And if you remember, I was pretty smitten, too. You're an easy woman to fall for, Jane. I couldn't believe my luck."

"Thanks, I think." She decided to let that one go. She didn't know what to do with it anyway. And it hit her that his friends—no, his colleagues, she reminded herself, classified her as "trusting" which was just a nice way of actually saying "easily duped". She wasn't sure that was a moniker she wanted to tack onto her psyche. Jane felt like she had a million questions she needed to have answered. "Did you fake playing tennis? Or was that part of your secret agent training?"

"Nah, I stink at tennis. But the ladies at the club loved the accent and how I flirted with them. The manager told me that more ladies came in than ever before because of me." He laughed. "And they spent a fortune on clothes in the pro shop that I said looked good on them. And they stuck around for long lunches with cocktails. So, it was all right with management that I had no real game. Funny that. So American."

"Aaannnnd… your cousins. How do you have Italian cousins? Oh… they weren't, were they?"

"I can't comment on them, but true, they aren't a blood relation of mine. It did help that you advised me they were trying a bit hard. That was some good feedback for them to cool it just a bit."

Jane looked away, her face a mask. Sarcastically she added, "They gave you that stupid Dutch oven. I bet you didn't sweet talk those TSA agents, did you? The ones who were stuck on the pot being a weapon."

He smiled shyly. "Nah. I had to call in the big wigs. When National told them to stand down, well they shaped right up."

"So, they knew who you were?"

"Hell no! They just knew I was one of them. And if you're one of them, then different rules apply to you."

"One of them? C'mon. TSA staff are not exactly secret agents."

"Well, the average traveler might not think so. Even the TSA agents themselves might not think so. But they sure did like it when I told them they were. And they let me right on through."

"And the whole event, you saving the day, never made the news."

The man who wasn't named Giovanni shrugged. "We weren't ready to blow my cover. So, my pictures couldn't end up on the news. But it was good, really good to be back in action again. It was a bloody beauty, even if it was just a passing song."

Jane put her face in her hands. "And you said you were well trained. That's how you could do all that."

"Well, that was true."

"Trained on the tennis courts. Agility training on the courts, you said."

"Oh, well, that part was false." He had such a roguish look on his face.

Jane gave a sarcastic snort and shook her head. "Your job was fake. Our marriage was fake. Our love was fake. You never really wanted kids." She gave him a sideways look. "Did you ever really love the dogs?"

He leaned towards her once again and took her hand in his, rubbing it in the way he always used to as she fell asleep at night. He would rub her hands, or stroke her arm, or massage her leg, almost absentmindedly, as she fell asleep snuggled against him. She had never felt so cared for. And it was all a lie. She had to admit she was impressed. He was fully a method actor when it came to his cover.

"I did love the hot dogs. Jasper and Horace, such cute little speckled buggers. And our marriage was both fake and it was real. You are actually married to Giovanni Romano. Or you were, because he is actually dead… from that explosion at the house… death certificate, life insurance policy, and all. You really are a widow. I can't change that and I can't come back. When we got married, it was a job. You were an assignment to create a cover for me and to establish me in America. But Jane, being married to you, I really fell in love with you. You're a kind person. You kiss in a way as to bewitch me. Your work ethic rivals mine. Hell, if you'd only been a DEA slick like I was, you'd be head of the agency by now. You never knew that when you were gone, I'd work like a dog." He smiled. "And you thought I was this playboy mooching off you the whole time, and you loved me enough to just let me enjoy life. You're a generous sheila, Jane. I knew it rankled you."

"It did. But you were my forever love. And I would do anything for you."

He looked at her for a long moment. "You did. I know that by the way you buried me when you knew I wasn't in there. By the way you gave me cover. You were so dignified when the press tried to follow you. And Janie—the Foundation!" Here he started to speak with his hands the way he always had. It was the first time since she kissed him that Jane really felt she was back in the presence of the man she had fallen in love with. "To help the underprivileged kids get to play the sport. To play tennis! Those poor kids! Oh Jane, you about ripped my heart out with that one. My Missus. You're my forever love too, you know. And, yes, I do love the dogs."

"And so, I guess our present circumstances make you a, a what? A widower? I mean, I'm not dead, but I guess it's not that much different."

He shrugged. "My new identity might be a widower. Might not. It'll be assigned. I'll take what I get." He nodded curtly. "We don't always get what we want, but that's the job, right?"

"Were you happy?"

He reached out and touched her hand. "Oh Jane, I've never been so happy. These were the best days of my life. But my life is about stopping the cartels and the organized criminals that are killing people by the tens of thousands. I can't leave that. It's my calling. My purpose. And I'm damn good at it."

She felt a sudden wave of anger. "We were trying to have a baby." There. She'd said it. She wasn't sure how she'd bring up that point but then she'd blurted it out and there it was.

He leaned back. He seemed awkward. A bit embarrassed. "I know… but… I can't…." He looked around him uncomfortably and rubbed the scruff on his chin. After taking a deep breath he said, "I can't have children, Jane. I have a, well, such a low sperm count that the buggers will never do anything. Doctors said it was one-in-a-million that I'd ever have a kid of my own. So, I thought it wasn't going to be a risk." Then he gave her his wink. "And the trying was a lot of fun."

"Ha! It was for you particularly! You didn't have to take your temperature constantly and track your ovulation!"

He just laughed at her with that new sounding voice of his.

"So, you're going back to that life. To an undercover-whoever-they-need-you-to-be. I'll miss you, whatever your name is."

"It's easier when you know you'll never have a family of your own. I'm a little older than you believe I am. Quite a bit older than I told you. I've done this for a couple of decades now. Not sure I'd be able to do anything else anyhow."

"I love you like I've never loved anyone." She could feel the tear as it slid slowly down her cheek. "I'm sorry that we only got a couple of years together. I'm sorry I worked so damn much of the time. I'd rather have spent it with you. You're about to disappear and I'm about to head back home… and it's just like losing you all over again. Like losing you twice."

He looked at her tenderly with a gentle smile. "I'll miss you too. And you know I'll always be Jane's loving husband. Father of two adorable fur babies. Taken too soon."

"One question."

"You can always ask it." He gave her his impish smile.

"Are you actually Australian?"

He picked up his wine glass and raised it in a brief toast before he took a swig, but he gave her no answer.

At the end of their meeting as she was about to leave the tent she stopped and turned. "Hey you."

"Yep?"

"If you ever retire, or quit the business, look me up."

* * *

Jane left their encounter with a queasy feeling in her stomach. A bit like butterflies, but different than the kind you have when you're falling in love. Suddenly she stopped short. "Well, damn. I'm the same girl I always was after all." She shook her head in disbelief and started walking again.

She went back home and had her first solid night of sleep since the accident. The next morning, she spent an extra hour in bed thinking about their conversation as she snuggled the dogs. He loved her. Enough to want to protect her. But not enough to leave that life. She decided she needed to throw up and went to the bathroom wondering how she could feel a sense of peace and yet have it make her feel so physically sick?

That evening she felt exhausted. She'd been feeling exhausted for weeks now with the emotional turmoil of it all, ever since the accident. She could hardly drag herself around the block as she walked the dogs. When she got back to the house, she went into the bathroom and stared at her pale face in the mirror. "Oh my God."

She pulled out the kit. Followed the instructions. Peed on the stick. Sure enough, the little pink plus sign materialized in front of her eyes. She sat down on the closed commode.

"One in a million." She looked at the little plastic test stick in her hand that told her future. "One in a million. You've got to be fucking kidding me."

Another sensation started to grow in her. While it couldn't quite snuff out the nausea, she eventually recognized it as excitement. She was going to be a mother. Maybe a single mother, but this was a role she never thought she'd get a chance to play. She had given Gio the chance to go underground again, start a whole new life. And he had given her the chance to raise her head away from the grindstone of work and experience life in a way she'd only dreamed about: as a family. Maybe he would keep tabs on her from afar. Maybe he'd see the child that was his, that family that could be his. Maybe. Or maybe it would just be the two of them, her and her baby. Mother and child.

She felt a sense of peace. The future would be what it would be. But it was a whole new horizon in front of her now. A world of love and excitement and experiences making up a journey that she was excited to take, and a little bit terrified as well. She had wanted the other side of the coin in her life, to flip heads and experience a true love, the real thing. She'd flipped that coin and it didn't come up heads or tails, Nicky or Giovanni. It came up motherhood—and there was no love that could be more real than that.

—The End—

Epilogue

Jane walked over to the car, her head absolutely spinning. In all her years, all the crazy experiences she'd been through, she hadn't actually seen this one coming. She was looking forward to some time alone so she could process it all and try to think it through.

"Hey, Mom, can I drive?"

She let go of the driver's side door handle and looked at her son running up to the car. "Uh, sure, Beckett, but I thought you and Dallas were going for ice cream after the big tennis showdown with Jordan High? Won't all the kids be there celebrating?"

"Yeah, and we were. But I told her I'd like to spend some time with my mom."

Jane could feel the smile growing on her face. "Well, that's something any mother couldn't hear enough of!" She tossed him the keys over the top of the car, ticking off in her mind her theories for what could possibly be going on with her son. At sixteen-and-a-half, "quality mom time" was not something that was typically high on his list. But how to broach the subject? As she walked around to the passenger side, she asked, trying to keep it light. "So, to what do I owe this honor?"

"Oh, you know, I'm only about halfway to getting my sixty hours of supervised practice, so this'll be a good chance to log some time, you know, if you want to drive around for a bit?" He sounded so casual as he tossed his racquet case and gym bag onto the back seat.

"Sounds lovely. And maybe you and I can go for some ice cream. I mean, I wouldn't want you to miss out, so I could probably suffer through some ice cream myself. You know, just for you."

Beckett wasn't usually interested in driving. It took some amount of nagging to get him behind the wheel, which is why he was so behind on his hours. She'd had to sign him up for the driver's ed classes since he never seemed to get around to it himself and then remind him that this was a real class that cost real money. The only thing that seemed to motivate him was the idea that he and Dallas could go on dates without Mom as a chauffeur once he passed that final driver's test.

As they pulled out of the parking lot, she gave him gentle coaching on his skills and tried, but failed, to avoid screeching "Red light! Red light!", although he did then stop and they did avoid getting into an accident. Her heart was racing. She wondered if he would ever get the hang of this or if she would spend the rest of her life in terror of him being behind a wheel? They finally got outside of Charlotte and into the surrounding countryside, where he could concentrate on the basics without the added pressure of high-volume traffic.

"You know, when you go to college you might enjoy a school in a big city." She tried to say it nonchalantly.

"You mean because you don't need cars there? And I wouldn't have to drive?"

"Ha! Big cities have lots to offer. Culture, arts, sports, entertainment, job opportunities, great restaurants. And not having to drive… eh, it's a benefit."

"You might as well not even try, Mom, you know I can always see through you."

Jane laughed. Beckett had always had this uncanny ability to key into what she was thinking and feeling. Just like someone else she'd known long ago. "Speaking of seeing through… is everything all right with you and Dallas? I mean, it's just that you don't usually choose me over her these days."

"Oh yeah. We're great."

"I thought so, you know, by the way you two were packing on the PDA after the match and all."

"Uh oh, here it comes." Beckett rolled his eyes.

"Here what comes?" Jane asked, her voice all innocence.

Beckett looked over at his mother and, as he spoke, started gesturing with one hand. "Mom, can we please not have the 'don't-have-sex-while-you're-still-in-high-school-talk' for the thirty-fifth time?"

"Ten and two, baby! Ten and two! Both hands on the wheel. Eyes on the road." She took in a few calming breaths and reminded herself that he was actually doing a good job at the moment. "You know, maybe you should have taken American Sign as your language fulfillment rather than Italian. You can talk without waving your hands all over the place. And you'll have to learn how to do that if you're going to successfully pass your driver's test!"

He sighed in an overly dramatic way.

"And, if you'll just do that, then yes, we can skip the mother-lecture about being too young for sex. But I do want you to tone it down with the PDA, especially in public, okay?"

"You know, Mom, technically that's really redundant."

Jane sighed. "You know what I mean. Doubly so. Beckett, it's not like you don't see Dallas five days a week."

"Well, yeah, but I can't kiss her at school."

"I'm glad to know that!" Jane laughed.

"Yeah, we got called into the principal's office one too many times. Coach had to give me a warning."

Jane stopped laughing. "Beckett! Oh my God, now the coach is parenting you. Please let that be my job, okay? Please let me be the one to nag and threaten you." She put her head in her hands and then quickly set her eyes back on the road.

"Nah, coach is cool. He was young once."

"Hey, I was young once! I remember those days."

"You got called out for kissing at school? Okay, I've got to hear this one!"

"Well, not that exactly. I got called into the office for other things."

"Other things like what exactly?" Beckett looked at her with one eyebrow raised, and it brought back a flood of memories. She couldn't speak. It wasn't high school that was on her mind anyways. "Yeah, I thought so."

She changed the subject. "So, what did stand-in-dad-coach say, anyway?"

"Oh, not much. It's not like me getting kicked off the team would hurt them."

"Don't say that! You're the heart and soul of the team. You might not contribute much towards points, but you make everyone gel." She couldn't lie about it—it was true. He wasn't very good at tennis. It was a mystery why he made the team the last two years, even at the JV level. It was a really good team, a contender for the state championship title, mostly due to the talents of two overly-tennis-obsessed players, but the coach had said that the whole team played differently when Beckett was there. He could help any player shake off a bad game and get focused again. Beckett was good for the team, even if Beckett was no good at the sport.

"Eh, he said I have a Spiderman build," Beckett shrugged as he drove. "Not the height and reach of some of the other guys. I'm quick but it's a lot to overcome not having the body size to capitalize on. And he said just because I couldn't reach for the shots tucked in the corner, it didn't mean I should be reaching for the easy shots off the court."

Jane was quiet for a few moments. Then she said, "I like your coach. Maybe you should follow his advice and keep your hands off of Dallas while you're at school."

"I hear ya, Mom. I hear ya." Now it was Beckett's turn to be quiet for a while. "Was my dad a stringy, Spiderman kinda guy? Am I like him?"

Jane sighed. "You've no idea. Hey, back to Dallas."

"Yeah?"

"How does she feel being named after a city? Just curious."

Beckett smiled broadly. "She likes it. She thinks it's cool. Wants to go to Texas and see it someday. Why?"

"Oh, it's just your Aunt Charlie always thought she was named after Charlotte. Your Grandee swears that's not true—and it's actually 'Charlotta', but my sister hated it so much she changed her name to Charlie. Said being named after a city was like being named after an inanimate object, like a roll of tape. So, Dallas is good with it?"

"Your sister, she's got issues mom. She's got serious issues." Beckett was quiet for a bit. "Dallas is pretty cool about most things. And uh, mentioned something to me."

Jane was wondering if they were going to have a discussion about birth control. Well, it was better to have it than not. She steeled herself and told herself to remain calm, practicing those annoying breathing exercises she'd read about and mostly ignored.

"She noticed that you were sitting with some guy at the match."

This caught Jane off guard. "Um, yes. I was."

"And that you seemed pretty, uh, happy."

Jane blinked a couple of times, trying to anticipate where this conversation was going. She had never dated after Beckett was born. With him around, she'd never felt incomplete. Lonely a bit, yes. She missed the 'before' and yet, the living in the 'after' had so much richness to offer. Now Beckett was reacting to her possibly being interested in a man? She acknowledged that would be a new experience for her son and could bring up complex feelings for him. Well, when he found out what was really going on, that was going to cause some fireworks for sure.

"Who was that dude?" Beckett asked, very direct.

Jane wondered how to phrase it. She wasn't sure what the right answer was. She took a stab at it. "A friend."

"And have you known him long?" Now Beckett sounded like the parent.

"Uh, yeah. I'd say... a pretty long time. Years and years." Jane shrugged as she said it and looked out her window, trying to hide her expression from him, afraid of what it would betray. She tried those breathing exercises again.

"So, where's he been? I mean, he's new on the scene, so if he hasn't been around, what's he been off doing? For, you know, years and years?"

"Oh him?" She was sure that innocent quality in her voice wasn't coming across as she hoped. "Him? Not sure. If I know him, he's probably been off saving the world. He's that kinda guy."

Beckett was quiet for an uncharacteristically long time. Jane struggled to think of what to say to break the tension of the silence. She would love to lighten up this interchange with some humor, but she couldn't think of anything remotely funny to say.

Then Beckett did it for her. "You seemed happy talking with him."

"I thought you were concentrating on your match. You know, that might be the problem you're having with your game, if you're watching the stands more than the ball." She laughed and Beckett joined in with a chuckle of his own.

"So, um, why does he limp like that?"

Jane took a few beats to answer. She'd only gotten part of the story. "He, um, he just came back from a war zone. He lost a leg. He's getting used to a new prosthesis. He's getting used to a lot actually. It's been a complex transition for him. He just, um, retired."

Then Beckett dropped a bomb Jane wasn't ready for. "I've seen him before."

She'd been idly looking out the window but now her head spun around and all the calmness she'd tried to pour into her voice had evaporated. It was a nearly breathless question she uttered back. "You have?"

"Yeah, he's been at the away matches all season. Like all the time. I always wondered who he was coming to see. The guys thought he was a college coach, scouting Bryce. You know Bryce is going to win the state title again this year. Surely, he's gonna get a scholarship. So, we all thought he was coming to see him. But that guy's not a scout, is he?"

Jane didn't know what to say.

"He's coming to see me. Isn't he?"

Jane nodded. She looked at Beckett steadily, wondering if this was the right moment for him to be behind the wheel. He seemed calm. In control. Like he'd maybe rehearsed this conversation in his mind quite a few times before coming to this particular opportunity. She thought that maybe it was better that it was him driving than her, actually.

"Is he my uncle or something?"

"Your uncle, huh? Why do you ask that?" Jane's heart was racing. She had to concentrate on Beckett's every word to make sure she heard it, given the pounding in her ears.

"Dallas took his picture at our last away match. He didn't see her do it."

Jane thought that was not likely. "And this picture?"

"Today, she put my picture through an age filter. After the match she showed me."

"And he looks like he could be your uncle?" Jane studied Beckett's face carefully.

"He looks like I could be him."

She made a noncommittal grunt.

Beckett was quiet for a while. "Dallas and I've been figuring this out. Figuring you out. She couldn't understand why I have no pictures of my dad. Not a one."

"Well, he died in the house fire before I even knew I was pregnant with you. Everything burnt up."

"Yeah. I know. That's the story. We take flowers to his grave on his birthday, and at Christmas, and every year on your anniversary. But you don't have any wedding pictures. Neither do Grandee or Grandpa John, and man, is their house stuffed with pictures! And his last name is my middle name."

"I've explained that before. We eloped and since I never changed my name, I thought it was best that you and I had the same last name. I thought that would be better since we were going to be the family, just you and me, a family of two. And you'd have your Donahue grandparents. Just what have you and Dallas been dreaming up?"

"We had decided that he never existed at all. That I never had a dad. And that you created a fake grave to cover that up." Beckett's mouth held a grim line. "From your antiquated sense of shame."

Jane was flabbergasted. "Not only do you kids have over-active libidos, you have over-active imaginations!"

"Do we? Really, Mom? Want to know what I was going to do after I grew up?"

"Sounds like you're going to become a secret agent. Or write for TV. Or write crazy fan fiction that you'll post online and no one will read. I mean, Beckett, you've got to be kidding me here."

"And just what would I find if I had that grave exhumed? Right. Just look at your face. It's empty. It's empty because I never had a father. At least that's what Dallas and I figured out."

Jane tried to laugh, but she knew it sounded strangled. "Yes, I admit it. You were an immaculate conception. You, Beckett, are a very special boy." *He's fantasizing about exhuming his father's grave?*

"Funny mom! After today I get it. The grave is empty because he didn't die. He just couldn't come home."

Jane felt her world rock. She tried to figure out her next move, and then she took the only path before her. "There's an old saying that apples don't fall far from the tree. You, Beckett, are my apple. My only apple. But you are the 'Mini-Me' of your father, who was a real person and who did not appear from a tube in a sperm bank, so you can allay that fear. It is in the shade of his tree where you are growing to be. You are his spitting image. And, apparently, you think like him as well."

"I want to meet him. This man."

Jane turned to look at Beckett, this time with an unstoppable smile on her face. Today had been complex. A surprise, both world-rocking and wonderful. So many years of wondering, of hoping and praying that Giovanni, or whatever his name was, would be safe while he faced those impossible odds in his dangerous calling. A new day was coming, and it brought with it a world of possibilities that she'd never dared to dream until now.

Beckett broke into her thoughts. "I want to know who he is to me."

"Oh Beckett, I think you already do."

Acknowledgements

As with any writing project, I am ever grateful for the support of my family. My boys in particular are asked to listen to plot lines and twists and turns of the story as I'm working them out. They are handed sections and manuscripts to read over and over again as the pieces get developed and polished. As a mother, I'm sure the talents of patience and poker-faced self-possession they've developed will serve them well in many facets of life. Alexander and Ethan are great supporters of my quest of the written word and storytelling journey, even when the genre represents a field different from the books that fill their own shelves.

I can't imagine a life partner who is more encouraging than Ruben. An ardent advocate since the very first novel-in-development that he read (without my knowing), he now listens not only to the stories as they are crafted, but also to a dramatically read-aloud final(ish) version of every book. This turns out to be a wonderful time for his keen wit or dry observation to come alive. There have been many moments when I'm completing one of my required six read-throughs after the manuscript is completed and before the work gets turned in for the galley copy, that I laugh at an engaging repartee of a character—only to remember that it came at Ruben's clever suggestion. If something makes you smile or laugh as you read it, there's a good chance it was his enrichment of the story.

Lucky for me, my family is not alone when it comes to reading and giving feedback. I am indebted to my Reader's Circle, which consists of dear friends, and sometimes even complete strangers who grow into dear friends. The Reader's Circle graciously read (and sometimes re-read and re-read) my novels in various stages, giving valuable critical feedback every step of the way, from extensive debates about cover art to story details to that final polishing stage of word choice or layout. For The Other Side of the Coin, special thanks go to Erika Lusk, Katie Rosanbalm, Ruben Fernandez, Laura Thomas, Alexander Fernandez, Linda Peterson, Bharathi Zvara, Michelle Abel-Shoup, Shannon Thielman, Barbara Marcum, Bekki Buenviaje, Sarah Kotzian, Angela Rosenberg, Katie Brandert, Susan Kermon, Amy Langenderfer, Dee Colello, Kimberly Allen, Debbie Jepson, Gary Glover, Anna Waller and Kathy Donnald. Some of these folks were part of the initial brainstorming of the Facets of Love series. Others participated in the work in development. Still others read finalized manuscripts. And others volunteered to be galley readers. There are also readers and supporters who want to maintain their privacy and remain unnamed—please know you are no less appreciated. My friends, I am grateful for all your encouragement and feedback on the story and particularly for your absolute dedication to detail. And, of course, a special thanks goes to Alison Williams, all the way over in Wales, editor on so many of my books.

A special shout out goes to my publisher, Beach Reads Books, with much gratitude for the support, the extra editing, the wonderful advice, and creating the pathway for this novel to make its way to the public. Beach Reads Books takes a strong interest in every aspect of the book, from story line to page layout to cover design, and their effort to bring together coherence from cover-to-cover shows impressive dedication to the art and perseverance of spirit.

Many thanks go to artists Shelley Hehenberger, who designed the cover, and to Danielle Hennis, who created the finalized cover for the book. All your artistic inspiration and skill is much appreciated. It was so much fun to see Jane come to life, both in her willingly blinded phase and her unknowingly blinded one.

Credits go to Harry Warren and lyricist Jack Brooks, author of the 1953 song Amore. Credit also to Steven Fink, author of Crisis Communication: The Definitive Guide to Managing the Message for the advice that "when there is a difference between perception and reality, perception always wins."

Notes From the Author

The Other Side of the Coin was a wonderful journey to embark upon. As the second book in the five-part *Facets of Love* series, it gave me the opportunity to explore relationships based on secrecy, camouflage, and betrayal. And to also discover the resilience and renewal that can grow from those experiences. Jane has an uncanny ability to find a truth underneath many layers of subterfuge. She can identify accuracy amidst lies, uncover beauty in darkness, and feel hope despite despair. And when all else fails, she can always run away and immerse herself in work. She is a heroine of resilience who has faith in herself—and when she can't face being the heroine any longer, being a workaholic is her salvation. I absolutely loved writing her story.

When Jane first appeared on the pages, she was part of a trilogy-in-one novel of three sisters and their troubled love lives. The story was a contrast of different experiences of love and my first title for it was *Millennial Women*. It was a fairly large manuscript, which my editor, Alison Williams, deftly pointed out needed to be reborn as three books. Having been under the impression that the story was finished, completed, and done—needless to say, it was difficult feedback to get. Plus, it meant having to discover what happened to each of the three sisters beyond their conjoined stories. In a more practical sense, it left three more half books to write!

Each sister experiences a different facet of love (hence the series title), which presents strikingly different life challenges that must be met and mastered, lest she succumb to despair. Breaking the sisters' stories into three different novels became an interesting challenge, since their life events are so intertwined. As one might imagine, keeping the timelines straight meant that the books needed to be written all at the same time. An unexpected outcome was that the original trilogy became a five-book family saga, bringing in additional twists of ill-fated love and challenges along the path to maturity, which almost required that the series be written backwards. Book five, *Taken by the Wind*, ended up being completed and published first, with the other series titles being created simultaneously. Jane's story, *The Other Side of the Coin*, is the second in the series to come out, although it was the last to actually be completed. Older sister Summer's story, *The Art of Summer*, and youngest sister Charlie's story, *Arc of the Dreamcatcher*, will follow shortly. *Love in the Fishbowl*, a facet of love as told from the male perspective, completes the series.

Jane is the only character to appear in all five of the Facets of Love books. In the original Millennial Women manuscript, her own love story initially ended with her return from her grand misadventure in Baja. When she had an entire novel dedicated to her growth beyond drama and heartbreak, the idea emerged that she wanted to experience the other side of the coin—from her perspective that was a peaceful and perfect love. There was little she wouldn't sacrifice to grasp at that dream, and much to which she would willingly turn a blind eye. Writing the second half of her love life was probably even more fun than writing the first half, since upping the humor and the drama became both a mechanism to explore Jane much more deeply and also a fun vehicle to catapult the story into another dimension.

My dear mother has always been a huge fan of mystery and murder genres. Despite the fact that those particular categories had not been the kind of literary playgrounds I'd delved into, at least until I wrote Holy Orders, my dedicated mother has read every romantic comedy I've penned. In particular, she related to Jane. This story has always been her favorite, although maybe that's because she was so enthusiastic that I finally wrote a book where explosions happen. Poor Jane.

About the Author

Ci Ci Soleil is a two-time national literary competition medalist who writes engaging stories exploring the thorny challenges of ethics and morals in daily life. Of particular interest are multi-volume stories that focus on an evolving cast of characters who themselves are evolving. Born an urban Northerner, she has now planted her roots in the New American South, where she lives with her husband, two sons, and yes—some of the longest living pandemic chickens. When she's not writing, Ci Ci is likely to be traveling, teaching, or painting.

Connect with Ci Ci at CiCiSoleil.com

www.ingramcontent.com/pod-product-compliance
Lightning Source LLC
LaVergne TN
LVHW010147070526
838199LV00062B/4284